When Paths Cross

Kim O. Davis

Independently Published

Disclaimer: *When Paths Cross* is a work of historical fiction. Apart from the well-known actual people, events, and locales that figure in the narrative, all names, characters, places, and incidents are the products of the author's imagination or are used fictitiously. Any resemblance to current events or locales, or to persons, living or dead, is entirely coincidental.

Printed in the United States of America.
Library of Congress Cataloging-in-Publication Data has been applied for:

ISBN 978-0-9913943-3-3 (soft cover)
ISBN 978-0-9913943-4-0 (hardback)
ISBN 978-0-9913943-5-7 (ebook)

FIRST PRINTING: December 2019

Cover Design: Kim O. Davis

Cover Photo: Cropped version of the painting by
George Caleb Bingham (American, 1811-1879).
Shooting for the Beef, 1850.
Oil on Canvas, 33 3/8 x 49 in. (84.8 x 124.5 cm).
Brooklyn Museum, Dick S. Ramsay Fund, 40.342

United States map, circa 1820, showing Arkansas Territory.

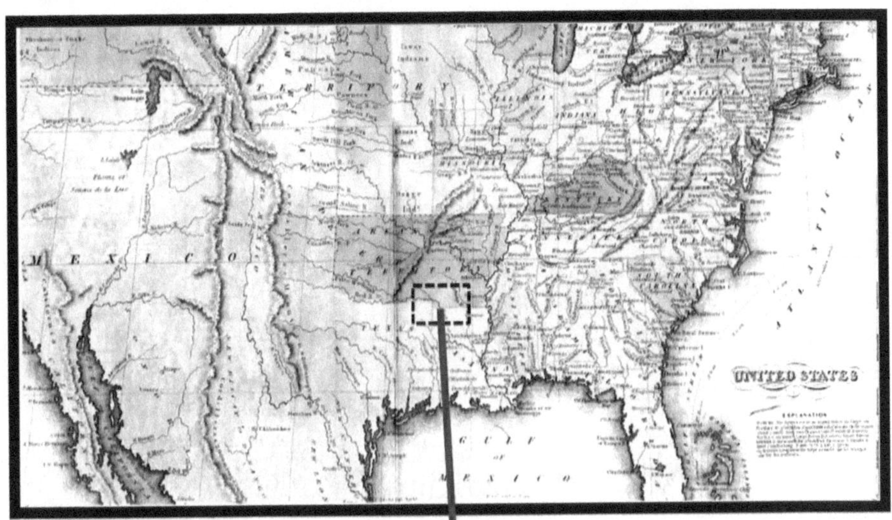

Source: Encyclopedia of Arkansas, Butler Center for Arkansas Studies, Central Arkansas Library System.

Area Detail circa 1830

Also by Kim O. Davis

Disfarmer: Man Behind the Camera

For Judy & Sydney

Acknowledgements

I would like to recognize the assistance of the following individuals who spent considerable time and energy in proofreading my manuscript and for providing invaluable feedback during the editing process: Odean Davis, Daniel Miller, Jesse Plant, Fredia (Turner) Plant, Mike Hartmeier, Chris Davis, Ms. Charlene Lawrence and Larry Lawrence. I would like to give a special thanks to William S. Elkins, a writing instructor with the University of Arkansas at Little Rock. The assistance provided by these individuals was critical in my quest to publish this novel.

Fame is a vapor; popularity an accident; the only earthly certainty is oblivion.

– Mark Twain

Fame is like a shaved pig with a greased tail, and it is only after it has slipped through the hands of some thousands, that some fellow, by mere chance, holds on to it!

– Davy Crockett

I have always been of the mind that in a democracy manners are the only effective weapons against the bowie knife.

– James Russell Lowell, American Romantic Poet, 1819-1891

WHEN PATHS CROSS

Summer 1819

Chapter 1

"I've made up my mind, Colin -- gonna make my mark out on the frontier. I'm leaving at daybreak -- traveling overland to the falls on the Ohio River -- then catching a riverboat down the Mississippi. Going all the way to Louisiana," said young Jimmy Black to his fellow apprentice. "You wanna join me?"

The two young men sat in their cramped, lean-to living quarters outback of Henderson's silversmith and plating shop. It was a moonless night. A whale-oil lamp seated atop a small table in the corner cast eerie shadows on the rough-hewn plank walls as the two roommates sat on straw-covered beds conversing. Having crossed paths under difficult circumstances some ten years earlier, the lads had grown close – like brothers – and Colin, not wanting to anger Jimmy, hesitated before replying. "I don't know. That's a fur piece off. I've never been outside of Philadelphia before. There's Injuns and outlaws out west, you know? Ain't you afraid to go off that far?"

"I'd be lying if I told you otherwise, but it's what I'm determined to do."

"Why am I just now hearing 'bout this? Springing this on me all of a sudden sorta doesn't sit well, us being friends and all," continued Colin.

"I've been dwelling on it for some time. Besides, I know'd how you'd react," said Jimmy becoming more agitated by the minute. "I've made up my mind, I told ya."

Colin pressed on, knowing how Jimmy might react if cornered. "But you've spent all this time 'prenticing as a silversmith? What about your family across the river in New Jersey? You willing to throw it all on the scrap heap?"

"You heard old man Henderson talking about the cheap silver-plate coming in from England. He's been grumbling for a while now about how that 1816 tariff didn't help silversmiths one bit. If he's said it once, he's said it a hundred times, 'I reckon the redcoats can't lick us in a fair fight so they'll try to starve us out by taking away our livelihood.' Besides, I ain't got no family. No sir. Now that I've completed my apprenticeship, I believe I'll try my hand at something different down south. I hear New Orleans is busting at the seams now that steamboats are plying the mighty Mississippi."

"Ain't you gonna stick around and tell the old man you're leaving?"

"Naw. You can do it for me, Colin. Tell him…tell him…tell him whatever you want. Now we best get some sleep. I'm pulling out at daybreak." Jimmy blew out the lamp and crawled under the ragged quilt atop his rickety bed.

* * *

The next morning, the sound of a nearby rooster roused Colin from his heavy slumber. He lay still momentarily, his mind slowly recalling his conversation with Jimmy the night before. He sat up in bed, looking across the way, hoping he was waking from a bad dream. Lying on the empty bed next to him was a note in plain sight. Colin quickly rose from his bed, crossed the room, and picked up the letter. *Old man Henderson may be a hard master, but at least he taught us to read and write a bit,* he thought to himself as he began reading.

Colin,

Never told you bout my famly. Too painful I spose. Mama died when I was small. My stepmama was mean as a snake. Beat me black and blu. Papa was a drunkard. He would watch or join in the beating. Run away from home when I wuz ate. Sherif brung me to mister Henderson. Tell him I am grateful for all. Will miss you.

Jimmy

Colin read the note again and again. In a couple of places, he noticed that the India ink appeared to be smeared by water drops. *Were those teardrops? Nah. As long as I've known Jimmy, I've ne'er seen him shed a tear. Good luck to you, Jimmy. I hope you find what you're seeking.*

* * *

South Louisiana, North of Vermilion Bay, and the Gulf of Mexico.

"Yep Jim, you and me will be wealthy soon, or we'll die tryin'," said Rezin Bowie to his brother. "I hear opportunity knockin', and we need to strike while the iron's hot."

It was a hot, steamy, summer day on the bayou. The two men sat in the shade of a sprawling, live oak tree heavily draped in Spanish moss on their father's plantation. They were drinking rum from a bottle -- passing it back and forth between them. The brothers knew their elderly father was near the end of his days, and according to English tradition, their oldest brother, John, would inherit the vast plantation.

"The planters moving to Louisiana need slaves. The government makin' it illegal to import slaves laid an opportunity at our doorstep. I hear the pirate, Lafitte, is selling slaves by the pound at his new encampment near Galveztown. Don't you have a friend that knows Lafitte?"

"Yep. D.C. Hall knows Lafitte. Hall met the pirate when he was at Dr. Long's filibuster camp – down on the Bolivar Peninsula – across from Galveztown," said Jim.

"I hear Lafitte doesn't want to mess with the slaves. When he captures a Spanish galleon in the Gulf, he's after booty to turn a quick profit. Spanish ships are often carrying slaves still traded in the West Indies islands. The slaves are a problem for Lafitte. Have to be fed and guarded and such. I have a plan to help Monsieur Lafitte with his little problem."

"What's your plan, Rezin? I'm all ears."

"Because Lafitte and his band of pirates helped win the Battle of New Orleans, federal authorities are giving him some leeway long as he's harassing Spanish ships. But he was forced to move his base of operations away from Grand Isle south of New Orleans over to Galveztown, where he's outside U.S. territory. What he needs is a partner with some cash that can buy the slaves and smuggle them into the United States. Lafitte doesn't want to press his luck with the authorities. That's where we come in, Jim."

"I like what I've heard so far," said Jim.

"You have quite a bit of cash from the sale of those forged Louisiana and Arkansas Spanish Land Grants. We know the swamps and bayous of South Louisiana better than anybody. And we have powerful connections from Natchez to New Orleans. So, we offer to take those slaves off Lafitte's hands. We're the perfect middlemen."

"How're we going to sell those slaves without getting ourselves hung or shot in the process?" asked Jim.

"That's the beauty of my plan," said Rezin. There's a reward paid by the government for capturing runaway slaves. Runaway slaves sold at auction become the legal property of the buyer. We can buy the slaves at auction, get half of our payment back from the authorities as our reward, then turn around and sell the slaves at a nice profit. I figure we can make a profit of a couple of hundred dollars per head."

"Phew...that's a tidy profit. How long do you think it'll be before the authorities catch on to us?" asked Jim.

Rezin quipped, "I know one of the federal agents, and he's not the straightest arrow in the quiver. A little kick-back to him now and then may keep this going long enough for us to accumulate a small fortune. The other beauty of this is we can get our hands on U.S. dollars – not some 'promise to pay' from some well-intentioned settler, or a note from some shaky bank in God-knows-where."

"Rezin, with your smarts and my guts, we're going to be as rich as those bastards living on the hill in Natchez," said Jim Bowie to his brother. "I have one last question."

"What's that?" said Rezin.

"When do we get started?" chuckled Jim.

"We need to track down that friend of yours, Hall, and get a letter of introduction to Lafitte. Then we head to Galveztown."

"We should head to New Orleans then. Last I heard, Hall was working for Lafitte selling stolen goods to merchants in the city. We can look up my old friend Caiaphas Ham while we're there. We may need another hand to help keep the slaves from escaping if Lafitte sells us some. Ham's a good hand, and I trust him with my life. Besides, spending a few nights in New Orleans sounds like a fine idea. A little gamblin', drinkin', and seeing some ladies I know there might get me in the right mind to take on this venture. Sounds like we'll be busy for a while."

Chapter 2

After spending a few raucous nights in New Orleans catching up on old times with Hall, Ham, and other old friends, it was time to sober up and get back to work. The Bowie brothers had laid out their daring plan for Hall and Ham over rum and cards. Hall wished them luck but said he needed to stay behind for business reasons. Jim suspected a woman was in the picture. Ham, having no ties to the Crescent City, decided to join the venture.

The following day, the daring trio headed due west on horseback. After several days slogging through the swamps and bayous of south Louisiana, the trio arrived at the Bolivar Straits near the barrier island of Galveztown. On the shore of the bay separating the island from the mainland, they located a local fisherman with a single-masted fishing boat. Rezin paid the fisherman in silver coins for the use of his small vessel for a couple of days. They would use the sloop to traverse the bay to Lafitte's Campeche – the encampment of pirates and their families – located on the nearby island. Jim's friend, D.C. Hall, had been to Campeche on more than one occasion. He had conveyed to Jim that Lafitte had as many as a thousand, well-armed, and cut-throat pirates living on his island paradise. Hall had given them a letter of introduction but said they were still at great peril.

At dawn the next day, the three men set out for Campeche. They left their horses with the fisherman to be watered and fed and as security for the safe return of the boat. The bay was choppy. The brisk breeze blowing inland from the Gulf provided much-needed relief from the sun rising steadily in the summer morning sky. Seagulls dotted the clear, blue sky. Many of the black and white birds quickly spotting the familiar boat flocked to the small fishing vessel seeking scraps of dead fish, shrimp, and squid. Making their way in a southwesterly direction, Ham steered the sloop towards the masts of several ships visible on the horizon. Approaching the docked vessels, they could make out a large African and a shirtless, olive-skinned man eyeing their approach. Both men were well-armed. The African held a musket and had a long sword attached to his waist. The olive-skinned man who wore a yellow bandana on his head cradled a musket in his arms and had two flint-lock pistols in his belt.

As the sloop drifted closer to the dock, the giant African pulled his sword from its sheath and began brandishing it in the air. The African yelled, "unless you have business here, you best turn that dingy around and head back from whence you came!"

Jim shouted back, "We're here to discuss business with Captain Jean Lafitte. We carry a letter of introduction from a mutual acquaintance – Warren D.C. Hall."

The African looked at the yellow-bandana man who nodded his head once, indicating his okay for the men in the boat to approach. "Come alongside then," said the giant African, "but keep your hands in plain sight. Are you armed?"

"We have a couple of pistols, a long-rifle and a knife," Jim replied.

Moored to the docks and anchored in the bay were about twenty or so ships and sloops of various sizes, a couple which bristled with canons. Lafitte's colorful flag of red, yellow, and green was popping in the stiff, gulf breeze blowing across the bay. White-capping waves were visible on the horizon where the mouth of the bay opened into the Gulf of Mexico.

As the three pulled along the dock, a couple of other leathery-skinned men approached the boat. Caiaphas Ham, standing in the bow of the boat, tossed a rope to the African man. Rezin and Jim climbed onto the dock, followed by Caiaphas. Rezin tossed a silver coin to the African who quickly snagged it out of the air with his massive fist. The African flashed a brief smile – a gold-tooth glinted in the sunlight. Rezin had a haversack slung over one shoulder and let the African know he wished to retrieve the letter of introduction from the bag. Rezin, reaching inside the canvas bag, slowly retrieved the letter, handing it to the African. As the African reached to take the note, Jim noticed a long, jagged scar on the man's forearm. Caiaphas saw it too but tried not to stare. Yellow-bandana also had several noticeable scars on his upper torso that looked like puncture wounds or cuts.

The African slowly looked the letter over, then said, "our visitors look thirsty. Take 'em down to the tavern while I take this letter to the Captain." The African nodded his head to the west towards a thatched-roof shack about a quarter-of-a-mile down a path from the docks. Yellow-bandana took off walking, motioning for the three visitors to follow. The other pirates fell in behind.

Yellow-bandana said to him, "What kind of knife do you have on your belt?" Jim unhooked the leather loop holding it in place and pulled the knife from its sheath. The blade was about twelve inches long. He gave it handle-first to Yellow-bandana, who grasped the knife by the handle, then held it up close so he could examine the blade. Yellow-bandana twisted it back and forth, the blade gleaming in the midday sun. He looked Jim in the eye and said, "this looks like a lady's kitchen knife to me." The men behind the visitors began to chuckle. He handed the knife blade-first back to Jim.

Rezin chimed in, "I gave Jim that knife after he was almost killed by a black bear back in the swamps of Louisiana. A blacksmith I know made it. Jim's pistol misfired, and that bear almost killed him. He told me afterward he'd never be caught without a reliable weapon again."

Yellow-bandana said, "We know a few things about misfiring guns and damp powder, don't we boys?" The other men mumbled their agreement.

When the group of men was about a hundred yards from the thatched-roof tavern, the loud sounds of the tavern crowd came wafting down the sandy path. The sounds of laughter, shouting, and cursing of men and a few loud, women, as well as that of a fiddle or two, emanated easily from the open-sided structure.

Yellow-bandana turned to the three visitors and said, "Nobody should give you any trouble as long as you're with me, but don't press your luck. Grog and ale sometimes make men get crazy ideas about who's the meanest one in a room."

Yellow-bandana stepped up to a large table where a group of pirates sat. He motioned for them to vacate the table. They did. The visitors and their escorts then sat down at the table. A man wearing an apron brought them a round of crock mugs full of ale. Jim gazed around the room. A makeshift bar made of wooden barrels topped with pine planks occupied one end of the rectangular tavern. Wooden tables, split-log benches, and roped-bottomed chairs filled the vast room. Rough-hewn men and a few, crusty women held all available seats while many patrons stood about the bar and tables.

The tavern-goers were light-skin, dark skin, and all shades in between. Some wore shirts, and some did not. Some sported hats, and some wore bandanas. Many had beards and long-flowing hair. Most had scars or were missing limbs or eyes. Some accessorized with earrings or necklaces while others sported pistols, swords, and knives. Quite a few showed signs of too much to drink.

The men that had been sitting at the table the visitors now occupied dispersed since no other tables were vacant. Caiaphas became uneasy when he noticed a couple of the displaced men glaring and pointing at them as they made comments to other patrons -- unhappy to relinquish their seats to some outsiders.

At some of the tables, the pirates engaged in games of chance. The sound in the room was deafening due to the loud laughter and boisterous conversations. As the visitors sat at their table, Rezin attempted to learn more from the hosts about Lafitte's pirate encampment. D.C. Hall had warned the Bowies not to use the word "pirate" in referring to Lafitte's band of rogues and scofflaws. D.C.

said Lafitte preferred the term "freebooter" or "privateer" to describe his enterprising brotherhood.

"How many freebooters do you have here at Galveztown?" Rezin asked Yellow-bandana.

"Captain Lafitte has about a thousand men in his service, give or take. And the Captain has named this end of the island Campeche," he replied. "We moved here from Barataria south of New Orleans after U.S. authorities became too meddlesome. The Spanish authorities leave us alone. They're too distracted with Mexican unrest, filibusters, and troubles in Europe to pay us much mind."

Suddenly, there was a commotion at a nearby table. A bearded man jumped up from his chair as he was reaching for a pistol stuck in his belt. A bronze-skinned man with a large gold earring sitting across the table from the man reaching for his gun quickly stood and, using both hands, flipped the table in the direction of the man drawing his flintlock. Cards, mugs, and gold coins went flying. The man with the earring lunged at the man with the pistol, using his left arm to deflect the gun up and away. The pistol discharged with a loud bang. A cloud of dark gray smoke filled the air leaving the smell of sulfur. The black powder gun launched its single lead ball harmlessly into the thatch roof. In one smooth, continuous motion, the charging pirate reached with his right arm, pulled a long-bladed knife from his waistband and swung his arm in a broad arc to his right across the midsection of the gunman. Then in a fluid backward slashing motion, he dragged the blade across the surprised gunman's neck, inflicting a grave and fatal wound. The shocked gunman dropped to his knees, then fell face forward, the gun still in his right hand hitting the floor with a thud. A pool of blood quickly formed around the dying man, turning the nearby cards and coins dark red. The dying man then made a gurgling sound as he drew his last breath. The tavern crowd was eerily quiet for a moment; then, the noise returned as everyone began drinking and having a good time. A few men turned the dead man face up on the floor. His guts were showing in a bloody gash at waist-level, and his nearly severed head dangled from his body.

Yellow-bandana got up and walked over towards the dead man. Jim Bowie followed close behind. The crowd of men stepped back, making room for Yellow-bandana. Bowie stood to his left. Yellow-bandana looked at the knife-wielding assassin and said, "You've got some explaining to do. You know the Captain won't be pleased."

The assassin calmly replied, "He was cheating. I called him out. That's when he went for his pistol." With the tip of his knife blade, the assassin pointed to the dead man's left sleeve. Some cards poked from beneath the sleeve near the dead man's wrist.

Yellow-bandana pointed at a couple of men standing near and said, "Get some men to help you bury him. Now drag him out of here. I'll let the Captain know what happened."

Bowie looked at our escort and said, "What kind of knife is that? I've never seen one like it."

Yellow-bandana looked at the assassin and said, "This man's here to see the Captain about some business. Tell him about your knife."

The assassin, approaching Bowie, swiped the open blade on the back of his pant leg, removing the drying blood of the unfortunate victim. He then held the knife to Bowie, handle first.

The knife was about two hands in length with the blade being half that length, a quarter-inch thick and slightly curved along its bottom. The razor-sharp blade shimmered with faint wavy lines that looked like ripples on water. On the top side, the blade had a straight, flat spine for three inches and a tapered clip point for three inches bringing it to a sharp point. The clip side was also sharpened, allowing the blade to cut in either direction. The fish-shaped, ivory-clad knife-handle was tapered and adorned at its tip with a silver-plated, beaded piece similar to a rattlesnake's rattler. Bowie, noticing the unique decorative beads, said, "It certainly has a bite like a rattlesnake – deadly," as he handed the knife back to its owner.

The assassin referring to his knife said, "She is a *navaja sevillana,* made in Spain from the finest Toledo steel. She will fold in half to cover the blade, but I carry her open in my sash for quick use. She saved my life yet again today." He kissed the knife on its ivory handle.

Bowie commented, “That arcing ‘v’ shaped slashing move you made, is that a move of your own making?”

“No, hombre. I sailed on a Spanish ship with a man that learned knife fighting in Seville, Spain, from Andalusian knife fighters greatly feared for their skills with the *navaja*. He taught me some of their secret moves.”

At that moment, the African that had carried the letter of introduction to Lafitte returned. “Cap’n will see you now,” he stated. “We must not keep him waiting.”

Chapter 3

Yellow-bandana escorted the visitors into the parlor of a two-story, white-washed, clapboard house. The nicely appointed room resembled a French Quarter home. An oriental rug covered the yellow-pine floor. The chairs and tables were of French design. Several swarthy looking men with flintlock rifles, pistols and sabers stood guard at the entrance to the home and in the large hallway that ran down the center of the house.

They had not been in the room for a long when the African man that had taken their letter of introduction entered through the double doors, followed by a handsome man that stood better than six feet tall. The man had dark, flowing hair, a dark, bushy mustache, and was well tanned. He wore a dark blue topcoat with brass buttons. The African man said, “This is Cap’n Lafitte.”

Lafitte said, “So which of you knows my old friend, D.C. Hall?”

“I do, Captain. My name is Jim Bowie. This is my brother Rezin and my friend, Caiaphas Ham.”

“Welcome to Campeche, gentlemen. Please have a seat,” said Lafitte. “Would you care for some chicory coffee or some brandy?”

“We have not had any good coffee in a while,” Rezin replied. “We gladly accept your offer, Captain.”

Lafitte nodded at a nearby servant who went quickly out of the room.

Lafitte then said, "And how do you know D.C., Monsieur Bowie?"

"I have a plantation and business dealings in Rapides Parish," said Bowie. "I have known D.C. for a long time. He has done legal work for the Bowie clan. And we have been on a number of adventures together over the years. We both volunteered to fight with Ol' Hickory at the Battle of New Orleans. Unfortunately, thanks to you and your men, the battle was won before we arrived on the bayou. D.C. and I also did some filibustering with Dr. Long."

Lafitte nodded his head. "I have great respect for D.C. He has done some favors for me in the past."

The servant returned with a two-wheel cart bearing a polished silver coffee service and fine china cups and saucers. The servant served the guests with aromatic cups of coffee. He then bowed to Captain Lafitte and exited the room, closing the sliding double doors behind him.

"So how can I be of service to you, Monsieur Bowie?" asked Lafitte.

Jim said, "I would like for my brother, Rezin, to explain our proposition to you, Captain."

"Very well," said Lafitte.

Rezin then sat forward in his chair and began, "We understand that you occasionally come into possession of some Africans as you conduct your business in the Gulf. We've heard you sell these Africans by the pound and would be interested in purchasing these Africans from you. We plan to transport them across the swamps and bayous of South Louisiana and sell them to planters we know near Natchez and New Orleans."

"You are aware that the government passed a law recently making it illegal to import slaves into the United States or its territories?" said Lafitte.

"We are," said Rezin. "Our plan takes advantage of that law."

"The price is two dollars a pound in gold," said Lafitte.

"We will pay a dollar per pound in gold and silver," Rezin countered.

Lafitte arose from his chair. He turned, stared out the front window a moment, and then turned again towards the table. "Your terms are acceptable. Are you prepared to take delivery today?"

Rezin looked at Jim. Both men stood. Rezin said, "Our father has a plantation on Vermilion Bay between here and New Orleans. We wish to arrange delivery of the first load of Africans by ship to Vermilion Bay on the next full moon."

"Very well, gentlemen. I look forward to doing business with you. Please work out precise details with Louis," said Lafitte as he nodded at the African man who had delivered the letter to Lafitte.

The Bowies shook hands with Lafitte, confirming their agreement.

"Will you gentlemen be staying with us this evening? I believe the men are roasting a few goats and pigs on an open spit tonight. I think you will find our banquet quite enjoyable."

"We appreciate your hospitality, Captain Lafitte, but we need to be on our way back to the bayou," replied Rezin. "We need to begin preparations for our new venture."

"Very well. Louis, escort our guests back to their sloop," said Lafitte to the giant African. "Oh, one other small matter. A man's word is his bond. Don't disappoint me. Au revoir, messieurs." Lafitte turned and left the room.

Spring 1825

Chapter 4

The young man stood at the rail of the steamboat, Enterprise, staring at the red, silt-filled wake moving outward from its bow. The captain was in the pilothouse keeping a careful watch on the side-wheeler's slow progress up the treacherous Red River. The packet boat had departed New Orleans several days ago for its final stop at Fulton, a port town on the banks of the river. The flat-bottom boat sat low in the muddy water loaded with sundries, barrels of whiskey, chickens, and a few other adventurous souls seeking a new life on the frontier. His final destination was not Fulton but a rapidly growing town some fourteen miles north by the name of Washington in Arkansas Territory.

The young man sat on some crates stacked on the boiler deck of the riverboat smoking a pipe – gazing at the muddy river and its tree-lined banks. Towering above the boat along the steep river banks stood giant cottonwood trees upwards of a hundred feet tall, large pecan, oaks, ash, and elm. Dense undergrowth of rattan, muscadine vines, brambles, grasses, and weeds covered the reddish loam and clay banks. With no sign of rock outcropping, the swiftly flowing water quickly eroded the sandy banks causing the towering trees and undergrowth to collapse into the river filling it with numerous trees, snags, limbs, and driftwood. In places, broad, expansive sandbars diverted the main channel into two or three more narrow channels. Captain sure is earning his pay navigating this snag-filled river, thought the young man.

Tired of sitting, the young traveler stood, stretching his legs. At that moment, a well-dressed man with a top hat walked up to him. The younger man had just turned twenty-five. The other gentleman, about ten years his elder, struck up a conversation. "It's easy to see why they call this the Red River."

"Maybe Rusty River would have been a better fit," the younger man remarked.

"Are you traveling from New Orleans?" the older man asked.

"No. I got on board at Alexandria," the young man quipped. "What about yourself?"

"Yes. I've been on a pleasure trip to New Orleans. I spent several days there gambling, dining, and shopping," said the stranger. "Where you heading?"

The younger man replied, "I'm on my way to a town called Washington in Arkansas Territory. I've accepted employment with a blacksmith by the name of Shaw. It seems Shaw's business has grown such that he can no longer keep up with demand."

The stranger energetically replied, "I'm one of the physicians in Washington. My name is Jones," said the stranger.

"My name is Black – James Black," replied the younger man as the two men shook hands. "Folks call me Jimmy."

"The town is bursting at the seams with new residents needing the services of blacksmiths, doctors, lawyers, and others. Are you a full-fledged blacksmith?"

"No, I hope to work as a journeyman for Shaw. I apprenticed to a silversmith in Philadelphia. After completing my indenture at the age of eighteen, I traveled by keelboat downriver to New Orleans and eventually Alexandria where I've worked as a riverboat deckhand and other odd jobs for a few years. I read a notice in a New Orleans newspaper that Shaw was looking for help."

"Shaw has a charming daughter about your age, as I recall. Might that have any bearing on your decision to move to Washington?" asked Dr. Jones.

"I've never met the man or his family," replied Black. "I accepted his offer of employment through the mail."

"Well, you made a wise decision moving to Washington. The town sits on a hill where several trails meet – an ancient crossroads for animals and Indians. Settlers can make their way up from New Orleans along the river route you have taken or overland down the Southwest Trail from St. Louis or Memphis. Washington is the last sizable settlement before you get to Mexican territory lying south of the Red and just west of here. The fertile Red River bottomland first attracted several cotton planters who were soon followed by merchants, lawyers, and doctors. It's a place where a young man can prosper if he's not afraid of hard work. Do you have transportation from Fulton to Washington?" asked Dr. Jones.

Black shook his head no.

"Well, I'm spending the night at the tavern in Fulton, and my servant will be picking me up tomorrow morning in my surrey. You're welcome to ride along with me tomorrow to Washington," said Dr. Jones.

"That's very kind of you, Dr. Jones. I accept your offer."

As Black was tapping his pipe on the railing to empty the ash into the muddy water, the captain blasted the shrill steam whistle announcing the approach to the river port of Fulton. The noise echoed for miles around. Looking upriver, Black could make out the town perched on a sandy bluff above the river. People were gathering near the landing, excitedly waiting to welcome the paddle wheeler from New Orleans.

Dr. Jones suggested the two meet at the tavern in town, and then he briskly turned to fetch his belongings from his cabin. It was nearing dusk. After grabbing his canvas duffel from his quarters, Jimmy made his way to the dock. Several Blacks began immediately unloading the crates, baskets, and containers covering every inch of the boat's decks. Along the riverbank were upwards of fifty to a hundred large bales of cotton ready for loading on the paddle wheeler for the return journey to the cotton market in New Orleans.

Jimmy weaved his way through the bales of cotton, wagons and mule teams, making his way up the riverbank. He followed a muddy road to the top of the embankment and then proceeded down the heavily rutted street running between about ten or so wooden buildings. Eventually, arriving at the tavern, he walked through the open doorway. Furnishings in the room consisted of a bar along the left side and some rough-sawn yellow pine and white oak tables and chairs. Several tables were occupied by customers drinking and eating. He walked up to the barkeep and asked if any rooms were available for the night. The barkeep replied that a private room was eight bits for the night, or one furnished with several bunk beds was two bits. Jimmy chose the bunk bed located on the second floor, first room to the right. Jimmy then took a seat at one of the empty tables to await Dr. Jones's arrival.

About a half-hour later, Dr. Jones arrived carrying a satchel along with a porter carrying a medium-sized wooden trunk. After securing a room for the night, Dr. Jones joined Black at his table. Jimmy said the tavern was serving venison stew and cornbread for supper with apple pie for dessert. The meal cost another two bits. The stew was filling, the cornbread hot and the pie tasty. The conversation was pleasant.

After the two men supped, Dr. Jones turned in for the evening. Black filled his pipe and had an evening smoke. While he sat smoking, he overheard two men at a nearby table discussing a man named Austin. It seems the town had been founded and platted by a Stephen Austin while Spain still controlled the land across the Red. Oddly, this Austin fellow had not lingered long in Fulton. Instead of remaining in the town he founded, the rumor was that Austin had fallen on hard times and moved south to Spanish-owned Texas with his father to start a colony of settlers. The two men at the neighboring table finally called it an evening. Black decided to turn-in also hoping to fall asleep before any snorers or obnoxious drunks joined him in the bunk room.

The next morning, Black awakened to the smell of bacon and coffee and the sound of conversation from below. A washbasin and pitcher of water sat on a nearby vanity. He shaved, washed his face, combed his hair, and then put on a pair of dungarees, a cotton shirt, and leather boots. He grabbed his duffel and headed downstairs. After a brief stop at the privy outback, he returned and seated himself at one of the tables to await Dr. Jones.

A young lady, presumably the wife of the tavern owner, approached Black's table and asked if he cared for any breakfast. He was famished and said, "yes." She brought him a steaming cup of coffee and a few minutes later, returned with a tin plate containing a soda biscuit, five thick-sliced strips of smoked bacon, and two fried eggs. She returned a moment later with a small crock jar containing some yellowish-brown jelly. Jimmy asked her what the pulp was. She smirked and replied, "muscadine, a wild grape that grows in these parts." Black was hungry, and he quickly cleaned his plate.

After finishing his breakfast, he went out front of the tavern to smoke his first bowl of tobacco for the day. The town was starting to come alive. The owner of the general store was sweeping the covered boardwalk in front of his store. A Black youth was brushing a horse in front of the livery stable, and a couple of others drove oxen-led wagons down the rut filled street, apparently returning to the plantation after unloading bales of cotton the day before.

Black was cleaning his pipe when he overheard the voice of Dr. Jones coming from inside the tavern. He stepped inside. Dr. Jones was chatting with the young lady that had served him breakfast. He saw Black enter and said, "Morning, Mr. Black. I hope you slept as well as I did on a cloud-like feather mattress."

Black replied, "Yes, quite well," rather than informing Jones he had slept on a rope-laced bunk bed in a room with five other men who had not bathed in a month.

Jones informed Black that his servant and surrey should arrive around noon after making the four and a half hour trip from Washington – a distance of some fourteen miles. Dr. Jones said he was going to visit a friend who lived in Fulton and asked Jimmy to meet him in front of the tavern a little before noon. Black had noticed there was a blacksmith shop near the livery stable and decided he would head there to talk with the local smithy about the type of work filling his day.

The blacksmith's shop had a slightly pitched roof and two large double doors that had been thrown open. Above the door hung a sign that said "Blacksmith" in large letters and written just below that, the words "Abner Scott." He had a Black and a young, freckled-faced boy working in his shop. The Black was working the large overhead bellows to get the forge ready for the day's work. The young boy was looking over a wagon wheel that needed repairing. The blacksmith was finishing a cup of coffee while directing his two helpers.

Black entered the shop through the open doors and said, "Morning. My name is Jimmy Black. I'm on my way to Washington to work for a blacksmith by the name of Shaw. Do you know of Shaw?"

"Of course," he replied curtly. "How can I help you today?"

"Well, I'm awaiting my transportation to arrive. I saw your shop and thought I might inquire about the type of work you undertake in this area."

The blacksmith drained his cup and stepped towards the door. "Let's talk outside where it's quieter and less distracting to my helpers." The two men stepped outside the shop. "The work I do is a tad different than Shaw's. Fulton being a river port, is less dependent on cotton planters and farmers than Washington. I suspect Shaw works a great deal on plows and such. I mostly shoe horses, fix harness, wagons, and carts, make and repair chain and work on parts for steamboats that pass through here three or four times a week. As with most blacksmiths, we fill our slack time making small fasteners, tools, and implements."

"Do you have any difficulty getting materials and supplies this far west?" Jimmy asked.

"Not really," said Scott. The steamboats that ply these waters make weekly trips to New Orleans. Goods from all over come through New Orleans. I can get iron, steel, tin, copper, silver, and coal – if I can afford to pay for it. Well, Mr. Black, the best of luck to you but, I need to get to work now."

"Good day to you, sir." Jimmy killed time walking around town. He stopped at the mercantile store and found it well stocked for a frontier town. He bought some venison jerky for a noonday snack and returned to the tavern where he sat out front and consumed the dried meat. A little before noon, Dr. Jones arrived back at the inn, followed shortly after that by a surrey driven by Dr. Jones's servant, a gray-haired Black by the name of Major. Sitting beside Major was a young Black about ten years old by the name of Little Charles. Major and

Little Charles loaded the bags and the trunk in the boot of the surrey. Dr. Jones and Jimmy got in the back seat while Major and Little Charles sat upfront. Two dappled gray horses pulled the surrey. Major popped the whip, and the team of horses leaned into the harness pulling the wagon north out of town for the last leg of Jimmy Black's journey to Washington, Arkansas Territory.

Jimmy sat quietly for the first few miles of the journey. He was anxious about what fate awaited him in the frontier town of Washington, about as far from his birthplace in New Jersey as one could be and still be in the United States. He wondered if he had made a wise decision, but he knew there were no guarantees in life.

On the long dusty, bumpy buggy ride north, Dr. Jones talked at length about the more prominent residents of the thriving community. Black quickly gathered that even though he was in the United States and not Europe, it was clear that a class system existed, and politics were ever-present. In the town of Washington and the surrounding community, the social elite consisted of the twelve or so large cotton planters that owned large tracts of land, and between a hundred and two hundred slaves each required to work the large plantations. The next rung down the social ladder ever so slightly were the doctors, lawyers and judges, and the successful merchants. Next came the small farmers that owned a handful of slaves. The next to bottom rung consisted of squatters and laborers followed by the freedmen of color. The very bottom rung consisted of a few Indians that remained in the area and of course, the slaves. Slaves were chattel property, although much more valuable than horses or cows. Even though all of the residents of Hempstead County had come to this crossroads on the edge of the new country chasing the same dreams, the old world-class system had also made the long journey.

After the four had traveled for about two hours, Dr. Jones instructed Major to make a stop under some shady trees at the edge of a large creek. There they stretched their legs, emptied their bladders, and washed their faces in the cool stream. The horses were watered and allowed to graze on the plentiful grass. Little Charles fetched a covered basket and a crock jug from underneath the front seat of the buggy.

Inside the basket were some corn dodgers and cured ham. The jug contained sweet tea. After Dr. Jones and Black had helped themselves, Major and Little Charles took the leftovers and moved away about twenty yards where they ate under a large oak tree.

The two men and the two slaves then loaded back into the carriage and continued their journey up the dusty, dim road. Late afternoon about two hours before sunset, the buggy crested a knoll. Dr. Jones pointed down the way towards the crest of a hill and said, "Mr. Black, yonder lies your new home, Washington of the West."

Chapter 5

Dr. Jones directed Black to Stuart's Tavern, where he "could get a decent room, a hot bath, and square meal, all at a fair price." Jones instructed his driver to drop young Jimmy off at the tavern. Dr. Jones said, "I'll have you over for dinner soon. Good luck to you and good day." Jones tipped his hat as the buggy pulled away.

After securing a second-story room for the night, Jimmy decided to take a bath, put on some clean clothes, and then take a stroll around the bustling frontier town. Several hours of daylight remained. After he dressed, he went downstairs to the tavern and introduced himself to the tavern owner, Elijah Stuart. Jimmy informed Stuart that he was in town to enter the employment of Mr. William Shaw, as a blacksmith. "How long you been here in Washington?" he asked.

Stuart replied, "I'm one of the first settlers in these parts and a founder of the town. I traveled overland down the Southwest Trail from the Duck River Settlement in Tennessee in 1821. Several of the other residents came in the same wagon train. Some in our party stopped at Bates Tavern and some in Little Rock rather than come all this way to the edge of the U.S. Territory. How about yourself? How'd you get here?"

"I came by riverboat from Alexandria up the Mississippi and Red rivers to Fulton."

"That's the safest way to these parts if you are traveling light and can afford the fare," said Stuart. If you wish to bring along your possessions, family, or livestock, the overland route is the cheapest. But it's a back-breaking journey and dangerous to boot. The road, if you' can call it that, is in bad shape – lots of ruts, sinkholes, fallen trees, and a few dilapidated bridges. There're bushwhackers along the way like that murdering John Murrell gang. And starving Injuns that will kill you for a horse or a slab of bacon. Of course, bear and panthers are the least of the varmints you'll encounter. During the warmer months, mosquitoes the size of your thumb swarm day and night and carry malaria. And I'll swear those darn biting flies surely must have a full set of teeth. There are few inns along the Trail, but occasionally you'll come across a settler's cabin that'll allow you to spend the night for eight or ten bits."

"How'd you land on the name of the town?" asked Jimmy.

"It was founded on the President's birthday – February twenty-second," replied Stuart.

"About how many call Washington home?" asked Jimmy.

"If you're talking about white folk, I reckon about a hundred and a half give or take," said Stuart. "There's probably close to four or five hundred slaves. We have a couple of doctors, a handful of lawyers, several merchants, about a dozen plantation owners, one blacksmith as you know, and the rest – small farmers, laborers, women and children – and some Injuns, mostly Choctaws."

"I think I'll take a stroll 'round town while it's still daylight," Jimmy replied. "When are you serving supper?"

"Supper is a little before dusk till shortly after sunset. If you are later than that, you might get some cornbread and buttermilk if you talk nice to the missus."

Black stepped outside the tavern onto the long, covered porch that ran the length of the building. It was a pleasant spring day. The bar and inn sat atop the crest of a hill near the intersection of the two dirt roads A covered water well stood nearby. Across the way, Black could make out the steeple of the small wood-sided church. More of the town appeared to lay straight ahead. He walked to his left down the porch past several half-log benches. The town was laid out in a typical grid with several streets crossing perpendicular to the main road that ran beside the tavern. Black walked north from the inn along a narrow, dirt street lined with residents' homes, some made of hand-hewn logs, and some made of rough-sawn lumber. Intermingled among the houses were a few commercial establishments.

Black passed a law office or two, a general store, a saddle, and leather shop, a couple of more homes, and eventually came to a young magnolia tree that was in bloom with large, cream-colored flowers. The breeze blew a smell much like lemons to his nose. Beyond the magnolia tree, the hill dropped off sharply. Across the road from the magnolia stood a two-story, clapboard building. Jimmy noticed several people gathered in front of the building staring at some papers tacked to a large, sign-like structure standing near the building. The free-standing structure had a roof-like structure running along the top to protect the bulletins from the elements. He walked across the street and up a steep incline to join the small gathering.

Black stepped up behind the people standing in front of the billboard. A man wearing a badge and a sweat-stained hat was tacking a handbill to the board structure, announcing a $200.00 reward for the capture and return of a runaway slave named Hank. The slave had recently fled one of the nearby plantations. The handbill contained a brief physical description of Hank and noted that he stood about five feet, ten inches, and had numerous scars on his back and a large scar that ran from just below the right nipple on his chest and curved downward around his right side. The thought occurred to Black that this was not Hank's first attempt at escape. Another notice caught his eye. It read:

Room for Rent – Meals Available – Terms Negotiable

One Mile West of Washington – Fort Towson Road

Ask for Ben Cooper

Black asked a man who was reading the handbills, "What building is this, sir?" The man replied, "It's the Hempstead County Courthouse."

"I'm new in town. Would you mind pointing me in the direction of Shaw's Blacksmith Shop?"

"It's two blocks east and one block north," said the man.

Black set off in the direction of Shaw's shop. About a block from the shop, he could hear the distinct "clang, clang, ping" of the blacksmith's hammer striking hot iron on the anvil. As he approached the shop, he noticed that business was brisk. There were a couple of ox-driven wagons and saddled-horses out in front of the shop. Several men sat under a large sycamore tree to the right side of the shop conversing. Standing near the wagons were a couple of Blacks, most likely slaves owned by the men under the tree. The shop was open on two sides such that the forge and bellows were visible from the outside. The right corner of the shop that was open to the outside had a rail fence enclosure to keep horses and customers from getting too close to the forge which was glowing red. Smoke was rising through a brick chimney from over the forge. A young boy about sixteen years old in a leather apron was standing near the forge where a Black was operating the large, leather, and wood bellows, forcing air into the forge. With each pull on the chain hanging from the bellows, the charcoal in the forge glowed orange-red, crackled and popped as the smoke was up-drafted into the brick chimney. A middle-aged man in a long, leather apron stood at the anvil, hammering on a piece of glowing iron.

Black stood by the wooden railing on the perimeter of the shop and watched the three work. It was hot, dusty, and smoky inside the shop. The men were all sweating and had black smudges on their faces, arms, and clothing. He waited for a bit until the blacksmith appeared to finish his work on the piece of metal before him. He then spoke to the man by the anvil and said, "I'm looking for Mr. Shaw."

The middle-aged man looked in his direction and said, "I'm Shaw."

"I'm your new hand, James Black. Most call me Jimmy."

Shaw gave him a good look over. "Come around to the left into the shop," said Shaw.

Just inside the open wooden door was a makeshift desk covered with work orders and other papers. Shaw sat down in an oak, swivel chair behind the desk. Then he directed Jimmy to have a seat on a log bench nearby.

"I trust you had an uneventful trip?" said Shaw.

"Yes, sir," said Black.

"You arrived none too soon," said Shaw. "We're considerably behind on our work. Many of my best customers are complaining and threatening to take their business to Fulton. Delays are costing them and me money. Are you ready to go to work?"

"I can be here at sun-up tomorrow," Black eagerly replied.

"Very well. Tell me the kind of blacksmithing you've done?" said Shaw.

"Sir, I was apprenticed as a silversmith in Philadelphia. While in New Orleans, I worked for about a year with an old Spanish blacksmith by the name of Peña. He forged knives in addition to normal smith-work and I applied handles and helped decorate some of the knives. I learned a lot about blacksmithing working with Peña."

Shaw's face became red as the embers in his forge. "That's all the experience you have? You lied to me about your credentials?" Shaw clenched his fists and tightened his jaw.

"Mr. Shaw, your notice in the New Orleans newspaper, stated you were seeking a journeyman blacksmith. I'm a quick learner, and my time spent as a silversmith's apprentice and working with Peña will allow me to become a productive journeyman in short order. Just give me a chance. I'll prove my worth to you. I know the meaning of hard work. I'm not married, so I can work whatever time the job requires."

Shaw sat quietly for a minute or two. He slowly unclenched his fists and jaw. His skin color returned to normal, as did his breathing. "Well, Mr. Black, I suppose I don't have a choice. I've been buying time with my customers by telling them I had help on the way. To disappoint them now will surely do irreparable harm to my reputation. Misrepresenting yourself is no way to begin a relationship, though."

Shaw rose from his chair and paced the floor briefly. "Very well," he said. "I'll pay you six bits a day, Monday through Friday, and 4 bits for a half-days work on Saturdays. We generally close at noon on Saturdays. After a trial period, if your work proves satisfactory, I'll reconsider your wages. Cash and coin are scarce in these parts. I'll keep a ledger of your earnings. We'll settle your account from time to time."

"Those terms are agreeable. You won't be sorry. See you at sunrise tomorrow, Mr. Shaw."

Chapter 6

True to his word, Black was at Shaw's shop before sunrise. Shaw and the two other men he had seen the day before showed up shortly after he had arrived. Shaw introduced "Jimmy Black" to the others as a journeyman from New Orleans. The young, white boy was an apprenticed lad by the name of Nathan Cook, who went by Nat. The Black was Shaw's slave, Willy. Shaw then gave out the work orders for the day. It was run of the mill – repairing plowshares, shoeing horses, fixing single-trees, repairing wagons and wagon wheels. The three wasted little time and got right to work. Willy fired up the forge. Nat began laying out the jobs. Jimmy put on a leather apron and some mule skin gloves that Shaw handed him. Jimmy familiarized himself with the layout of the tools and the area around the forge. Shaw went out front to talk with a man on a wagon.

Willy began working the bellows and got the coal in the forge glowing red-hot. Smoke began rising up through the brick chimney overhead. Willy used a rag to wipe large beads of sweat from his brow. His work shirt quickly became sopping wet with sweat.

Jimmy asked Nat what the first job was that required forge work. Nat retrieved a plowshare from the nearby workbench that was cracked. Jimmy was hesitant to undertake such a repair as his first effort. It surely would garner a close inspection from Shaw. Jimmy said to Nat, "have you got something a bit smaller that needs some forge welding?"

Nat replied, "I got dis slave shackle dat needs mending." Nat handed it to Jimmy, who looked it over. He had never seen anything quite like it. It was a pair of shackles made out of used mule shoes. The open back of the mule shoes had a link from a chain welded to each prong of each shoe. The open side of each shoe had a sturdy piece of metal connected to one of the loops forming a hinge that could be closed and secured with a metal brad. A chain about two feet in length was used to connect the two shoes together, forming a set of shackles. One of the loops of metal securing the chain had worn thin and broken. Jimmy asked Nat what kind of animal was hobbled with such a device.

Willy piped up, "Masser Jimmy, dem shackles is used on slaves dat have run away befoe. They's called 'runners.' They don't run no mo' when dem shackles is placed around they feet."

Jimmy looked carefully at the hand-made shackles. The chain loop attached to one of the shoes that held the length of chain in place had broken due to repeated rubbing against the chain link. It was clear to Jimmy that the "runner" must have been shackled by the reused mule shoes for quite a while to wear the chain link in two. He took the shackles over to the anvil, took a chisel and hammer in hand, then cut away the badly worn chain-link loop. He asked Nat to bring him a short section of chain from outback where scrap materials were kept. Using the hammer and chisel, Jimmy severed the chainlink at the end of the chain. He then took the shackle and the new chain section to the forge. Jimmy directed Willy to work the bellows up and down a couple of times. The hot charcoal crackled, and embers popped and flew in the air.

Using a pair of tongs, Jimmy held the chain link and the end of the shoe in the hottest part of forge until the chainlink was glowing orange-red. He then quickly moved to the anvil. Using the tongs to position the link next to the end of the mule shoe, he then began to hammer away at the link. After the link started to cool and change color back to dull gray, he returned to the hot forge and reheated the link to an orange-red glow. Then back to the anvil, he went for more hammering. He repeated the process until the weld appeared complete. Jimmy then connected the new chain section to the old chain. He heated the severed chain link in the forge and then hammered it on the anvil, repeating the heating and hammering until the gap in the link was welded closed. Jimmy examined the repaired shackles with his naked eye, unable to detect where the welds had been made. He then handed the shackles to Nat, who placed them in a bin holding completed jobs.

Jimmy wiped the sweat and smut from his face with a handkerchief. He walked to the water keg underneath the large sycamore tree growing near the shop. As he was downing his second gourd-full of water, he could see Shaw carefully inspecting the shackles. Using both hands, Shaw gave the two halves a robust and swift tug. And yet again. Satisfied that the weld was holding, he returned the shackles to the finished jobs bin. Shaw showed no expression on his face that would indicate if he was pleased with Black's work. The fact that he did not complain left Jimmy to conclude that Shaw was reasonably satisfied with the quality of his first job.

The gang worked hard until about noon, then broke to eat. Nat and Shaw sat in the shop and ate from their pales. Willy sat underneath the sycamore tree and ate corn dodgers and dry salt meat. Having just arrived the day before, Jimmy had nothing to eat, so he walked down the road to Abraham Block's Mercantile.

Running one of the general stores in Washington, Mr. Block was a very prosperous merchant, as evidenced by owning one of the finest homes in town. It was rumored that his wife had refused to move her young family to the frontier town until she had a proper home with the finest of furnishings and conveniences. Mr. Block was behind the counter when Jimmy walked into the store. He introduced himself as Shaw's new blacksmith. Block replied that he had heard rumors of Jimmy's pending arrival. As a leading citizen of the community, Mr. Block was delighted Jimmy had chosen to make Washington his home. Block said great things were in store for the thriving town, and he was glad to have young craftsmen like Jimmy arriving to help the settlement grow.

Jimmy grabbed a handful of saltine crackers from a barrel and had Mr. Block cut him a thick slice of yellow cheese from a large hoop on the counter. "How much do I owe you?" asked Jimmy.

Making a shooing motion with his hands, Block said, "Your money's no good here today. Please, consider this a small token welcoming you to our fair city."

Jimmy thanked him and left. He ate his cheese and crackers on the way back to the shop but dared not tarry. The look on Shaw's face back at the shop had let Jimmy know his boss was not pleased that he had not brung his noon meal to work. When he returned to the shop, the others were already at work. Jimmy quickly donned his apron and joined the others.

Jimmy worked tirelessly through the afternoon on many different jobs. Shaw carefully scrutinized all of his work before accepting it as finished. Every muscle in Jimmy's body ached. He was sweaty and covered with soot and coal dust from head to toe. He smelled like a polecat. Just before sunset, Shaw said it was time to close up shop. They did so with great haste. Jimmy then ambled toward Stuart's Tavern, where he hoped to get a bath and a hot meal. There was no doubt that he would sleep soundly on his second night in an unfamiliar town.

Chapter 7

It was mid-morning on Saturday, and Shaw announced they would close shop at noon. After work, Jimmy decided to walk west of town on the Fort Towson Road to check on the room for rent he had seen advertised on the bulletin board outside the courthouse. It was too costly for him to continue sleeping and eating at Stuart's Tavern. At noon, Shaw came into the forge and told the men it was time to close up shop. They quickly doused the forge and returned their tools and aprons to their proper places.

When all was done, Jimmy walked into Shaw's office. "Mr. Shaw, I wish to draw some of my wages in cash or coin today if it's not too much trouble? I'm inquiring about a room for rent out on the edge of town, and I may need to make a deposit."

Shaw looked put out. "I suppose, but don't make a habit of this. You need to give me more warning." He went behind a wall and returned lugging a metal strong-box by both handles. He took a key from his pocket and opened the box. "How much do you need?"

"Well, sir, would five dollars be okay?"

Shaw fished around in the box and withdrew three Spanish Real silver coins, eight bits of a Real, and a one-dollar banknote drawn on a Little Rock bank. "Here, take these. I'll make a notation in the ledger. Hope you can make do with this for a while."

Jimmy thanked Shaw, grabbed his haversack, and left the shop. He began walking back towards the center of town. He mumbled to himself. "Shaw. What an ass. Acts like I'm putting him out asking for my own money." He stopped at the covered well – dropped the bucket down the well by – then pulled it back to the top by the attached rope. He grabbed the gourd ladle hanging on the side of the well and took a long drink. The sun was straight-overhead. He was hot, and the water was cool. He got another ladle of water and drank it down. He then took off his leather hat, leaned forward and poured a scoop of water over his head to help him cool down and to wash some dust and grime off his face.

Black walked to the main cross-roads near Stuart's Tavern then headed west on the Fort Towson Road. There was a breeze blowing from the southwest, which helped make the noon sun tolerable. As he walked, he retrieved his haversack slung around his neck and opened the flap. Inside, he had some venison jerky and some stale corn dodgers. There were no other travelers on the road as he walked and ate, enjoying the peace and quiet.

Down the road apiece, he could see a red-tailed hawk sitting on the top branch of a tall, dead tree. The bird of prey was intently scouring the natural prairie lying either side of the road. Suddenly, the hawk leaped from the branch and went streaking down toward the grass-covered field. The bird pounced on something hidden in the tall grass. In a moment, the raptor flapped its wings and lifted from the ground with a small rabbit in its sharp, deadly talons. Black reflected on the moment. *Life could end suddenly out here on the frontier. One minute you are basking in the sun minding your own business and the next...*

Jimmy walked on, enjoying the beauty of the natural prairie. He watched scissor-tails, blue-jays, red-winged blackbirds, and buzzards flying over the landscape. A myriad of butterflies and dragonflies fluttered over the wildflowers growing along the rutted, dirt road. And he listened to the varied songs of the great bird imitator – the mockingbird.

Black had walked near a mile or so when he came upon a dog-trot log cabin on the north side of the road atop a low hill. The locals called it a "dog-trot" because it had a large opening in the center that split the structure into two separate rooms under one roof. The passage between the two structures created a draft allowing a breeze to blow or the dogs to trot unfettered through the middle of the cabin. A long porch ran the length of the cabin. There were several out-buildings behind the cabin. One of the buildings looked like a smokehouse, the other a barn, one a corn crib, and the fourth possibly a kitchen set off from the main house in case of fire. To the left of the cabin was a split-rail fence forming a corral that contained several horses, a mule, and a some of cattle. A creek running east to west crossed in front of the cabin and through the corral. On the right side of the cabin, the stream widened out into a sort of watering hole with some willow trees and cattails growing around the edge of the water. A few ducks were swimming in the watering-hole. A big hog and some suckling pigs were wallowing in the mud nearby. Goats and chickens meandered about the cabin and its outbuildings.

Jimmy turned off the main road and followed a trail that headed toward the cabin. A few split-logs formed a walkway over the muddy creek, and he crossed over them. Approaching the log structure, Jimmy could make out an old man with a long gray beard sitting in a willow rocking chair on the front porch. He appeared to be carving something. Sitting on the edge of the porch nearby was a white-haired, Black man puffing on a corncob pipe. A Kentucky long-rifle leaned against the front of the log structure within arm's length of the gray-bearded man. Jimmy noticed a couple of hound dogs lying in the open space between the two structures. As he approached the cabin, both men appeared to pay him little to no attention.

Black walked up to the cabin and stood in front of the two men. He said, "I'm looking for a Ben Cooper 'bout a room for rent. I saw a bulletin in town at the courthouse. Do you happen to know Mr. Cooper?"

"Maybe," said the gray-bearded man. "Depends on who's asking. Are you thirsty?"

"Yes, sir. That walk from town made me a might thirsty," said Jimmy.

"Grab a gourd full of spring water from that bucket." The gray-bearded man pointed to a wooden bucket sitting in the shade on the front ledge of the porch.

Black took the gourd ladle in hand and scooped up some water. He gulped the water down. It tasted much better than the well-water in town, so he helped himself to a second gourd-full.

"Come on up and have a sit," said the gray-bearded man. "Now who the dickens are you, and what brings you to our doorstep?"

"Name's James Black, but folks call me Jimmy," he said as he clamored up the uneven, split log steps and sat in a nearby willow chair. *Hmmm, the chair is more comfortable than it looks*, thought Black. "I just moved to Washington 'bout a week ago to work at Shaw's blacksmith shop. I'm his new journeyman."

"I'm Ben Cooper," said the gray-bearded man, "and this old coot is Henry," as he pointed his carving knife at the Black man. "Most call me Ol' Ben cause I'm old. That's a fact. Before you get any ideas, Henry ain't my slave. He's a freedman. Henry's former master, Challie McCrary, was a friend of mine. Me and Challie used to fox-hunt and coon-hunt a little and drink a lot. Henry was Challie's house servant and would join us on those hunts. Just before Challie died, he declared Henry a freedman and gave him a signed paper to that effect. After Challie was buried, his eldest son took over the plantation, which is not far from here. Henry wanted nothing to do with the no-account son – can't say as I blame him -- so I asked him to come over here and live with me. You see, Henry is the best dang cook in these parts. I needed me a cook, so he lives here free of charge. Sleeps in the loft of the kitchen that sits outback. Don't reckon you got a problem eatin' next to a former slave, now do you boy?"

"I reckon not," replied Jimmy. "Now is your room for rent?"

"Hold your horses, young Jimmy," said Ben. "Whoops, I see you got nary a horse." Henry let out a chuckle at Ben's jab. "Why don't you tell us a little something about yourself?" said Ben.

Black proceeded to tell the two old men about his short life, including how he ended up in Arkansas Territory. He told them about running away from home in New Jersey and becoming a silversmith's apprentice in Philadelphia. Ol' Ben was particularly interested in hearing more about Jimmy's time spent with the Spanish knife maker in New Orleans and the men who bought the knives.

"How long you been in these parts?" Jimmy asked Ol' Ben.

Ben carved a couple more strokes on the piece of wood he held in his hand. "Well sir, I first came to these parts with the Freeman-Custis Red River Expedition that was commissioned by President Jefferson shortly after the Louisiana Purchase. I was living in Natchez, Mississippi, at the time. I joined the expedition 'cause it sounded like a great adventure to explore uncharted territory on behalf of the U.S. Government. We were supposed to trace the Red to its headwaters, thinking it might open a trading route to Spanish held Santa Fe. The expedition was doomed from the start. A jackass by the name of Wilkinson got word to the Spanish authorities about the expedition. We had traveled a few hundred miles upriver when we were intercepted by 'bout two hundred Spanish soldiers near Pecan Point not far from here. Pecan Point is the site of an ancient river crossing for large herds of buffalo. Thanks to a parlay and bluff by Freeman, the Spaniards allowed us to turn around and head back down river rather than being shot on the spot or imprisoned. On our way back to Louisiana, we established trading contacts with the Caddo and Choctaw Indians that lived along the river."

"Being a young man full of piss and vinegar, I saw opportunity in this area, so I later returned here. I trapped beaver mostly along the creeks and streams flowing into the Red. I hunted buffalo, bear, and deer for their hides and meat. A man by the name of Levi Davis operated a trading post on the Red 'bout a day's ride east of Pecan Point. I traded hides and meat with Levi or with the local Injuns. Eventually – I got too old to sleep under the stars, so I rode over here to visit my old friend, Challie. We grew up together back in Virginia. He found his lifelong dream of being a large plantation owner raising cotton just down the road from here. He told me about this place with its spring-fed creek. I purchased forty acres and built this here cabin and farm. It's not much, but I'm living off the land and my wits still."

Ol' Ben paused a bit, staring off into space.

"Henry? Why don't you tell young Jimmy what brought you to this place?" said Ben.

Henry had not said a word since Black had arrived. "Ohhhh, Misser Ben, you done heard my story," said Henry chuckling. "White folk don't care nutin' about an ol' slave's life anywho."

"Tell it anyway, Henry. Besides, you're a freedman now," urged Ben.

"Well, suh, I don't rightly know a lot 'bout my early years. I can tell what I know, I 'spose. My firs' recollection is about my Mammy. I was 'bout 5 years ol' workin' on a plantation on the Alabama River. Us chillins had to work da cotton fields jess like big folk. We had to pick da cotton and put it in a big sack. Dat cotton look soff, but it war prickly – cut my fingers till they bleed. Da boss man sho' 'nuff don't like us slaves bleedin' all over dem white cotton balls. When we got back from da field, we went into the slave quarters. Mammy heard me a cryin'. She went off somers and came back with a big leaf rolled up. Inside dat leaf was some salve she had mixed up wif some yarbs and some bar fat. She rubs dat salve on my fingers, and while she did, she sang me a song till I fell asleep. I never knew my pappy. Mammy never say nutin' 'bout my pappy. She told me her mammy's mammy came on a slave ship from Africa. Dat's all I 'member 'bout my family."

"When I was 'bout twelve years old, some white men came and took me away from my Mammy. I was a cryin' for dem not to take me, and my Mammy was a cryin' and a fightin' to get me away from dem men. Some of t' other slaves was tryin' to get my Mammy to calm down. I was placed on a wagon with some other slaves, and we drove off. I never seen my Mammy again." Henry paused for a moment and puffed hard on his pipe, blowing a smoke ring in the air.

"We traveled for 'bout two or tree months and finally ended up on Masser McCrary's plantation down da road a piece. I worked the cotton fields til I wuz 'bout twenty-five years old. Masser McCrary had a bunch of hound dogs that he use to go huntin' wit. One day, dem hounds got to chasin' after a deer. Dem dogs chase dat deer into da swamp down by da bayou. Well, all dem dogs came back da nex day 'cept for Masser's bes' hound dog. Da Masser was bery upset. He told da boss man to get all da slaves and go into da swamp to find dat dog."

"Most of da slaves were 'fraid of dat swamp cause of snakes and gators an' such. Shoot, I weren't 'fraid of no swamp. Rather be in dat swamp dan in dat hot cotton patch. I backtracked where dose dogs had been and found Masser's best dog, Ol' King, lying in da' swamp. His front leg was all swole up from where a big ol' cottonmouth done bit him. I carried Ol' King out of da swamp back to da slave quarters. I mixed up some dat salve my Mammy used to put on my fingers and put it on dat dog's leg. Next day, I took Ol' King to the Masser's house. Ol' King was a waggin' his tail when he seen da Masser. Dat day, Masser McCrary said I was gonna become his personal servant in da big house. I never chop or pick cotton another day of my life. And now I is a freedman sittin' on dis porch talkin' to you white folks. Da good Lord works in mysterious ways. He sho do."

Jimmy sat speechless for a few minutes. *Here I thought Henry was mute. Henry could talk the hind legs off a donkey.* Henry repacked his corncob pipe, lit a match, and began to puff away, blowing another smoke ring into the air. He poked at the smoke ring with the pipe stem. Jimmy watched the smoke ring drift out of sight, then turned to face Ben.

"Well, Mr. Cooper, I've enjoyed the story tellin', but I guess I need to be headin' back to town before dark. Is that room for rent or not?"

Ben looked at Henry, who was puffin' away on his pipe and staring into space. Henry gave a wink back at Ben. "I suppose it is. Let me show you the room."

Ol' Ben got up from his rocker and began walking towards the dogtrot. Black rose up from his twig chair and followed him. Ben opened the door into the room on the right side of the dogtrot. The room was furnished with a rope bed, a large wooden trunk sat at the foot of the bed, a small table holding a washbasin, and a ladder-back chair sat by a front-facing window. A fireplace was on the end wall opposite the door.

"This is it," said Ben. "Taint much but beats sleepin' on a bedroll on the ground."

"How much?"

"Depends," he said. "If you're willing to do some chores 'round here when asked, I'll require five dollars a month. If'n you wish to eat some of your meals with me and Henry in the kitchen, it'll cost you an additional two dollars a month. I know you have a full-time job in town and I'll not over-work you with chores. It's just that me and Henry are not as spry as we used to be, and we need some help from time to time. I assume you can shoe horses, help with the garden, patch a leaky roof, that sort of thing?"

"Mr. Cooper, those terms seem fair to me. When can I move in?"

"The room is yours," he replied. "And call me Ben like everyone else. Deal?"

"Deal," said Jimmy as the two men shook hands. "How about if I move my things tomorrow morning?"

"You know tomorrow's Sunday," said Ben. You, not a church-going type?"

"No, sir. Never found time for religion," said Jimmy.

"We'll be expecting you. Pardon my jest earlier, but since you walked here from town, I take it you don't own a horse?" quizzed Ben.

"No, sir, I haven't yet saved enough money to buy one."

"Well, let's go over to my pasture and pick you out a horse. I have an extra saddle, bridle, and such in the barn. You're welcome to it. We can work out payment later."

Jimmy's jaw dropped, and he stood motionless with mouth agape. "I don't know what to say. How do you know I'll pay my debt?"

"Young Jimmy, one thing you need to know about Ol' Ben Cooper, don't cross me 'cause I can be your worst nightmare. I'll get my payment out of your hide if need be."

Jimmy followed Ben out of the room, down the steps and along a path to the corral. There were several horses in the pasture. Some were showing a little age. There was a sorrel gelding with a blonde mane and tail and what looked like white socks on the back legs. It caught Jimmy's eyes immediately. That was the one. Ol' Ben walked up to where Jimmy was standing with an apple in one hand and a rope in the other.

"Have you picked one out?" he asked.

"How 'bout that sorrel horse with the white socks?" Jimmy asked.

"You got a good eye for horseflesh," Ben replied. "That's the one I expected you'd take."

Ol' Ben gave a whistle and held out the apple. The gelding sauntered to the rail fence. Ben slowly lifted a rail, climbed over the fence and held the apple to the horse's mouth. As the horse was sniffing the apple, Ben slipped the rope around his neck. He started leading the horse towards the log barn. Jimmy followed. After the horse was saddled and bridled, Jimmy put his foot in the stirrup and mounted the colt. Ol' Ben rubbed the horse between his eyes and said, "You take good care of this one, or you'll have hell to pay with me later."

Jimmy was grinning from ear to ear. "Does he have a name?"

"Never gave him one," mumbled Ben.

"Think I'll call him Socks." Jimmy then directed Socks down the path to the bridge over the creek and back onto the road. He twisted in the saddle and waved back at Ben and Henry, then turned east and headed back to town. As he rode Socks toward Washington, his mind wandered back to the two very different men living on a small farm on the edge of the territory. *One man had lived a life of total freedom away from civilization. The other lived as a slave for most of his adult life. An odd pair, to say the least. And here he was now...sitting on the back of the most beautiful horse in the territory because of the generosity of a near-total stranger. Maybe his luck was about to change.*

Chapter 8

Bowie Plantation, Louisiana.

"Rezin, I'm heading back to Texas," said Jim Bowie to his closest brother.

"Whoa, there hoss. Why, Jim? You finally have this plantation you've always wanted. Why sacrifice what you've worked so hard to build?"

"I don't own this place outright," said Jim. "The noteholders are demanding payment. I can't hold 'em at bay much longer. I'm cutting my losses and selling out before the buzzards pick my bones clean."

"What happened to all the money from our slave-trading venture?" asked Rezin.

"You know how I like to live it up. What money I didn't lose on land speculation, I lost gambling on horses and cards or frittered it away on women and rum. Let's face it, Rezin – I'm not cut out for planting – or stock raising. I'm a hunter -- an opportunist. All those years, I envied those planters living in their fine summer mansions up on the bluff at Natchez, looking down on the ne'er do well Under the Hill. Well…I say be careful what you wish for, that's all."

"Jim, don't make a hasty decision here. We can figure this out. We can find a way to get our hands on more money or buy some time with the lenders. Don't you think it's time you settled down?"

"I'm afraid there's more to the story, Rezin. The Federal Land Commissioner and U.S. Marshals are hot on my trail. They've figured out those Spanish Land Grants I've been selling are forgeries. I broke in the Land Office at Alexandria the other night -- stole and burned all the documents I could find. Left them no evidence against me. That'll slow 'em down a bit, but it's best I put some distance between me and those I duped. Need to let things cool off a bit. May have to do the same up in Arkansas soon."

"Why Texas of all places, Jim? You know Texas is a powder keg with the fuse lit. Tensions are running high. The Mexican Government's attitude toward white settlers shifts like the Texas wind. The Mexican Army could decide overnight to seize those Texians' properties, run 'em back across the border to the U.S., or worse – slaughter 'em like sheep. Besides, I hear settlers have to pledge allegiance to the Mexican Government and convert to Catholicism. You're a God-fearing Presbyterian, Jim. Our Scottish ancestors risked everything coming here to escape Catholic persecution in Ireland. Are you willing to up and forsake your ancestry, your country and in the blink of an eye, become a Catholic?"

"My loyalties are to ol' Jim Bowie. All that turmoil in Texas creates opportunity. It's a big game of chance, and I like my odds. The Mexicans are giving away vast parcels of land for practically nothing. Several of our old neighbors from up in Missouri are down in Texas, cashing in while the opportunity lasts. You remember Moses Austin and his boy Stephen from when we were young 'uns? After his lead mines went broke a few years back, Moses set his sights on Texas. Seems he convinced a Spanish governor to let him start a colony on the Brazos River. Like his name-sake – Moses led folks to the promised land in Texas but never lived long enough to see his vision through. His son, Stephen, honored his father's death-wish and moved from Arkansas to continue what his father had started. And you remember that bunch of Trammell's from Missouri? Well, old Nick Trammell cut a trail from Arkansas across the Red River down to Nacogdoches, Texas. Folks call it Trammell's Trace. Seems old Nick's been trading contraband with the Indians and Mexicans in Texas for years. Goods like horses and salt. Why shouldn't I join our old Missouri neighbors seeking fame and fortune in Texas, Rezin?"

"Jim, you've always been drawn to adventure like a moth to a candle."

"Yep. Remember when we were younger, and we'd rope and ride 'gators in the swamp? I guess I just want to catch and ride a bigger and meaner ‘gator. I thrive on seeing what lies around the next bend in the river or over the next hill. Some might say I suffer from an itchy foot. Maybe I do. It’s my God-given right to pursue freedom and opportunity.”

“I’m wasting my breath. Your mind’s made up, but I may let you ride this ‘gator by yourself this time,” said Rezin. “My family needs me here in Louisiana.”

“Don’t blame you none. If I had a family of my own, I might sit this one out too, Rezin. But I don’t. So, I’ve gonna rope and ride this gator.” *This ‘gator might get the best of me – time will tell*, Jim thought to himself.

Fall 1825

Chapter 9

A few months had passed since Jimmy began working for Shaw. Shaw seemed pleased with Black's work, although he had not said so directly. At least he had not complained. Jimmy deemed that progress.

With Black's help, Shaw was caught up on the backlog, and work was getting done on-time for a change. And the quality of the work was much improved. Word had spread, and business was brisk. Because of the increased workload, Shaw had recently hired his son, Thomas Jefferson Shaw, to work at the shop. Shaw wanted Tom to learn the family trade.

It was a slow day, and Shaw was gone in the wagon to Fulton with Willy to pick up supplies arriving from New Orleans. Jimmy, Nat, and Tom were taking a break from their tasks. The three young men, all about the same age, had much in common and were becoming fast friends.

"Where did you learn to blacksmith so good?" asked Tom.

"I spent some time in New Orleans working for a blacksmith," said Jimmy. "The blacksmith was an old Creole by the name of Diego Peña. Peña learned his skills from his grandfather, who was a full-blood Spaniard from some town in Spain known for its steel and knife making."

"I thought you was from out East? Philadelphia or some such?" said Nat.

"I was born in New Jersey. When I got a might older, I didn't get along with my stepmother, so I ran away from home to Philadelphia. Sheriff there caught me, and I was apprenticed to a silversmith when I was about fourteen. After I turned eighteen and had completed my apprenticeship, I decided to head south. I hired on as a deckhand on a keelboat and floated down the Ohio and Mississippi to New Orleans. One day, I stumbled across Peña's shop in the French Quarter. He was making fancy knives for wealthy merchants and planters. I convinced him I could do some silver inlay on his knives that would add to the price they would fetch. Peña agreed to pay me per piece if my work was good."

"What kind of knives was he making?" asked Tom.

"Peña made fixed blade knives and folding knives that gentlemen could carry in their pockets," Jimmy replied. "Peña told me they've been making knives in Spain before the time of the Romans. Because of his skill, a Spanish governor brought Peña's grandfather from Spain to Louisiana when it was part of Spain."

"Did he make knives full-time?" quizzed Nat.

"Peña had a thriving shop with a couple of blacksmiths working for him. They did all kinds of smith work. Peña spent most of his time making knives."

"We get quite a few folks stopping by here inquiring if Shaw makes knives," said Nat. "A lot of pioneers headed across the Red to Texas are looking for knives. Shaw turns away their business. Says he has no time to waste on knife making. I think its 'cause he don't know nothin' 'bout knife making. Did you learn any knife making while you worked for Peña?"

"I watched him make a lot of knives while I was there," said Jimmy. "I never actually made a knife from start to finish, but I think I could if I tried. If he was making a knife for a wealthy merchant, a gambler, or a planter, he would give me the knife to add some silver touches to the handle or some inlay on the blade. He would then double or triple the price of the knife."

Nat paused and looked down at his feet. "Mostly the men passing through here are looking for a heavy-duty knife for skinnin' animals or for protection. But I think a fellow could make a nice livin' makin' and sellin' knives. Maybe you should try your hand at makin' one or two in your spare time, Jimmy."

"I'll think about it," said Jimmy. "I guess we best get back to work. Shaw will be madder than a hornet if he returns and finds us loafin'."

The three young men returned to work. They repaired some farm implements, made some kitchen pot hooks for one of the ladies in town, made some split shoes for a team of oxen that would be shod later in the week, and worked on a few other odd jobs. The sun was straight overhead, so they decided to stop for their noon meal.

Jimmy had brought his noon meal. He grabbed his knapsack and went out under the big sycamore tree next to the shop and sat on a half-log bench. Reaching into his pack and pulled out a biscuit, some salted pork and a hunk of cheese. As he sat in the shade of the tree enjoying his meal, he noticed a young lady walking down the road toward the shop. She looked to be about eighteen years of age. She was wearing a colorful calico dress, and her shoulder-length, chestnut-colored hair glistened in the noon-day sun.

The young lady was strolling along the road, taking in the sights along the way. As she approached the shop, she saw Jimmy watching her from underneath the big sycamore. She began to walk a bit more briskly and came up to where he was sitting.

Jimmy set his morsels on the bench and was getting ready to stand when she said, "Please keep your seat and finish your meal. You must be Mr. Black, the new blacksmith."

Jimmy almost choked on his hard biscuit. "How do you know my name?"

"My father's your employer. I'm his oldest daughter, Anne. I've heard him speak of you on several occasions. He speaks highly of your skill as a blacksmith."

Black's jaw dropped.

"You're going to catch flies if you're not careful, Mr. Black," she giggled.

Jimmy quickly closed his mouth. "You can call me Jimmy," he replied. "May I call you Anne?"

"Why what else would you call me?" she said.

Jimmy looked a bit dumbfounded. "Would you like to sit down? How about something to eat? I have ample."

"No, thank you, Mr. Black, err...Jimmy. I can't stay long. I will say hello to my brother, Tom, then be on my way. I'm off to look at some fabric at Block's Mercantile. Besides, Papa doesn't like me visiting the shop so I best not tarry. Papa has a terrible temper, and I do not wish to incur his wrath. Nor give him a reason to be angry with you." Anne twirled on her toes and briskly walked towards the entrance to the shop. She was about five feet, six inches tall. Her shapeliness was quite apparent even under her calico dress.

"I hope to see you again sometime," Jimmy called out to her.

She did not hear him or simply chose not to let on that she did. Jimmy tried to finish his meal, but the biscuit and pork he was chewing seemed to swell and toughen in his mouth. His mouth became dry as cotton. He put the remnants of his meal in his knapsack and went to the water bucket where he drank a gourd full of tepid water. His palms were sweaty, and he wiped them on his pants. He remained under the tree until Miss Shaw exited the shop and continued her stroll towards Block's store. She did not waive or look his way as she strolled up the lane.

Jimmy entered the shop and found Nat and Tom sitting calmly finishing their meals. Black paced the floor in front of them.

"Did you meet the boss's daughter?" asked Nat. He clearly did not notice young Jimmy's agitated condition.

"Er...uh...yes, we talked briefly outside," he said.

"She has the old man wrapped around her finger. She's his pride and joy," said Tom.

"How old is she?" asked Jimmy.

"She's eighteen," said Tom.

"Do you know if she is seeing a beau or promised to anyone?" Jimmy asked.

Tom looked up at Jimmy with a concerned look on his face. "Why all the questions of a sudden? You just met the girl. Pa is very protective of his children and Anne, most of all. You best think of her as the boss's daughter and let it end there. Else Pa will come down on you like a hammer on an anvil."

Nat threw Jimmy his apron as he began putting his back on. "We best get busy," said Nat. "When the old man shows up tomorrow morning, there'll be hell to pay if he thinks we've been lollygagging."

Jimmy put on his apron and headed back to the forge. As they worked and sweated through the hot afternoon, his mind kept wandering to thoughts of the young and graceful Anne. *Surely Shaw would not have a problem with me courting his daughter. After all, Shaw spoke highly of my work in her presence. I'm gainfully employed in an honorable and essential trade. I'm not a drunkard. She could certainly do worse by someone else.*

Black made up his mind that afternoon. *I'm going to get better acquainted with Miss Anne Shaw even if she is the boss's daughter. Surely I can prove myself a viable suitor if given the opportunity. Although I'm not a man of means, I have much to offer Anne. Shaw's a reasonable man.*

Chapter 10

The men at Shaw's Blacksmith Shop generally worked six days a week. They never worked on Sundays – Shaw said that was the Lord's day. On Saturdays, if they were caught up on work, Shaw would usually close the shop at noon. It was on one such Saturday that Shaw announced at mid-morning, they would be closing at noon. Black had been waiting on such an occasion. He went to Shaw, who was at his desk looking over some papers. "Mr. Shaw, I have a favor to ask?"

Shaw, a bit apprehensive, looked at Jimmy with raised eyebrows.

"I want to practice some knife making skills I saw when I was working in New Orleans. I'd like to use the forge this afternoon if it's okay with you. I'll close up proper afterward," said Jimmy.

Shaw thought about it for a moment, then agreed. How could he refuse the young man's request? After all, Black's enhancing his skills would make him more valuable to Shaw. Shaw, Nat, Tom, and Willy called it a day, leaving Black alone at the shop.

Jimmy had been preparing for this opportunity after he, Nat, and Tom had discussed knife making. Jimmy had stored some materials and other items in a safe place in the back of the shop. The old Creole, Peña, in New Orleans had taken a liking to Jimmy and had shared many details of his technique, which had been taught to him by his grandfather. Peña and his wife had no children. Jimmy always thought he was looked at as the son Peña and his wife never had. Or maybe Peña simply wanted his knife making technique to live on with Jimmy.

Peña's knife making was a lengthy, multi-step process that relied on technique and skill. Black recalled the process but definitely had not mastered Peña's technique nor his expertise. That would only come with a lot of practice and patience – trial and error.

The first step was to get his hands on some steel. At Shaw's, they typically worked with wrought iron, not steel. Peña had shown Jimmy how to create steel from ordinary wrought iron. Peña had made something called blister steel. Black had set aside five pieces of iron about six inches in length by two inches wide by three-quarters inch thick. He had purchased a crock jar with a tight-fitting crock lid from a local potter. After placing the pieces of iron inside the crock jar, he then packed the jar with pulverized charcoal, surrounding each of the iron plates with the grayish powder. The lid was firmly placed in the mouth of the crock jar. Jimmy then sealed the top in place with some wet clay to keep out any air.

Jimmy went to the forge that was still hot from the morning's work and pumped the large bellows several times until the coals glowed red. He then raked the coals away from the center of the forge, creating an indention where he placed the crock jar. Next, the young blacksmith piled charcoal around the container leaving only the top visible. Now he simply needed to keep the coals hot but not too hot – for a couple of hours.

Using an hourglass, he let two hours pass. He then took a large pair of tongs and lifted the crock crucible out of the forge. He set the jar on the ground and let it cool down a bit. He then removed the lid and emptied the contents onto the sandy floor. Magically, the iron plates were now covered with grayish blisters. The iron had become blister steel. Jimmy dropped the hot bars of steel into a bucket of water to quickly cool them off.

While the plates were cooling in the water, he added more charcoal to the forge and made sure his tools were in order. He fetched a wooden bucket containing a mixture of powdered limestone and fine sand that he would use as a flux and poured some into a wooden tray. He then retrieved the metal plates from the water bucket.

The next step in the process involved forge welding the plates together into a billet. Jimmy decided he would first weld three plates together which needed to be reasonably clean. He used a stiff brush and a file to clean the scale from the plates. Next, he coated the steel bars with flux by rolling them around in the wooden tray containing the mixture of fine sand and powdered limestone.

Next, he pancaked the three metal plates together and with the long tongs, placed them in the middle of the forge. He worked the bellows until the plates glowed bright orange. He grabbed the three bars with the tongs and carried them to the anvil, where he proceeded to hammer the plates down the center and then hammered outward towards the edges of the plates. As Jimmy struck the hot metal, sparks flew into the air as the flux worked its way out from between the rectangular bars of steel, removing the impurities and scale in the process. As he hammered, the plates began to cool to a dull, gray color. Black repeated heating and striking the chunk of metal several more times. The plates were slowly welded together into a single billet of steel. Heating the metal in the charcoal fire also added carbon to the crude steel.

The next step in the process again relied on the forge, anvil, and hammer to create layer upon layer of steel, all-welded together into a single piece of flattened metal. Beginning the process, the blacksmith would again heat the welded-metal billet to a reddish-orange color. Next, using the anvil and tong, the metal billet was bent and folded in half, then beaten till welded into a single piece of metal. Black then reheated the metal bundle to welding temperature and hammer-welded the metal, drawing out the steel into a thinner, longer, and broader piece. Again and again, he reheated the billet to a bright orange color and began to draw out the metal to extend its length and width. He repeated the process multiple times, resulting in a fused, single piece of steel composed of 48 layers of blister steel.

Black was tired, sweaty, dirty, and hungry. The sun was getting low in the sky. He felt like he had accomplished quite a bit and decided to call it a day. Besides, tomorrow was Sunday, and there was going to be a pot-luck dinner on the grounds following the morning service at the Methodist Church. Although Jimmy was not the church-going type, he was planning to attend the service and dinner afterward because he had overheard Shaw telling Nat about the event and that the entire Shaw family would be in attendance. Jimmy thought to himself about how the day might go. *It'll be a perfect opportunity to bump into Anne there without raising any eyebrows. Besides, many of the important people in town will be there. It never hurts to rub shoulders with such folks. Those acquaintances may come in handy down the road.*

Jimmy carried the crock jar and metal billet to his safekeeping place outback. He then returned all of the tools and materials to their proper places, doused the forge, and closed up shop. He saddled Socks and headed west to his new home at Ben Cooper's cabin on the edge of town.

Chapter 11

The Methodist Church was one of the oldest buildings in the young town of Washington. It was a white, clapboard sided structure with a tall steeple. The Reverend Stevenson, who founded the church, was one of the earliest settlers to make Washington his home. Jimmy was on the edge of town when he heard the church bell clanging away. *Looks like I'm going to be a tad late for the prayer meeting*, he thought as he gently kicked his heels into the side of his gentle horse, Socks. "Giddyup, boy. Preacher's not waiting on us today."

The church was surrounded by a stand of oak, sweetgum, and hickory trees. In preparation for the dinner-on-the-ground following the service, several make-shift tables had been set up under the trees to the right of the chapel. Buggies, wagons, and horses were tied-up to the trees around the church. A group of Blacks was gathered in the shade of a large catalpa tree with its distinctive, large, heart-shaped leaves. The slaves had driven some of the wealthier planters and townsfolk to the service. A couple of the Blacks were smoking corn cob pipes. Black reined Socks to a halt, leaped to the ground, and quickly tied the horse to the nearest tree. He then walked briskly to the front entrance of the chapel.

He gently opened the large oak door and slipped into the sanctuary. He squeezed into a seat next to a rotund woman on the back pew. She was sweating profusely as she fanned herself with a pasteboard fan. The church was packed with local citizens – most dressed in their most elegant outfits. Many of the women wore hats or bonnets. The well-to-do men of the community had on suits with string bow ties. Jimmy had on a pair of well-worn but clean, dark pants and a white shirt. His shoes showed some wear but had been carefully shined with some bear tallow and lampblack.

It was a hot, muggy July day, and the windows on both sides of the sanctuary were opened wide. Like the woman next to Jimmy, many of the women were fanning themselves in a feeble attempt to stay cool. The service began with the congregation being led in the singing a few well-known hymns. The music was provided by a little gray-haired woman playing the upright piano that set to the left of the pulpit.

While the singing was underway, Jimmy craned his neck, peering around the hats and heads in front of him, trying to catch a glimpse of Anne Shaw and the rest of her family. He knew Shaw was among the congregation because he had noticed Shaw's buckboard outside under a shade tree. Black finally spotted Shaw on a pew on the right-hand side of the church, about five rows from the front. Middle of the bench, he could make out the back of young Anne's head. From the movement of her head, she appeared deeply engaged in the singing.

At the end of the sixth hymn, the music conductor stepped down from the pulpit and took a seat on the front pew. Reverend Stevenson arose from a chair behind the pulpit and stepped up to the lectern. He asked the congregation to rise – then led the group in prayer. After the prayer, he motioned for the congregation to be seated.

"Brothers and sisters, we are gathered here today to celebrate this beautiful Sabbath the Lord has made." Several "amens" were uttered by some of the deacons seated as a group in reserved pews to the left of the pulpit. "The Lord has blessed us with this glorious day on which to celebrate Him through the study of His word and through the fellowship following the service where we will break bread together. As you know, we are having a potluck dinner on the grounds after the service, and everyone is welcome to attend. Before we feast on the wonderful dishes lovingly prepared by the women of the church, let us feast upon the Word of the Lord, our God, and Savior, Jesus Christ."

Reverend Stevenson opened his Bible, extracted several loose pages, and laid the pages on the lectern. He then placed his Bible next to his sermon notes. He paused with his head bowed and then raised his head and looked out over the congregation.

"I look around the congregation today, and I see many familiar faces. But I also see many new faces as well. Our young town sits on the western edge of the United States in this territory known as Arkansas. Naturally, as a town on the edge of the frontier, we have many new arrivals in our community. Some are settlers looking to make their home in our fair town. Others are merely passing through on their way to Texas in search of cheap land. All are seeking a new life for their families. My old friend from Missouri, Moses Austin, and his son, Stephen, went to Texas a few years, so I know of what I speak. Texas colonists are required to pledge allegiance to a new flag and to forsake their religion for a new one. For those of you headed to Texas, I beg you to think carefully about what lies ahead for you and your families. But enough about Texas."

"Children of God, I see strife in our midst. Many of you have found a new and abundant life for your families here. As pioneers to Arkansas, some of you have prospered. Others are less fortunate. Following the many paths leading to Washington by land or river has been an arduous journey. Many have died along the way – taken by disease, starvation, unfortunate accidents, or at the hands of bushwhackers or renegade Indians. Just like the Israelites in search of the Promised Land, many more will journey to our town. Some will choose to stay helping our town thrive and prosper. Others will choose to face more hardship and continue their journey to Mexico. How we treat these sojourners may sway them to stay or go. Our Heavenly Father, through His written word, provides us guidance on how we are to treat our fellow man."

"Let us now read the word of God from the New Testament. Open your Bible and turn with me to Galatians, chapter three, verses twenty-six through twenty-nine, 'For you are all children of God, through faith in Christ Jesus. For as many of you as were baptized into Christ have put on Christ. There is neither Jew nor Greek, there is neither slave nor free man, there is neither male nor female; for you are all one in Christ Jesus. If you are Christ's, then you are Abraham's offspring and heirs according to promise.'"

"Now let us take heed of the Ten Commandments. In Mark, chapter twelve, verse thirty-one, the Lord told Moses, 'The second is like this, 'You shall love your neighbor as yourself.' There is no other commandment greater than these.' Let us not forget the golden rule. In Matthew, chapter seven, verse twelve, 'Therefore whatever you desire for men to do to you, you shall also do to them; for this is the law and the prophets.'"

"We will now turn to the Old Testament and read from Leviticus, chapter nineteen, verses thirty-three through thirty-four, 'If a stranger lives as a foreigner with you in your land, you shall not do him wrong. The stranger who lives as a foreigner with you shall be to you as the native-born among you, and you shall love him as yourself, for you lived as foreigners in the land of Egypt. I am Yahweh your God.'"

"Brothers and sisters, the word of God is clear. We are to love our neighbors as ourselves. We are equals in the eyes of God, and He loves each of us the same. His precious son, Jesus, died on Calvary's cross so that each of us, no matter our lot in life, could receive the gift of salvation. The gift of salvation is available to all that believe. It matters not whether you are Jew or gentile, man or woman, rich or poor, free or slave. So as you leave this house of worship today, embrace God's word and show kindness to your neighbors and those that are sojourning in our town. We'll dismiss a tad early today so that we can fellowship with one another over a hearty meal. Please bow your heads as we pray. Dear Heavenly Father, thank you for this opportunity to study your word. Help each of us take your word to heart. As we break bread today at your house, allow us the opportunity to get to know any strangers in our midst. Help us show love and respect to our neighbors, as you have commanded. Thank you for sending your son to die on the cross so that we might have everlasting life. In Jesus's name, we pray, Amen."

A chorus of amen's echoed across the church. Reverend Stevenson made his way to the back of the church. He stood at the top of steps just outside the door to the church and shook hands and spoke briefly with all in attendance as they exited the building. Once outside, Jimmy noticed a bustle of activity as the women and younger ladies in attendance busied themselves retrieving baskets of food from nearby wagons.

The dishes were quickly spread across the makeshift tables under the shade trees. It was July, so there was a large selection of fresh vegetables arrayed – Indian corn, yellow squash, red tomatoes, and several types of beans. The meats included wild game – venison, bear steak, roasted quail and squirrel. There were smoke-cured hams along with loaves of bread and wedges of cornbread. There was cheese, pickles, butter, and honey. Some green-striped watermelons were ready to be sliced for dessert. Plates were a mixture of woodenware, stoneware, and tin.

Once all the food was on the tables, Reverend Stevenson asked everyone to gather around for the blessing of the meal. After the blessing, everyone began to form a line. Men were served first, and the women and children were served last. Because of the number of horses and oxen present, a large number of flies, horseflies, and gnats were also in attendance.

In spite of the Reverend's heartfelt message and closing prayer admonishing those in attendance to make visitors feel welcome, no one went out of their way to extend hospitality toward Jimmy. He noticed a few others that appeared to be searching for a friendly face as well. Families and old acquaintances seemed clumped together. Jimmy wondered to himself if the sermon had fallen on deaf ears.

Jimmy saw Shaw and his family gathering under a large oak. Anne had yet to notice that he was in attendance. Jimmy was not to be put-off easily. He got a plate of food and walked toward the Shaw family. As he approached, Shaw saw him coming and stood up. The two men shook hands.

"Jimmy, I didn't expect to see you here today. Didn't know you were a Methodist," said Shaw.

"I'm not a Methodist," replied Black. "Not really the church-going type, I reckon."

"Let me introduce you to my family," said Shaw. "This is my wife, Elizabeth. Of course, you know Tom. These are my other children, Charlotte, Anne, Elizabeth, Ellis, Sophia, John, Sarah, and the baby is Mary. Family, this young man is James Black, my new blacksmith. We call him 'Jimmy.'"

"Pleased to make your acquaintance," Jimmy replied.

"Would you care to join us?" said Elizabeth Shaw.

"Thank you kindly, Mrs. Shaw," he replied. "I'll gladly join you if it's not an imposition."

Anne spoke up, "Please join us, Mr. Black. You are a visitor to our church, and the Reverend has asked us to make visitors feel welcome. Right, Papa?"

"Um...uh...you're right, Anne. Glad to see you were paying attention today and not staring out the window," said Shaw.

Jimmy sat on the ground near Anne and her siblings. They all began to eat. Jimmy said, "This food is quite good. Nice to get a break from my usual midday fare of cheese and crackers."

Mrs. Shaw asked, "So Mr. Black, how do you like our Washington so far?"

"It seems to hold a great deal of opportunity for a young man willing to work. For the most part, people are nice here."

"Well, we need young men like yourself that are not afraid of work. We want Washington to grow and become a center for trade and agriculture," said Mrs. Shaw. "My husband thinks highly of your work. He seems much more relaxed in the evenings now that you are helping him with his growing business."

Jimmy waited on Shaw to chime in, but the older man remained tight-lipped. They continued to make small talk while finishing their meal. Jimmy looked at Anne and asked, "Would you care to get a slice of watermelon?"

She replied, "Yes, I love watermelon."

The two walked away from the group and went over to where a couple of men with long knives were slicing open the bright red melons. The clear, sugary juice was flowing everywhere, and the flies were swarming. A man waiting on a slice of watermelon said to one of the men wielding one of the knives, "Can that Arkansas toothpick carve anythin' besides a melon?"

The carver grinned, "Man, bar, hog, or melon. Makes no difference." The men in earshot of the conversation all laughed loudly.

Anne and Jimmy each grabbed a slice of melon and walked a short distance away from the rowdy crowd to enjoy the sweet, juicy melon. They leaned forward as they ate to keep the juice from dribbling on their clothes.

Anne looked at Jimmy and said, "I bet I can spit a seed farther than you can."

"You're on," Jimmy replied.

The fair-skinned girl leaned back and then quickly leaned forward, spitting the seed forcefully from between her puckered lips. The seed launched in an arc and landed about twelve feet in front of her.

"Looks like you've had some practice at this," Jimmy said.

"Oh, my brothers are always trying to outdo me at something. I happen to be better than them in most of our competitions," she replied. "Now it's your turn."

Having never spit watermelon seed before, Jimmy tried to mimic her technique. He leaned back, then quickly forward and spit with pursed lips. The seed landed at his feet. His face turned redder than the watermelon he was holding.

Anne broke into laughter. "You better stick to blacksmithing."

About that time, Jimmy heard Anne's mother calling for her, "Anne, it's time to go, dear. Your father is loading our dishes into the buckboard."

Anne looked at him and said, "I have to go now, Jimmy. My father will be angry if I tarry."

"May I call on you sometime?" Jimmy said, his face still flushed.

"I suppose," she replied as she turned and walked hurriedly towards the buckboard. Her father was already in the driver's seat. The rest of the family were climbing into the wagon. Tom, the oldest boy, mounted a nearby horse. As Anne approached, it appeared that Shaw had some sharp words for her. He flicked the reins and said "giddy-up" to the horse, and off they went in a cloud of dust.

Black, in a daze, sauntered to his nearby horse, mounted Socks, and began the long ride back to his new home on the outskirts of town. Lost in his thoughts about the beautiful Anne Shaw, it felt like he was floating along on one of the cotton-like clouds overhead rather than riding on the back of a horse. The time on the road passed quickly. Jimmy was soon gazing at the log cabin lying just ahead. *I can't wait to see her* again, he thought to himself. *I wonder if she feels the same?*

Chapter 12

It was Tuesday following Black's visit to the Methodist Church. Shaw had only made shop talk with him – not saying anything to Jimmy about their encounter at the dinner-on-the-ground. Jimmy was dying to know what Shaw's family thought of him, especially Anne. Jimmy was at the forge with Nat. The two were working on some farm implements. Tom and Willy were outside in the corral shoeing some oxen.

An oxen-drawn wagon moved deliberately down the dirt road and pulled up in front of the shop. The burly, bearded driver who was smoking a stogie, got down and walked in to see Shaw. A few moments later, Shaw brought the stranger into the forge area.

"Boys, this here is Mr. Taggart," said Shaw. "Him and his family are traveling through with a bunch of families headed to Texas. He damaged the rear wheel on his wagon and needs it fixed so he can rejoin the other wagons camped down on Town Creek. Drop whatever you are doing and give Mr. Taggart a hand." Shaw turned and abruptly went back to his office.

"This here is Nat, and my name's Jimmy."

"Pleased to make your acquaintance," replied Taggart. "Let me show you the wheel that needs fixin'."

The three men walked out of the double door and followed Taggart to the right, rear wheel of his covered wagon. Taggart grabbed the wheel with both hands and gave it a hard shake. The wheel wobbled and creaked. Taggart said they were crossing a creek about twenty miles back up the Southwest Trail when the wagon hit a large rock. Jimmy asked Taggart to unhitch his team and take the oxen around to the side of the shop where the large sycamore tree stood. There was a watering trough there, and the oxen could stay cool in the shade. Jimmy and Nat then rolled a big stump of wood into position behind the wagon. Nat placed a long pole across the top of the stump and underneath the rear axle of wagon. The two men then pressed down on the free end of the pole and lifted the wagon wheel about six inches off the ground. Taggart quickly shoved some blocks of wood under the axle. Jimmy and Nat then eased up on the lift pole. The wheel could now be safely slipped off the wagon's axle. Jimmy and Nat paused to catch their breath after the strenuous effort.

Taggart pulled another stogie out of his vest pocket and lit it. He took a couple of puffs on the thin cigar while Jimmy and Nat were resting. Taggart said, "I guess I'm lucky to make it this far. Some folks call that rabbit trail we just crossed the Congress Road. I got news fur 'em – it's a fur piece from a road. Then again, I reckon it's only fittin' that they name such a monstrosity after those big bugs in Washington City. They's chug holes big enough to swallow a wagon, team, and all. Places where the so-called bridges are nothing more than a few logs laid across a crick. Them skeeters can bleed a horse dry overnight. And those darn bitin' flies surely must have a set of teeth. Least we had enough folks in our caravan to keep the bushwhackers and highwaymen at bay. Just south of Bates Tavern, we came across a couple of families that were traveling by themselves. They was murdered – all ten of 'em, including the women and children. Their horses and livestock were taken, and the wagons burned. Probably the work of that devil John Murrell and his Mystic Gang. He's known to operate in that big swamp between Little Rock and Memphis. Folks say he fools people into believin' he's a preacher. He'll hold a church meeting, and his gang will be outside stealin' the congregation's horses. Like I said, I guess we can count ourselves lucky to make it this far with only a busted wheel."

"What's drawin' you to Texas?" asked Jimmy. "Just curious. There's plenty of good land to be had around here. And you won't have Mexicans and near as many Injuns to contend with here. We have a few Choctaws and Caddos occasionally causing folks trouble, but renegades are usually dealt with swiftly and severely."

"Well sir, I hear tell them Mexicans will let settlers have about four thousand acres for almost nothin'. All you have to do is pledge allegiance to Mexico and become a Catholic. Then make some minor improvements to a parcel of land. The last piece of land we occupied back in Tennessee was full of rocks, and the soil was worn out. I couldn't make a decent crop of cotton, so I had no hope of payin' off the loan against the deed. I wrote across my note 'Gone to Texas' and nailed it to the door of my cabin the day we left. Besides, Texas is a lot closer and easier to get to than headin' way out west – crossing the Rocky Mountains. If'n things don't work out for us in Texas, it's not too fur for us to make our way back here. If'n, a man, takes a notion to uproot his family and head way out West to Oregon or Californy, he's biting off more than he can chew. Once you make that move, there ain't no turnin' back."

Nat and Jimmy worked for another couple of hours repairing Taggart's wagon. After the wheel was back on the wagon, Taggart hitched his team of oxen back to the double-tree. After he had settled his account with Shaw, he shouted "so long and thanks" to Jimmy and Nat, and he headed off in the direction of the encampment down by Town Creek. The two young men headed back inside to the forge.

Shaw came over to where the two were working. "How's that knife making coming?" asked Shaw. "While he was paying for his wheel repair, Taggart asked me if I had any knives for sale. Taggart saw several along the Southwest Trail sporting large knives strapped to their sides. He was willing to pay good money for such a knife. Unfortunately, I have nary a one to sell."

"It's coming along," Jimmy replied. "I've been able to get through most of the steps. I just need a bit more practice. If you wouldn't mind me working on my knife-making a bit during slack-time at the shop, I could make faster progress. Just working on my off days has limited my mastering the skills."

"Alright then," said Shaw. "Seems a worthwhile investment of time. You can work on the knives so long as it don't interfere with your other work. But any knives you make on shop time are mine for the selling, understood?"

"Yes, sir."

Shaw returned to his office. It was late in the afternoon, and the men were pretty well caught up on their work. Jimmy looked at Nat, and the two knew what each other was thinking. Jimmy went to the back of the shop and returned with a knife he had recently begun making. Jimmy had drawn the knife out to about a foot and a half in length – the blade being about twelve inches and the tang about six. The spine of the blade was about three-eighths of an inch thick along the spine. It was straight – and there were no visible cracks in the blue-gray metal.

The next step was critical and one that the new knife-maker was having difficulty with – the quench. The quench involved reheating the knife blade to critical temperature and then quickly immersing it in a liquid like water or oil. The quenching process causes the metal to take on an exceptional hardness. Without the quench, the knife would not hold an edge.

Old Peña had made smaller knives than Black was attempting to make. Peña quenched his knives in the briny water. Peña had shared stories his grandfather had told him about bladesmiths in Spain using animal blood to quench their steel. The knife makers thought quenching in blood would give the blade magical power – causing it to seek out the blood of the knife-wielder's enemies.

The key to getting a good quench was to heat the blade to the right temperature before the quench. Too hot and the metal would crack. Not hot enough, and the quench would not work. Peña had said that the color of the metal should be reddish-orange. Peña would shutter his shop windows so he could see the exact color of the metal during the heating process. Too much sunlight would wash out the true color of the heated metal.

Jimmy had tried quenching his knives in water, and the blades had warped or cracked. *Maybe the length and thickness of the blade have something to do with it, or perhaps I am overheating*, he thought to himself. He decided to do a couple of things different this time around.

He said to Nat, "Ya' wanna help me with this knife I've been working on? The next step is critical, and one that's been giving me fits."

"I'd be glad to," said Nat.

"Alright, then. A little before dusk when it's still light enough to see, I am going to need that forge ready. I want you to get the forge ready. I'm going to Block's Mercantile to fetch a keg of bear oil. I won't be gone long."

"You want it to burn in a lamp?" asked Nat.

"It's not for burnin'."

Black got in the shop wagon and headed to Block's. When he returned with the bear-oil, it was almost dusk. He carried the keg of oil into the shop and set it on the ground by the forge. Nat had the forge glowing brightly. He was working the big bellows feeding air to the charcoal. Jimmy took a chisel and pried the top off of the wooden keg. He then took a pair of tongs and grabbed his knife blade by the end of the tang. He placed the blade in the center of the hottest part of the forge while Nat kept the bellows going at a steady pace. It was getting dark in the shop, but the forge provided enough light for Jimmy to see. Black kept a keen eye on the blade in forge. It changed color, slowly moving from gray to red to reddish-orange. He waited patiently. The reddish-orange color worked its way from the point of the knife towards the tang.

When the entire edge of the knife, including the point, was glowing reddish-orange, he removed the blade from the fire and went quickly to the keg of bear oil. He then thrust the entire knife into the open mouth of the barrel, fully submerging it in the oil. A hissing sound erupted as the oil began quickly cooling the metal evenly throughout.

Jimmy listened carefully for another distinctive and un-welcomed sound. He heard none. He let out an audible sigh of relief and said, "Nat, you may have just witnessed a perfect quench."

"A what?" said Nat with a puzzled look on his face.

"I didn't hear a ping when I dunked the knife in the bear oil. If I'd heard ping when I quenched the knife in the oil, it would have meant the blade had cracked."

Jimmy pulled the knife from the oil and held it up near the forge – the glow from the coals illuminating the knife. He examined the knife from every angle. It was straight – no warping – and showed no cracks. He let out a loud "whoopee."

"Yessiree, Nat. That was a perfect quench. This knife should hold an edge."

Summer 1829

Chapter 13

It was a typical Saturday, and Jimmy had to work at the shop until noon. Ol' Ben had given him a list of needed supplies before he had left the farm that morning. Ben had told Jimmy to hitch up his mule to the buckboard and drive it into town so he could pick up the supplies. On the ride into town, Jimmy had concocted a little scheme. First, he would work on his latest knife in progress after the shop closed. Afterward, he would pick up the supplies at Block's Mercantile, then drop by the Shaw house – unannounced. He planned to pop in on Shaw at his home under the pretense of showing progress on his latest knife. Of course, his real intent was to see Anne. *It's a good plan,* he thought to himself.

After the shop closed and everyone had left, Jimmy went to the back and retrieved a wooden crate containing his latest knife creation. Jimmy had been working on it feverishly for several days. Black was confident he had a great knife in progress. After drawing out the blade on the anvil to the desired shape, Jimmy used a foot-operated grinding wheel to refine the form and add a decent edge. Painfully, he had learned that he needed to refine the shape before the quench. After the quench, the blade was hardened and much more difficult and time-consuming to work.

After grinding the knife to the desired shape with a decent edge, Black had successfully quenched the blade in the bear oil. He had then applied a handle made from black walnut secured to the tang with brass pins. *The knife is looking really good*, he thought to himself. The same had been opined by Nat a day or so ago.

Today, he would perform the next to last step in his knife-making process – honing the edge. He would complete the final step, polishing, another day when he had more time. Today, he was in a hurry to see Anne. Jimmy had traded for a Hot Springs wet stone at the local leather shop. Folks swore that the native stone from Hot Springs was best for putting a razor's edge on a knife. The stone was a black rock with a fine-grain texture and was a prized possession of knife owners lucky enough to own one.

Black retrieved the prized stone from his wooden crate and laid it on his workbench. He spit on the black stone, took the blade in both hands, and began to draw the edge against the stone – applying downward pressure as he did so. He continued scraping the blade edge back and forth across the novaculite – spitting and flipping the blade over frequently during the process. An abrasive, rasping sound was emitted by the friction of the steel as it scraped against the sandy-textured stone. After about a half-hour of honing the edge of the blade, Jimmy held the knife edge against his forearm at a forty-five-degree angle. He slowly scraped the blade along his skin, shaving the hair from his arm as if it was a barber's razor. *I'm ready to show the knife to Shaw*, he thought as a smile crossed his face.

He carefully put the wet stone back into his wooden crate. He then wrapped the knife in a cotton cloth and placed it in his knapsack. Black poured a bucket of water on the forge and closed up the shop. He hitched up Jake the mule to Ben's buckboard and headed toward Block's Mercantile.

Block's was a busy place. It was Saturday after all. Several men were sitting or standing in front of Block's store swapping tales, spitting tobacco juice in every direction while some whittled on twigs just passing the time. A couple of young boys sitting on burlap sacks of seeds were playing a game of checkers while other lads stood anxiously awaiting their turn to take on the winner. Dogs of all shapes and sizes ran yapping through the streets or lay in the shade scratching fleas. Inside the store, women were milling about looking at all the goods on the tall shelves around the walls of the store. Several young children were ogling hard candies and the few toys that were tucked away safely behind a wood and glass case. Behind the glass case stood Mr. Block and his long-time partner, Mr. Johnson.

Jimmy didn't have time to waste if he wanted to get to Anne's house before the family sat down for supper. He walked up to the counter. Mr. Block was engaged in a one-sided conversation with a talkative woman. Black quickly turned to Mr. Johnson instead, telling the other proprietor that he was there to pick up some goods on account of Mr. Ben Cooper. Mr. Johnson flipped open a large ledger book to a page that had Ben Cooper's name at the top. Jimmy handed a list of supplies to Mr. Johnson, who slowly read the list. Johnson replied that all the items were in stock and jotted them down in the ledger. After he finished noting the details in the ledger, he added the prices and totaled the bill. The total came to a little over eight dollars. Jimmy said that Mr. Cooper would be in to settle the account later. Mr. Johnson said that Mr. Cooper's credit was good. Johnson then called his slave, Sam, from the backroom to come help load the goods into the buckboard out front as Johnson fetched the items off the shelves and bins.

While Jimmy waited for the goods to be picked and loaded, he stood back out of the way and eyed the other shoppers. Black overheard two women talking about the upcoming Fourth of July a week from today. One lady said to the other that there was going to be dance and celebration at the Hempstead County Courthouse. That piece of news got Black's immediate attention.

After the goods were loaded, Jimmy said "thank you" to Mr. Johnson, and he hurriedly left the store. Suddenly, two hound dogs began fighting just off the boardwalk in front of the store, causing Jake, the mule, to start braying and pulling to get loose from the hitching post. Jimmy quickly untied Jake and led him away from the dogfight. He then climbed onto the driver's seat and snapped the reins to get Jake moving away from the fight. Jake was happy to oblige. As he was pulling away, Jimmy overheard two men toting Kentucky rifles having a heated exchange of words. One man threatened to shoot the other's dog for chewing the ear off of his "best bar dog." Jimmy didn't wait around on the outcome as Jake made quick strides towards Shaw's residence.

Jimmy pulled up in front of the Shaw place, got down from the wagon and tied Jake mature catalpa tree near the street. Not hearing any gunshots from town, Jimmy guessed the dog owners had settled their dispute peaceably. He grabbed his knapsack out of the back of the buckboard and walked the short path to the front door of the Shaw home. It was a white-washed, one-story house with clapboard siding. It had a wide porch that ran the width of the house. He stepped up on the front porch and knocked firmly on the door.

Mrs. Shaw answered his knock. "Why, Jimmy, what brings you to our doorstep today? Is something wrong at the shop?"

"No, ma'am," he replied. "I came to see Mr. Shaw about a small matter. Is he home this afternoon?"

"He's away for the moment, but I'm expecting him home soon. Would you care to wait?".

"Yes'm, that would be fine. I'm in no hurry. Would you mind if I waited here on your front porch?"

"Make yourself comfortable. William should be home soon. Would you care for some water or tea while you wait?"

"No, ma'am. I'm not thirsty at the moment. Is your daughter Anne, home by chance? Perhaps she could join me on the porch till Mr. Shaw returns?"

Mrs. Shaw hesitated for a moment, looking a bit nervous.

Then from inside the house, Jimmy heard Anne say, "Tell Mr. Black I'll join him momentarily, mother."

"Very well, Jimmy. Please have a seat. Anne will soon join you."

There was some willow furniture at one end of the long porch. Jimmy made himself comfortable in a willow chair with a broad, heart-shaped back. Even though it was a hot summer day, a slight breeze was blowing across the porch, making it quite comfortable. Jimmy began to think about what he would say when Anne joined him. His palms were sweaty, and his mouth became dry. After a brief wait, Anne joined him and sat in willow settee conveniently angled, so she was facing Jimmy.

"How are you, Anne? It's been a while since I last saw you at the church dinner."

"I'm fine, I suppose," said Anne. "Why have you not been by to see me sooner?"

Jimmy was a tad startled by her response.

"Er...uh...well, I've been busy at work and with chores at the boarding house where I'm staying. I've been working after hours at the shop to master some knife making skills. That's partly why I'm here today. I came to show your father my latest work. I think he'll be pleased."

"Is that the only reason you're here today?" she asked, with an elfish smile on her face.

"No, not totally. I was hoping I might see you as well," Jimmy blushed.

"Well, I'm glad you stopped by," said Anne gleefully.

There was a brief period of silence. Jimmy sat, staring at his feet, trying to clear his throat without making his nervousness visible. "While I was at Block's Mercantile earlier today, I overheard two women talking about an Independence Day dance at the courthouse next Saturday afternoon. I was thinking about attending. Might you be attending as well?" Black asked.

"Hmmm. That could be a problem. You see, one of the planters from down in the river bottoms is throwing a party at his summer home here on the hill. He invited our family along with many other prominent families for a grand Fourth of July celebration. I believe they will be roasting a pig. Papa is insisting I attend. I'm sure he expects there'll be many eligible bachelors there."

"I see," said Jimmy dejectedly. "It sounds like quite a celebration."

There was an awkward moment of silence. "Hmm...perhaps, I can attend both," said Anne. "I can spend some time at the Royston's home – then maybe I can slip away and join you at the courthouse dance."

Jimmy's mood uplifted instantly. About that time, they heard a horse and buggy approaching from down the street. It was Shaw. As Shaw turned off the road taking the buggy to the carriage house out back, he glanced at the two sitting on the porch. Shaw had a stern look on his face. A few minutes later, he made his way through the house and to the front porch.

"What brings you to my home on your day off, Jimmy?" said Shaw, his jaw muscles clenching.

"I have something to show you," Jimmy replied. He reached into his knapsack and retrieved the cloth-wrapped knife. He removed the cloth and held the knife up by its handle. Jimmy proceeded to shave a spot of hair from his forearm, then handed the knife to Shaw. "It's almost finished," he said to Shaw. "I just need to polish the blade a bit with some fine grit. What do you think?"

"Oh, what a beautiful knife!" exclaimed Anne. "Did you make that yourself?"

"Yes, I did. As I mentioned earlier, I've been working for months attempting to master the skills to make such a knife. There've been many missteps along the way."

Shaw took the knife from Black and began turning the blade over in his hand, looking at it from every angle. He seemed pleased.

"Anne, go inside and help your mother get supper on the table. I need to talk business with Jimmy if you don't mind," said Shaw rather firmly.

"Yes, Papa," said Anne soberly.

She extended her hand to Jimmy, and the two shook briefly. She gave him a light, reassuring squeeze and then went inside the house.

"What do you think?" Jimmy asked Shaw.

"I think we can sell 'em like hotcakes," replied Shaw. "Have you tested the knife? Will it hold its edge?"

"Not yet," Black replied. "It should be quite durable. I believe Diego Peña himself would be pleased with my work. It's strong steel. Hardened to hold an edge and tempered to remove any brittleness. I'd be happy for you to put it to the test."

"Very well. I'll do so on Monday. Now, if you don't mind, it's approaching supper-time, and I need to wash up. I'll see you at the shop on Monday," said Shaw rather curtly.

He handed Black the knife, turned quickly, and went into his home, leaving Jimmy standing alone on the porch. Jimmy re-wrapped his precious creation in the cloth, then placed it in his knapsack and ambled to the buckboard. He untied Jake, climbed onto the wagon seat and said: “giddy-up.”

As he was pulling away, Jimmy thought he overhead Shaw speaking loudly to his wife and daughter. Puzzled, Jimmy headed Jake west out of town on the Fort Towson road. He reflected on his brief conversation with Anne. He wondered, *Did she mean what she said about meeting up with me at the dance next Saturday? She seemed sincere. I guess I’ll have to wait and see. A week sure seems like a long time.*

Chapter 14

Saturday, July Fourth, 1829.

Life on the frontier is not for the weak or the timid. Most folks living on the edge of civilization are searching for something – a new opportunity – a new life. But some are fleeing something – a past run-in with the law or a creditor whose patience has worn thin. Some are loners. Some are adventurers with a general dislike for civilization and the rules and regulations that come with it. On the frontier, when paths cross between such men, one or both lives will likely take an unexpected turn – sometimes for the better but more often, for the worse.

There is a sheriff in Washington, but he has a fondness for whiskey and loose women. Some speculate he has a bit of a yellow streak. Maybe he does. Or perhaps he’s just better at drinking and chasing women than he is at keeping the peace.

Saturday is “go-to-market” day. The farmers living on the edge of town come in to trade produce for things they need but can’t grow or make on their own. Goods are often bartered or sold for credit since money is scarce. The wealthy planters come to town with several wagons driven by slaves to acquire supplies but also to take advantage of the social opportunities. And as usual, there are always many strangers in town. Many of the trappers or traders that live in the wilderness are hungry for a bit more socializing than they usually have with Indians, other trappers and traders or worse, their horse. Some want a hot bath and a home-cooked meal. Some just want to visit one of the taverns in town where they can gamble, get drunk, and sleep in a real bed with a real woman.

On a typical Saturday, after Shaw closed the blacksmith shop at mid-day, Black frequently worked a few hours in the afternoon, perfecting his knife-making skills. But this Saturday was the Fourth of July – Independence Day – so Black had decided to take the afternoon off and rub elbows with all the others in town celebrating. He had high hopes of seeing Anne at the courthouse dance later that day. Jimmy went to the back of the shop, washed up, changed clothes, and combed his hair. He then mounted Socks and headed toward the center of town.

The streets were bustling with horses, wagons, and people. Dogs were barking. The children were playing. Dust was billowing. As he approached Black Bear Tavern, Jimmy could see a gathering of people outside the tavern door. Jimmy recognized Nat from the shop standing near the crowd, so he rode Socks over to where Nat was standing.

"What's all the commotion, Nat?"

"There's been a stabbin'," replied Nat. "Happened at a card game. Not sure if it involved cheating or too much grog. Anyways, a young man's trip to Texas was cut a might short. That Arkansas bible led to the death of another poor man."

"Arkansas bible? What are you talking about?" asked Jimmy with a puzzled look on his face.

"You mean you never heard 'em call a deck of cards an Arkansas bible?" asked Nat in disbelief.

"Can't say I have. What happened to the man wielding the knife?" asked Black.

"According to a man at the card table, the man that did the stabbin' stood up, wiped his bloody blade clean on the dead man's shirt – then finished off his mug of ale. He paid for his ale and that of the dead man and just strolled out the tavern door. He then mounted a bay-colored horse and slowly rode down the Trail toward Fulton. Probably headed to Mexico across the Red. I heard someone say the killer's a half-breed called Lightnin' Billy. Said he's called that 'cause he's fast with the knife. Wears a hat with a big eagle feather stuck in the headband."

"Did anyone go for the Sheriff?" asked Jimmy.

"Sheriff's nowhere to be found. Speculation is he's sleeping one off over at Stewart's Tavern," said Nat.

"Did anyone know the dead man?"

"No one's claimed him yet," said Nat.

"You weren't hanging out in Black Bear, were you Nat?"

"I was headed here after leaving the shop, but I think my thirst has been quenched. Where you off to?" asked Nat.

"I'm on my way to the courthouse. There's supposed to be a dance there later this afternoon. I'm hoping to run into Anne there. You wanna go with me?"

"Might as well," said Nat. "Maybe it'll get my mind off the stabbin'."

"Give me your hand. You can ride behind me. Easy, Socks. Easy, boy."

Nat gave Jimmy his hand as the rider backed his foot out of the left stirrup. Nat inserted his left foot into the stirrup, then reached up and took Jimmy's left arm. Jimmy tugged, and Nat gave a leap, swinging his right leg over Sock's rump. Nat settled comfortably behind the saddle on the edge of the thick blanket covering Sock's back. He grabbed Jimmy around the waist for stability, and off they rode.

The two soon reached the courthouse lawn. People were milling about. Young men were firing pistols and rifles into the air to mark the day. Children were playing chase and hide and seek. Horses and buggies were tied to trees and hitching posts. A group of men in the shade of the courthouse were passing a jug around. The sound of a fiddle emanated from the open door and windows of the courthouse.

Jimmy helped Nat dismount from the back of Socks. Then Jimmy dismounted and tied Socks to a bush so the horse could graze on the green grass. The two young men then strolled toward the courthouse door. Inside, the courtroom had been turned into a dance hall. The benches had been moved around the perimeter of the room.

There was a small group of musicians standing in one corner. There were a couple of fiddlers, one person playing the dulcimer, one the banjo, and one person was keeping time on a washboard. They were playing a catchy tune, and several couples were dancing in the middle of the courtroom on the shiny, pinewood floor.

Jimmy looked around the room for a familiar face. He recognized several of the townsfolk, but there was no sign of Anne. He turned to Nat and nodded towards an empty bench off to their left. They walked over to the bench and took a seat.

Nat said, "Quite a turnout – looks like everyone's having a good time."

"Looks that away," Jimmy replied as his eyes continued to search the room for Anne. He noticed that several of the town's more prominent citizens were not in attendance. He guessed they were at the Royston party that Anne had mentioned last Saturday. Jimmy stared down at his feet.

Nat looked at him and said, "What's the matter, Jimmy? Thought you were looking forward to coming to the dance? Don't seem too happy to be here?"

Jimmy didn't respond right away. "I'm okay, Nat. I was hoping Anne might be here. That's all."

"It's still early. Anne may still show," replied Nat half-heartedly.

Jimmy relayed to Nat the story Anne had told him about the wealthy planter having a Fourth of July celebration at his summer townhome. He told him Anne said she would try to slip away from the party and join him at the dance.

"Those highfalutin critters," grumbled Nat. "They're too good to rub shoulders with the rest of us. Act like they've been rich all their lives. Most of 'em didn't have a pot to piss in when they came to this country."

"Yep. How quickly people change when they get a little money," Jimmy replied.

"Look over there. I think I know that girl across the room," mumbled Nat. "The one in that blue dress. I wish I had nerve enough to ask her to dance."

"Go on. Ask her. That little girl won't bite," chuckled Jimmy. "Wait till I tell Shaw that big ol' Nat was afraid to ask a little girl to dance."

"Oh, alright," said Nat. "You best not say anything to Shaw. You hear?"

He got up off the bench and slowly made his way across the room to where the girl was standing with her friends. Jimmy could see Nat talking with the young lady. Her head came about to Nat's chest and stood looking up at him. Nat then took her by her hand and walked onto the dance floor as the musicians started in on the next ditty. Poor Nat had two left feet, but the girl didn't seem to notice. The couple made their way around the dance floor – laughing and talking like they had known each other forever. Watching them, Jimmy thought to himself, *I sure wish Anne was here.*

Jimmy decided to walk outside to take his mind off of Anne. The group of young men firing guns into the air was still at it. The old men passing the jug were now sitting around a fire laughing and swapping tales – the contents of the jug apparently having its desired effect. Kids were still running here and there and had been joined by a pack of yapping dogs, significantly adding to the noise and confusion. *Why am I not celebrating like everyone else?* Jimmy thought, knowing the answer to his rhetorical question. *Cause I'm not spending time with Anne.*

Jimmy slowly walked back inside the courthouse. Nat walked over and introduced his dance partner to Jimmy. The young lady's name was Elizabeth McAllister. Her father was part owner of the leather shop along with Mr. Daniels.

Nat said, "Elizabeth has a friend here if you'd like to meet her?"

"Maybe later," Jimmy replied.

Nat and Elizabeth went back across the room to join her group of friends. Jimmy guessed he had been at the dance for a little over an hour. *Maybe I should go to the Royston party? Perhaps I can just blend into the crowd, and no one will notice. Nah, that won't work – Shaw will be there. Maybe I should just head back to the boarding house.* Suddenly, a group of young people walked through the courthouse door. Anne was in the group. She wore a long, billowy, yellow dress with a matching bow in her hair.

She quickly made eye contact with Jimmy. Jimmy casually walked over to her, not wanting to appear in a hurry.

"Hi, James," she said.

"Hello, Anne," he replied. "I was beginning to think you weren't going to show."

"Well, we had to wait till the older folks were distracted by brandy and cigars. I persuaded my group of friends to leave with me. I convinced them this dance would be more fun than that stuffy party," said Anne.

"It's good to see you. You look beautiful."

"It's nice to see you too, James. I was concerned you might have left by now."

"The thought had crossed my mind. I was just about to leave when you walked in."

"I'm glad you didn't. Well, aren't you going to ask me to dance?"

Jimmy blushed then said, "May I have this dance?"

"Why, James, I thought you would never ask."

He took her by the hand, and they walked onto the dance floor. The couple began to move in circles to the time of the music. Jimmy felt like he was floating on air. He looked into Anne's green eyes, and she looked into his. His strong, calloused hands weren't sweating this time. The two said very little as they danced, but their eyes spoke volumes.

Jimmy and Anne danced several dances and then took a break. She held his hand as they walked outside, away from the prying eyes of their friends. Outdoors, things had calmed some. They found a large tree stump and sat down. They sat quietly for a minute or two.

Jimmy broke the silence. "Anne, I would like to come calling on you. I wish to ask your father if he'll allow me to court you."

"James, I'd like that very much, but I'm afraid my father will not consent. He will only permit me to court the sons of nearby planters. Or maybe the son of one of the doctors or lawyers in town. He claims he only has my best interests at heart."

"But your father knows me. He knows what I can do with my hands. I've made him a great deal of money working at his shop. He has more business now than he ever had before I arrived here. And he saw the quality of the knife I just made. With all the settlers passing through on their way to Texas, he knows we can sell all the knives I can make at an attractive price. Surely, he recognizes my potential for success in my trade?"

"I suppose you're right, James. But Papa is headstrong. Once his mind is made up, he's stubborn as an old mule."

"Are you trying to be polite? Or are you just not interested in me calling on you?" he asked. "Just say so."

"Of course, not silly. Why do you think I snuck away from the party to come here? That party was brimming with most of the eligible bachelors in this part of the territory. Papa will be furious if he finds out what I've done."

"Your father is a reasonable man. Surely I can persuade him that my intentions are honorable. I'll speak with him this week on the matter," said Jimmy. "Now, let's get back to the dance."

The two stood up and turned to head back to the courthouse. From behind came the sound of a horse galloping at top speed toward the courthouse. As the horse approached, Anne said, "Why that looks like my brother Tom's horse."

The two stood watching as the horse rode up to them. The rider pulled back hard on the reins causing the horse to dig in its heels. As it suddenly came to a stop, the passenger jumped down from the panting horse. It was Anne's brother, Tom.

"Thomas, what's wrong? Why are you riding like a mad man?" shouted Anne.

"Anne, you best get your friends and head back to the Royston house," replied Tom. "Pa was beginning to make inquiries as to your whereabouts. I told him that you and some of your friends had taken a stroll around town. If he finds you here, he'll be furious."

"Very well," said Anne. She scurried inside to gather her friends and return to the Royston party. Tom stood holding his horse, trying to calm him. The horse was breathing hard and sweating after the fast gallop. Jimmy and Tom were well acquainted with each other from working at the shop.

"I knew my sister was coming to see you, Jimmy," said Tom. "She likes you, and I like you. My father likes your work, but that doesn't mean he approves of you seeing my sister."

"Anne told me as much just now. She said your father wants her to see only the upper crust," Jimmy replied. "I hope to persuade him otherwise."

"You have a long row to hoe in front of you," replied Tom.

Anne and her friends quickly exited the courthouse. Jimmy waved bye to her as the group scurried in the direction of the Royston house. Tom climbed onto his horse and tore off in the same direction, hoping to keep his father from leaving the party. Jimmy went inside the courthouse and found Nat, who was still talking to Elizabeth. Jimmy told Nat that Anne had left and that he was heading home to the boarding house. "I'll see you bright and early Monday," said Jimmy as he left the courthouse.

Outside, Jimmy untied and climbed on the back of Socks. As he headed west, his eyes were blinded by the setting sun. *Maybe I'll see more clearly on Monday about how to approach Shaw about his daughter. I can reason with him. Surely, Shaw will allow me a chance to court Anne.* Lost deep in his thoughts, the next thing Jimmy knew, he was snapped back to the present by the clomping of Sock's hooves over the narrow bridge crossing the creek in front of the boarding house. I guess I'll go see if Ol' Henry has any leftovers from supper. Come to think of it, I haven't eaten since breakfast. I should be starving, but I'm not. I don't want to answer a passel of questions from that old coot. I'll grab a biscuit and some bacon and tell Henry I'm tired and gonna hit the hay early.

Chapter 15

Though he was not a God-fearing man, Jimmy attended Reverend Stevenson's church on Sunday after the Fourth hoping to speak with Anne briefly after the service. Sadly, the Shaw family was not in attendance. Jimmy returned to Cooper's farm and spent Sunday afternoon at the cabin catching up on his chores. While he worked, he mulled over how he would approach Shaw about his desire to court Anne.

Jimmy wished he could talk to Ben about his approach but decided against it. *What would an old beaver trapper know about my situation anyhow? Ben had never married. I think he may have spent some time with a squaw or two after trading some beads and blankets to the chief. I wonder what it would take to convince Big Chief Shaw to let me court his eldest daughter? Certainly a lot more than some beads and blankets. If only it were that easy.* He pondered the matter the remainder of the day.

For supper that night, Henry made vegetable soup and cornbread with honey for dessert. It was one of Jimmy's favorite meals, but he picked at his food. Ben and Henry did most of the talking as Jimmy sat quietly, stirring his soup.

Ben said, "You sick, boy?"

"No, sir. Just tired, I guess. Been working pretty hard today."

"Look like de love bug done bit him," chuckled Henry. "Yassir, bad case if'n ya' ask me."

Ben nodded his agreement. "Who's the gal?"

"I told you, I'm just tired. You two old coots think you know everything...well, you don't."

"Henry, looks like you caught the scent, and you're hot on the trail," said Ben.

"I'm going to bed," Jimmy replied. "I got to work 'bout twelve hours tomorrow while you two just sit on the front porch, spitting and picking your nose."

He pushed his chair back from the table, rose, and walked out of the kitchen door.

* * *

Jimmy rose at first light to the shrill and annoying crowing of the red-bearded rooster that strutted the yard daily. *One of these days, I'm going to wring that old cock's neck. He might be a bit tough to eat, but I'll enjoy every bite.* It was still dark in the room, so he lit the bear oil lamp on the nightstand. He staggered over to the washstand in the corner, poured some cold water from the porcelain pitcher into the matching washbowl. He splashed cold water into his bleary eyes a couple of times. He looked in the mirror and decided he needed a shave. Jimmy took the shaving mug and brush in hand, lathered up the lye soap, and smeared it over his cheeks and neck. Then he took the straight razor, slapped it a couple of times across the strop hanging on the side of the washstand, and scraped it up from his neck to his chin. A few more strokes and his neck was done. Then he took some sweeping swipes from his ears across his cheeks. He scraped the razor down from the bottom of his lip to below his chin. He saved the upper lip for last.

"OUCH!" *I hate shaving my upper lip. Never fail to knick it.* He splashed water from the bowl onto his face a couple of times and took the cotton rag from the rod on the side of the washstand and wiped his face and ears. He combed his hair, slipped on his dungarees, boots, shirt, and suspenders. He took one last look in the mirror. Except for the bloody lip, He looked ready to face the day. *If only I felt like I look,* he thought.

He was famished, having left his supper half-eaten last evening. He thought about the conversation at the supper table. *I guess those two old buzzards know more about women than I imagined.* He blew out the lamp and stepped into the breezeway, shutting the door behind him.

A breeze was blowing from the back of the house. To his surprise, the aroma of black coffee and bacon frying immediately struck his nostrils and just the faintest hint of buttermilk biscuits fresh out of the Dutch oven. Jimmy looked outback. The lamp was on in Ol' Henry's kitchen. *What's he doing up at daybreak? He's usually not awake for a couple of hours. I sure could use something in my stomach.* Jimmy walked to the kitchen and rapped on the door.

"Get on in heah," said Henry. "I thought I was gonna have to roust you outta dat feather bed dis moanin'."

"What's the matter with you? You sick? You don't usually rise with the chickens," said Jimmy.

"Well, young Jimmy, it's lak dis. I reckoned you'd be a might hungry dis moanin' since yo' don't eat all yo' supper las' night. And I reckon you got sumptin in-store today that needs yo full strength. When I was workin' for da masser back in da big house, Ol' Henry could always tell when masser was havin' some big goings-on da nex day by da way he's actin' at supper da night befoe."

"Are you going to stand there flapping your jaws, or can I get some of that coffee and some of those biscuits and bacon?" said Jimmy tersely.

Henry let out a chuckle. He poured Jimmy a steaming hot cup of coffee. Then he set a plate in front of him with several slices of thick, hickory-smoked bacon, two fried eggs, sunny side up, and two large, biscuits, golden brown on top. On the table was a small crock jar of blackberry jam and another with the honey from the night before.

"Aren't you going to eat?" Jimmy said to Henry.

"I done et," he replied.

The plate of food was no match for Jimmy's knife and fork. He was soon finished with the meal and working on his second cup of coffee. Henry busied himself in the kitchen, not saying a word while Jimmy ate and thought about what the day would bring.

"I reckon I best get to town," Jimmy said. "I think I'm ready for whatever comes my way today, thanks to you, Henry. That was a mighty fortifying breakfast."

"Now get on outta here. I gots work to do, and yo' is in my way," said Henry with a gleam in his eye.

Jimmy went to the barn, saddled up Socks, and headed toward town. As he rode east, the wind was kicking up from the southwest. He glanced in a southwesterly direction and noticed a dark cloud on the horizon. *It looks like a storm brewing today. No matter. Today's the day I talk to Shaw about Anne – man to man. No more stalling.*

* * *

Black arrived at the shop a tad later than usual. The boys were busy near the forge, getting the fire started for the day and laying out some of the jobs that needed working. Jimmy headed towards the office, where he knew he would find Shaw. Shaw was at his desk, looking over some papers. He looked up at Jimmy.

"'Bout time you showed up," snapped Shaw.

Jimmy walked up to the desk.

"Sorry, I'm a tad late. I'll make up the time by staying late today," Jimmy replied. "Looks like a storm is heading our direction. Winds blowing a might strong from the southwest."

"So I noticed," said Shaw.

"Mr. Shaw, I'd like to visit with you sometime today about a matter. Whenever it's convenient for you."

Shaw stared at him for a moment. "I reckon now's as good a time as any. What's on your mind -- besides work?" he said sarcastically.

"Mr. Shaw, I won't beat around the bush. You know me, and you know my work. I've been in your employment for about four years now. I'd like your permission to court your daughter, Anne. My intentions are honorable towards your lovely daughter."

Shaw sat quietly. His complexion began to redden ever so slightly. He twisted his head side to side as if he were trying to stretch his neck muscles. His breathing became more rapid. He fidgeted in his chair. He stared at Jimmy intently as if he were seeing through the young man. The silence was most uncomfortable for both men. Finally, Shaw spoke. "Jimmy, I need some time to consider your request. Can't give you my decision on the spot."

"I understand, sir. I'll await your response." Jimmy turned and went into the shop where Tom and the others were already at work. Suddenly, the wind began to howl around the building, and the trees began to sway. Dust and ash started to blow in their faces. The embers began to glow and pop as the gush of air struck the forge. A flash of lightning lit up the shop, followed by a tremendous clap of thunder. Then it began to rain in sheets.

"Whooeee...looks like a sho' 'nuff frog strangler is coming," said Willy.

Jimmy stood quietly in awe of the power of the storm, deep in thought.

Tom walked up to him and said, "How'd it go? Did you talk to Pa about Anne?"

"I did, and it didn't," replied Jimmy somberly.

"What do you mean?" quizzed Tom.

"He said he needed some time to consider my request. Not exactly what I expected."

"Well, at least he didn't say no," said Tom.

"Maybe he was saying no," said Jimmy, "and just stalling for more time to come up with an answer."

"Maybe," replied Tom quietly. "Just give him some time. After all, Anne is his favorite daughter. Maybe he's just fearful of losing her."

Jimmy pondered that for a moment. *Maybe Tom was right. Perhaps I'm jumping to a conclusion. Maybe Shaw just needs some time.* "Yeah, I suppose. We best get to work, or we'll have hell to pay. What's the first job, Nat?"

* * *

For Jimmy, the week rolled along slowly. Each day seemed it would never end. Still no word from Shaw. Not a "yes" or "no" to my request to court Anne. It might be my imagination, but Shaw seems to be avoiding me. He stays in his office. The few times I've seen him, he won't make eye contact. Jimmy was beginning to fill in the blanks on his own. No answer is his way of saying "no." He's trying to avoid conflict with me.

On his ride back to the boarding house after work, Jimmy had a one-sided conversation with his horse. "Socks, you're right! Shaw's not answering me means 'no, you may not court my daughter.' I want to hear the answer from Shaw. He owes me that much. Man to man, he owes me his answer – and an explanation. Why does he not want me to date his daughter? He knows me. He knows I am dependable. He knows I'm a skilled blacksmith. I can provide for his daughter if this goes where I hope it will. Shaw owes me an answer! Tomorrow I'll demand his explanation."

* * *

Jimmy awoke before sunrise -- no rooster needed to wake him from a fitful sleep. He saddled Socks and headed east at daybreak. The sky ahead was glowing bright reddish-orange like the charcoal in a hot forge. *Is that a good omen? The forge can join two pieces of metal together as one. Is that my fate?*

Jimmy arrived at the shop before anyone else. He opened the large wooden doors and closures over the windows near the forge. He placed his hand over the charcoal in the forge. There was some heat. He worked the bellows, and the charcoal came to life. He added more charcoal to the forge. Sparks began to rise up the flue. He placed a pot of coffee at the edge of the forge near the hot coals. Out of the corner of his eye, he saw Shaw and Tom pull up in the buckboard. Shaw went through the front door and into his office. Tom unhitched the horses and took them around to the corral at the back of the shop. Jimmy poured two cups of coffee and headed towards the office. Shaw was sitting at his makeshift desk.

"I thought you might like a cup of coffee," said Jimmy.

Shaw nodded his head in agreement but kept his eyes on the papers in front of him.

"Mr. Shaw, about our conversation earlier this week, I wish to..."

Shaw cut him off mid-sentence. "I will not grant you permission to court my daughter. I know this may come as a surprise to you, but that's my final decision. Now I wish to put this matter behind us, and let's get on with our work. I want you to focus your talents on making those large knives. We can surely sell all we can make. I'm raising your salary by a dollar a day, and I'll give you ten percent of all knife sales. How's that?"

"No...I mean, yes, the offer is fair but, why will you not permit me to court Anne? I demand an explanation, sir. You owe me that."

"I don't owe you a damn thing. I've given you my answer," said Shaw. "Now why don't you get busy making those knives so we can both make some money. Let's strike while the iron's hot."

Black had anticipated as much. It was still hard to hear never-the-less. He felt like he had been gut-punched and patted on the back at the same time. He started to argue his case but decided it was pointless. *Shaw has his mind made up, but this matter's not over yet.* Black turned and walked toward the forge. He was dazed. *Maybe I should just quit and tell Shaw he'll be sorry. No, I need to think this through. Now is not the time. Shaw's a hothead. If I argue with him, this could turn ugly, ruining any chance I have of seeing Anne again.*

Tom met Jimmy at the forge. He could tell Jimmy was upset. Jimmy stood by the forge, trying to calm down. He was breathing hard, and his face was red.

Tom said, "I guess you talked to Pa about courtin' Anne?"

"Yep, didn't go well," replied Jimmy.

"I heard him arguing with Anne t'other night. They were yellin' at each other pretty good," whispered Tom. "Anne started crying and ran to her room. Mama followed, trying to calm her down."

"So why does your pa not like me? Any idea?"

"We shouldn't be talkin' 'bout this," said Tom. "If Pa hears us, he'll tan my hide. It's not that he don't like you. He knows you're a skilled blacksmith. I think you remind him of himself when he was your age. He just doesn't think you're right for Anne. He says he has worked hard all his life to get to where he is. He has built up relationships with planters, merchants, lawyers, and such. He thinks the big plantation owners in the area see him as an equal. He wants Anne to take advantage of his relationships. He doesn't want her to settle for less when more is within her reach. Now I've said enough. We best get to work, or we'll both be lookin' for a job."

Tom walked off. Black went to the workbench and grabbed a billet of blister steel he had made in his crucible. It was the start of his next knife. He took the long tongs, placed the hunk of steel in the forge until it was glowing reddish-orange. Then he walked over to the anvil, grabbed his hammer and began to whale away at the metal. Sparks flew. *It's going to be a long, long day.*

Chapter 16

Jimmy stayed close to the boarding house that Saturday and busied himself with chores. Work was a distraction for him, but his thoughts kept returning to Shaw's refusal to allow him to court Anne. He became more angry and agitated as the day wore on. His anger consumed him. After mulling his situation over in his mind for hours on end, he decided his only course of action was to leave Washington. Just as he had done in his past, he would flee the unpleasant situation. *What's the point in sticking around here and fighting with Shaw for the right to court his daughter? Might as well leave this wide spot in the road. No sense in sticking it out here. I've got no roots in this place. Well, I might as well tell Ben and Henry. They'll try to talk me into staying, but my minds made up. Come daybreak, I'm pulling out.*

Jimmy was out at the barn rubbing some bear grease onto some leather harness when he heard Ol' Henry clanging a wooden spoon on the bottom of a metal pot. He knew that sound well -- supper's ready. Ordinarily, Jimmy would be moving at a fast pace towards the kitchen. Ol' Henry always managed to put on an excellent spread no matter how limited the larder might be on any given day. Today was different. Jimmy didn't have much of an appetite, so he dawdled on his way to the kitchen outback of the main house. His stomach churned at the thought of breaking the bad news to the two old coots.

When Jimmy walked into the kitchen, Ben and Henry were already seated at the table eating. Henry had cooked a pot of beans with hog jowl. A saucer of sliced onion sat in the center of the table next to a steaming plate of cornbread cut into pie-shaped wedges. Jimmy quickly filled a bowl full of beans and sat down in his usual chair. He poured himself a cup of milk from a nearby pitcher and began to consume the tasty brown beans. Jimmy sat quietly, avoiding the usual banter with the two elderly men unsure how to break the news that he was leaving town.

"Cat got your tongue, boy?" asked Ben. "Your not your usual run-on-at-the-mouth self."

Jimmy reached for a slice of cornbread and onion. He dipped the tip of the cornbread into the bean juice, then placed it in his mouth and began to chew. He took a swig of milk from the tin cup to wash it down. "I guess I might as well spill the beans."

"Now, why you wanna spill a perfectly good bowl of beans?" said Henry.

"I didn't mean...oh, you know what I mean," said Jimmy.

The two old men chuckled at the young man's reaction to the jest.

"You two old buzzards are always trying to get under my skin. Well, I ain't in the mood for no joshing today. I'm heavy burdened today."

"Now just calm down," said Ben. "You know Henry was just messing with you. We're all ears. Ain't we, Henry?"

"Yessir. Just like the two old mules, we are all ears," retorted Henry.

"Mule-headed, sure enough," said Black. "That fits you much better than me calling you buzzards. Now don't make this any harder than it is. I'm leaving here tomorrow. Pulling out in the morning. Time for me to start fresh somewhere else."

"I suppose this sudden departure is related to Shaw's daughter? It's usually a woman that makes a young man act foolishly," said Ben. You've been moping around here for better than a week now. Me and Henry been wondering how this might go."

Jimmy knew they would pester him relentlessly until he told them about the girl, so he proceeded to fill in Ben and Henry on his interactions with Anne and Shaw, especially the events of the past week. Ben offered to go into town and beat some sense into Shaw's head – said that would give him immense satisfaction. It seems Ben had held a strong dislike for the man for some time, having had Shaw do some blacksmithing for him over the years. Jimmy liked the idea but told Ben he might break his hand for naught or, worse still, get thrown in jail. Jimmy laid out his plan to move west about thirty miles to a place on the Rolling Fork River. There, he planned to build a grist mill on the mountain stream to take advantage of the settlers moving to the area who would need their corn ground.

Ben gave Henry a sideways glance with an eyebrow raised. Henry nodded back at Ben. "Have you thought long and hard about this, boy?" said Ben. "Sounds like a speculative venture. I know that area like the back of my hand. Trapped up and down those rocky streams and hills for years. That ain't good land for raising row crops. Too rocky. Seems to me you are running away from something rather than to something. Sometimes a man has to know when to stand his ground and fight for what he wants. It's not always best to tuck tail and run."

Jimmy could feel his face growing red as he clenched his hands into fists. He tried to control his anger, but it was uncontrollable at times like this. It happened to him more than he liked to admit. It was like Ben had punched him in the nose. He fought hard to regain his composure out of respect for these two men who had taken him under their wings. "My mind's made up. No use trying to change it. I'm leaving here in the morning. Can't stomach Shaw another day. And it's too painful for me to be this close to Anne. I've pulled up stakes and moved before. I can take care of myself. Now, if you don't mind, I need to finish my chores." Jimmy pushed back his chair and left the kitchen, banging the door closed behind him.

* * *

The following morning, Ben went to Jimmy's room and knocked on the door. He hoped Jimmy would join them for one last breakfast. Hearing no reply, he pushed open the door and entered the room. It was empty. Looking around the room, he noted that all of Jimmy's belongings were gone. The old trapper spotted a piece of paper lying on top of the washstand and picked it up. Scribbled in charcoal across was a brief note:

Ben and Henry,
Thanks for everything. Sorry about last night.
Don't know what gets into me sometimes.
I know you were trying to help.
Maybe our paths will cross again someday.
I will take good care of Socks.
Jimmy

* * *

Even though it lay in the opposite direction from where he was heading, Jimmy decided to return to Washington briefly. He wanted to pick up some of his things at the shop, including a couple of his knives. More urgently, though, he wanted to see Tom and get word to Anne about his sudden departure. As Jimmy sat in the saddle with Socks plodding along the familiar path to town, his mind wind-milled on the unfamiliar that lay ahead. *Anne must know my plan includes coming for her once my new venture is underway. Don't think I could stand saying bye to her face. Not sure I could handle her reaction. Would she cry or say good riddance? Would she say she was cutting her losses and setting her sights on a wealthy planter's son? What if she said she would never move to some tiny cabin on the edge of nowhere? I must believe Anne will join me later on the Rolling Fork. That belief might see me through the hard days ahead. To think otherwise might be more than I can bear.*

Fall 1829

Chapter 17

It was an unseasonably, warm fall day. Jimmy Black sat on a tree stump, wiping his brow with a soiled kerchief. The stump protruded from a low hill near the Rolling Fork River that curved through the Washita Mountains about thirty miles west of the town of Washington. The ancient, rolling hills were thickly forested with hardwood trees in the early stage of changing colors from shades of green to the earth-tones of burnt orange, yellow, red, and tan. The hill on which Black sat was dotted with the stumps of numerous trees he had felled during the construction of his tiny cabin, which stood nearby. He was taking a break from the back-breaking work of building a rock dam across the spring-fed creek that emptied into the more significant mountain stream. After the coffer-dam was complete, he planned to build a grist mill on the river for grinding the corn for the settlers moving into the area.

The idea for the grist mill had come to him back at Ben's boarding house one night as he lay tossing and turning, stewing over his plight with Shaw and Shaw's daughter, Anne. Just thinking about his former employer sent him into a rage. His face grew red, his palms began to sweat, and he unconsciously clenched and unclenched his hand into tight fists. Jimmy cursed Shaw under his breath, calling him every bad name he knew.

I hope that old goat's business is suffering without me around to help, Jimmy thought to himself. *I hope he realizes how lucky he was to have me around. Losing all his customers and being forced to close up shop would suit me just fine. What do I care? It was hot, dirty, back-breaking work anyhow. At least when I get my grist mill built, I can let the water in this stream do the hard labor for me. All I'll have to do is take people's money. Maybe after I get some money coming in, I can get Anne to marry me and move out here and leave that old goat behind. That'll fix his wagon for sure. Shaw doesn't know who he's messing with. I've been kicked around all my life and by a lot worse than the likes of him. I guess I best get back to building this dam. It ain't gonna build itself.*

As Black rose from the stump, he was suddenly startled back to reality by the sight of a horse and rider stepping out of the underbrush onto the east bank of the Rolling Fork. Black quickly looked around for his long-rifle, which was leaning against a sapling at the edge of the creek about twenty paces away. Jimmy began to sprint towards the rifle when he was hailed by the rider across the way.

"Whoa there, mister. No need for your gun. I'm the sheriff of this here county. Besides, if I aimed to harm you, I would have shot you while you sat lollygagging on that there stump. Easy pickin's, I reckon. Now you hold on -- I'm coming over."

Jimmy stood still as he watched the horse and rider forge the rapids of the flowing mountain stream. The big, painted horse was sure-footed and appeared comfortable stepping gingerly through the white water cascading over the moss-covered river rocks. Jimmy carefully observed the man riding atop the big horse. The bright sun glinted off a shiny object on the left breast of the rider's buckskin shirt. *It looks like a badge he's wearing.* Jimmy began to relax a bit. Rider and horse approached the spot where Jimmy was standing.

The rider dismounted. "Name's Sanderson. Will Sanderson. As I said, I'm the sheriff of Miller County. Are you a fellow by the name of Black?"

"I am," replied Jimmy. "How'd you know my name?"

"A land surveyor by the name of Conway gave me your name. Said I'd find you building a dam up this way," said Sanderson.

"Care for anything to eat or drink?" asked Black. "Got some stale coffee over to the cabin."

"No, sir. I best not tarry. I've got a couple more squatters to see afore sunset. No reason to beat around the bush, Mr. Black. Afraid I've got some bad news. You're going to have to pull up stakes and move back east of here. On account of this new survey, this here land is no longer part of Miller County. It's now part of the Indian Territory. The politicians back east in Washington City are making plans to relocate a bunch of Choctaw Indians from east of the Mississippi over here soon. So I'm telling all the squatters out here they have to move several miles back east of here to Arkansas Territory."

Black's jaw dropped, and he stood in disbelief of what the authoritarian figure in front of him had just said. After a long pause, Black finally spoke. "You can't do that! This must be a joke...some kind of a mistake!"

"No, sir. I wouldn't josh about such a thing. I can see you've put lots of sweat and back-muscle into building this here cabin and this cofferdam. I'm sure sorry to give you this bad news."

"What if I refuse to leave?" said Black.

"In that case, I guess I'll have to arrest you. Now I'll be back through here in about a week, and you best be gone. Understood?"

Black stood stoically silent. He felt his face reddening.

"Good luck to you, Mr. Black. I trust things will work out better for you next time." The gruff sheriff mounted his big horse and headed off to the north.

Black just stood there in a daze, staring in the direction of the sheriff as he rode away. He felt as if he had been clubbed over the head. *This can't be happening. Not again. How much bad luck can a man stand?* Jimmy slowly turned and shuffled his way back to the nearby stump. Reaching it, he slumped down, rested his elbows on his thighs, and rested his head in his open hands. *This is not fair...just not fair.* Black sat lost in his thoughts, overwhelmed by his feelings.

Minutes stretched into hours. The shadows grew long. The wind kicked up and began to howl through the nearby trees, making a low, lonesome moaning sound. Though he had not eaten or drunk anything for several hours, he wasn't hungry. His mouth grew parched in the dry wind. He slowly rose from the stump and stumbled as he turned towards his tiny cabin. His legs were numb from sitting too long in one place. He was light-headed as the blood had settled in his legs and feet. He stopped, regained his balance and feeling in his legs, then continued his slow walk to his cabin.

Upon entering the one-roomed cabin, he lit a bear-oil lamp sitting on a crude shelf that ran along the mud-chinked log wall. From the ledge, he grabbed a wooden mallet and a bowl containing some black walnuts he had gathered a few days earlier in the nearby woods. Jimmy carried the dish and mallet a few paces, then placed them on a log bench that sat near a mud and twig fireplace. Even though he knew it would grow colder during the night, he had not the energy to start a fire in the hearth. Walking back to the shelf, Jimmy retrieved a crock jug of grog, then straddled the log bench. He popped the dried, corncob stopper from the mouth and the jug, placed the opening to his lips, tilted back his head, and took a long draw off the liquor. He slowly put the jug on the floor near his feet.

Pulling the walnut-laden bowl near him on the bench, he took a nut and smacked it hard with the wooden mallet. He sat and plucked the meat of the walnut from the fractured hull. He plopped a morsel of the walnut into his mouth and began to slowly chew. The walnut left a pungent, bitter taste in his mouth. Black questioned whether the nut was more bitter than usual or if his mood contributed to the bitter after-taste. After consuming the meager contents of the hard-shelled nut, Black placed another on the log surface and gave it a hard whack with the mallet. Shards of the hull and inner flesh flew in all directions – the nut virtually disintegrating in front of his eyes. *Well, it looks like I smacked that one a bit too hard.*

He sat absorbed in his thoughts, contemplating his unfortunate fate. Frequently, he would take another swig from the nearby jug in between bites of the earthy-tasting nuts. It grew dark outside. The wind continued to howl around the corners and through the poorly chinked seams of the log shelter. After consuming half the contents of the jug and the wooden bowl, Black found himself nodding off. He slowly stood, lifted one leg over the bench, then staggered across the room and fell onto a bearskin lying in the corner that served as a bed. He was soon sound asleep and snoring loudly.

* * *

Black awoke from a fitful slumber well after daybreak. His head was pounding, and the taste of bile was in his mouth. Mother nature was calling, so he quickly rose from his bed, walked briskly outside the cabin, and relieved himself. As he stood in the brisk morning air, he suddenly felt ill and wretched. Shakily, he returned to the cold cabin where he was at least shielded from the wind. He walked over to the back wall of the cabin, where a wooden bucket sat on a ramshackle table. He took a nearby gourd dipper and scooped water from the bucket. He gulped down the contents of the gourd. He scooped another gourd-full of water. Leaning forward in a half-stoop, he poured the water over his head. He grabbed a nearby rag and dried his face and head. He walked over to a buckskin pouch hanging from a wooden peg. Opening the bag, he plucked out some venison jerky and some hardtack. He sat on the wooden bench and began to consume the meager breakfast, which seemed to have a calming effect on his upset stomach.

The groggy night's sleep had distilled his jumbled thoughts from the previous day. In light of the eviction notice delivered by the no-nonsense sheriff, he had but one course of action. *My mind's made up. No looking back now.*

He grabbed his long-rifle, his knife, and his few items of clothing and removed them from the cabin placed them on a large stump forty paces from the cabin. He walked back to the cabin, retrieved his saddle and bridle which he carried out to the nearby rail fenced corral where his prized horse, Socks, stood chewing on some grass watching Jimmy's movements. He placed the saddle over the top rail of the fence, climbed over, and walked up to Socks. He then bridled the gentle horse. He tied the reins of the bridle firmly around the fence's top rail. He then returned to the cabin and went inside.

He remained out of Sock's view for only a few minutes. After exiting the structure, Jimmy strolled over to the corral and turned to face the cabin. A yellowish glow could be seen flickering inside the doorway. The glow slowly grew brighter. White smoke began to waft from the door as it made its way skyward. Suddenly, tongues of orange-reddish flames began to lap the edges of the wooden shingled roof. Then the entire structure erupted into a roaring blaze, the heat from which was quickly felt by Black and Socks. The horse began to buck and tug, but the bridle kept the horse from bolting from the small enclosure. Grayish white smoke billowing into the air glowed orange as it reflected the bright, hot, flames below.

Jimmy stood solemnly by watching the bonfire engulf the dwelling that he had called home for the past few months. *If I can't live here, then nobody can. Don't want my handiwork falling into the hands of some ungrateful Injuns.* He stood mesmerized by the beautiful but destructive flames of the all-consuming fire. The log house and its contents were quickly consumed, and the walls eventually collapsed. The embers continued slowly burning, sending smoke skyward. The trail of smoke rose high into the fall air and traveled downwind for miles.

Black had one remaining task to perform at his frontier home. He walked down the hill towards the stream where he had spent months building the rock dam. He waded into the stream on the low water side of the dam. The cold water took his breath away. He slowly made his way to the center of the stream where the cold, clear water was streaming over the dam. Standing knee-deep in the icy water, he turned to face the damn and placed his two, leather stocking clad feet firmly among the slippery rocks. Using both of his heavily muscled arms and calloused hands, Black reached forward, grasped a large rock wedged into the dam, and pulled. He quickly jumped to his right to avoid being struck by the falling rock, which landed at his feet. He again turned to face the rock dam, grabbed hold of the large rock to the left of the newly created gap, and tugged. The rock splashed into the stream bed. Next, he pried on the stone to the right of the gap, which tumbled into the stream. Black, drenched from head to toe by water rushing through the gap and the splashing from the falling rocks, slowly created an ever-widening gap in the center of the dam.

Wet, cold, and tired, Jimmy decided to take a break from his labor. *Tearing down may be easier than building something but not nearly as gratifying*, he thought to himself. Slowly making his way back to the eastern bank of the stream, Jimmy stumbled up the bank and slumped onto a fallen log to catch his breath and rest. It was nearing noon, and he was hungry. He arose from the wooden seat and sauntered uphill to where his cabin once stood. Standing near the smoldering embers, he stretched out his arms and began to warm his icy hands. The warmth from the dying fire felt good on his face and exposed skin. The glowing embers were mesmerizing and lulled Jimmy into a trance-like state.

Suddenly, Black was jolted from his dark thoughts by the loud snorting and stamping of hooves by his nearby horse, Socks. He turned to see what was alarming Socks. On the far side of the clearing, making its way down the dim road, a team of oxen lumbered along, pulling a wagon. Sitting atop the cart was a bearded man and a young boy. Jimmy recognized his distant neighbor, Daniel Davis, and his teen son, Andrew, coming across the clearing. He had gotten to know the two reasonably well over the past few months. Young Andrew's mother was dead, and the boy rode over quite often to spend time with Jimmy. The elder Davis was calling out commands to the oxen as he tugged on the reins, guiding the team down the pot-hole filled dirt road. The driver and wagon slowly made their way to where Black was standing.

"Whoa," yelled the driver to the big oxen, as he pulled back on the leather reins. The team came to an abrupt stop. "What happened here?" said the bearded Davis. "The boy here saw the smoke, and we came quick as we could."

"Climb down, and I'll tell you," said Black. "You fellows want some venison jerky and hardtack? I was just getting ready to eat my noon meal."

"We'uns et," said the elder Davis as he climbed down from atop the wagon. Having jumped to the ground from his perch, the much nimbler, younger Davis was already standing next to Black as the elder Davis walked to where the two were standing. Surveying the scene, he said, "Looks like your cabin's a total loss. Did you get soaking wet trying to put out the fire?"

"I burned my cabin. Got wet, destroying my dam."

"I told the boy here that you might have done something like this. Sheriff stopped by our place yesterday after he stopped by here. Can't say as I blame you. So what are you gonna do now?"

"Guess there's only one thing I can do. Don't have no money. Guess I'll go back to Washington. May have to crawl on my belly back to Shaw and see if he'll give me another chance to work for him. I'd rather be horsewhipped, but that's the only idea I came up with. What about you two? What are your plans?"

"We'll be packing our belongings and heading to Texas. Young Andrew here feels a calling to be a preacher. Spreading God's word to the heathen south of the Red. You're welcome to join up with us. I'll lend you a hand till you can get back on your feet. They'll be needing a good blacksmith down in Texas. Lots of folks heading down that way. You've been a good friend to the boy here for the past few months. What do you say?"

"Yeah, come with us, Jimmy," said young Andrew.

Black stood silently for several minutes as he pondered the offer. "That's mighty nice of you, Daniel. And Andrew reminds me of someone I knew back in Philadelphia but, I've made up mind. I need to head back to Washington. I got some unfinished business back there. I can't keep running away from fights like a cur dog, with my tail tucked between my legs. No, sir. No more running."

"I know we've talked about this before, but you need the Good Lord on your side. Lean on Him, and He will give you strength. Ain't that so, Andrew?"

"Yes, sir. Jimmy, you need the Lord on your side. He will be a lamp unto your feet," said Andrew.

Black stared at the two men in silence. "No disrespect, but I need to get back to work. Got a lot to do before sunset. I'm pulling out at daybreak."

"Let's load up, Andrew," said Davis. The man and the boy climbed back onto the wagon seat. "May the Good Lord go with you," said Daniel.

"Take care, Jimmy. I hope you find what you're looking for," said Andrew.

"Hee yah!" yelled Daniel at the team of oxen as he slapped the long reins. The oxen leaned into the harness, and the wagon began to move. Daniel pulled the long leather straps to the right, and the cart started a slow turn. The wagon carrying the two men headed back south down the road.

Jimmy, waving to the two men as they rode out of sight, thought to himself, *What's God ever done for me? Not a damn thing.*

Chapter 18

Jimmy rode into the town he had left a few months earlier. He was angry, sad, and anxious -- angry at the politicians in Washington City for giving his land to a bunch of Indians, sad life was not going as planned, and anxious about his bleak future.

Best get used to the taste of crow 'cause I've got a heaping helping to eat, he thought to himself. *Guess I'll stop by Shaw's shop first. See if he'll hire me back. Worst he can say is "no." Then I'll go to see Ben and Henry. See if my room's still for rent. I hope so even though I'll hear "I told you so" for about a month. I wonder if Anne has found her a rich beau yet? Wouldn't fault her if she did. Can't worry about that now. Gotta get my ox out of the ditch.*

As he rode within sight of Shaw's shop, he could see the smoke rising from the forge. As he approached, he thought about what he would say to Shaw. *Might as well just tell him the truth. See what happens.* He rode up to the front of the shop. Tom and Willy looked out from the forge and saw Jimmy sitting on his horse. A smile broke across Tom's face. Jimmy dismounted from Socks and tied the reins to a nearby hitching post. He brushed the dust from his shirt and pants, then moved slowly toward the front entrance. It was a crisp, fall day, and the double doors to the shop were opened wide. As he entered, he paused to let his eyes adjust to the light inside the shop. Shaw was sitting at his desk, looking over some papers. Black cleared his throat. Shaw looked up, and the two men made eye contact. Shaw rapidly blinked his eyes as if they were deceiving him. Shaw's visage quickly turned to a scowl. Jimmy, undeterred, closed the space between them.

"Hello, Mr. Shaw. I reckon I'm the last person you 'spected to see today."

Shaw grunted his agreement.

"Before you toss me out on my tail, hear me out. I got thrown off my land west of here. Seems the Federal Authorities plan on moving some Choctaw Indians there. Bad luck, I reckon. I burned my cabin and have no money. I need my job back."

Shaw sat quietly for several awkward minutes, staring a hole through Black. "Boy, you got a lot of sand in your craw. I'll hand you that." He paused for an awkward minute. "Against my better judgment, I'll say 'yes' with strings attached. Your pay will be reduced to what I'm paying Tom. And as for those knives you were making before you left, I'll keep seventy percent. Take it or leave it."

"I'll take it. Now, if you don't mind me asking, why did you agree to hire me back?"

"Strictly business, boy. I got more business than I can handle. And the sight of more money allows me to tolerate the sight of you. Understood?"

"Understood," said Jimmy.

"Now go tell Tom and Willy you'll be here at daylight," said Shaw. "Don't dawdle -- they've got work to do. And don't be late tomorrow."

"Yes, sir." Jimmy briskly walked out to the forge where Tom and Willy were hard at work. Seeing Jimmy, Tom quickly laid his hammer on the anvil and extended his arm to shake his friend's hand. "Looks like you boys could use a real blacksmith to show you how it's done."

"Yeah, do you know one?" replied Tom with a big grin on his face. "How you been, Jimmy? Didn't expect to be laying eyes on you today."

"I've been better. But that's a story for another day. You boys are in luck. I'll be here tomorrow bright and early to show you how it's done. Now I best be going before Shaw changes his mind about giving me my old job back. And Tom, please tell Anne I'm back and hope to see her soon." He exited the shop, mounted Socks, and headed toward the center of town. At the crossroads, he turned west down the Fort Towson Road.

As Black rode into the afternoon sun down the road to Ben's boarding house, he watched two Cooper's hawks circling in the blue sky, gliding lazily in big, sweeping circles. His mind gently wandered like the two birds. It had been tough to swallow his pride and ask Shaw for a job. But he had conjured a new plan -- to continue working for Shaw and honing his knife making skills. He would take his cut of the knife sales and save his money. If the knife sales took off as he thought it might, he would eventually demand a bigger cut of the sales from Shaw. *In about a year, maybe I'll have enough money to open my own blacksmith shop. Then Anne might see me as a bona fide suitor. Perhaps I can even convince Shaw I'm a worthy suitor -- a long shot for sure.* Black's mood elevated suddenly, soaring like the hawks overhead. *I can stay in touch with Anne through Tom, letting let her know my intentions. We can meet without Shaw knowing...I wonder if Anne will bide her time for a whole year?... She must or...*

* * *

As Jimmy approached the familiar dog-trot log house he had called home prior to his foolish move to the Rolling Fork, he felt butterflies in the pit of his stomach. *I hope my old room is not rented out. Ben and Henry are sure going to be surprised to see me.* As he rode Socks across the log bridge over the creek in front of Ben's cabin, a couple of hound dogs lying on the front porch began to bark loudly. As he approached the house, Ben suddenly appeared on the porch with his long-rifle in hand. "Don't shoot, Ben. It's me, Jimmy."

"Lordy, lordy," said Ben. "You could knock me over with a feather. I sure didn't expect to lay eyes on you today."

"How are you, Ben? And how's Ol' Henry?"

"He's out back in the kitchen cooking. Now crawl down off that horse, boy, and let's go see what's for supper. Henry ain't going to believe his eyes. He moped around here for weeks after you left...saying he'd probably never see you again."

"Looks like I timed it just right," said Jimmy. "I've missed that old coot's cooking."

Jimmy climbed down off his saddle and tied the horse to a nearby post. He stepped up on the front porch and reached out to shake Ben's hand. Ben extended his arm, clasped Jimmy's hand and pulled him to his chest, and gave the young man a bear hug. "How are things working out for you over on the Rolling Fork?" asked Ben.

"Not so well, but that's sort of a long story," said Jimmy. I'll tell you and Henry about it over supper. I'm hungrier than a stray dog."

"Sure, boy. Let's go see Henry. I can't wait to see his face when he sees you."

The two men turned and walked through the breezeway on their way outback of the cabin. As they walked, Jimmy asked Ben, "Is that spare room rented out? I may need a place to stay for a while."

"It is," said Ben.

Jimmy stopped mid-stride and stared at Ben with his mouth agape.

"By you," continued Ben as he let out a chuckle and slapped Jimmy across the back.

"Why you...you...you almost gave me a heart attack," as he let out a sigh of relief.

"Let's go tell Henry he'll have to set an extra plate at the table for a while," said Ben as they continued on their way outback.

* * *

Wednesday, a week later.

On the prior Monday, Shaw had left town with Judge Eskridge, a local planter, to accompany him on a trip to the territorial capital at Little Rock -- something to do with politics. It would take about two weeks for them to make the round trip, depending on how long they were in the capitol. Jimmy had gotten word through Tom for Anne to drop by the shop while her pa was out of town.

Jimmy sat eating his noon meal under the big sycamore tree outside the shop. Just like the first time he'd laid eyes on her, Anne came strolling down the lane towards the shop at a leisurely pace as if she had not a care in the world. Her attitude was vexing. As she walked up to where he was sitting, Jimmy rose from his seat. "Hello, Anne. How've you been?" His mouth was dry as cotton.

"Sit and finish your lunch, James. You wouldn't want to take advantage of my father's generosity by taking an extra-long noon break, now would you?"

Jimmy didn't reply. He sat back down, and she sat on the other end of the bench.

"Would you like something to eat?" he asked her.

"I'm not hungry at the moment."

"Me neither," he replied.

"I'm still angry at you for leaving town without saying good-bye," said Anne. "I cried for days afterward."

"I can't blame you for being angry," he said as he dropped his chin and stared at the ground.

"You know your selfish actions simply aided my father in saying that you are shiftless and will never amount to anything, don't you?"

Jimmy squirmed uncomfortably on the bench. His skin grew flushed as if he was seated on hot coals. "Well, I plan to prove your pa wrong."

Anne stared off into the distance. "From the first time we met, I never expected Papa to treat you like you're some shiftless ne'er do well. He values your skills as a blacksmith. I've seen a side of my father that saddens me."

The two sat in uncomfortable silence for several minutes.

"Did Tom fill you in on my plans?" said Jimmy.

"He did. Said you were going to keep working for Papa till you can make enough money to open your own shop if that's what you mean."

"Well, what do you think?" he asked her.

She didn't reply. She continued to stare off into the distance.

"Anne, I know a year is a long time. So I need to know – am I wasting my time? Are you willing to give me some time? Otherwise, I...I don't know what else to do."

"Papa is insistent on me courting one of the planters' sons. He doesn't really care which one. There are several my age in the area. He wants the best for me, and he thinks to be a wife to the heir of one of these large plantations is in my best interest. Part of me believes it's not really about me."

"Well, why don't you then?"

Anne sat silently for a moment. "Most are snobbish," she said. "They think they're better than most simply because they own a lot of land and slaves."

"Is that the only reason?" he asked.

"James, why are you asking me all these questions?"

"Because, Anne, I have to know if I'm wasting my time. If I am, tell me now. To make this work is going to take a lot out of me – out of both of us. I'm ready to try if you're willing to give me some time."

"James, you remember the church dinner? I knew there was something about you that day that made you different. The times I've seen you have not changed my feelings. I can't predict what may happen down the road. Regardless of what happens with us, if you can open your own shop a year from now, isn't that worth the effort?"

"Anne, just tell me. Are you willing to give this a try?"

"Like you said, what other option is there?"

"Are you willing to see me without your father knowing?" he asked.

"I'm here today, aren't I?" She stood up. "I have to go now. Mama will be looking for me."

Jimmy stood and stepped close to her. He looked into her eyes, reached out, grabbing her around the waist with both hands, and pulled her towards him. At first, she resisted, placing her hands against his chest and pushing backward. Then her resistance faded. He bent his head downwards and kissed her on the lips. The first kiss was ever so brief. He kissed her again. This time he lingered. Anne then pushed him backward. Her face was flushed. She broke free of his embrace.

"I best go now. Keep in touch through Tom. He likes you, James. Now get back to work. You need to make lots of money quickly. I won't wait forever." She turned and walked briskly back up the road toward town. After she had gone about twenty paces, she turned and waved good-bye.

Jimmy waved back and watched her until she was out of sight. *Am I on another fool's errand? Only time will tell.* He picked up his knapsack and returned to the shop. The boys were already hard at it. He put on his leather apron and joined them.

* * *

About a week after his meeting with Anne, Jimmy was at the forge working on a knife that was nearing the end of the lengthy process. The long blade had been through the quench. It was a good-looking knife free of defects. But without the next step, it would be brittle. Jimmy had the forge at a lower temperature. He had made a metal box with a lid about two feet in length, about a foot wide and about a half-foot deep. Placing the blade in the box, Jimmy put the cover in place and set the container on the edge of the coals in the forge. He needed to keep the temperature of the box between 200 to 400 degrees for about two hours.

While the tempering process was underway, he took some blades not yet quenched to the grinding wheel. The grinding wheel operated like a spinning wheel. Applying foot-power to the pedal would spin the large grindstone. Once the stone-wheel was in motion, it was reasonably easy to keep it turning. He picked up a blade and then began to taper the edge. He then worked around the tang to refine the shape of the handle. Occasionally, he would check the forge and apply a small amount of air with the bellows to maintain the temperature. He kept the coals smoldering but not red hot.

Two hours later, he removed the metal box from the forge and popped off the lid. The knife blade needed to cool down slowly until it could be handled. No quench was required. Jimmy went about his grinding on the other knives that had not yet been quenched. After quenching, the metal became too hard to work with the grinding wheel.

Jimmy used Nat and Tom to help him with some of the less critical steps of the knife-making process like polishing and sharpening, but he never let them help with the forging, quenching, or tempering processes. He never discussed these critical steps with the others in the shop. Those steps were Jimmy's trade secret carefully protected. To help keep those essential steps from prying eyes, he had a large leather curtain that he would unfurl around three sides of the forge. The curtain also reduced the external light so that he could better maintain the color of the metal during the heating process. Heating the metal to the right color was critical in maintaining the proper temperature.

It was just about quitting time. Jimmy removed the knife that had been cooling from the metal box. He twirled the lethal weapon while carefully examining it for imperfections. It was a keeper. It would be ready for the final few steps tomorrow. He would apply the handle. Then, using the wet-stone, he would hone the edge and clip point to razor-sharpness. He would get Nat or Tom to help with the polishing and sharpening tomorrow.

Chapter 19

It was harvest time on the many large plantations and small farms surrounding the town of Washington. Hundreds of slaves were busy picking cotton that covered the planters' fields like early snow. The more impoverished farmers had their wives and numerous children cutting stalks of corn and placing them in shocks around their small plots. Both efforts required the unfortunate laborers to toil from dawn to dusk with little rest.

Judge Cross, the owner of Marlbrook Plantation, was in town checking on his cotton that was being deseeded and pressed into bales at Dr. Jones's cotton gin. While in town, the Judge stopped by Shaw's to pick up a knife he was having made.

"Is my knife ready?" the Judge asked Shaw.

"It is. Let me get it for you," said Shaw. Shaw went to a wooden cabinet where finished knives were stored. He returned and handed the knife to Judge Cross. At the Judge's request, Jimmy had inlaid the knife handle with silver. The Judge had paid twice the going price for the custom work. Judge Cross looked the knife over carefully. The expression on his face let Shaw know he was pleased with the craftsmanship. "Jimmy did an outstanding job on my knife. She's a beauty. I'd like to personally thank him."

"He's at the forge," said Shaw.

The Judge walked to where the forge was located. Jimmy was hard at work on another knife. He was at the anvil hammering away on a hot blade in the making. Seeing the Judge, Jimmy laid down his hammer and pulled off his gloves. The two men approached each other and shook hands.

"Jimmy, you outdid yourself on my knife," said the Judge. "I'm very pleased."

"Glad you like it. I thought it turned out to be a nice piece."

"Saturday night, I'm hosting a husking bee at Marlbrook. I'd like you to come. It'll be great fun. We'll have lots of food. People from all over the county will be there. Who knows, you might meet an attractive young lady there."

"That sounds like fun, Judge. But pardon my ignorance, what's a husking bee anyhow?"

"I see you haven't spent much time on a farm," said the Judge. "This time of year, when the corn is ready to harvest, stalks, ears and all, are bundled teepee style and left to dry in the field. After the ears are dried, the ears are shucked and stored in the corn crib. A husking bee is a social event where folks get together to shuck corn and have fun."

"I figured you'd make your slaves do the shucking?" quizzed Jimmy.

"I could, but my slaves are busy harvesting my cash crop – cotton. It'll be a load of fun, I promise. So will I see you there?"

Jimmy was hopeful a certain young lady might be in attendance. "Yes, sir. I'll plan on it."

"Very well. You'll be glad you came," said the Judge. "I'll see you on Saturday." He then made his way out of the shop, climbed into his surrey, and rode off in a cloud of dust down the lane.

* * *

Saturday after the shop closed at noon, Jimmy mounted Socks and headed north of town. Marlbrook Plantation was about five miles out. After he had ridden about three miles, he was snapped out of his daydream by what sounded like singing up ahead. He couldn't make out the words until he rode closer to the source. As he rounded a curve in the dirt road, the brush on the side of the road gave way to the white rows of cotton on both sides. There looked to be about a hundred or so slaves of all ages picking cotton on both sides of the road. The slaves were dragging long, canvas sacks behind them that were slung around their necks by wide straps. One old, white-haired slave would sing a line, then the rest of the slaves would join in the chorus.

"All them pretty gals will be there,
Shuck that corn before you eat;
They will fix it for us rare,
Shuck that corn before you eat.
I know that supper will be big,
Shuck that corn before you eat;
I think I smell a fine roast pig,
Shuck that corn before you eat."

The slaves paid no mind to the lone rider passing slowly by. Several white men on horseback were positioned throughout the fields along with massive wagons pulled by teams of mules. Some of the slaves were emptying the sacks of cotton into the wagons. Each horseman carried a Kentucky rifle with a pistol or two stuck in their belts. Some had long, leather whips coiled and slung over their saddle horns. One of the riders nodded his head at Jimmy as he rode by. Jimmy nodded back. The singing continued until he was out of earshot of the slaves.

It seemed he had been riding past the white fields of cotton for a couple of miles when he finally arrived at a whitewashed, wooden sign with black lettering that read "Marlbrook Plantation." He reined Socks to the right down a tree-lined lane. After riding about a hundred yards, the trees cleared as he topped the crest of a low hill. He was looking down on a hollow with the main house and a large number of outbuildings lying between two ridges.

Judge Cross's home is not quite what I expected, thought Jimmy. I was hoping to see a large, white structure with columns in front like those plantation homes over in Louisiana. Instead, the Cross's home was similar to the boarding house he lived in – only much larger with a second story and large brick fireplaces on both ends. A large porch wrapped around three sides of the house. Behind the main house, Jimmy could make out a kitchen, springhouse, a smokehouse, a carriage house, a stable, a large, chicken coop, and several barns. Standing about a hundred yards or so behind the main house, were several small log structures with crude doors and windows. Hmmm, those must be the slave quarters. Near the slave quarters were some small garden patches where the slaves raised their own food. Near the log, barn structures were several split rail fences creating corrals for mules, horses, pigs, sheep, and goats. Inside one of the fenced-in enclosures was a large vegetable garden. In front of the largest barn, he could make out a group of people milling about.

Jimmy had gotten word to Anne through Tom that he was going to the husking bee at Marlbrook. He was hopeful the Shaw family was invited. At least he hoped Anne was among the crowd even if the old man wasn't. Jimmy rode down the hill towards the main house. As he approached the house, a young Black boy approached and said he would take care of "Masser's horse." The young Black then directed Jimmy to walk around behind the main house to where folks were gathering at the large barn. Jimmy dismounted and gave the reins to the boy who led Socks toward the stable.

Jimmy proceeded around a path to the right in the direction of the sounds of people talking, laughing, and of young children playing. As he approached the barn, he could make out the faces of several people he knew from town. As his eyes searched the crowd for Anne, Jimmy made out a very familiar face. It was Dr. Jones whom he first met on his trip up the Red on the paddle wheeler. Dr. Jones had remained in contact with Jimmy, but the two men had not seen each other in a while.

As their eyes made contact, Jimmy walked briskly to where Dr. Jones was standing and reached out to shake his hand.

"Dr. Jones, how are you? I didn't expect to see you here today."

"Likewise, Jimmy. Edward showed me the knife you made him. It's a beautiful piece of work, especially the silver inlay on the black walnut handle. I've been meaning to come by Shaw's and talk to you about getting one for myself. How are knife sales going by the way?"

"Knives are selling like hotcakes. I can't keep up with demand."

"That's a good problem to have, I would think," said Jones. "Last, we talked, you were seeking permission from Shaw to court his lovely daughter. Has Shaw given you his permission yet?"

"No, sir. He has not."

"That's unfortunate but not surprising. Shaw's a stubborn old coot. I'm surprised you continue to work for him under such conditions," responded Jones.

"It's difficult, I'll admit. Dr. Jones, may I confide in you?"

"Of course, Jimmy. What's on your mind?"

Jimmy proceeded to the doctor of his plans to open his own shop, thereby proving to Shaw he was a worthy suitor for Anne. Jimmy told Dr. Jones he'd been diligently saving his money and that in six months or so, he should be able to make his move.

"How's Anne with this plan?" said Jones. "That's quite a lot to ask a young beauty like her to while away her time while being pursued by several eligible bachelors in the area."

"She seems willing to give it a try. She urged me not to tarry. Do you have a reason for me to think otherwise?" Jimmy asked.

"I know that more than one young man of means has been calling with her father's permission," said Jones.

"I know time is not on my side. I am at a loss as to how I can speed up the process, though," Jimmy lamented.

"Have you been able to keep in touch with Anne, given her father's stance?" asked the doctor.

"Well, I'm able to exchange messages through her brother, Tom. Tom likes me. On occasion, I've been able to see Anne briefly. The brief encounters are stressful for fear of being caught. I'm hoping I might see her here today, as a matter of fact. Have you seen any of the Shaws here?"

"No, I haven't. But it's still early." Dr. Jones sensed Jimmy's dejection. "Have you considered a partner for your new venture?"

"Not seriously. I thought about asking Ben Cooper, my landlord, but he's been generous to me already. I don't want to take advantage of him. I'm not sure he has much money anyhow."

"Well, Jimmy, I might be interested in being your partner. How would you feel about that?"

Jimmy's jaw dropped, and he stood silently for a moment. "Dr. Jones, I couldn't possibly take a handout from you."

"It's not a handout, Jimmy. I've seen your handiwork. I expect to be fairly compensated for my investment. Besides, I've never cottoned to Shaw. He's an ass. How much money do you need to supplement your stake?"

Again Jimmy paused. "Well, sir, I'm not rightly sure. Perhaps I can put pencil to paper and drop by your office next week. We can negotiate terms then. Is that acceptable to you?"

"That'll be fine," replied Jones.

"Thank you for your consideration, Dr. Jones. I didn't expect this turn of events when I rode out here today."

"Jimmy, I recognized you as a young man with ambition the first time I met you on the riverboat. I consider myself a pretty good judge of character. It's another mark against Shaw in my book that he cannot see the same."

Jimmy stood blushing like a schoolboy.

"Have you been inside the main house yet?" asked Jones.

"No, sir, I have not."

"Come along, Jimmy. Mrs. Cross is proud of her home. She's from Virginia, and Judge Cross has gone to great expense to create a Virginia plantation here on the frontier. You'll be impressed with the furnishings. Most all purchased in New Orleans and brought upriver. Have you ever seen a Persian rug? She has one covering her parlor floor, and it's one of her prized possessions."

* * *

After a brief tour of the main house, Dr. Jones and Jimmy returned to the large barn where a crowd of people had gathered and were milling about. Jimmy set about to see if he could locate Anne. *Surely Shaw would not miss an opportunity to have Anne hob knob with the county's elite.*

He ventured inside the barn. In the center of the dirt floor was a large mound of corn ears to be shucked by the guests. It looked to be several wagon-loads of corn. The pile of corn was ringed by long, half-log benches and large, white oak baskets. Several slaves stood in one corner of the barn talking.

Jimmy went back outside the barn and continued his search. To the right of the barn, a couple of slaves were roasting a whole pig on a spit over a pit of hot charcoals. The smell of the smoke rising in the fresh air made his mouth water. Underneath a lean-to shed that adjoined the barn, several slave women with bandana-wrapped heads busied themselves, setting out plates, cups, and tableware on long, makeshift tables covered with tablecloths. On a low table near the front of the shed sat several crock jugs and urns. Jimmy overheard some men standing near the table saying the urns contained apple cider for the womenfolk, and that hard cider was in the jugs for the men. They then proceeded to pass the jug. People began gathering near the barn. Children were running, screaming, and playing games. It was late afternoon. Jimmy saw no sign of Anne or the Shaws.

About that time, a man standing in the back of a wagon blew on a long cow horn to get everyone's attention. Hello-o-o! Hello-o-o! It was Judge Cross. "Welcome, ladies and gentlemen! Welcome to the annual Marlbrook husking bee. Mrs. Cross and I wish to welcome you to our humble abode and are so happy you could join us this afternoon. For those who've not been here before, please allow me to go over a few things. The husking bee will begin momentarily. It's open to boys and men of all ages. Anyone finding the red corn ear earns the chance to kiss any girl or woman in attendance today so long as she does not strongly object. Ladies, we hope you honor the spirit of the contest. After the husking is done, supper will be served. After you sup, we will light the lamps in the barn, clear the floor, and dance till midnight. Now, please join me inside the barn for the contest."

With the help of a couple of men, the Judge climbed down from the wagon and made his way to the barn. The crowd began to elbow its way into the barn. The young boys and men seated themselves on the benches surrounding the mound of corn. Jimmy found a seat between two fellows about his age. The women and girls stood back out of the way behind the benches.

The Judge shouted, "Now men, on the count of three, go at it and may the best man win. One – twoooo – THREEEEE!"

Hands began grabbing corn. Husks began flying. Dust filled the air. A few startled mice under the pile of corn began to run for cover. As the mice scurried for cover underneath the long dresses and petticoats, the even more startled women began to shriek. One elderly woman swooned into the arms of her friends, who started fanning her face. Nothing distracted the men from the task at hand. The search was on for the all-important prize – the red ear of corn.

Jimmy was doing his dead-level best to keep up with his two neighbors. Having never shucked an ear of corn in his life, he was severely disadvantaged. He was just getting the hang of it when he heard a familiar voice behind him.

"And whom might you plan to kiss if you find that red ear, Mr. Black? You might find yourself in a pickle."

Without looking around, he knew it was Anne goading him. His face turned as red as that most sought after ear of corn. *She was right, though. What would I have done if I found that red ear and Anne had not shown up?* He looked around briefly, but she had quickly slipped away. Jimmy continued to shuck. He was sweating profusely even though it was a chilly November afternoon. He glanced quickly around the barn while furiously shucking. Anne was standing across from him with a small group of her friends. She was laughing and pointing at him as if taking glee in his predicament. He kept shucking.

The mound of corn was shrinking rapidly. A shaft of afternoon sunlight beaming through an opening above the barn door illuminated the dust that filled the room like smoke. Some of the older women fled the barn to escape the dust or mice or both, but most women remained steadfast.

Finally, the suspense was over. A lad of about twenty shouted at the top of his lungs as he leaped into the air, "I found it! I found the red ear!"

People around him patted him on the back. He was grinning from ear to ear. Judge Cross walked to where the fellow was standing and shook his hand. Then the Judge took the ear of corn from him. "Ok, men. Keep shucking! We can't quit till the job is done. Who knows, there might be another red ear in that pile!"

Finally, the last ear was shucked. The oak baskets were filled and overflowing with the mottled purple and gold corn. The husks were cast aside.

Judge Cross carried the red ear back and handed it to the lucky fellow and said, "Okay, Robert, who's the lucky lady gonna be?"

Robert made a beeline towards the group of girls where Anne was standing. The young girls were giggling with delight. Jimmy stood petrified. Robert, with the red ear in hand, walked up to Anne and said, "Miss Shaw, may I kiss you?"

Anne stood swaying side to side. Her smile slowly faded. She looked slowly around the room as if searching for an answer. All eyes in the room were on her. She briefly glanced at Jimmy. "Why, of course, Robert, why not."

Robert took her right hand in his and then slowly leaned forward until his lips met hers. He lingered for a moment. Then the two stepped back from each other. The crowd let out a loud whoop and began to clap their hands. Anne curtsied, turned, and walked outside the barn with her friends following behind, cackling like a bunch of chickens. Jimmy sat back down on the bench, not sure what to do next. He still had not seen hide nor hair of Shaw. As he sat staring at the ground, someone came up behind him and placed a hand on his shoulder.

It was Dr. Jones. "Jimmy, I expect to see you at my office this week with an offer. Like I said earlier, time waits on no one."

"I'll be there. You can count on it," Jimmy responded, determination in his voice.

"By the way, Judge Cross informed me that Shaw was unable to attend the bee today – some sort of conflict. If I were you, I would find that young girl and spend some time with her."

"Thank you, Dr. Jones. Thank you. I ..."

"Stop dawdling. Go," said Jones.

Jimmy quickly rose from the bench and bolted from the barn. Most people were in or around the shed, either filling their plates or eating. He promptly spotted Anne with her group of friends and walked up to her. "Would you care to get something to eat? I have some great news to share."

"Why, James, I thought you would never ask. I'm famished."

It was turning dusk. Blacks were lighting bear-oil lanterns under the shed and in the barn. Others were stoking a large bonfire in the pit where the pig had been roasted. The young couple filled their plates with roasted pig, brown beans, baked yams, and hot, buttered cornbread. They seated themselves on a log near the bonfire. They sat quietly, eating for several minutes.

Jimmy broke the silence. "I was afraid you were not coming. I looked all over for you before the husking began."

"I rode here with some friends. They were running late."

"I'm glad you came," said Jimmy. "I have some good news, I do believe."

"Well, out with it. I need some good news."

"I talked to Dr. Jones here today. I filled him in on my plans to open my own shop. He's interested in becoming a silent partner. I'm supposed to drop by his office this week and negotiate terms with him. With his help, I should be able to open my shop much sooner than I had planned. No more waiting."

Anne sat calmly, eating.

"Well, aren't you glad to hear the good news?" Jimmy asked.

"Why, of course, James. That is certainly encouraging news. I'm just thinking about what Papa's reaction will be, that's all. I was just not prepared for this moment to come so soon. That's all."

"Me neither. I guess we'll know soon enough. That's assuming I come to terms with Dr. Jones."

"Have you thought about where you'll locate your shop? And how you'll get the necessary tools and so forth?" she asked.

"I've had my eye on a piece of land just north of town. It's a good location and will let me take advantage of the travelers passing through on their way to Texas. As for tools and whatnot, I suppose I'll have to make a trip to New Orleans to purchase what I need. I'll come up with a firmer plan after I work out the partnership with Dr. Jones. He may have some ideas to help me get started. He has connections in New Orleans. But enough of that for now. Let's enjoy this evening while we can."

"I hope you know what you're doing, James. Lots can go wrong. You know this will not go easy."

"Anne, since I ran away from home when I was still wet behind the ears, nothing's been easy."

The sounds of a couple of fiddles wafting from the barn door got everyone's attention. People began making there way to the barn for the dance. Jimmy carried their empty plates to a Black woman under the shed, and then the two made their way into the barn. The barn floor had been cleared of the baskets of corn and husks. The table of cider jugs was now standing in the corner of the barn. A small band of musicians stood at the far end of the barn.

People were dancing a Virginia reel. The bear oil lamps cast moving shadows across the floor and on the walls. Jimmy grabbed Anne's hand, and the couple made their way onto the dance floor. Jimmy felt as if his feet were not touching the ground. Anne did not take her eyes off of Jimmy. They danced until they were winded and made their way to a nearby bench. Jimmy fetched them each a tin cup of apple cider. The couple sat quietly, drinking the cider, holding hands, and keeping time to the music. Jimmy wished the night would never end, but it was getting late.

Anne's friends approached her and said they best get home. Even with the harvest moon in the sky, it would be a long ride back to town. She squeezed Jimmy's hand gently and rose from the bench.

Jimmy stood and looked into her eyes. "I don't have a red ear of corn, but I would like to kiss the most beautiful girl at the dance."

She smiled back and said, "You don't need a red ear of corn, silly. But you will need to follow me outside to claim your kiss."

They walked outside the barn and stepped into the shadows. Anne's friends made their way towards their wagon. Anne called out to them that she would be along in a moment. Jimmy put his arms around her waist. She placed her arms around his neck. He leaned down and kissed her lips. They remained steadfast for what seemed like minutes.

She finally pulled away and said, "I have to go now, James. My friends are waiting."

With heart pounding in his chest and ears and hands sweating profusely, Jimmy watched as she walked away. He wanted to run after her but resisted the urge. "I hope the next time I see you, I can tell you more about my plans. Keep your fingers crossed," he yelled.

"Bye, James. Good luck."

She climbed into the wagon with her friends. Watching as they rode out of sight, Jimmy thought, *Bye, Anne. You seem to have more faith in me than I do. I hope I don't botch this like most other things in my life. I would hate to prove Shaw right about my being an unworthy suitor for his precious daughter.*

Chapter 20

True to his word, Jimmy met with Dr. Jones Monday following the husking bee. So as not to raise any eyebrows, he met with Jones after Shaw closed-up shop. The two men reached mutually agreeable terms for their new partnership. Dr. Jones would supply the land and a building through a long-term lease to the business. He would also loan working capital equal to the amount Jimmy had saved, which was to be repaid in one year. In exchange, Jones would receive twenty percent of the profits for five years. After that, Jimmy would simply continue to pay Jones rent on the building and land. Jimmy agreed not to draw a salary but would simply live off his share of the profits. Jimmy thought the deal was overly generous, but Dr. Jones seemed more than satisfied. The good doctor agreed to have his lawyer draw up the contract for signing a few days hence.

As it turned out, Dr. Jones owned land on the north-side of Washington that was an ideal location for the new shop. Settlers traveling down the Southwest Trail would lay eyes on the new shop when entering the settlement. It was far enough from Shaw's shop to lessen the threat to Shaw's business, but the competition was inevitable. Jones instructed his lawyer to hire some locals to construct the shop to Jimmy's specifications. While the shop was under construction, Jimmy made plans to travel by steamboat to New Orleans to secure his tools, anvil, and other supplies that he would need to properly outfit his shop.

Only one matter remained…for Jimmy to tell Shaw, he was quitting. It should become clear to Shaw that his own actions had forced Jimmy down this path. Jimmy could no longer stomach working for Shaw under the present conditions. *Shaw has left me with no choice. I can leave town or strike out on my own. Then again, I could be fanning the fire by competing with him. Besides, there's plenty of work for two shops. There are more than one tavern, lawyer, and doctor in town. It's too late for cold feet -- the die is cast -- no turning back now.*

The next morning, upon arriving at Shaw's shop, Jimmy went straight in to see Shaw. "Mr. Shaw, I need to talk to you."

Shaw looked up from his desk. "Yeah? What's on your mind?"

"No sense in hem hawing around. I'm making plans to open my own shop on the northside of town. I aim to show you I'm a worthy suitor for your daughter. I think there's plenty of work in the area for two shops. Besides, I plan on focusing on my knife making. You gave me a good start here in Washington for which I am grateful."

Shaw's face turned bright red, and veins bulged in his neck and head. He squeezed both of his hands into fists and slowly stood from his desk. Jimmy braced himself, expecting Shaw to take a swing at him.

"Well, I'll be damned," he grumbled. "This is how you show your gratitude? You plan to steal food off my table? I curse the day I ever laid eyes on you, boy! I know you've been sneakin' around behind my back, seeing my daughter. Word travels. It'll be a cold day in hell before I ever let you court my Anne. Fetch your things and get out o' my sight before I beat you like the cur you are! LEAVE NOW!"

Jimmy glared back at him. He opened his mouth to speak but decided against it. Now was not the time. He turned and walked out of the office. Jimmy walked to the forge, where the boys were readying themselves for the day ahead. He went to the back of the shop and retrieved the wooden crate containing his crucible and other things. He placed a few items in his knapsack and walked back to the forge.

"Boys, it's been nice working with you. I'll be opening my own shop soon on the north side of town. Drop by and say hello sometime. Take care of yourselves."

As he walked to the door, Jimmy nodded his head at Tom to meet him outside. Jimmy went outside and began saddling up Socks. Tom walked out to where he was standing. "Tom, tell Anne your father did not cotton to my plans. No surprise. I'll get word to her soon. In the meantime, I have to go to New Orleans to get some tools and supplies for my shop. Tell her I'll be gone for about three weeks. You've been a good friend, Tom. I hope we'll remain such."

"You know it, Jimmy. I'm sorry things haven't worked out between you and Pa. He's stubborn like a mule and ornery as a bear. Hang in there."

Jimmy mounted Socks, pulled back on the reins, and headed the horse toward home.

* * *

A couple of months later.

Jimmy's blacksmith shop had been open for business for about a month. After Jimmy returned from New Orleans with two wagon-loads of equipment, tools, and supplies, he was pleased to find that Dr. Jones's attorney had seen to the completion of the shop. Jimmy quickly fitted out the shop. The shop construction was true to Black's specifications. It was a sturdy, log structure with a wooden shake roof.

Shed-like structures ran along both sides and in front of the shop. Vertical log posts about a foot and a half thick supported the sheds, which provided outdoor work area and storage well protected from sun and rain. The forge area was on the interior of the shop with only a single doorway and a couple of window-like openings to the outside. A sturdy plank door and shutters were hung on the outside of the openings. Inside, the openings were fitted with leather curtains that could quickly be drawn shut. Having the forge in the interior of the building accomplished two of Jimmy's objectives. First and foremost, he could control the amount of light entering the room, enabling him to carefully monitor the changing color of metal heated in the forge. Second, he could keep prying eyes from stealing his trade secrets.

The business was brisk. As planned, being located near the main road into town from the northeast gave Jimmy first shot at the travelers heading southwest to Texas. Many folks in the area not particularly fond of Shaw began to trade with Jimmy. Rumors about his knife making skills spread throughout the territory and into Texas and business was booming.

It was midmorning at the shop. Jimmy was out front in the shade of the front shed, repairing a plowshare. He heard some riders approaching. Looking up, he saw three men on horseback. The lead rider sat astride a big bay and wore a hat sporting an eagle feather in the hatband. Jimmy walked out to meet the riders. The riders reined to stop, and the one in front dismounted. The other remained mounted.

"Morning," said Jimmy.

The one that dismounted said, "Are you the smithy by the name of Black?"

"I'm Jimmy Black. How can I help you?"

"Name is Lightnin' Billy, and I'm lookin' to buy one of them Arkansas toothpicks folks is talkin' 'bout."

"I sold my last knife earlier this week. It'll be a week or so before I have any more to sell."

"Now you ain't pullin' ol' Billy's leg are you, mister?"

"No, sir. I wish I had a knife to sell you. I need the money. I just opened this shop about a month ago."

Billy stared at Black intently with cold, dark eyes. Jimmy felt like he was staring into a deep well. A chill ran down his spine. “Well, alright, then. I’ll take you at your word. We have some dealings west of here. We’ll be back in a week or so. I ‘spec you ‘ll hold me one of them knives, now won’t ya’?”

One of the mounted riders reached down and pulled a dirk from inside his boot and began to clean dirt from underneath the fingernails of his left hand.

“Sure, I’ll hold you a knife. Now I have work to do if you don’t mind. Jaw-boning won’t pay the rent.” The blacksmith turned his back to the strangers and walked back to the plow underneath the shed.

Lightnin’ Billy mounted his big bay. “Now, don’t forget about ol’ Lightnin’ Billy’s knife now. Ya hear?”

Jimmy nodded his head at Billy, signifying his understanding. The three riders turned their mounts and continued down the road towards town.

* * *

A week later.

Jimmy kept in touch with Anne through Tom. His plan to show Shaw that he could succeed on his own had driven a deeper wedge between the two men. Shaw was now convinced Black was intent on putting him out of business. Anne and Jimmy both agreed Shaw would never consent to his courting her -- so the couple decided to elope. Quietly, they were married by the County Judge at the Hempstead County Courthouse. Dr. Jones attended the ceremony, as did Tom, Nat, and a couple of Anne’s closest friends. The newly wedded couple bought a house in town. Jimmy gathered his belongings from the boarding house and said good-bye to Ben and Henry. He told them he would keep in touch. Shaw was furious when he learned of the unsanctioned wedding. Anne’s mother cried for days.

The young couple attended Reverend Stevenson’s church the first Sunday after they were married. Reverend Stevenson’s timely sermon was on forgiving those who have transgressed against others. He spoke about how the Great Redeemer had died so that sins could be forgiven. He talked about the greatness of God's love for those that continue to disobey his will due to their sin nature. He reminded all in attendance that they should follow God's example and love their neighbors as themselves.

Anne and Jimmy sat on a pew near the back of the church, so they were some of the first ones outside after the service. After shaking the Reverend's hand and thanking him for the message, they stood outside the church. Anne wanted to get a glimpse of her family. Her family brood eventually exited the church. Her father stormed past them, never looking their way. Anne's mother came over, with tears streaming down her face and gave Anne a long hug. Anne's sisters and brothers stopped by and said they missed her and wished she would come home. Tom gave Jimmy a nod and a wink. The clan then joined Shaw in the wagon, and off they rode.

The young couple returned to their little cottage. Anne attempted to make Sunday dinner. Her cooking skills were sorely lacking, and the meal was definitely not up to her mother's standard. With faked enthusiasm, Jimmy raved about how great everything tasted. He said Ol' Henry could not have done any better. Anne knew he was sparing her feelings. They sat at a tiny table in the kitchen and picked at their plates. Anne was very quiet. Then she began to cry.

Jimmy tried to calm her and asked, "What's wrong, dear?"

"Everything," she uttered with tears streaming down her cheeks. "I miss Sunday dinner at home with my family. Mama is a great cook, and I miss her food. They are probably enjoying fried chicken or venison steak with grits and gravy. Sunday dinners will never be the same again," she lamented.

Jimmy listened intently and responded, "I understand being sad and all. Things will get better. You'll see. You'll become a better cook with a little practice. Besides, we'll have a family of our own someday. Surely as some time passes, your pa's attitude towards me will change. Then maybe we will get invited by your ma' for Sunday dinner. Or we can invite them over here so you can show off your cooking skills."

Anne slowly ceased sobbing. They finished their noonday meal, and she began to clear the table. Jimmy sat by the fireplace. He stared into the fire, the flickering flames had a hypnotic effect, and he wondered to himself, *Will Anne's pa' truly ever change his mind about me?*

* * *

Monday, Jimmy was at his shop, putting the finishing touches on a new batch of knives. Sitting underneath the shed on the side of his shop, he was polishing the blades using a sheepskin that he had attached to the outside of his grinding wheel. Jimmy heard what sounded like several horses approaching from the south. He looked down the road and could make out three riders leading a string of about eight or ten horses. As the caravan got closer, Jimmy could make out the distinctive eagle feather in the hat of the leader – *Lightnin' Billy*. Jimmy put down the knife he was polishing and walked out from underneath the shed and stood in front of his shop.

The caravan pulled up and halted. Some of the pack animals were mules. All three of the riders dismounted. The two unknown riders led the horses and mules over to a watering trough to the side of the shop. The pack animals were saddled with large, leather bags with large leather flaps. The large bags were supported on each end by an "X" shaped wooden frame and were bulging with their hidden contents.

Lightnin' Billy walked up to where Black was standing. "We're back, jus' like I told ya,'" said Billy.

"Those are some large saddlebags," Black replied. "Don't think I've ever seen any quite like them."

"Mexicans south of the Red call 'em 'ciaxes' or somethin' like that," quipped Billy. Great for hauling goods south of the Red. Trammell's Trace is a proper name for that rabbit trail into Texas. We been o'er to the salt works west of here. We're haulin' a load south to trade with the Caddos."

"I thought it was illegal to trade salt to the Indians?" Jimmy quizzed.

"Only if'n you get caught," Billy smirked. "You got me a knife ready like I asked?"

"Just finishing up a batch. I've got a few for you to choose from this time. Come inside the shop."

Lightnin' Billy followed Black inside. Jimmy had three finished knives lying on his workbench – each with a slightly different look and feel. One had a stag horn handle, one had a black walnut handle, and one had a bone handle. Billy picked up the one with the staghorn handle and held it close to his eyes. The gleam of the blade reflected in his coal-black eyes. He clasped the knife in his right hand as if gauging its weight. He made a couple of paring moves with the weapon. Then he thrust the blade forward. A smile slowly came across his face. "She's a beauty, a real beauty, jes' like a woman – sharp-tongued and ready to cut your heart out. How much?"

"Twenty dollars," Jimmy replied.

"I'll give you fifteen Spanish reals," he countered.

Jimmy thought about it a moment. "Throw in a bag of that salt you're toting, and we have a deal."

Billy shoved the knife in his belt. "The coins are in a saddlebag on my horse."

Jimmy, a bit leery, followed Billy outside. Billy untied some rawhide ties and opened his saddlebag. He pulled out a small leather pouch and poured out some coins. Billy counted out fifteen silver dollars, handed them to Jimmy, and then called at one of his men to give a large bag of salt to the knife maker. "We're square. Mount up." Billy flashed a gap-tooth smile, touched the brim of his hat, and gave a slight nod of his head to Jimmy. "Let's hit the trail, boys. We're burnin' daylight." The caravan headed south in a cloud of dust.

Fall 1831

Chapter 21

Around noon, a white man with dark wavy hair and a Black man wearing a floppy, sweat-stained hat, rode up from the south of town on horseback. The white man sat upright on the back of a large, dappled, gray horse. The older Black man rode slumped in the saddle on a medium build, spotted horse. They stopped at the well near Stuart's Tavern, watered the horses, then walked across the open ground to the tavern. They left the horses to graze on the grass out front of the inn. The Black sat down on the edge of the front porch in the shade, pulled out his corncob pipe, and began to smoke. The white man strolled into the tavern to see about a room for the night. Once inside, the man stepped up to the bar and said, "My name's Bowie, and I need a room for the night. And I need a place for my servant to bed down for the night."

The tavern owner replied, "Welcome, Mr. Bowie. I'm Elijah Stuart, and I'm the owner of the oldest tavern in town. I have a room on the second floor – number two. It's four bits a night. Don't have a room for your servant, though. Check over at the livery stable. The owner, Moore, sometimes lets Blacks bed down in the loft at no charge if you stable your horses there. We serve a hearty meal at dusk, and breakfast is served till 'bout an hour past sunrise."

"I'll take it," said Bowie. "Now I need some information, Mr. Stuart. In my travels in Texas, I've run into several settlers that passed through here carrying knives made by a local blacksmith named Black. Can you direct me to this Black?"

"Go out in front of the tavern and follow the main road to the northeast. It'll take you to the blacksmith shop."

Bowie turned and walked out of the tavern. He motioned at his servant to bring the horses. "Mount up, Sam. We're off to see a blacksmith."

* * *

Jimmy was in front of the shop, shoeing a horse. The two riders rode up and dismounted. The Black man held the reins of the horses while the white man walked to where Jimmy was shoeing the horse. "I'm looking for a knifemaker by the name of Black."

"I'm James Black. Folks call me Jimmy. Give me a few minutes to finish shoeing this horse, and we can talk."

Bowie nodded his head, turned, and walked out to where Sam was letting the horses graze on the sparse grass. Bowie and Sam took a seat on a log bench shaded by a grove of black walnut trees. They had not waited long when Black joined them.

"My name's Jim Bowie. This here is Sam, my servant. Sam's been with me through thick and thin."

Sam nodded his head in agreement and said, "Sho' 'nough, Masser Jim. We seen da' good and da' bad."

"What brings you to town, Mr. Bowie, if you don't mind me asking?"

"Call me, Jim. I've been living down San Antonio-way in Texas for the last few years. I'm on my way to check on some landholdings in Arkansas northeast of here – toward the Mississippi."

"What brings you to my shop, Jim?"

"Awhile back, I was appointed by Stephen Austin to lead a group of Rangers to travel around the Mexican state, keeping the peace between the Indians and the settlers. In my travels, I've met a number of settlers that passed through here that were sportin' large knives they called Arkansas toothpicks. They told me you made those knives. That true?"

"I suppose it is. I've sold quite a few knives to those passing through on their way to Texas."

“They told me your knives hold a keen edge after considerable use. And are tough to boot. They claim you’ve mastered some old world know-how – some secret skill in tempering the metal.”

“I picked up some knife-making skills from an old creole in New Orleans who learned from his Spanish grandfather. I’ve honed those skills. I’ll put my knives up against anybody’s for strength and durability.”

“I’ve got something to show you.” Bowie got up from the bench and walked over to his horse. He untied the leather straps holding his saddlebag in place, lifted the bag off his horse and returned to the seat. He opened the pouch on one side and pulled out an object wrapped in cloth. Unwrapping the item revealed a knife-shaped object carved out of a piece of red cedar, the aromatic smell of the cedar struck wafted to their nostrils. “Here’s a carving of the type of knife I’d like you to make me, Mr...er...Jimmy. You see, I’ve had a bit of experience using knives over the years. When I was a boy, I used to hunt and skin gators and bears in the swamps of Louisiana. I’ve been in a couple of scrapes where a knife was the only thing that kept me alive. I once witnessed one of Lafitte’s pirates use a knife to gash a card sharp’s gut and throat before the unlucky man could fire his pistol. I’ve carved features into this piece of wood that’ll make my knife useful for killing man or beast.”

Bowie handed Black his wooden knife prototype. Jimmy twisted and turned the wooden blade over in his hands, examining it from every angle. The blade portion of the knife model was about a foot in length, and the handle was half again as long. It had a distinctive “C” shaped guard open towards the blade. The bottom edge of the blade made a long, sweeping curve from the bolster upwards to the pointed tip and was sharpened along the entire length. On the top side, the last four inches slanted downwards to the point of the knife and was sharpened. The handle had a bulging center with a large, rounded pommel end.

Bowie explained the functions of his design. “This ‘C’ shaped guard protects my hand in a parry by catching and deflecting the opponent’s blade. With some luck, I might twist the opponent’s knife out of his hand. The sharpened, top, front edge makes the knife effective in a back or forward slashing motion. The pointed tip is useful when thrusting. This oval-shaped handle with the bulging center and the large, rounded pommel end makes the knife easier to grip. The pommel will also put a nice bump on a man's head."

Jimmy nodded his head in approval.

"Can you make such a knife?" asked Bowie.

"Jim, I can turn your design into a knife like no other."

"Very well. I'll be in eastern Arkansas for about a month. Me and Sam will be ridin' back through on our way to Texas after that. Will that give you time enough to make the knife?"

"More than enough time."

"Do you require a good faith payment today?" asked Bowie.

"That won't be necessary, Jim. If you fail to return, I won't have any problem selling such a knife, I assure you."

"Very well, Jimmy. If I'm not back in six weeks, you're free to sell the knife. But I'll be back, and I want that knife." Bowie extended his right arm, and the two men shook hands. "Sam, we need to get the horses stabled, and you bedded down for the night. I'm staying at Stuart's tavern. How's the food there?"

"You'll get a hot meal at a fair price. If you're lucky, they might be serving bear steak tonight. And Mrs. Stuart makes a larapin apple pie."

"See you in about a month then," said Bowie. He and Sam got on their horses and headed in the direction of Moore's Livery Stable.

Chapter 22

The ideal knife Bowie had carved out of soft cedar was a bit longer, broader, and more substantial than any of the knives Black had previously made. Jimmy quickly realized he would have to add more steel to the billet. Otherwise, when he drew out the metal, the blade would be too thin and likely warp during the quench. The sharpened clip point was similar to knives Peña had made. He decided to start work on Bowie's knife right away. It might take several attempts to get it right.

Jimmy had heard about Bowie and his knife fight on the Mississippi sandbar near Natchez. Such stories quickly made their way upriver spread by word of mouth. Jimmy never let on he knew Bowie by reputation, but having Bowie carrying one of his knives would be better than any advertisement money could buy.

Black's business had grown such that he had brought on an apprentice by the name of Daniel Miller. Dan was a medium build lad with reddish-blond hair, bright blue eyes, and a quick wit. Jimmy and Dan were near the forge, preparing to place the crock crucible into the hot coals to make some blister steel when they heard an oxen-drawn wagon approaching the shop. The driver was shouting orders to the team and popping a whip. Jimmy instructed Dan to tend the crucible. Dan had helped Black before and knew what to do. Black stepped outside to greet the wagon driver.

The driver climbed down from the wagon. "How do," he said. "Name's Richard Boatright. This here's my eldest son, Lewis. Tip your hat boy." A young boy about six sitting next to him, did as he was told.

"I'm Jimmy Black. How can I help you?"

"Well, sir, I got some animal traps in the back that needs repairin'. There's a plowshare, and some harness needs mending as well. Lewis, fetch them traps and whatnot from the back."

"Yes, Pa," said the boy as he clamored to the back of the wagon.

The elder Boatright walked around behind the wagon and began to let down the tailgate. The boy handed his pa the traps and other items. Boatright laid the traps on the ground, followed by the plow and the harness. Young Lewis hopped down from the wagon.

"Where you folks from?" asked Jimmy. "Don't believe I've seen you around."

"We was livin' north of here on the Washita River -- near the Hot Springs. We settled thar some time ago. Been trappin' beaver and huntin' buffalo and bear. About a week ago, Sheriff came and ran us off our land. Seems we' uns and some of our neighbors had been duped in a land scheme – bought some forged land grants. Nothin' left for us to do but load up our belongings and head southwest till we can sort out where to go next. My wife and the rest of our party are camped on that big crick north o' town."

"That's a tough break," said Black. "You folks should consider settling here. It's a growing town. Lots of good land and even better people here."

"Some in our group might settle here 'bouts. I'm leanin' towards headin' to Texas with my family. Lotsa folks settling south of the Red."

"That's a dangerous proposition, Mr. Boatright, especially for someone with a young family like yours. The Mexican Army makes random patrols to harass white settlers. Several Indian tribes call Texas home – Comanches, Kiowas, and Wichitas being some of the meanest. Then there's outlaws and renegades operating over there out of reach of the authorities. You might think twice about calling Texas your next home."

"Thank you kindly for the information, Mr. Black. I'll mull it over. Now when do you think I can pick up my traps and such?"

"Call me Jimmy. You can check back in a couple of days. I should have everything repaired by then."

"Alright, then. Get in the wagon, boy. We best get back to camp." The two climbed onto the driver's seat. Boatright popped his whip, slapped the reins, and yelled "giddy up" at the team of oxen. The oxen leaned into the harness, and off they lumbered, the wagon creaking and clanking behind them.

Black stood and watched as the wagon rumbled north and pondered. *What makes such men with so much to lose risk it all? Heading southwest across the Red into a dangerous place like Texas? It makes no sense. The lure of cheap land, I guess. The odds seem against them, but off they go.*

He went back inside the shop to the forge where Dan was gently working the bellows. "How long has the crucible had been in the fire?"

"About a half-hour," Dan replied.

It would take another hour and a half for the blister process to work. Jimmy told him to keep at it, then he went out front and brought

Boatright's traps, plow and harness into the shop. They would tackle those next after the crucible was out of the forge.

* * *

Three days later.

Saturday afternoon, Jimmy was in the shop late working on Bowie's knife. He was working on the second of two knives he was planning to show Bowie. The two versions would have slight variations. He was at the anvil drawing out the blade from the billet of steel. It was an arduous and backbreaking process -- lots of hammering required. His clothes were wet with sweat. His face and arms were smudged with soot. Jimmy glanced up from the anvil and was startled to see the outline of a man standing across the anvil from him. He drew back his hammer in a defensive posture. Then his eyes focused on the semi-dark and recognized Tom Shaw standing in front of him.

"Tom, you scared the piss out of me. I almost struck you with this hammer."

"Didn't mean to startle you, Jimmy. Guess I'll need to make some noise next time. You were really focused on pounding that piece of metal."

"Yeah, I guess I was taking out some anger on that blade. When I'm here by myself working a piece of metal, my mind wanders to my problems. It may not surprise you, but I was thinking about your pa. I found Anne crying last night. When I asked her what was wrong, she refused to say. I knew the answer – her pa."

"Sorry to hear that," mumbled Tom.

"I thought after the birth of his only two grandchildren with a third one on the way, Shaw would have a change of heart about his daughter and me. Not William Shaw. That is one angry, hateful man. I sometimes imagine his face on my anvil as I wail away on a piece of iron."

"I'm as surprised as you are," said Tom. "He forbids the mention of your name in his presence. He seems more withdrawn and angry as time passes. I think this started out about you and Anne, but now it's more about you. He knows you're having success with your knife making. He's jealous of your skills and feels betrayed by both of you. He sees you like the dog that bit the hand of the man that fed it."

"I guess all of Shaw's trips to church on Sunday are just for show," replied Black.

"Mama prays for him daily," said Tom. "And she prays for you, Anne and the children. I know she slips over to visit Anne and the grandchildren every chance she gets."

"Enough about that," said Jimmy. "I'm sure that's not why you dropped by today?"

"I was just checking in to see how business is faring," said Tom.

"Business is booming. I brought on an apprentice. I could use an experienced hand, though. Why don't you come to work for me, Tom? I'll give you a nice raise in pay."

"Now you wanna kick the hornets' nest that you knocked out of the tree? I swear, Jimmy, you beat all."

"It's a crazy idea, I reckon."

"That's a rather large knife you're working on. Isn't that bigger than most knives you make?" asked Tom.

"Matter of fact, it is. I'm making a knife for a man named Bowie who passed through here a few days ago."

"Bowie? Bowie...isn't that the feller that was caught up in a brawl following a dual on a Mississippi River sandbar?" asked Tom.

"Yep. One and the same."

"No, kidding! My recollection of the story is that Bowie was shot two or three times and stabbed several times. Bowie still managed to kill two men...one a former Louisiana sheriff that he stabbed with a butcher knife. Most people said it was a miracle that Bowie lived. He wants you to make him a knife?" asked Tom.

"He was passing through on his way to some business dealings in the eastern part of the Territory. He carved a wooden knife resembling one he wanted me to make for him. Said he'd be back in about a month. I told him I'd have it ready. I plan to have a couple of knives for him to choose from."

"Well, don't screw it up. I best get out of here so you can get back to work. Tell Anne and the boys 'hello' from Uncle Tom."

"Will do. Stop by anytime, Tom. I miss talking to you and Nat."

Tom then turned and left the shop. Black went back to the forge, heated the half-made knife until it was red hot. Then he wailed away with his hammer. Tom could hear the clanging of the hammer on the anvil after he was well down the road.

Chapter 23

"We done good, Sam," said Bowie as he warmed his hands over the campfire. He took a sip of coffee from a pewter cup. "Breaking into that Land Office was easier than I thought it would be. I'll sleep better tonight than I have in a while." Bowie leaned back on his saddle and stared up into the night sky. Orange glowing sparks from the campfire rose in the cool air as if being drawn upwards by the millions of stars overhead. "Yes sir, I think my troubles in Arkansas are finally behind me."

Sam sat by the fire, roasting a rabbit skewered on a pointy stick. "Mmmm, Masser Jim. This here rabbit sho' gonna taste good tonight. He a fat one."

Bowie poured another cup of coffee from the pot sitting on the edge of the fire. Sam drew the rabbit skewer away from the flames and pried at the charred flesh with the tip of a long, slender knife. "Ol' rabbit ready to eat, Masser Jim." Sam began to carve the rabbit into pieces and placed them on two metal plates. Steam rose from the blackened carcass. "Wish we had some yams and greens to go with dis here rabbit." Sam handed a plate to Bowie.

The two men sat quietly as they quickly devoured the rabbit. After he consumed his portion of the rabbit, Bowie let out a loud belch, then finished his cup of coffee. Sam pulled out his corncob pipe and filled it with tobacco. He then lit one end of a twig in the fire and lit his pipe. He puffed and watched the smoke drift into the night sky.

Bowie rose up and walked over near the horses, which were tied to a rope stretched between two saplings. He returned with a bulging saddlebag and a crock jug. He sat back down near the fire. "Throw some more wood on the fire," Bowie said. He then untied the leather ties on the saddlebag. He held the bag over his head and emptied out a bunch of documents onto the ground. Bowie waited until the fire was blazing. Then he began to throw the papers onto the fire. As the documents caught fire, large pieces of glowing red ash floated into the air and slowly drifted out of sight. Bowie grabbed the crock jug sitting on the ground, popped the cork from the mouth of the jug and poured his cup full. "Hand me your cup," he said to Sam.

"Masser Jim, you know I don't drink none o' dat John BarleyCorn."

"Hand me your cup, damn it!" said Bowie. "You can drink a sip. We're drinking a toast. We're celebrating being rid of the Federal authorities once and for all."

Sam reluctantly handed Bowie his cup. Bowie poured some of the contents of the jug into the cup and handed it back to Sam. Bowie lifted his cup in the air. Sam followed Bowie's lead. The two men clanked the tin containers together, and each took a sip. "Here's to the last time I lay eyes on these forged Spanish Land Grants once and for all. It was a good run while it lasted," said Bowie. He drank down about half of his cup and wiped his mouth on the sleeve of his buckskin shirt. Sam poured the remaining contents of his tin cup onto the fire -- a hissing sound emitted as steam rose into the air.

Bowie kept slowly tossing the fake land grants into the fire, making sure each was entirely consumed by the flames. Bowie mumbled to himself while he stared into the campfire. "That bunch in Little Rock will have a helluva time prosecuting me for forged land grants without any evidence." He rubbed his hands together and then held them towards the fire for warmth. He took another drink from his cup as he stared at the flickering flames dancing in front of his dark eyes.

"We'll arrive back in Washington tomorrow at about noon. I wonder if that blacksmith has my knife ready?" said Bowie. He looked over at his faithful servant, who sat slumped over fast asleep. Bowie walked over and gently lifted Sam's head, pulled his saddle over, and rested the servant's head on it. Bowie then covered Sam with a quilt. "Good thing you didn't drink more than a nip," mumbled Bowie.

Bowie then lay back on his bedroll with his head on his saddle, pulled the blanket up to his chin, and stared at the stars overhead. He thought about his family back home in San Antonio and wondered how they were getting along without him. He said a short prayer for them before dozing off to sleep.

* * *

The next day.

Black was standing out front of his shop talking to a customer when he saw two familiar horsemen approaching from the north down the Trail. He said, "thanks" to the customer who climbed into his buckboard and rode off. Jimmy stood watching the riders as they approached. The riders reined their horses, and both men dismounted.

"You're back a little sooner than you estimated Mr. Bowie er...Jim," Black said.

"We wrapped up our business a little quicker than expected," said Bowie. "The people we met with were easier to deal with than I expected. Sam, take our horses around to the watering trough."

"Yassir, Masser Jim," replied Sam. He took the horses by the reins and walked them around to the side of the shop.

"Did you have enough time to make my knife?" quizzed Bowie.

"I did. Matter of fact, I made two knives – one like your model and one with a slight variation of my own design. Come in, and I'll show 'em to you."

The two men walked into the shop to some wooden bins where Jimmy stored finished jobs. He tugged open one of the drawers, reached in, and pulled out an oily cloth concealing the contents. He walked to a nearby workbench and unrolled the cloth. Inside were two shiny knives about eighteen inches in length. Black grabbed one and handed it to Bowie. "I made this one after your model."

Bowie took the knife and began to twist and turn it in his hands, examining the knife from every angle. A smile slowly broke across his face. He stepped away from Jimmy and began to make some thrusts and parries as if he were fighting an invisible man. He stopped the deadly dance and then rubbed his thumb across the edge of the blade. Before Black could stop him, Bowie was wiping blood on his breeches.

"It's razor-sharp," Jimmy said. "You can shave with it."

"So I see. Jimmy. You've exceeded my expectations. This is one helluva knife. She's a thing of beauty and lethal to boot."

Black pointed to a hemp rope hanging from a rafter nearby. "Walk over to that rope and take a downward swipe at it with the knife."

Bowie walked over to the inch diameter rope. He held the knife above his head and made a downward chopping motion, bringing the knife in a swift slicing action across the rope, cleaving it in two. Bowie nodded his head in approval. He walked back to where Jimmy was standing. "What about the other knife?" He laid the one knife down, and Jimmy handed him the second knife.

"This one is similar to your model, but I altered the length of the handle and made the pommel end a bit larger to give the knife better balance. I also added a slight curvature to the clip point."

Bowie again examined the knife from every angle. He held it in his hand as if he were weighing it, checking the balance in his hand. He again made the same thrusting and paring gestures. "I want 'em both. You are the master of your craft."

Black walked to the cabinet, retrieved a leather object from the bin, and handed it to Bowie. "I had Mr. Daniels down at the leather shop make a belt and scabbard for your knife. The scabbard will fit both knives."

Bowie inserted the first knife in the leather sheath. It was a snug fit. "How much do I owe you for both knives and he scabbard?"

"I'll take twenty dollars apiece for the knives and five for the scabbard."

"That's a fair price," said Bowie. "My money's in my saddlebag outside."

Bowie fastened the belt with the knife and scabbard around his waist. Black rolled up the second knife in the oily cloth and handed it to Bowie. Bowie led the way outside, where Sam was tending the horses. Bowie reached into his saddlebag and pulled out a leather pouch. He untied the string around the neck of the bag and reached inside to retrieve his payment. He counted out twenty-five Spanish reals. "Will you take the balance in a twenty-dollar banknote issued by the Canal Bank of New Orleans?"

"That'll be fine," Black replied.

Bowie handed him the banknote and the silver coins.

"Staying in town tonight?" Jimmy asked.

"There's plenty of daylight left," said Bowie. "It'll be pushing it, but we can make Fulton before we call it a day. We'll spend the night there. Then tomorrow, we'll catch the ferry over to Texas and head down Trammell's Trace to Nacogdoches. I need to get back to San Antonio and see my wife and boys. Been away too long." The two men mounted their horses. "I may be back this way again," said Bowie.

"Safe travels to San Antonio," said Jimmy. "Hope those knives serve their purpose."

The two horsemen rode south down the Trail towards Fulton.

Winter 1832

Chapter 24

Trammell's Trace, East Texas, Mexico.

"Sam, barring any difficulty, we ought to be back in San Antonio de Bexar in about three weeks," said Bowie. "Course down here in Mexico, it's hope for the best but expect the worst. We'll be travelin' through these piney woods for few days till we reach Nacogdoches. We'll camp for the night at the Caddo Village just a few miles ahead. The Caddos, or what's left of 'em, are friendly towards Whites. They've been tradin' with French and American trappers for a long time. An impresario by the name of Felisola has started a settlers' colony just west of here. There's quite a few settlers in the area but, it's still dangerous here."

"I hope you is right, Masser Jim. I ain't lookin' to lose my scalp to no renegades," said Sam.

"We're more likely to get robbed or murdered by some outlaws than we are Injuns," said Bowie. "It's a good place south of the Red to escape the law. Or we could run into some Mexican soldiers patrolling the border to curtail illegal immigration. The Mexican government passed a law about a year ago to stop any more U.S. settlers from coming into Texas. The Mexicans are afraid the white settlers will grow in number -- then start a revolt. I think that horse is out of the barn. Across a big bayou just ahead is a large Caddo Village. I hope the ferry's operatin' today, or we may have to swim the horses across."

"Now Masser Jim, you knows I can't swim. Water's fur drinkin' – not swimmin'."

"You're horse can swim. Just hang on to that saddle. Besides, if you fall off, 'gators 'ill probably eat you 'fore you drown," chuckled Bowie.

"That ain't funny, Masser Jim. Nary a bit. You might be good at wrasslin' gators but ah ain't."

"Calm down, Sam. Them Injuns probably done et all the gators in this here bayou – least I hope so. I ain't wrestled a gator since I was about eighteen." laughed Bowie. The two rode over the hill, and the pine thicket cleared on the other side, revealing the wide, muddy bayou. "Looks like we're in luck, and you won't have to swim or wrestle a gator today, Sam. Ferry appears to be operatin' today."

The ferry lay across on the other side as the two men rode up to the bayou's edge. Jim put his hands up to his mouth and hooted loudly to get the ferry operator's attention. To aid the ferry in traversing the stagnant water, a long rope was strung tautly between two large, oak trees on either bank. The ferry operator began slowly tugging on the line, pulling the ferry across the muddy water toward the two riders. As the boat approached, Bowie yelled out, "How much to cross over?"

The copper-skinned, dark-haired Caddo boy operating the log ferry replied, "Two bits for horse and rider – or we'll trade a ride for sumpin' of value."

Bowie handed the boy four bits. The boy waved the two riders to come aboard the log raft. Once on the raft, Bowie and Sam dismounted. The young Caddo boy began tugging on the rope, slowly pulling the crude ferry back across to the other bank. Bowie stared across the bayou, observing smoke rising from the many campfires of the Caddo village. Upon reaching the far bank, the two travelers mounted their horses and rode up the muddy bank toward the encampment.

Several beehive-shaped huts stood on both sides of the Trace. The shelters consisted of a series of limber, wooden poles stuck in the ground in large circles, then tied together at the top to form domed structures. Saplings stripped of their limbs were woven in and out of a the of posts in evenly spaced horizontal rings from top to bottom. Reeds and grasses were layered in a thatch-like fashion over the structures forming the roofs and walls of the distinctive lodges. Caddo women were busy cooking over open fires or cleaning hides. Young, scantily clad children, ran here and there playing games. Several dogs roamed the village or were lying about. A few Caddo men were visible skinning deer or small game.

Bowie and Sam rode on until they came to the southern edge of the village where a log structure stood. A string of horses and mules stood in front of the building. The horses and mules carried large leather bags attached to "X" shaped wooden frames. The bags looked empty. The two men rode up to the front of the crude log building and dismounted.

Bowie said to Sam, "This is Pascal's Trading Post. It's owned by a crusty old Frenchman that's been in these parts for most of his life. Stay with the horses while I go inside. We're running low on supplies, and we still have about three weeks till we get to Bexar."

Sam nodded his head in agreement, then led the horses over to a nearby watering trough.

Bowie stepped through the front door. It took a few minutes for his eyes to adjust to the dim interior of the windowless trading post. The interior of the trading post consisted of one large room. There was a doorway in the back wall that led to a lean-to structure on the backside – most likely Pascal's living quarters. The large room was lit by bear oil lamps placed around the interior. Bundles of animal hides stood in piles throughout. More animal pelts packed a loft structure that extended from the middle of the room to the back wall. A makeshift ladder provided access to the loft. Dry goods and other sundries stocked the rustic shelves that covered the interior walls. Rough-hewn planks of cypress lay on top of four oak barrels forming a makeshift bar along the left side of the room.

Three men stood at the bar drinking from crock mugs. One of the men wore buckskin breeches, a buckskin shirt and sported a felt hat with a large eagle feather stuck in the hatband. He wore a woven, leather belt that supported a large knife sheathed in a leather scabbard on the left side and a flintlock pistol stuck in his belt on his right-hand side. The other two men wore dirty cloth breeches, sweat-stained shirts, and floppy hats. Both were armed with pistols. A gray-bearded man sat on a tall stool behind the bar. All eyes turned towards Bowie as he entered the room. Without hesitation, Bowie walked up to the bar.

"Care for a drink, monsieur?" said the man behind the bar. "We have rum, ale, and whiskey."

"Rum," said Bowie. "Are you the owner of this place?"

"Oui, Name's Pascal. And to whom do I have the pleasure of speaking?"

"Name's Bowie, Jim Bowie."

"Are you here to trade hides or simply to drink this fine day?" asked Pascal.

"Just need a few supplies. Headin' home to Bexar and runnin' shy on some victuals," said Bowie.

"After you finish your drink, monsieur," said Pascal. "Then we can walk over to the other side of the room to fill your bill."

Just then, the man with the feathered hat slowly reached his hand down to his right legging and pulled out a small dagger. He quickly clasped the knife by the blade, then snapped his arm and wrist, flipping the dagger across the bar where it stuck with a thud in a log just above a shelf holding several bottles of rum.

"Damn! Just missed him," said feather hat.

"What the hell are you doing, Billy?!" yelled Pascal.

"I was tryin' to kill that big roof rat that was about to sample your rum. Hate vermin," said Billy.

Out of the corner of his eye, Bowie had seen Billy reaching toward his leggings. Bowie had placed his hand on his knife just in case the man had bad intentions. He now took his hand off his weapon.

"Monsieur Bowie, meet Lightnin' Billy," said Pascal. "Says he's called 'Lightnin' Billy 'cause he's fast with the knife. I guess being fast is better than being accurate, hey Billy?" Pascal said with a laugh.

Billy's face turned red. He walked around behind the bar and pulled his knife from the log. Billy held his blade in front of Pascal. "See those rat hairs and that spot of blood? I was aimin' to give that rat a close shave," said Billy. "Looks like a got a might too close."

The two men with Billy began to laugh and snort. "Yeah. He was just givin' that ol' rat a close shave," guffawed one the dirty men. "You smart off ag'in, and he might just give you one."

Pascal spat some tobacco juice on the ground. "Get out from behind my bar, Billy."

Billy grinned at Pascal. Then he turned and walked back to the other side of the bar. He wiped his knife blade across his breeches and placed the knife back inside his leggings. Billy looked over at Bowie. "Say, are you the feller had that knife fight on a Mississippi sandbar a few years back?"

Bowie turned up his cup of rum and looked sharply at Billy. "You oughta mind your own business. Now let's get them supplies," Bowie directed at Pascal.

"You boys have had enough to drink today," said Pascal. "Bar's closed." Pascal stepped out from behind the bar and crossed the room. Bowie followed. Billy and the other two men stood glaring at Pascal, cursed and grumbled, downed their mugs, and headed towards the door.

Pascal yelled out, "Stop by anytime you have more salt or other goods to trade." The three men exited the building. "That half-breed's always looking for trouble. One of these days, Billy's gonna cross paths with the wrong fellow. Now, what supplies do you need?"

"Coffee, salt pork, dried beans, cornmeal, and a bottle of rum. I also need some black powder and lead shot."

"Well, sir, I can help you with all but the coffee. I have some black tea. I'm out of coffee till the next steamboat arrives."

"Steamboats make it this far?" asked Bowie.

"During the rainy season. Boats come up the Red and through the bayou over to this point. Are you traveling alone?"

"My servant's outside tending the horses."

"If you are camping nearby tonight, a minister is passing through that's gonna hold a meeting about dusk down by the river. Hear he's a real fire and brimstone preacher. Can get the crowd worked up. He's trying to convert the heathens and the Anglos that have settled in the area. Are you a God-fearing man by chance?" asked Pascal.

"I was raised Presbyterian but converted to Catholicism when I moved to Texas and married my wife. She's catholic. Might see ya' later at the preachin'." Bowie paid for his supplies, gathered what he could carry in his arms, and headed towards the door. Pascal helped tote the remaining supplies outside to Sam and the waiting horses.

Sam was napping under a tree. Bowie, seeing Sam asleep in the shade, squalled like a bobcat, startling the unprepared servant awake. Sam jumped to his feet as if shot. "Mount up, Sam. We'll camp down by the river tonight. Going to a preachin' tonight. Hear 'bout Jesus."

"'Spect I need to go hear 'bout Jesus since you done scared him out o' me jes' now," grumbled Sam.

Bowie and Pascal laughed heartily at the poor servant's expense. Bowie and Sam mounted their horses, and the two rode off toward the river. "Au revoir," Pascal called out to the two men as they rode away.

Chapter 25

Bowie and Sam made camp near the bayou not far from the ferry crossing. They decided on an early supper so they could attend the preaching that evening. Sam built a fire and roasted some fresh venison that Bowie had bought off some nearby Indians. The two men sat quietly, devouring the fresh venison and downing the last of their coffee. Bowie sat, observing several men gathering in a clearing on the other side of the ferry landing. The distant men were busily building a large bonfire. Several of the men were sticking long torches in the ground in a wide arc around the fire. Some were dragging logs inside the arc, apparently forming crude benches. A little before sunset, more people began to appear – Indians and Whites – men and women – children and dogs.

After polishing off the last of the roasted venison and coffee, Bowie and Sam wandered over to the clearing. Approaching the makeshift chapel under the stars, Bowie made out some all too familiar faces – Lightnin' Billy and his two cronies were standing at the edge of the glow cast by the torches drinking from a jug. From their actions, Bowie guessed the three scoundrels had been steadily drinking since leaving the trading post.

Suddenly, a man dressed in buckskin breeches and shirt standing in the back of a buckboard near the bonfire began clanging a big, wooden spoon on a large metal pot. Most of the crowd started to quiet down and take seats on the logs and ground.

"Friends, brothers, and sisters in Christ, my name's Sumner Bacon. I'm a Presbyterian circuit rider here to share the Gospel with you today. Before you get any notions about me – let me tell you – I'm one of you. I came to this place on the edge of the frontier from Fort Smith, where I served in the army and then as a laborer. Just like you, I'm a sinner. I once cussed and drank with the best of 'em. Just like you, I came west searchin' for a better life for my family. Lord knows it's hard living out here on the edge. Friends, let me tell you where I'm different than many of you – I don't walk this narrow path alone. In my search for a better life, I found Jesus. Now the Holy Spirit walks it with me."

A few "Amens" rose up here and there from the dispersed crowd.

The stump preacher continued, "As the Psalmist David said, 'Even though I walk through the valley of the shadow of death, I will fear no evil, for you are with me. Your rod and your staff, they comfort me.' I feel the Lord's presence with us here today. I feel the power of the Almighty working amongst us today. Some of you folks is believers, and some of you ain't. Many of you never heard the Word of the Lord about his Son, Jesus Christ, who God sent to earth to save all sinners from eternal damnation. I'm merely a vessel on this earth carrying His message. Heed His word 'afore it's too late. You have a choice. You can walk with Jesus and live with him throughout eternity in a mansion in the sky, or you can suffer eternal damnation in the lake of fire. Do you see this roaring fire? It's but a candle compared to the lake of fire. Imagine the constant smell of burning sulfur, with nary a drop of water to quench your thirst and the endless screams of those in eternal agony?! You have a choice, good people. Live eternally in the bosom of Jesus in Heaven above or spend eternity in the lake of fire? Which will you choose?

A voice from the back of the crowd said, "They got any rum in that there Heaven?" said Lightnin' Billy. His two cronies joined him in laughter. One of the two said, "That's right, Billy. We ain't interested in going if they ain't got no rum and whiskey."

Bowie quickly weaved his way through the crowd to where Billy was standing. "You still ain't learned when to keep your mouth shut, have you Billy?" said Bowie. "You and your boys need to take your jug and clear out – NOW. Else I'll shut your pie hole for you."

Billy started reaching for his knife, strapped to his side. Several men from the crowd quickly stepped forward and stood near Bowie. Billy slowly took his hand off his dagger. He reached down, nearly falling on his face and grabbed his jug. Billy then stood erect, steadying himself by grabbing the tree he stood under and glared at Bowie. "Come on boys. Let's go some'ers quieter to drink. 'Sides, it stinks around here. Smells like a pig wallow."

Bowie replied, "It'll smell better when you and these two other skunks find a hole to crawl into."

Lightnin' Billy let go of the tree and slowly clenched his free hand into a fist. His face grew red as a beet either from anger, the effects of the rum, or both. "Bowie, I got a little piece of advice for you. Watch your backside." The three men turned and staggered into the darkness.

The crowd let out a brief cheer. The preacher shouted, "'Behold, I send an angel before you, to keep you by the way, and to bring you into the place which I have prepared. Pay attention to him and listen to his voice. Don't provoke him, for he will not pardon your disobedience, for my name is in him. But if you indeed listen to his voice, and do all that I speak, then I will be an enemy to your enemies, and an adversary to your adversaries.' Exodus, twenty-three."

The young farmer preached for another hour. A chorus of "amens" and "hallelujahs" rose up from the crowd throughout the sermon. Some in the group fell to their knees and prayed to Heaven. Moved by the fiery preacher and the Lord's Spirit, many in the crowd stepped forward to shake the preacher's hand and to let all know they were accepting Jesus as their Savior. Bowie and Sam stayed until the preaching was over – then returned to their camp as the crowd slowly disbursed.

At daybreak, Bowie and Sam drank their remaining coffee, ate some cold, venison, and corndodgers. They rolled up their beds, stowed their belongings, and mounted up. They headed south towards Nacogdoches back through the Caddo village. Smoke was rising from most of the huts. Other than a few mangy dogs looking for scraps of food, the village was quiet. Some of the women were outside the huts talking to each other. Most of the horses and braves were nowhere to be seen. *Probably out hunting,* thought Bowie.

The two men rode along the well-worn trail in silence for close to an hour. Finally, Bowie said, "I'm ready to get home to the wife and boys. Been gone too long – near forgot what they look like. What about you, Sam? You ready to sleep in your own bed for a change?"

"Sho' 'nuff, Masser Jim. Deez ol' bones ready to lie down on sumptin' soffer den de ground."

The two riders crested a small hill. About a hundred yards ahead, at the foot of the rise, lay a wide creek that snaked its way through the thick pine timber and dense undergrowth. At that moment, a flock of ducks lifted off from a wide spot in the creek, their wings popping the air. The ducks quickly headed east away from the two riders. Bowie held up his hand, and the two halted on the trail. Bowie cocked the flintlock on his Kentucky rifle. "Something spooked those ducks," said Bowie. "I think we're a might far away to have done it." They stood quietly, watching the line of trees on either side of the creek. It was eerily quiet – too quiet – no birds chirping – nothing stirring. Bowie motioned to move ahead slowly. Just as they reached the bank of the creek, three horsemen came galloping from behind a stand of cane. Bowie and Sam wheeled around to face the three riders headed towards them at a gallop. The lead rider had a familiar hat with an eagle feather flapping in the wind. The three men had their flintlock pistols drawn and pointed at Bowie and Sam.

"Looky here, boys. It's the high and mighty Jim Bowie and his negro," said Lightnin' Billy. "You talk big when they's a bunch of men around to help you out. You still feelin' cocky this mornin'?"

"We're not looking for trouble, Billy. You boys best move on. It'll be better for your health," said Bowie.

"Dat so?" said Billy. "You done sassed me twice, Bowie. Dat's two times more than most get away with. I think you need to learn a little respect for Lightnin' Billy. Ain't that right, boys?"

"Dat's right, Billy," said one of the ride-alongs.

"You gonna find dealin' with me a little harder than carvin' up some decrepit old sheriff on a sandbar at night," said Billy.

"You got me a little out-numbered, don't you think? My man-servant don't carry a weapon. How's this a fair fight? If you're as good as you think with that knife, let's me and you settle this one-on-one. Knives only. On one condition, if you kill me, you and your men promise to let Sam go free?"

"Here's my condition – you and me with knives. My men 'ill stay out of it. But after your dead and gone, your property becomes my property. Boys, keep your guns on 'em," said Billy as he dismounted.

Bowie slowly climbed down from his horse. He looked up at Sam as his back was to the others and gave him a wink. Bowie and Billy each drew their knives and squared off. The two men then began to slowly circle each other. Bowie waited on Billy to make the first move. Billy glared at Bowie with a half-grin, half-sneer. Bowie showed no facial expression as his face slowly turned redder and redder. Then Billy made a lunge at Bowie – his knife thrusting straight ahead. Bowie jumped to one side. Then Billy turned in a full circle, his blade slicing through the air. Bowie arched his back, allowing the tip of Billy's knife to slice a small hole in the front of his buckskin shirt. Bowie brought the pommel end of his knife down hard on the back of Billy's neck as he circled in front of Bowie. Billy let out a grunt. Billy cursed Bowie but regained his footing. Billy made a little fake as if he was going to lunge at Bowie. Bowie jumped backward. Billy immediately came at Bowie with a full lunge. Bowie made a slight step to the right, using his own knife to deflect downward, Billy's thrusting blade. Bowie drew the clip point of his knife backward in an arcing motion, slicing across the cheek and ear of Billy, who let out a squeal like a stuck pig. Blood ran down the front of Billy's shirt. Stunned by the sight of his own blood and the pain, Billy stood still for one moment. In one quick motion, Bowie made a broad swipe with his big blade across Billy's stomach, opening a large gash. Then with a backward movement, he sliced the clip point across Billy's throat, severing his jugular vein. Billy fell to his knees, clutching his throat, his guts spilling through the gash in his shirt.

Quickly, Bowie did a forward shoulder roll across the ground, coming up standing on the right side of the closest horseman. The stunned man swung his pistol to shoot Bowie, but Bowie quickly stabbed the rider through his chest, piercing his lung. The gun fired – the ball hitting harmlessly in the dirt in front of Bowie. The frightened horse reared into the air, throwing the now dying rider to the ground. Bowie came around behind the bucking horse and lunged at the remaining rider, knocking him off the horse. Bowie slapped the horse across the butt, and the horse leaped forward. Bowie lunged for the rider now on the ground striking him in the head with the large blade, splitting his skull open. Bowie slowly stood up, trying to catch his breath. He looked around for Sam, but Sam was not on his horse. Then he saw Sam standing next to Bowie's horse. Sam was pointing the Kentucky rifle in Bowie's direction.

"Sam, what in tarnation are you doing?" yelled Bowie.

"I was gonna shoot one of 'dem men if'n I had to. No way was I gonna be a servant to dat man," said Sam.

"There for a minute, I thought you were going to shoot me," said Bowie.

"Yassir. I thought 'bout it fur a minute. But knowin' how mean you are, I figured I'd just wing ya' and you'd stab me with dat big ol' knife." Both men began to laugh.

Bowie walked over to where Billy lay on the bloody ground. He picked up Billy's knife. "I swear, this knife looks like it was made by that blacksmith in Arkansas. Don't think Lightnin' Billy will need this one anymore."

Chapter 26

It was mid-morning on a cold, cloudy January day, and it looked like it could snow at any time. Jimmy had all the openings in the shop fastened shut, trying to stay warm. The wind was whistling through every little crack and fissure. He was at the forge, working on a new batch of knives. Dan was helping.

A man's voice from outside yelled, "Yo in there! Anybody here?"

Dan walked over and opened the front door of the shop. The wind blew up a cloud of dust from the floor. The man quickly entered. Dan leaned into the door with his shoulder pushing against the wind – soundly closing the door. The visitor wore a long overcoat and military hat. He walked over to the forge and began to warm his hands. The stranger unbuttoned his coat, letting in the warmth from the glowing coals revealing a military uniform underneath.

"I'm Lieutenant Kerr with the Bureau of Indian Affairs. I'm leading an advance scouting detachment under orders from Captain Gaines. I'm in the area securing civilian contracts to aid in the relocation of Choctaw Indian tribes from east of the Mississippi to their new home west of here near Fort Towson. Which of you is the proprietor of this shop?"

"I am. Name is Black. How can I help you?"

"In about three days, there'll be about thirty wagons through here pulled by teams of mules. We'll need some repairs to the wagons and harness. Some of the mules will need shoeing. Are you interested?"

"Yes, sir, I am," said Jimmy.

"Very well. What are your rates?" inquired the young officer.

I'll shoe the mules for two bucks a head. The work on the wagon will depend on the type of work, but I'll be more than fair. Work's a bit slow this time of year."

"Sounds fair." The lieutenant extended his hand and the two men shook. The lieutenant stayed by the fire warming himself. "Mind if I have a cup of your coffee?" as he eyed the steaming pot sitting on the rim of the forge. Dan poured and handed a cup of steaming coffee to the lieutenant.

"Thank you kindly." The lieutenant took a couple of sips of the coffee as he stared into the hot embers. "About twelve hundred Choctaws or what's left of 'em will be traveling with the wagons in a few days. Most will be on foot. The old, the sick and the young will be in the wagons. A few weeks back, about two thousand left Vicksburg. The lucky ones traveled by steamboat down the Mississippi, up the Red and the Washita to John Camden's Post east of here. The unlucky ones left Vicksburg on foot and got lost. A search party found 'em wandering in the swampy lowlands 'tween here and Vicksburg. Many died of cholera, starvation, and the cold before they reached Camden's Post. God knows how many will make it to Towson before it's all said and done. In any event, my men are in the area securing contracts for food, so when the Indians get here, they'll have something to eat. Do you know any farmers or planters we can contact?"

"Talk with Abraham Block over at the Mercantile. He can supply you with names of those likely to help you."

"Thank you, Mr. Black. I'll be on my way now– no time to tarry. I'll see you in about three days." He buttoned his coat and headed out the door. The wind again gusted in blowing dust and soot in all directions.

Jimmy looked at Dan and said, "Let's break for our noon meal. I'm hungry." They grabbed their food and returned to sit on a wooden bench close to a cast-iron stove in the corner of the shop. The wind continued howling through cracks in the building. "I guess the government didn't waste any time booting the Choctaws off their land east of the Mississippi. I got my hands on a stale copy of the *Arkansas Gazette*. It had an article about the Indian Removal Act. Old Hickory couldn't wait to sign it into law. Looks like just a matter of time before the last of the so-called Five Civilized Tribes will be making new homes in the western part of the Territory. Sounds like the Seminoles down Florida way are putting up a helluva fight, though."

"I'm pullin' fur the Seminoles," said Dan.

"Why's that?" Jimmy quizzed, a bit perplexed.

"My grandmother is part Cherokee," he said.

"Truth be known, there's more around with a little Injun blood in 'em than lets on," Jimmy said as he tore off another piece of venison jerky with his teeth and chewed it slowly. He took a gulp of coffee from his tin cup to help loosen up the dried venison. The two sat quietly for a minute or two, eating. "Well, we best get back to work. These knives aren't gonna make themselves. Besides, we'll be extra busy in a few days and will not be able to work on them for a while. Throw another stick or two o' wood in the stove – gettin' a might colder outside."

* * *

It was dark out as Jimmy headed home. Coming down the street toward his house, he could see the yellow glow of the bear oil lamps through the curtained windows. When he entered the front door, his two young boys ran to greet him. They all three made their way to the backroom kitchen. The fire in the fireplace was blazing. Anne was busily putting the final touches on supper.

"Mama, Papa's home," yelled William, the eldest son.

Anne wiped her hands on her calico apron and brushed a stray strand of hair out of her face. Jimmy walked over and gave her a hug. "What's for supper?" he said. "I'm starvin'."

"Venison stew and cornbread," she replied. "Wash up and have a seat. It's ready."

Jimmy and the boys quickly washed their hands at the nearby washbasin. Jimmy sat in his chair, and the boys promptly sat on the wooden bench beside the table. Anne walked over to the fireplace and used a metal hook to swing out a cast iron pot hanging from a rod over the fire. She took a big wooden spoon, filled a bowl with steaming hot stew and set it in front of her husband. She repeated the process filling bowls for the boys and herself. Anne sat at the table opposite from Jimmy. A plate of cornbread sat at Jimmy's elbow. He passed the cornbread plate to the boys and lastly to Anne. He then took a slice and crumbled it into his stew.

"How were things at the shop today?" she asked. The boys were slurping down their stew and cramming hot cornbread in their mouths. "Guess you weren't the only one hungry," she laughed, watching the boys wolfing down the hearty stew.

"Well, we had an unusual visitor today," Jimmy responded. "A young lieutenant with the Bureau of Indian Affairs stopped by. He told Dan and me a bunch of Choctaw Indians will be passing through town on their way to Fort Towson. Lieutenant said there'd be upwards of a thousand or so. Some will be in wagons, but most will be on foot. He hired me to repair wagons, harness, and shoe the mules that need it."

The boys perked up, and they stopped slurping their stew. "Papa, did you say a bunch of Injuns is coming through town?" said William. "Are they mean Injuns?"

"Are they gonna scalp us?" chimed in Grandison.

"They're not on the warpath, boys. These Injuns are civilized. They've been livin' near white folks over in Mississippi. The government agents are just moving them to their new home west of here."

"What's wrong with their old home?" said William.

"Well Billy, I guess it's 'cause too many white folks been movin' to Mississippi. The white folks want the Injuns land, so the Injuns have to find a new one."

"But weren't the Injuns there first?" asked Billy.

"You boys ask too darn many questions. Now eat your stew before it gets cold."

"It sure is terribly cold out for a bunch of women, young children, and old men, even if they are Indians, to be traveling cross-country looking for a new home," said Anne. "How are they feeding all those Indians?"

"That's partly why the lieutenant and his men are in town," said Jimmy. "They're scoutin' to find farmers and planters that'll sell food to the agents so they can feed the Injuns when they arrive."

"James, you know as well as I do, food is scarce this time of year. It's disgraceful to be moving those poor Indians in the dead of winter," said Anne.

Jimmy finished off his first bowl of stew. Anne asked if he'd like some more. "Of course," he replied. She quickly refilled it and sat the steaming bowl in front of him.

"Do we have any of that honey left?" he asked. "I think I'll slather a piece of cornbread for somethin' sweet."

"I think so." She went to the cupboard, returned with a crock jar, and set it on the table next to him. Jimmy finished off his second bowl of stew, then slowly spooned honey onto his cornbread. He sat quietly, savoring every bite. The boys did likewise.

"President Jackson has fought so many Injuns over the years," said their pa. "I guess he still sees them all as savages even though some have tried to adopt our ways. I guess the government knows best. It looks like you boys are finished eating. Drink the rest of your milk, and I'll tell you a story before bedtime."

The boys downed the last of their milk. Their papa moved his chair over by the fire. He grabbed his corncob pipe off the mantelpiece and stoked it with tobacco. He then grabbed a long twig he kept near the fireplace, lit the twig in the fire and then lit his pipe. He took a few drags to make sure it was well lit, blowing the smoke in the direction of the hearth. The two boys sat cross-legged on the floor in front of the warm, glowing fire. The only sounds heard were those of the crackling fire and the clanging of dishes as Anne washed them in a large wooden tub

"Boys, I'm gonna tell you another story about Moses. You remember the story about baby Moses and how his mama placed him in a basket in the Nile River in Ancient Egypt? And how he was rescued by Pharaoh's daughter? Well, this is a story about Moses when he became a man. God spoke to Moses one day through a burning bush. God's voice said, 'Moses, I have chosen you to lead my people, the Israelites, out of slavery in Egypt to the promised land – a land flowing with milk and honey.' But God warned Moses that taking the new land would not be easy because it was occupied by some pagan Indian tribes. These tribes were called the Canaanites, Hittites, and Jebusites. Before the Israelites could build homes and farms in this new area, they would have to fight those tribes and drive 'em off their land. But the Israelites were a long way from getting to that Promise Land. You see, the Israelites were still held as slaves by king Pharaoh." Their papa proceeded to tell his boys about the plagues that God inflicted on Egypt. "It's getting late, and you boys need to go to bed now. We'll finish this story later. No whining. Now go."

"Yes, Papa," said Billy. The two boys slowly headed out of the room, talking among themselves about Moses and the mean Pharaoh.

Anne and Jimmy sat by the fire and talked after the boys had left the room. Jimmy made a point to spend time each day, asking Anne about her day. Even though she loved the boys immensely and enjoyed spending time with them, she was still struggling with her father's continued absence from their lives.

"Mama dropped by unannounced today," said Anne. "As usual, she did not tell Papa she was coming to visit. She told me Papa wishes to see the boys very badly, but he's unwilling to show weakness. Mama said 'William Shaw is a proud, stubborn man and would not relent – at least not yet.' When Mama got up to leave, James, I broke down and cried. Mama gave me a long hug and told me she loved me and the boys very much. She told me to be patient and not give up hope on Papa having a change of heart."

"Let's go to bed, dear," said Jimmy. "We've both had a long day." He placed his arm around his wife's waist and helped her to the bedroom. That night, Jimmy lay awake, thinking about Shaw, about Anne, the boys, and the mess he had created. Then his mind wandered to those poor Choctaws sleeping out in the freezing cold on the trail somewhere between Camden's Post and Washington. *I bet my long day didn't hold a candle to theirs*, he thought to himself.

* * *

Three days later.

Jimmy and Dan were in the shop repairing some farm implements and shackles that had been dropped off by one of the local planters. Hearing the shouts of men driving several wagon teams up the road, he opened the front door and stood watching them approach the shop. He made out five sturdy wagons, each pulled by two teams of mules. A couple of soldiers bringing up the rear each led a string of mules. Another couple of soldiers on horseback rode alongside. *I guess the Choctaws have finally made it to Washington*, thought Black.

One of the riders galloped up to the shop and quickly dismounted. It was the young lieutenant. "We finally made it, Mr. Black. We have five wagons that need some work. There's harness in the back of the first wagon that needs repairing. Ten mules that need shoeing. My men will help you any way they can."

"Let's start with the mules," Jimmy said. The lieutenant motioned for the riders in back with the mules to come forward. Dan went into the shop and retrieved the farrier tools. Jimmy went to work on the first mule. He first trimmed and cleaned the mule's hoof with a rasp, a nipper, and a pick.

The lieutenant stood close by and watched. He said, "We're camped on that big creek that runs just a little north of here. Tough trip over from Camden's Post. We lost another thirty or so Choctaws on the trail – mostly women and children. Many are sick with cholera, typhus or dysentery. Some of the pregnant ones didn't fare well in the cold. We couldn't stop long enough to give 'em a proper burial, so we just left them alongside the trail."

"How about feeding the ones that made it? Were your men successful in securing contracts for food with some of the locals?" Jimmy asked.

"My men were successful at securing food contracts alright. The only problem is many of those that agreed to supply food haven't lived up to their end of the bargain. Some of your locals saw fit to pile ears of corn alongside the trail. Others staked some old cows or crippled oxen by the road. The Indian women had to grind the corn and make cornmeal mush to eat. The braves had to slaughter the cows or oxen before they could eat. The oxen were so tough, the old men with bad teeth couldn't chew the meat. I've seen enough pain and suffering on this journey to last me ten lifetimes."

To Jimmy, it seemed the young lieutenant had aged since he'd seen him a few days earlier. "Lieutenant, it's going to take Dan and me a good three to four days to finish all of this work by ourselves. As bad as I'd like to take all your money, I think you should take about three of these wagons and half of these mules over to William Shaw's blacksmith shop. He's my father-in-law, even though he will deny that to your face. Tell him I sent you. With his help, we can get this work done in half the time so you can get these Indians on their way to their new home. The longer they camp down by Bois d'Arc Creek in this weather starving, the more death and suffering you'll surely see." Jimmy gave the lieutenant directions to Shaw's place.

"I appreciate your integrity, sir," said the lieutenant. He turned and began barking out orders to his men. The last three wagon teams and two of the riders headed off toward Shaw's place. *I hope that ornery cuss will accept the work,* thought Black.

* * *

As Jimmy suspected, Shaw's need for cash overcame his pride. By splitting up the work, Shaw and Black finished all the repairs and shoeing the mules by late afternoon the following day. The lieutenant paid Black for his services with U.S. banknotes. He told Black they would pull out at dawn the next day. Shortly after daybreak, the caravan of wagons and Indians would travel through the middle of town on their way west down the Fort Towson Road. Jimmy decided he would be there watching when they rolled through town. He mentioned his plan to Dan, who said he would also be there. The two closed up shop and headed home.

* * *

Jimmy awoke at his usual time the next morning but, instead of going to the shop, he rode to the water well in the center of town and sat on the rail fence. The Fort Towson Road lay in front of him. He had only been seated a few minutes when Dan joined him. Dan nodded but did not speak. Word must have spread about what was happening today because many of the local citizens were beginning to line the road. It was another cold, cloudy winter's day. The wind howled through the leafless branches of the trees, making a low, mournful sound. The sun rising behind the clouds caused the sky to appear blood red.

The first ones appeared over a rise in the road – a group of young bucks led the caravan. They walked erect with their heads held high -- their long, black, hair blowing in the wind. They wore beaded vests and buckskin leggings with fringe down the sides. Some wore animal skins draped over their shoulders. Weapons were conspicuously missing. The solemn Indian braves trudged slowly by on the muddy road, flanked on both sides by soldiers on horseback carrying Kentucky rifles with flintlock pistols in their belts. The soldiers were spaced out evenly about fifty feet apart.

Jimmy overheard some townsfolk nearby, shouting obscenities at passers-by. Some yelled out, "Dirty Injuns, go home! We don't want you here! This land is for white folks – not a bunch of savages and pagans!" He saw several men, and some of the women spit at the Indians as they ambled by. The Indian braves stared straight ahead and walked with heads held high. Jimmy felt some movement at his side. He turned in time to see Dan quickly mount his horse and then gallop off towards the shop. *I guess Dan has seen enough.*

Next came the younger women and older children. Some wore leather moccasins. Many were barefoot – their feet were caked in mud. The women wore buckskin or course woven skirts. Some had blankets or skins draped over them for warmth. Their clothes were tattered and dirty. Their hair had a greasy sheen to it as if unwashed for weeks. Some had makeshift scarves tied around their heads. Many of the women walked along, holding hands with their young children, helping them traverse the muddy road. Many of the children had their heads drooped, staring at the ground while others stared blankly ahead as if in a trance. Some of the women were heavy with child. Many walked with the aid of a stick or with a limp or shuffled their feet. One woman stumbled and fell to the ground. A woman and boy near her helped her get up. The woman with the now mud-covered dress slowly regained her footing and continued trudging on.

Next came the old, gray-haired men, or what was left of them. Their ranks were thin compared to the other groups. Their skin was ashen and wrinkled. Their gray hair was wispy and blew about their heads. Many wore beaded headbands and strands of beads hung around their necks. In the middle of the pack of old men, one old man stood out. He carried a long spear adorned with feathers and beads. A bear claw necklace hung around his neck. Several braves proudly followed closely behind the old man. *A chief?* Some of the old men chanted some unintelligible song or prayer to their gods.

Last came the thirty or so wagons. About half of the wagons were filled with the old women, the sick, the young, and the babies. The sound of babies and children crying could be clearly heard over the clomping of the mules, the clatter of the harness, and rattle of the wagons. Low moans and coughing could be heard over the squalling of young babies. An old woman leaned her head over the tailgate of the wagon and puked.

The last fifteen or so wagons carried tents, bedding, and supplies. Dragging up the rear were several soldiers pulling strings of spare mules. The young lieutenant was riding up from the rear after checking on the progress of the caravan. He suddenly saw Jimmy and came galloping up to where he was sitting. "Mr. Black, it's nice to see a friendly face in the crowd. Thank you again for your help and your advice. You were right. Mr. Shaw said he didn't have a son-in-law. But he didn't think twice about accepting our work or our money. We'll be back this way in a few weeks. We may need some more work from you."

"Glad to help, Lieutenant. Good luck to you on your journey."

The lieutenant tipped his hat and rode off at a brisk pace towards the front of the long line of Indians. The caravan continued it's slow, steady pace west towards Fort Towson. *A more disturbing sight I have not seen in my lifetime,* thought Jimmy. He watched until the last mule walked out of sight. He was unable to turn his eyes away from the spectacle. He slowly rose up from his seat on the rail fence, and as he turned to leave, he caught a glimpse of a light-colored object lying in the middle of the muddy road. He walked out to where the object lay, reached down, and picked it up. It was a child's doll made from a corncob with a corn-husk dress. The tiny baby splattered with mud and manure had a face drawn with charcoal. Just below one of the babydoll's eyes was a spot of dirt. It looked as if the doll was crying. He carefully placed the tiny baby in his coat pocket and walked to his horse. "Socks, let's go to the shop. I need to hammer on something."

Spring 1833

Chapter 27

It was mid-afternoon in late May, and signs of spring were everywhere. The hardwood forests and fields reflected nature's shades of green. The green fields and roadsides provided a welcoming canvas for the abundant wildflowers in bloom. Mustard-yellow Black-eyed Susan and fiery orange-red Indian Paintbrush dotted the landscape in bright, warm clusters of color. Against this backdrop, two familiar riders rode into town from the south and stopped at Stuart's Tavern. After dismounting, the Black man stayed with the horses while the stocky white-man with the dark, wavy hair walked into the tavern.

"Welcome, Mr. Bowie." said the man behind the bar. "What brings you back to Washington so soon?"

Bowie ignored the question. "Need a room for a few nights, Mr. Stuart. Not sure how long I'll be in town. And call me Jim."

"The only bed available Mr. Bowie is an upper berth in the bunk room. Sorry but that's the best I can do. I've never seen so many strangers in town at one time."

Bowie looked put out. "Is a fellow by the name of Sam Houston staying with you tonight?" asked Bowie.

"Yes, sir. He checked in a couple of days ago."

"In that case, I'll take that bunk bed. If there're any snorers in the bunch, they might find themselves tossed out that second-story window tonight. Put me atop your waiting list should a room come available."

"Will do mister...er...Jim. Will you be eatin' with us later? I believe the missus is cooking something special this evening? You don't want to miss out."

Bowie nodded his head "yes" at Stuart, then turned and walked out of the tavern. He walked the length of the porch that ran along its front. Sam was sitting on the edge of the porch smoking his pipe. The horses were grazing on the tender grass. A couple of robins scurried across the ground. Bowie reached into a front pocket of his vest, pulled out a twist of tobacco, and bit off a chaw. Bowie chewed the dark stringy leaves, then spat into the grass. "We've got time to kill before the card game starts," said Bowie. He walked over to his horse, lifted its front, right leg, and inspected the bottom of its hoof. "I think my horse is about to throw a shoe. Let's head over to that blacksmith's that made me those knives. I'll get him to look at my horse's hoof." The two men mounted up and rode off in the direction of Black's shop.

"I reckon I be sleepin' in dat livery stable hayloft jes' lack last time, Masser Jim?" asked Sam.

"Reckon so. That a problem?"

"Naw suh, reckon not, 'cept dem horseflies is big as sparrows with a full set of teeth. When day bites you, day draw blood."

"I'll talk to the knife maker about you staying in his shop tonight. Maybe he won't mind," said Bowie.

As the two riders approached Black's shop, Dan, who was out front working on a wagon tongue, greeted the two men.

"Is Black in?" asked Bowie.

"Yes sir, he's inside repairing some hardware for this here wagon," said Dan.

Bowie and Sam got down off their horses. Bowie handed the reins of his horse to Sam, turned, and walked into the open door of the shop. Sam walked the horses over to the nearby watering trough. When inside, Bowie spotted Black at the anvil next to the smoking forge. Black was hammering on a large iron ring attached to a doubletree being held by one of his helpers. Another young man was working the bellows feeding air to the glowing coals. Bowie walked up and stood next to the man in the charcoal and sweat-stained apron. Bowie waited until Black stopped hammering -- then called out, "Don't mean to startle ya'."

Black looked up and saw Bowie. "Jumpin' Geehosafat, Jim. I didn't expect to see you back in Washington so soon. You must have one helluva horse and a calloused back-side to boot as much time as you spend in the saddle."

Bowie smiled back. "You're right on both counts."

"What brings you back to Arkansas, if you don't mind me asking?" quizzed Black.

"I'm here to meet up with a man by the name of Houston. Sam Houston.," said Bowie.

"Yeah, I heard the former governor of Tennessee is hold up over at Stuart's Tavern. Word around town is he sleeps all day, drinks and plays cards all night. Some say that's just a cover, though. That he's in town makin' plans to start a revolution down in Texas and overthrow the Mexican Federales. Some folks say that many of the travelers in town are recruits for an army he's formin'. Any truth to that, Jim?"

"I wouldn't know anything about that, Jimmy. All I know is that he's agreed to pay me to show him around Texas," said Bowie.

"Well, I'm glad to hear that, Jim. 'Cause Governor Pope has declared it illegal for anyone to be plotting the overthrow of the Mexican government in Texas. Anyone involved in such a plot could find himself behind bars. Seems Ol' Hickory himself asked Pope to put a lid on any such activities."

"That's good to know," said Bowie. "But if a revolution breaks out in Texas, it won't be because some outsiders from the U.S. decide to make it happen. It'll start when the Texians living there get their fill of the Mexican government. Its constantly changing policies and harassing settlers it once courted with open arms is wearing thin. Once a man gets a taste of freedom, he'll fight to the death to keep it. Just like a wolf that'll gnaw off its leg to get free of a trap. Didn't you tell me you came from Philadelphia? Did you feel trapped back there?"

Black stared at the floor for a minute. "Yep, I was looking for an opportunity – a better life. I reckoned the frontier offered more opportunity than staying put in Philadelphia. Course a mean step-mother had a little something to do with my leaving."

"Looks like things worked out for you," Bowie replied. "You got a wife, a houseful of children, this blacksmith shop sitting on the doorstep to Texas, and you make the best damn knives I've ever laid hands on. Speaking of knives, did you, by chance, ever make a knife for a man called "Lightnin' Billy? Wore a big eagle feather in his hat?"

"Lightnin' Billy? Yeah, I made a large knife for him awhile back. Didn't really cotton to a man like Billy toting one of my knives."

"Why's that?" asked Bowie.

"Billy was a two-bit outlaw. Always up to no good – smuggling – picking fights to prove how tough he was – cheatin' at cards. Billy killed a man over at the Black Bear Tavern in a card game a while back," said Jimmy.

"Then why'd you sell him one?"

"I reckon I was afraid of what he might do. Not to me, but to my family. Why do you ask if I made him a knife? I hope he's not a friend of yours," said Jimmy.

"I crossed paths with Billy south of the Red a few months ago, on my way to San Antonio. Let's just say you don't have to worry about Billy carrying your knife around anymore."

Black stared at Bowie a moment, trying to comprehend what the dark-haired man had just said. Then his eyes widened as reality set in. "Are you still pleased with those knives I made you?"

"What price is a man's own life worth?" said Bowie. "That's how much those knives mean to me."

"I thought maybe you were here to get your money back."

"I'm here to ask you a favor, Jimmy. I'm staying in town a few nights down at Stuart's Tavern. Last time I was here, my servant, Sam, slept in the loft of the livery stable. He's not too keen on swatting horseflies and smelling horse manure all night. Would you mind if he were to bunk here at your shop for a few nights? I'll pay for your trouble."

"Jim, your servant's more than welcome to bed down here anytime you're in town. I've got a rope bed in the back room just in case me or one of my assistants ever needs to work into the night. Your servant can throw his bedroll on there. No charge."

"Thank you, kindly, Jimmy. It's getting late, and I'm keeping you from your work. We need to ride down to the local mercantile and pick up some supplies. Sam 'll be back a little before dusk if that's okay."

"That'll be fine. I'll show Sam the bunk when he returns. I close up shop about sundown. By the way, meet my new hand. Tom. Come over and meet Jim Bowie." Tom walked over to where Bowie was standing. "Jim, this is Tom Shaw. He's my wife's brother." Bowie and Tom shook hands. "Tom's been working for his pa till a couple of weeks ago. I finally convinced him to come work for me. Got so busy, I needed his help."

"Bet that makes for some happy family gatherings," said Bowie.

"We don't have any of those to worry about. You see, Tom's pa never consented to my marrying his daughter -- thought I wasn't good enough for her even though I worked for him at the time. That's a big part of the reason I opened my own shop. To show Shaw, I could succeed and partly 'cause I could no longer stand being around him. That's enough about my troubles. I'm sure you've got more important things to do than stand around here, jawboning with me."

Bowie nodded his head in understanding. "My wife's of Mexican descent. Her father was not too keen on me either." The two men shook hands, then Bowie turned and walked out of the shop. Bowie shouted at Sam, who was tending the horses under the big shade tree. "Let's ride, Sam. We need to head to the mercantile and fetch you some victuals."

Sam walked the two horses over to where Bowie was standing. The two mounted up and headed towards the center of town.

"Looks like you won't be swattin' horseflies tonight, Sam," chuckled Bowie. Mr. Black said you could sleep at his shop – on a rope bed no less. Your old bones ought to rest easy tonight."

* * *

After sending Sam on his way to Black's shop for the night, Bowie headed back to Stuart's Tavern, where he dropped off his gear. He then rode his horse to the livery stable and afterward walked back to the tavern. The tavern was crowded. It was dusk, and the bear oil lamps were lit about the main room. The room was hazy with smoke from pipes and from the oil lamps.

Elijah Stuart stood behind the makeshift bar of yellow-pine planks across oak barrels, filling crock mugs with ale and grog. Yellow-pine shelves covered most of the wall behind the bar except for a rectangular space in the center where a print of George Washington hung, the town's namesake. Each shelf supported a variety of crock jugs plugged with corn cobs and dark-green, corked glass bottles. An assortment of mugs hung from wooden pegs running along the wall beneath the bottom-most shelf.

Crude wooden tables were arrayed haphazardly throughout the room. Some were long, rough-hewn tables with long benches on opposite sides. Others were square or rectangle tables ringed with four to six ladder-back chairs with cane bottoms. Most of the tables were occupied. At a couple of tables, card games were underway. At one table, four elderly men with lengthy, gray beards were playing dominoes. Most everyone was drinking. The spittoons placed around the room were covered in dark brown spittle as was the surrounding floor. A young boy wearing a well-stained apron was busy waiting on the patrons.

Bowie walked up to the bar. Stuart nodded his head at Bowie. "How about a drink?" said Stuart.

"Got any Scotch whiskey?" asked Bowie.

"Wish I did," said Stuart. "Hard to get what I little I have this far upriver from New Orleans. Got rum, hard cider, and grog."

"Gimme the rum," said Bowie. "Any rooms open up for the night?"

"'Fraid not. You're still in the bunk room."

Bowie turned his mug up, taking a long drink. He wiped his mouth with the back of his hand. "Know where can I find Sam Houston?"

"He's sitting right over there," said Stuart as he pointed at the table by the window. "He's in that Injun looking garb."

Bowie turned to his right and saw a tall, thin man with long, salt-and-pepper hair sitting at the table with two other men. He was dressed in buckskin head to toe. The buckskin shirt was fringed down the sleeves with tiny, colored beads sewn onto the front in a pattern.

The buckskin breeches were fringed down the sides. Bowie made his way across the room and approached the three men.

"Governor Houston. I'm Colonel Bowie of the Rangers."

Houston stood up, towering over Bowie by several inches. The two men shook hands. Houston used the freemason's handshake. Bowie reciprocated.

"Have a seat, Colonel Bowie. This here's Claiborne Wright and John Nail. You're among friends here."

"I've come to the aid of the widow's son. Call me Jim."

"Very well, Jim. Have a seat," said Houston as he pointed to the open chair. "We were just about to order something to eat. Care to sup with us? I think they're serving squirrel stew – maybe venison, not sure."

"Believe I will," replied Bowie.

The young boy in the stained apron walked up to the table. "Y'all need anythin' to drink or eat?" said the lad.

"Bring us another round," said Houston. "I believe we'll all try a bowl of stew and some of your mama's fine cornbread. How is the stew, by the way?"

"It's larapin," said the boy. "Them squirrels was fresh kilt by my oldest brother this mornin'. They's young squirrels, not them tough ol' boar squirrels. And Mama is one of the best cooks in these here parts. They's dewberry cobbler for dessert."

"You're a natural-born salesman," said Houston with a grin. The other three men let out a chuckle. "Bring us the stew, a platter of cornbread and butter if you have any. Set aside four servings of that dewberry cobbler."

The boy quickly turned and headed towards the open doorway next to the bar.

"I'm glad you could join me," said Houston to Bowie. "I'm looking forward to travelin' with you down to Texas -- maybe as far as San Antonio."

"The locals call it Bexar," said Bowie.

"I understand you have a wife and children down in Bexar?" said Houston.

"That's right. My wife, Ursula Maria, is from Bexar. And we have two boys."

"I understand your wife is the daughter of a prominent Mexican citizen," said Houston.

"My wife's maiden name is Veramendi. Her father is Juan Martin de Veramendi. He is vice-governor the Province of Coahuila y Tejas."

"Such a connection may prove useful down the road," said Houston. "Mr. Wright and Mr. Nail have families with plantations at Pecan Point just west of here. Are you familiar with Pecan Point?"

"I've heard of it," Bowie replied.

"Pecan Point is a large peninsula of land surrounded by the ever-shifting Red River," continued Houston. "It's a place where buffalo have crossed the Red for God knows how long. About 1818, fifty or so pioneer families settled at Pecan Point. They built plantations and farms there. At that time, Pecan Point was part of Miller County, Arkansas Territory. That is until the Adams-Onis treaty was signed with Spain in 1819. Henceforward, Miller County was deemed Spanish Texas – and now Mexico. The U.S. Army told settlers there they had to leave Pecan Point. The settlers petitioned the U.S. Secretary of State to keep their landholdings. Sadly, to no avail. They were disbursed by Federal troops. Some moved north of the Red to Arkansas. Some headed further south into Texas. Some hardy souls stayed put."

The young waiter returned with a tray of straw-colored crock bowls full of steaming-hot stew, which he set in front of the four guests. He then returned with a tin plate full of cornbread and a crock jar of creamy butter. Houston passed the tin of cornbread to the other men then helped himself. The men began to devour the soup and bread.

Houston continued, "Those brave men who settled at Pecan Point were the first white settlers in Texas. Most think it was Austin's Colony down on the Brazos. Rightfully so, those Pecan Point men feel betrayed by those back in Washington City. But enough about that for now. Jim, you've been down in Texas for a while. How's the attitude of the ex-patriots living down Texas way?"

"Flustered," said Bowie. "The Mexican Government changes its attitude toward the white settlers as often as the wind changes direction on the Texas plains. One minute the Mexican Federales want more white settlers. The next minute they don't. One minute, it's okay for Whites to own slaves, the next, slavery is outlawed. Rumor has it that Generalissimo de Santa Anna is exerting his influence to shift the government from a federal structure to a centralist one, which will further restrict the freedoms of its citizens. Mixing the political situation with the lack of protection for its citizens from raiding Indians and you've got a tense situation. Texas is a powder keg just waiting for someone to light the fuse."

Houston used his spoon to scrape the bottom of his bowl. "Men, I've lived with the Cherokee Indians on and off over the years, and I've eaten a lot of wild game stew, but I don't recall eating any better than this. I'd have another, but I best save room for that dewberry cobbler -- and cream, I hope."

The young lad returned to check on the four men. The bowls and mugs were empty. Only crumbs remained on the tin plate.

"Bring us another round of drinks and four bowls of that cobbler. Don't skimp on the cream," said Houston. The boy turned and scurried away.

Bowie then said to Houston, "Governor Houston, as you probably know, I'm not a meek man. So I'll get to the point. You're the focus of much gossip around town. What brings a former governor of Tennessee and a close friend of the sitting President to this little trail-crossing on the edge of Mexico?"

"Let us discuss that upstairs, shall we. I have cigars and a deck of cards in my room. Some things are best said in private."

The four men finished off the cobbler, and cream then rose from the table. Houston walked over to the bar and said, "Mr. Stuart, put that fine supper on my account and add a couple of bottles of rum. I'll take the rum now." Stuart handed two olive-green, corked bottles to Houston. The four men walked out of the tavern and up the outdoor stairs to the second floor.

Chapter 28

Houston opened the door to his second-floor room and allowed his guests to enter. He followed the three into the room and set the bottles on a sturdy, oak table in the center of the room. Bowie set the four mugs brought from the tavern in front of Houston. Houston popped the cork, poured the mugs half-full of rum, and handed them to the men. He raised his mug in the air and said, “Men, join me in a toast.” The others raised their mugs in the air. “Here’s to much success in our future endeavors.”

“Hear, hear,” chimed in Wright. All four took a drink from the crock mugs.

“Have a seat,” said Houston as he pointed his mug at the table surrounded by ladder-back chairs. “I had Stuart bring us up a table, some chairs, and a couple of decks of cards. Told him I had some old friends coming to town for a game of faro.”

Each man took a seat. Houston gently set the bottle on the table. He looked the other men in their eyes one at a time and said, “We’re all Freemasons. Each of us joined the brotherhood of our own free will. As such, you’ve sworn an oath of secrecy under the penalty of death. What I’m about to tell you is to be held in the strictest confidence and only discussed with fellow Freemasons. Understood?”

Each man nodded his consent.

“Very well,” said Houston. “Jim, you asked me a question downstairs. I’ll attempt to answer your question best I can. When I was about fourteen and living back in Tennessee, I ran away from home. My brothers were quite mean to me, and I finally had my fill. While wandering in the wilderness, I stumbled on a hunting party of Cherokee braves. Fortunately, they did not kill me but carried me to their chief, Oolooteka. The old chief took a liking to me and gave me the Cherokee name of ‘Colonneh,’ which means Black Raven. I lived with those Cherokee for about three years, eventually returning home to my white family. A few years later, I fought with General Jackson in 1814 at the Battle of Horseshoe Bend in Mississippi Territory. Even though it was during the War of 1812, we fought against the Red Sticks, who were Creek Indians. I had mixed feelings about fighting those Creeks, but I justified it on the grounds they were the sworn enemies of the Cherokees. I suppose it was due to my own blind ambition. Old Hickory took a liking to me, and I basked in his approval. As you surely know, with Jackson's support and encouragement, I eventually ran for political office in Tennessee. I served the people of Tennessee as their congressman, senator, and governor. While serving as governor, I let my love of the bottle and of women cause me to shame my wife and the Office of Governor. So I resigned from my office and moved to Dardanelle just north of here on the Arkansas River, where I served as a Government Agent for the Cherokee people. It was there that I married my current wife, a Cherokee by the name of Tiana Rogers."

"Which brings me to why I'm here today. I aim to find a permanent home for my Cherokee family. They deserve a home, and I intend to secure one for them. They're one of the Civilized Tribes and don't deserve being forced to live on top of the warring Osage, their sworn enemy. Even though Old Hickory and me are friends, we don't always see eye to eye on things – the treatment of the Cherokee is one of those – and the Indian Removal Act is another. Now before you go calling me 'Indian lover' or worse, allow me to explain. Texas is a vast frontier. I believe there's room for Whites, Indians, and Mexicans to live as neighbors without getting in each other's way. I'm looking for men like yourselves who can share my vision for a new way of living in Texas."

"So you're talking about a revolt against the Mexican government?" asked Wright.

"And is President Jackson aware of your plans? Does he support it?" asked Bowie.

Houston downed the last of his rum and refilled his mug. He held up the bottle offering a refill to the others. Bowie shoved his cup towards Houston, who quickly filled it. "It's a fundamental principle of Freemasonry that all men have a God-given right to live free from tyranny. Freemasons were behind the Colonies declaring independence from the Crown. Texas should be no different. Awhile back, I met in private with President Jackson at Hermitage, his plantation home in Nashville. He's sympathetic to the cause, but politics are such that he cannot be seen publicly supporting us. Those in Washington City don't want war with Mexico. Abolitionists in Congress are afraid Texas would eventually become a slave state altering the balance of power between free and slave states. We have to keep our plan secret, and we cannot count on the President to openly aid our cause."

"You keep mentioning a plan. Do you have a plan?" asked Wright.

"I do, but my plan will not happen overnight," said Houston. "It will require a longer-term commitment. That's why I'm looking for men like you – men with a backbone – risk-takers. If all goes well, Texas will become a new country, and you men stand to benefit greatly. Are you interested?"

The three men made eye contact with one another. A simple head nod affirmed they were. "Let's hear your plan," said Bowie.

Houston uncorked the second bottle and refilled each man's mug. He stood, gained his balance, and padded in his leather-clad feet over to the door. Yanking the door open, Houston glanced outside. Satisfied no one was eavesdropping, he returned to the table. "My plan has been in motion for over a year now. The heart of the plan is to get enough settlers into Texas so that when a declaration of independence from Mexico is signed, we can muster enough men to defeat Santa Anna's considerable army. Old Hickory has secretly been aiding my efforts. He pushed Congress to pass a bill to fund improvements to the Military Road, which runs from Memphis and Missouri down to our current location. The stated reason for the bill was to prepare the road for use in relocating the Civilized Tribes from lands east of the Mississippi to the western part of Arkansas Territory. The unstated reason for the bill was to funnel money in the form of wages to poor folk wishing to buy cheap land in Texas. With little oversight of the roadwork, many of the workers simply drew their wages, then headed to Texas. Having just traveled that so-called road, I can attest that there was little work done in exchange for money."

"I've been back east for months holding meetings in Freemason Lodges. In those meetings, I urged folks to raise money and stake those in their communities interested in migrating to Texas. Those meetings resulted in several wagon trains making their way west to Texas."

"As we speak, a wagon train from North Carolina is camped on the edge of town, ready to cross into Texas. Staying in town tonight are about two dozen Georgia men that made there way here to join up with us. That's where you all come in. In a couple of days, we'll head west on Fort Towson Road. Claiborne and John, I want you to escort the wagon train south to Jonesboro across the Red from Fort Towson. You all know that area of Texas like the back of your hand. Help those settlers find land in that part of Texas. I'll ride with you to Jonesboro. Then I'll head south on my own. I plan to stop at the cabin of James Clark just south of Jonesboro. Judge Trimble here in town told me I should meet Clark – a man of some influence just south of the Red. I studied law under Trimble's uncle, Judge James Trimble, back in Nashville. The Trimble family and mine are kin and owned adjoining plantations back in Old Virginia. After spending some time with Mr. Clark, I'll head south to Nacogdoches, then over to Austin's colony on the Brazos River and maybe on to Jim's home in San Antonio. Excuse me, Jim, I mean Bexar. I want to scout the country. See with my own eyes how many people are there and what their attitude is towards the Mexican authorities."

"Jim, I want you to ride on to Fort Towson with the two dozen or so that are here from Georgia. I'd like for you to make contact with some of the men stationed at the fort. See if you can interest any of them in relocating to Texas once they're discharged. We'll need some real soldiers to help train our volunteer army when the time is right. After spending a few days at Fort Towson, you can lead the Georgians down to Bexar. Help them find a place to settle. You men good with that?" All agreed.

Houston rose from his chair and crossed the room to where his saddlebags lay on the floor. Picking up the bags and placing them on the rickety bed, he rifled through the contents of one pouch and pulled out a folded document. Returning to the table, the governor began unfolding the paper and spreading it on the table. It was a crude map of Arkansas Territory, the State of Louisiana and Texas.

"Jim, you know Texas. I want you to point out the trails I'll need to follow to get me to my destination," said Houston. He returned to his saddlebag and retrieved a small stoppered, crock jar, and a quill pen. He returned to the table. "Use this India ink to mark the trails."

Bowie took the quill pen in hand. He began to examine the map. "The first trail to mark is Trammell's Trace," said Bowie. "Old Nick Trammell's been running horses and contraband into Texas before any Whites settled there." The four men continued to pour over the map late into the night as Bowie described the trail to San Antonio de Bexar and the perils that awaited travelers on such a journey.

"All sorts of trouble lies around every bend in the trail," said Bowie. "Of course there's ordinary bushwhackers looking for easy prey. Then there's Comanche, Kiowa, and Wichita Indians roaming the Red River valley looking to steal horses and take a few scalps along the way. You have Mexican army troops patrolling – looking for interlopers and illegal immigrants. Texas watering holes are far-and-few-in-between, rivers are mere streams, and in summer months, more dry than wet. So you best keep plenty of water with you at all times."

"Sounds like a veritable paradise," cackled Nail. "And remind me again, why are we going there?"

"The grassland rolls on forever," replied Bowie. "It'll allow a man to graze cattle, horses, and all sorts of livestock. The land is fertile and will grow any crop – corn, cotton, sugar cane, or what-have-you. The land is cheap, and you can secure large tracts for little or nothing. As the good Lord told the Israelites, it's a land flowing with milk and honey."

"Well said," responded Houston. "How about another round of rum? All that talk of lack of water makes me a might thirsty."

"None for me," said Bowie.

"Nor me," chimed in Wright. "I believe I've reached my limit, or you'll have to carry me to my room."

"Since I'm in my room, I believe I'll have another," said Houston. He tipped the bottle over the top of his mug, and the last bit of rum trickled out. "Looks like our meeting just came to an end."

The three men chuckled. Houston yawned and stretched his arms in the air. "Tomorrow, I'll get word to our Texas sojourners we're pulling out at daybreak in two days. You all have any questions?"

The other three men stood and pushed back their chairs. Bowie replied, "None from me." The other two nodded their agreement.

"Very well," said Houston. "Let's call it a night. Oh, and remember, we've been playing faro, and I lost big. It'll take a lot of luck and a couple of nights to win back my hard-earned money. And we'll need a lot of luck and money before this venture is over."

Chapter 29

Black sat at a contraption of his own making, polishing a recent knife creation. Necessity is the mother of invention, and buffing and polishing his knives by hand had driven him to invent a better solution. By attaching a sheepskin to the perimeter of the stone wheel on his treadle powered grinding wheel, Jimmy had considerably cut the time and energy expended in polishing his knives and improved the quality of the process as well. A paste of bear grease and fine grit acted as a polishing compound.

Jimmy rubbed his latest blade with the bear grease compound. He then started the stone wheel into motion with a push of his hand. He kept the wheel in motion by pumping his feet up and down on wooden pedals connected by rods to a crankshaft running through the center hub of the wheel. Once the heavy stone wheel was in motion, it took little effort to keep it spinning at a goodly pace. Applying gentle pressure, he held the compound covered blade against the rapidly spinning sheepskin. After a half-hour of buffing, the metal began to shine like new money. He held the knife up, visually inspecting his handiwork. Satisfied, he stopped the spinning wheel.

It was getting late, and he was tired. *Sharpening this one can wait till tomorrow*, thought Jimmy. He yelled at Dan and Tom, "let's call it a day, boys." Dan poured a bucket of water on the smoldering charcoal in the forge. Steam billowed out, hiding him from view. Tom closed the shutters over the windows. The three men walked outside, and Tom closed the shop door.

"See you tomorrow, Jimmy," said Dan as he walked toward town.

"It'll be here before you know it," Jimmy replied. "Tom, you're welcome to come eat with your sister and me tonight."

"I best get home tonight," replied Tom. "I've got some chores to do when I get home. Don't need to goad Pa any more than I have by coming to work for you."

As Jimmy rode home, he thought about a traveler from Texas that stopped by the shop earlier in the day. Turns out the stranger knew Jim Bowie quite well, having run in some of the same circles down in Texas. The traveler had shared some interesting and some disturbing news from Texas. *I'll have to tell Anne all about it tonight at supper.*

He rode Socks around to the small corral back of his house, where he unsaddled his horse. He placed the saddle, blanket, and bridle inside the small barn. He went to a large barrel, scooped up some grain in a dried gourd ladle and poured it into a trough under the lean-to attached to the barn. Socks eagerly began to chomp on the grain.

Black entered the house through the back door and was greeted by a delicious aroma and by the squeals of small children. "Is that apple pie I smell?" he said to Anne, who was busy in the cramped kitchen. He walked over to the hearth and saw the Dutch oven sitting near the fire with the lid covered with hot coals. Pork chops were sizzling in a skillet. A pot of beans with ham hock was steaming in a cast iron pot hung over the fire. "Anne, I'm truly the luckiest man alive to have you as my wife." He grabbed her around the waist and gave her a kiss.

The kids all chimed in, "Oh Papa, quit that. Yuck."

Anne smoothed the front of her apron. "You and the kids best go wash up. Supper will be on the table soon," she replied.

"You heard your Mama, you little billy goats." He herded the kids over to the washstand in the corner. He grabbed the bar of lie soap –

washed the boys' hands – then his own. They returned to the kitchen table and took their seats. The plates and forks were on the table. Anne served them each in turn. She first carried her husband's plate to the hearth and plopped down a big scoop of beans, then stabbed a pork chop and nuzzled it next to the beans. Anne set the plate in front of her husband. She did the same for each of the children, serving herself last. As usual, a plate of crusty, golden yellow cornbread sat in the center of the table. A bowl of sliced onions sat next to the bread. The kids had forks in hand and were ready to dig in.

"Now hold on, boys," said their mama. "We need to ask the Lord's blessing on our meal. Now bow your heads. Dear Lord, thank you for this fine meal that you have placed before us today. Thank you for our many blessings. And Lord, we especially thank you for my dear husband and father of these fine children. Amen."

Not being the religious type, Jimmy squirmed in his chair and fidgeted with his fork. The boys did not waste a minute. They grabbed their pork chops off their plates and began to gnaw away like ravenous wolves. Jimmy helped himself to a wedge of cornbread and a crisp slice of onion. He then used his fork to stab some of the beans on his plate. Anne sat and ate her meal quietly. A smile crossed her lips as she watched her family devouring the meal she had lovingly prepared.

"You boys need to slow down before you choke or get the belly-ache," she said. "How were things at the shop today, James?"

He finished chewing a bite of the pork chop then took a drink of water. "Well, I have some sad news, assuming it's true. You remember me talking about Jim Bowie, who bought a couple of knives from me awhile back? It seems his young wife and precious children all died in a cholera outbreak in San Antonio. I'm sure he's devastated. I know I would be."

"Oh, James, how dreadful. How did you hear this?" Anne asked. "Are you sure it's true?"

"A traveler from Texas stopped by the shop today. He's on his way back east on some important business. It seems he's a courier for Governor Houston. The traveler recently attended some sort of constitutional convention held in a place called San Felipe. He said

Bowie was there along with Houston and Stephen Austin. Seems Bowie was still mourning the loss of his lovely wife and children. The courier had asked Bowie about the large knife strapped to his side. Bowie told him I made it for him, so he stopped by the shop to buy one for himself. Bowie told him the knife had saved his life in East Texas, where he was attacked by three assassins."

"Do you believe the man?" asked Anne.

"The traveler had no reason to make up such a story. And he sure did know a great deal about Bowie," her husband replied.

"Poor man," mumbled Anne. "I'll say a prayer for him. How could he put something like that behind him so soon?"

"I honestly don't know. I think life would no longer be worth living. But Jim Bowie, he's a different sort. The man seems to thrive on adversity. Nothing seems to get him down. When he's in difficult situations – and he's been in several – he's at his best."

Jimmy pushed his empty plate away. The boys had cleaned theirs as well. "Now, how about some of that apple cobbler? It shore does smell good. How 'bout it, boys? You ready for some cobbler?" The boys nodded their heads in agreement.

Anne went to the hearth and used a metal hook to lift the lid off the Dutch oven. The steam rose from the cast-iron pot filling the room with the smell of cinnamon and apples. The boys were squirming in their chairs, waiting to dig into the sweet concoction. Anne used a big wooden spoon to dip each a bowl of dessert. As they gobbled down their cobbler, the only sound was that of spoons clanking against the sides of the dishes. Black sat quietly, thinking about Bowie. *What pushes a man like Bowie? How does he keep going after such adversity? God only knows. I wish I had a tenth of his strength.*

"Boys, it's almost time for bed. Go get ready for bed. I'll come up to the loft shortly to tell you a story. Now git."

Anne began taking away the dishes to be washed and put away in the cupboard. After the boys left the room, Jimmy said to Anne, "there's something else that the traveler told me. He said the men attending the constitutional convention had signed a resolution for Texas to declare its independence from Mexico. Austin agreed to carry the document to Mexico City. Sounds like a battle for Texas independence is nigh at hand. I suspect Bowie will be right in the middle of it. The man never runs from a fight. He seems drawn to conflict as a moth to a flame. I best get up to the loft and tell the boys a story, or we'll not hear the end of it."

Fall 1834

Chapter 30

Two men on horseback followed by a lone man in a Dearborn wagon slowly and arduously made their way down the Southwest Trail towards the frontier town of Washington. It was mid-morning on a sunny fall day. The leaves of the trees in the vast hardwood forests were turning warm shades of burnt umber, orange, mustard, and fiery red. The two men on horseback rode in silence as they made the best of the time-consuming and challenging journey. All were tired and hungry. The young man driving the wagon concentrated on keeping up with the two horsemen. Judge Cross of Marlbrook Plantation was escorting an important visitor to the territory -- George W. Featherstonhaugh, who was on U.S. Government business rode along beside the Judge. Featherstonhaugh's son of the same name was driving the wagon and team.

The Judge broke the silence. "Only you Red Coats could possibly pronounce your name as 'Fanshaw.' The spelling's nothing like that."

"How quickly you colonists have lost your grasp of the King's English," said Featherstonhaugh.

"Mind if I call you G.W.?" asked Cross. "Rolls off the tongue a might easier."

"If you insist. By the way, I'm beginning to believe the hearsay back east about this so-called Military Road."

"What might that be?" asked Judge Cross. "I relish any news from Washington City."

"President Jackson signed into law, several military acts to pay for improvements to this miserable rabbit trail," said Featherstonhaugh. "It's rumored that Old Hickory wished to kill two birds with one stone. Publicly, he pressed Congress to improve this road in preparation for moving the Civilized Tribes to the western part of this territory. Privately, he's aiding his old friend Sam Houston's efforts to overthrow the Mexican Government in Texas. With an improved road, Virginians, Kentuckians and Tennesseans would hopefully find the treacherous overland journey to Texas a might easier."

"By Jehoshaphat, that was money well spent," chuckled Judge Cross.

"Precisely why I'm now inclined to believe the hearsay. The payments also served as a bounty enticing poor settlers to make the journey south of the Red River where large tracts of land can be bought on the cheap. Political chicanery on a grand scale by the President to simply encourage squatters and freebooters to aid Houston's cause."

"Sounds plausible," replied Judge Cross. "But isn't the official position of the U.S. Government to oppose any subversive activities toward the Mexican Government?"

"Yes," said G.W. "For many reasons, not the least being fear by the Northern States that Texas will upset the balance of power in Congress by becoming a future slave state."

"Enough about politics for now. What led to your appointment as the first geologist of these United States?" asked Judge Cross as they rode along a section of the old trail barely wide enough for the Dearborn wagon to traverse. Here, the many travelers down the ancient road had worn a wide gash through the hill. Over thousands of years, herds of buffalo, ancient Indians, and now European settlers traversed the clay and crushed shell hill, slowly eroding away the surface. On either side, dirt embankments rose above their heads, exposing the roots of trees growing on top.

As they rode along, Featherstonhaugh scanned the embankments looking for rock outcroppings or fossils. "I was born in England but grew up on the North Sea in a town near York. As a child, I would climb the nearby cliffs in search of bird eggs and fossils. After my studies, I became a fellow in the Geological Society and the Royal Society of London. Being the restless soul that I am, I moved to the United States shortly after the Louisiana Purchase intending to study the languages of Native Indian tribes. Recently, I was appointed as the first U.S. geologist by the War Department, which sent me here to study the minerals and natural resources of the elevated land between the Missouri and Red Rivers. Hence, I find myself in your presence on the edge of this vast western frontier."

"So what is your impression of Arkansas thus far?" asked Cross.

"Candidly, my encounters with some of the inhabitants of this territory have proved far more interesting than my geological observations," said Featherstonhaugh. "Granted, I was not commissioned to study the region's inhabitants, but, my observations will undoubtedly make it into my journal."

"Care to share some of your more interesting encounters thus far?" asked the Judge.

"Without a doubt, the Barkman clan near Magnet Cove is at the top of my list. I had heard tales of travelers' compasses going haywire due to some magnetic disturbance near a settlement lying near the confluence of the Washita and Caddo Rivers. We decided to swing by Magnet Cove on our way to the Hot Springs, lying further to the west. There, we sought out overnight accommodations at the home of a well-known trader in the area by the name of Barkman. After a tiring journey up the Washita fighting our way through dense canebrakes, we stumbled onto a most unexpected sight – a brick house standing in a clearing on the riverbank. Mr. Barkman was not home, but we did meet his unforgettable wife. It seems Barkman's wife was the daughter of a hunter in the area by the name of Davis. The locals call her old Davis's 'She-Bar.' Beyond her nickname, there was nothing ladylike about her. She drank whiskey, smoked a pipe, chewed tobacco, cursed and swore more heartily than any four of the worst scoundrels – doing all of these in rapid succession. I was told she was much refined now compared to her younger years before she was married. That's a picture I shan't soon forget."

"You seem surprised to encounter such folk here on the frontier?" queried Judge Cross. "After all, we are a long way from civilization, G.W."

"No, not really surprised," said Featherstonhaugh. "Stories back east prepared me for what I might encounter here in Arkansas. The frontier's a hard, dangerous place. I fully expected to find people here of such character."

As the riders made it over the crest of the hill, a large stream came into view. The horsemen and wagon made their way down the gentle slope and stopped at the edge of the stream. The bed of the stream was strewn with rocks and small boulders. There was no bridge. On the other side of the rapidly flowing stream was a dense, head-high, cane break.

"This is the Caddo River," said Judge Cross. "We should be able to cross the stream without too much difficulty today. Fortunately, we haven't had rain in these parts in about a month."

A disturbance downstream suddenly got the trio's attention. The men turned their heads left just in time to see a large black bear galloping across the stream, his massive paws striking the water as he ran. Upon reaching the far side of the stream, the bear ran into the cane break, causing the tops of the can to snap to and fro. Off in the distance, the men heard the distinct sound of a pack of hound dogs in hot pursuit of the big animal.

"Aaargh, aaargh, aaargh, aaargh!"

"Aaoooo, aaooo, aaooo!"

"Yawp, yawp, yawp...yawp, yawp, yawp!"

From the distinctive sounds of the yapping dogs, there were at least six or eight hounds on the trail of the fleeing bear. The barking of the dogs got louder as they approached the place in the stream where the bear had recently crossed. The lead dog was a large bluish, gray speckled and spotted hound. The blue-tick hound slowed at the edge of the Caddo River. With his nose close to the ground, he sniffed the riverbank. The hound ran back and forth next to the riverbank, sniffing and barking. After catching up with the leader, the other dogs slowed their pace at the water's edge. Each dog wandered in circles, smelling the rocks and grass, yapping incessantly. Suddenly, the lead dog darted into the stream and began to slosh his way towards the far bank. The other hounds quickly followed suit. When the lead dog reached the other side, he locked onto the scent of the bear and was off. The other dogs picked up the trail in no time.

The astute judge had been keeping watch upstream to the right, thinking the wily old bear might re-cross the river in an attempt to throw the hounds of his scent. Sure enough, about a quarter of a mile upstream, Judge Cross made out the shape of the black bear crossing back onto the northeast side of the river. "That's a sly, old bear, gentlemen. He just crossed back to this side of the river about a quarter-mile upstream of us." As the men stood observing the hunt in front of them, a man on foot ran out of the trees downstream to the spot where the dogs had crossed a few minutes earlier. Judge Cross put his hands together in front of his mouth and let out a loud "oooh!"

The hunter following the dogs looked in the direction of the judge and the other two men. Judge Cross waved his arm in the air and then pointed upstream from where he was sitting on his horse. "The bear's back on this side!" he yelled.

The hunter rapidly trotted towards the three men. As the hunter approached, Featherstonhaugh recognized the man. "I say, aren't you a brother to the woman called 'She-Bar' who lives north of here?" he asked.

The winded hunter stood trying to catch his breath. Then he spits a large dark stream of tobacco juice onto the ground in front of him. "That's rat, mister. Name's Davis. And you's that Anglish feller here looking fer rocks. Find any yet?" he laughed as he stared at the rocks covering the scene around them.

Featherstonhaugh was not amused.

She-Bar's brother was dressed in leather head to toe made from skins of animals he'd killed. Slung over his right shoulder was his heavy long-rifle, over his left hung a fringed, leather knapsack, and around his neck, hung a powder horn. On his left side, hanging from his belt, was a large knife housed in a leather scabbard. On his head, he wore a coonskin cap. His feet were clad in leather moccasins. His hands were dirty, and he was sweating profusely. He reached in his knapsack and pulled out a plug of dark, brownish-black tobacco. Biting the plug, he tore off a sizeable portion and commenced chewing. "So you saw that ol' bar crossed upstream?" asked Davis.

"Yes," said Judge Cross. "We first saw the bear as he crossed over the river near where you came into the clearing. Your dogs went across in hot pursuit. Just as the dogs crossed over to the other side, I saw the bear cross back to this side about a quarter-mile yonder," as he pointed to his right.

"That old sow's a smart 'un. My dogs been trackin' her pert-near all mornin'," said Davis. "'Nough of the chit-chat. I got me a bar to kill."

"Care if we tag along, old chap? My son and I've never been on a bar...er...bear hunt before," said Featherstonhaugh.

"So long as you don't git in my way or that bar's," said Davis. "One of us might hurt ya. You best leave them horses here. They spook easily at the sight of a bar." Davis turned north and was off at a rapid pace.

The two men quickly dismounted, and young Featherstonhaugh climbed down off the wagon. They tied the horses to some nearby saplings. As they headed in the direction pursued by Davis, they saw the pack of hound dogs making their way back across the river. Once on the north side of the river, the dogs quickly picked up the scent of the bear and continued their pursuit. Davis joined right on their tail. The three other men scurried to catch up and filed in behind the yapping dogs. The dogs trailed the bear for another half-hour or so. Suddenly, the low-toned baying sound made by the dogs hunting the bear turned into a series of short, high-pitched yelps followed by fierce growling.

"Let's hurry, gents. I believe the hounds have run the bear to ground," said Judge Cross.

The three men moved through the dense undergrowth as fast as possible. The limbs and thorn-covered vines tugged and tore at their clothes and exposed skin. Up ahead, they could now make out the sounds of dogs growling mixed with the sounds of the angry bear. The three men hurried on, finally breaking free of the thicket into a small clearing. The old bear was backed against a rocky bluff. The pack of hounds ringed around the cornered bear. Davis was standing close by calling encouragement to the dogs. "Get him, Blue, get him!"

The dogs inched closer and closer to the bear. The bear became more agitated as the minutes past, growling and swatting its front paws at the dogs. The old blue hound led the charge and went around to the left of the bear. Blue lunged at the bear's hind legs. The bear turned its head and swatted its big paw at Blue, just missing the dog. A black and tan hound ran at the bear's right haunch, nipping at the bear. The bear turned quickly, catching the dog with its big paw, sending it flying and yelping in agony. The black and tan hound landed on the ground with a thud. Three or four of the dogs moved in close to the bear, barking, and growling.

A white dog with a big black spot on its side lunged at the bear from the front. The bear reared up on its hind legs at that instant. The white dog dove into the chest of the bear, which quickly hugged the dog with its front paws. The bear grabbed the dog on the back of its neck with its powerful jaws, shook its head back and forth violently, then slung the dog about five feet in the air. The dog fell lifeless to the ground a few feet away.

Davis suddenly dropped his rifle to the ground, unsheathed his large knife, and moved up to the right of the bear. All of the dogs were barking, growling, and running at the bear. Davis yelled a command at Blue. Blue went around the left side of the bear again and lunged at the bear's hindquarter. Blue bit into the bear's back leg. Just as the bear turned on Blue, Davis jumped astride the bear from the back and sunk his knife hilt-deep into the bear's neck and throat. The bear let out a loud growl and then stumbled forward with Davis hanging on for dear life. The bear fell forward onto its belly into the rocks and dirt, not moving. The pack of dogs moved in for the kill, but the bear was dead. Davis climbed off the bear and called his dogs to his side.

The three men stood silently for a few minutes in a state of shock over what they had just witnessed. Finally, they moved forward to where Davis was standing, catching his breath and calming his dogs. Davis was looking a bit pale and appeared to be choking on something.

"Are you hurt, son?" Judge Cross asked Davis.

"I reckon not. Jes' swallowed my tobaccy in the middle of that scuffle. Guess I won't be wormy for a while," said Davis.

"I have never witnessed anything like that in my life," said Featherstonhaugh. "Fascinating. Why didn't you use your rifle on the beast?"

"It's like this. Two things can go wrong when you use a rifle in that situation. The gun can misfire. Or the ball can miss the mark, and the bear could have kilt me or two or three of my dogs. He done got one of my best dogs and hurt another. The knife seemed best to me at the time. Hard to beat a knife in a close fight," said Davis. "Can't afford to lose another one of my bar dogs. They's worth more than gold to me. You fellers ever eat any bar meat?"

The Judge nodded yes, and the Featherstonhaughs said, "no."

"We'll if'n ya'll help me get this bar skin't and cut up, we'll feast on some bar meat tonight. I growed up eating it. Once you taste fat bar meat, you can't get enough. I guess it's cause bars eat acorns and berries and such that makes it taste so good. Now one o' you go fetch one of the horses and bring him here. I'll make us a sled, and we'll haul the carcass down to where yore wagon is. Bring back a pick and shovel too. Need to bury my dog where he died. The other two of you go pitch camp down by the river. Gather some far wood. We'll camp here tonight."

* * *

After he skinned the bear carcass, Davis cut it into sections. He carved out some tender pieces and fed his dogs well. The dogs devoured the meat and lay around the camp, licking their front paws. The sections that were not needed for supper were hauled up into a nearby tree to protect it from wild animals and the dogs.

The fire, having been built for some time, had created a nice pile of hot coals – better for cooking than an open flame. A pot of beans sat steaming on a rock on the edge of the campfire. Davis used a large, cast-iron skillet to pan-fry the greasy bear meat. Davis served everyone a heaping helping of beans and "bar" before serving himself. Young Featherstonhaugh was gracious enough to share some of his precious coffee to cap off the feast. It had been a long day. The men were tired but famished and made short work devouring the hearty meal. Davis was pleased to see everyone enjoying his favorite meat.

"Well, how was it?" asked Davis.

"Splendid," said Featherstonhaugh. "Truly a feast fit for a king."

"Words fail me," said Judge Cross.

Featherstonhaugh looked at the Judge, unsure if the Judge was paying the cook a backhanded compliment. *Remember never to play poker with the Judge*, G.W. thought to himself. The Judge pulled out a handsomely carved burl pipe, packed it with tobacco then, lit it with a twig from the fire. The Judge sat quietly, puffing his pipe.

The junior Featherstonhaugh said to Davis, "You cooked, I'll clean." Junior gathered up all the dishes, went to the rear of the wagon, and began cleaning up.

"More coffee?" said Davis to the other two men.

"Don't mind if I do," said the Judge.

"Here, here," said G.W.

Davis poured their cups full of the dark brew, the steam rising in the cool, fall-night air. It was just past sunset. A large, blood-red moon hung in the sky, illuminating wispy, willowy clouds slowly drifting across the night sky. The bright moon cast shadows on the ground.

The Judge stared up at the moon as he puffed on his pipe. "I believe some call that a Hunter's Moon," he said.

"Fitting," said G.W., "after what we saw today. Again, one of the most amazing feats I've witnessed in my life. Man against beast. Quite remarkable. Pray tell us about yourself?" said G.W. to Davis.

Davis threw more twigs on the fire, keeping one sprig in his hand, which he used to poke at the glowing embers. "You think that bar hunt today was somethin'?" said Davis. "Y'all should hear some of my Pa's tales. They'd curl your hair. Some said they's whoppers. But I know'd better. He might stretch the truth a might now and then. Pa once fought an angry buffalo with nutin' but a knife for nigh on all day. Buffalo is easier to kill in the herd. You get one of them big critters off by itself, and Katie bar the door. You got a fight on your hands. Pa got a might too close to the critter after losing his rifle. The buffalo ran Pa up a young sapling, which is the only thin' that saved his life. All Pa had was an Arkansas toothpick like mine. That old bull would use his big head and horns to push on that tree a tryin' to knock Pa out. Pa'd swing down from that sapling, twirling 'round its spindly limbs like a monkey. He'd take a swipe at that old buffalo with his knife, cuttin' him all over the head and back. Finally, after several hours, the old critter laid down on the ground – all tuckered out from the loss of blood and just being tard, I reckon. Yessiree Bob, nobody tougher than my Pa. Taught me everthin' there is to know 'bout living out here on the frontier." Davis stared into the fire and grew silent for a moment as if in deep in thought.

G.W. said to Davis, "Mind if I have a look at your knife. It's different looking than the other knives I've seen men carrying in these parts."

Davis unsheathed his knife, grabbed it by the blade and gave it handle-first to G.W. "Careful, it's sharp as a razor," he said. "Had that there knife for several years. It holds an edge like no other knife I ever owned. I can chop clean through a piece of wood, and it'll still shave the hair off my arm."

G.W. looked the knife over from every angle, admiring the craftsmanship. "This is the most unique knife. I don't recall seeing one quite like it. How did you come by it, if I might ask?"

"Traded some hides fur it from a man travelin' to Little Rock. The man said he bought it from a blacksmith by the name of Black down in Washington."

Judge Cross piped in, "I know Black. He's been to my plantation before."

"I'd like to visit this Black while we're in Washington," said G.W. "Maybe he'll share some of his forging technique with us."

"You fellers headed to Texas?" asked Davis.

"We might venture across the Red River," said the judge. "I'll leave that up to the wishes of my guests. We plan to see the Red for sure."

"Might like to go to Texas, my own self," said Davis. "Sounds like my kind of place."

"How so?" said G.W.

"'Cause I heard there ain't no such thing as a government down thar and no varmint lawyers in the whole doggone place. Nobody there tryin' to steal a man's hard-earned land from him or accuse him of bein' a squatter."

"You're welcome to ride with us," said G.W. "We can use a man of your skill on our journey."

"That's a mighty tempting offer, Mr. G.W. I ain't never been nowhere further than 30 to 40 miles from my birthplace. I have a hankering to see some fur off places." Davis again staring into the fire quietly for a few minutes. "Naw, sir. Now's not the time. The bars are fattenin' up gettin' ready to hibernate. Can't leave my bar huntin' rat now."

"Very well. You may change your mind by morning. I think I shall retire for the evening," said G.W. "It's been an extraordinary day, but I find myself sinking fast."

"I'm plumb tuckered out myself," said Davis.

G.W., Junior, and the Judge climbed into the back of the wagon where their bedrolls awaited them. Davis lay down next to the fire and placed his knapsack beneath his head for a pillow. "You fellers sleep all cozy like in your wagon. My dogs 'll wake you if'n any bars or varmints venture close tonight," Davis chuckled.

* * *

At daybreak, the men in wagon awoke to find that Davis and his hounds had already cleared out. The coals in the fire pit still smoldered. After a quick breakfast and a short break in the nearby bushes, the men knelt by the cold Caddo river for a quick shave, face washing and teeth brushing. The water and weather were too brisk for a bath, so they saddled the horses and hitched the team of oxen to the wagon, then forged the Caddo River. The trio continued their journey from the previous day in a southwesterly direction down the Military Road towards Washington.

Chapter 31

Mid-afternoon, six days later.

The two horsemen and the wagon rode into Washington. The streets bustled with activity for such a small town on the edge of nowhere. The men rode up to Elijah Stuart's Tavern for accommodations only to learn it had no vacancies. Stuart directed the travelers to the Black Bear Tavern instead.

After securing rooms at Black Bear, each man paid for a hot bath and a shave. They met up in the Tavern groggery for drinks and supper. The groggery, as expected, was noisy, smokey, and fragrant with the body odor of patrons who had not bathed in awhile. Serious poker games were underway at a couple of the tables. Most everyone was drinking or drunk. The three men found a table in the corner and sat down. A young boy of about thirteen walked up to take their orders.

"Do you serve tea?" asked G.W.

"Yes, sir," said the lad. "It's black tea."

"Very well, tea it is," said G.W.

"Rum for me," said Junior. Judge Cross nodded his agreement with Junior.

A few minutes later, the young boy returned with the drinks. As he placed the mugs in front of the men, he asked, "Y'all in town to play cards with Governor Houston? Most strangers in town are."

"No, son, we're here on other business," said Judge Cross. "This is George Featherstonhaugh and his son. Mr. Featherstonhaugh is the first U.S. Geologist on a military expedition to the Territory to study our minerals."

The young waiter had no response. He turned and faced another table where the patrons were loudly shouting, "more rum."

"Young man, do you have any sugar to go with my tea?" asked G.W.

"Huh...uh...I'll check, sir. Sugar's hard to come by, but we may have some honey," said the waiter as he scurried away.

"Well, that explains why they're no rooms at Stuart's Tavern," said Judge Cross. "Houston is back from Texas. He purports to gamble and drink all night. Such a facade. No doubt there's much drinking and some card play but, most locals know what he's up to."

"As does Old Hickory, I suspect," said G.W. "The President puts up a convincing front that he opposes a Texas revolt. Publicly, reminding us we're at peace with Mexico and any act of sedition against Mexico is a violation of the neutrality act. But many question his sincerity. His desire for Texas is widely known. He tried to buy Texas for one million dollars, but Mexico rebuffed him. Old Hickory may be called a lot of names, but 'quitter' is not one of them."

"Quitter? Old Hickory? Nope, I agree with you there," said Cross. "Our territorial governor has adopted the party line for the time being. He's let it be known anyone supporting an insurrection in Texas is breaking the law."

"You being a man of the bar, are you familiar with the neutrality act, Judge?" asked G.W.

"Only vaguely," said the Judge.

"Houston's been back east seeking financial aid and recruiting settlers willing to relocate to Texas. Some barristers...er...lawyers have advised those willing to meet with Houston that in so doing, they're not breaking the law. These counselors say the neutrality act only forbids men from joining a military group intent on engaging in a revolt. From the looks of the number of pioneers in town, it appears his efforts have been successful. I've heard he's found a large number of sympathizers in the southern states of Georgia and Alabama. Not surprising, really. Wealthy planters see the potential for Texas to become its own country where slaves can be imported again. Not constrained by the U.S. law prohibiting such. Or at the very least, the largest slave state in the Union."

"Well, we certainly wouldn't want that to happen, now would we?" said Judge Cross sarcastically.

"I say old chap, I forgot that you are a slaveholder," said G.W. "I did not wish to offend you. Please accept my sincere apology."

"Good show, Father," said Junior. "No one will ever call you a diplomat."

"What say we order some supper?" said G.W. "We're weary from the long trek down that wide game trail, and tempers are flaring. Judge Cross can show us around town tomorrow. And I wish to pay a visit to that smithy. I believe his name is Black. Yes, James Black."

* * *

The three men slept a little later than usual, rising about an hour past sunrise. After the morning constitutional, a quick shave and dressing, they ate a hearty breakfast consisting of hominy grits, fried eggs, a rasher of thick, smoked bacon, and several cups of black coffee. Judge Cross then took them around town and introduced G.W. and Junior to his many friends in town.

Mid-afternoon, the three finally made their way to Black's shop. As they rode up to the blacksmith shop, Black was out front talking with Dan, his assistant. Black made eye contact with the Judge and broke off his conversation. "Judge Cross, what brings you to town? It's been too long. How're things at Marlbrook?"

"Fine, just fine, Jimmy. Good to see you. Word around town is that your business is booming. I was telling these gentlemen on the way here about how you and Dr. Jones formed your partnership at a corn husking at my plantation. Er...how rude of me. Allow me to introduce my guests. This is George W. Featherstonhaugh and his son, George, Junior." The judge continued with the introductions. "On our journey here, we ran across a bear hunter near the Caddo River, who was carrying one of your knives. We witnessed the hunter downing a bear with the help of that knife and a pack of hounds. G.W. wished to make your acquaintance and talk knife making. So here we are."

"Welcome to Washington, gentlemen," said the blacksmith. "This is my able assistant, Dan. Would you all care for a cup of coffee?"

"Jimmy, I'll pass on the coffee. I'm going back into town. Have some business to transact with one of the attorneys in town. I'll leave the Featherstonhaughs in your capable hands for a while if that's okay with you?"

"Of course," said Black. "Let's go inside and get that coffee. Dan just made a fresh pot. Then we can talk about my knife making. Hope you like your coffee on the strong side." As Judge Cross headed toward town, the four men went inside the shop. "Have a seat, gentlemen," as he directed them to cane-bottom chairs placed near a large cast-iron stove. Dan grabbed a pot from atop the stove and poured each a steaming cup of coffee. "Did you see anything interesting in town today?" asked Jimmy.

"We met a doctor today by the name of Nathan Smith," replied Junior. "He raises mulberry trees on which he grows silkworms. He then uses silk from the worms to stitch up his patients. I never expected to find that out here on the edge of the frontier."

"I'm guessing you expected to find a bunch of rough-hewn, downtrodden folks or outlaws here. Am I right?"

"Quite," said G.W. "And we've seen our fair share of those, to be sure."

"Were you surprised at the number of doctors, lawyers, judges, and merchants we have here in Washington?" asked Black.

"Yes, indeed. That was rather unexpected," said G.W., "given the stories we heard back east."

"Have you found any interesting rocks or minerals on your trip?" asked Black.

"I haven't found any gold or silver if that's what you mean," said G.W. We have observed some exciting geological features, though. We visited the Hot Springs lying north of here. Quite a fascinating geological feature it is. The water from multiple artesian springs must come into contact with some volcanic fissure deep in the earth. The Indians that once dwelled there and now the current white occupants believe the hot waters have healing power to cure all forms of ailments. Then Judge Cross took us across one the fields on his plantation where we found fossils of ancient sea creatures – crustaceans and cephalopods – very similar to those I observed back in England."

"If you're interested in shell fossils, you need to visit a place about thirty miles west of here. I've seen it with my own eyes," said Jimmy. "A little south of the Fort Towson road. There's a white bluff there on the north bank of the Little River. The high bluff is made of some sort of chalky, soft rock. The ground at the base of the cliff is covered with seashell-shaped rocks. The Indians must have believed it to be some sort of sacred ground as large burial mounds are lying between the bluff and the river."

"Hmm…sounds like a limestone bluff similar to the White Cliffs back in England," said G.W. "That would certainly make sense given what I know about this area. This part of the territory once lay beneath a shallow sea. Limestone forms in a shallow sea. We should make an effort to travel there," G.W. said to Junior as he drank the last of his coffee.

"Care for more coffee?" asked Dan.

"None for me," said G.W. "So what prompted you to start making knives?" as he looked at Black.

"That's a long story," said Jimmy. "The short answer is this. A lot of travelers pass through town on their way to Texas. Shortly after I moved here and went to work for my father-in-law as a blacksmith, pioneers passing through would ask if we had knives for sale. We did not. I tried my hand at knife making in my spare time more to see if I could. You see, I was a silversmith's apprentice in my youth in Philadelphia. I eventually made my way to New Orleans, where I worked for an old Creole knife maker who had learned his skills from his Spanish grandfather. Through trial and error, I developed my own technique. Then life took one of its interesting twists. A man named Jim Bowie stopped in the shop one day. He showed me a wood carving of a knife he wanted me to make him. I made one like his model and a similar knife with a few of my own alterations. Jim liked them both. As fate would have it, three would-be assassins attacked Jim down in the Texas piney woods. He dispatched all three with nothing but his knife. Well, sir, after word spread throughout these parts about Bowie and the knife I made him, I can't make knives fast enough to meet demand."

"Bowie. Yes, I've heard tales about Bowie," said G.W. "Mostly the one about the dual on the Mississippi sandbar. So when's the last time you saw this Bowie fellow?"

"About a year ago. Jim was in town to meet up with Sam Houston here in Washington. The two men, along with some others, rode to Texas together. Last time I saw Jim."

"Interesting," mumbled G.W. "So Houston and Bowie appear to be compatriots in their cause. Do you have any of these 'Bowie' knives on hand? I'd like to see one."

"You're in luck. I just put the finishing touches on one," said Black. He retrieved a knife about a foot and a half in length from a nearby table. Jimmy meticulously explained the unique features of the weapon to Featherstonhaugh. He then handed the knife to G.W., who held the knife in his right hand and flexed his wrist as if feeling its balance.

"The design's sort of a cross between a Scottish dirk and a Spanish navaja," said Black.

"It seems you two have collaborated to create a distinctive American weapon perfectly suited for life on the frontier. Can you tell me how you go about making such a knife?" asked G.W.

"It's a multi-step process – takes me about a week to complete. I've gained some efficiency by working on small batches. But still, it's a labor-intensive process."

"What's the secret to your tempering of the metal?" the visitor asked. "The bear hunter up the road told us his knife would hold its edge after rigorous use."

"Well, Mr. Featherstonhaugh, if I were to tell you about that, I'd have to kill you. That's my trade secret."

G.W. stood with his mouth agape, not expecting such an answer.

"I'm joshing, Mr. Featherstonhaugh. Not everyone in Arkansas is a ruffian or outlaw. Even if I were to tell you my process, step by step, I doubt you could actually repeat it. It's sort of like having a famous artist show you how to paint a masterpiece. It looks easy till you pick up the brush."

"Point taken," said G.W. as he handed the knife back to Black. "By the way, were you aware Bowie's confederate, Governor Houston, is back in town?"

"Not much goes on in a small town without everyone knowing it."

"Do folks here really believe he's simply in town to playing games of chance and drinking all night?" asked G.W.

"Maybe the first time he was here, but not now. It's commonly known he's plotting to take Texas away from Mexico."

"Are most of the locals' sympathizers with Houston's cause?" asked Featherstonhaugh.

"I can't speak for most," replied Jimmy.

"Can't or won't?" quizzed Featherstonhaugh. Not pausing for an answer, he continued. "I, for one, am not. These freebooters oppose governmental authority of any kind. They despise the ruling class. That's one of my major dislikes about this country – the breakdown of the class system prevalent in England and Europe."

"No disrespect, Mr. Featherstonhaugh, but that's what makes this country great. A person's only limitations are the size of his dreams and his willingness to pursue them. I'm living proof that by hard work, a can-do attitude, and a little luck, a person can change his status in life – sometimes rather dramatically."

"A class system has benefits for society. It provides stability and order," said Featherstonhaugh. "It mirrors nature – birds of a feather flock together."

"Our system seems to be functioning pretty darn well," said Black. "You chose to move here for some reason, Mr. Featherstonhaugh. And why was that?"

"If your system is so great, how do you justify slavery?"

"I never said it's perfect. Perhaps slavery will be abolished someday. Many are pushing for that," said Jimmy.

"Tt's growing late Junior, and we should retire to Black Bear Tavern for the evening."

"Be on your guard there," said Black. "Black Bear seems to attract a rowdy clientele. Or the crowd may simply reflect the owner's attitudes."

"Thanks for the bit of advice," said Junior. "I trust my father's bluntness has not offended you."

"Not in the least," said Black. "Free speech is a right in this country, thanks to our Constitution."

"Your knives are most impressive," said G.W.

"Please take this knife with you," said Black. "Consider it a gift." Black handed the knife and a leather sheath to Featherstonhaugh. Featherstonhaugh stood speechless, his mouth agape, but no words escaped.

"It's a rare occasion to see my father speechless," said Junior.

"I'm indeed honored and humbled," said Featherstonhaugh. "How can I repay you?"

"Just do this. When you submit your report to your superiors, remember to report that we are not all scalawags here in Arkansas. And one more thing, do not engage in a knife fight if you can avoid it. Simply having this weapon does not make you a Jim Bowie."

Junior let out a loud chuckle. "Good advice, Mr. Black. Father does think highly of his defensive skills. I hope he heeds your warning." The two men exited the blacksmith shop, mounted their horses, and rode off in the direction of Black Bear Tavern.

* * *

After entering the tavern, the proprietor handed a note to G.W. The letter informed him that Judge Cross had accepted an invitation for dinner at the home of a friend and would not be joining the Featherstonhaughs until the following morning at breakfast. The Featherstonhaughs decided to have some rum before dinner. The tavern was full, so the two sat at a table of strangers. After the exchange of introductions, G.W. learned that the other men at the table were local residents.

After several rounds of rum, the conversation eventually turned to discuss the real reason Sam Houston was hold up at Stuart's Tavern. Featherstonhaugh being Featherstonhaugh, loudly proclaimed his distaste for insurrectionists and freebooters. He went on a tirade that Houston had disgraced himself enough by humiliating his young wife back in Tennessee with his philandering and drunkenness, resigning his office as the duly elected governor of Tennessee and then fleeing to live with the Cherokee Indians in Arkansas Territory. G.W. and Junior failed to take notice of two men seated at a table next to them that seemed content to drink rather slowly, not talking but intently listening to the conversation at the table next to them. After dinner, the Featherstonhaughs stumbled up the stairs to their meager beds on the second floor of the tavern.

* * *

The following morning.

Judge Cross was seated at a table reading a back edition of the *Arkansas Gazette* printed in Little Rock, the territorial capital. G.W. was the first to join the Judge for breakfast.

"You look pale, G.W.," said the Judge. "Are you ill?"

"My head feels like I was kicked by my horse," mumbled G.W. "Too much John Barleycorn, I'm afraid. I suppose that's why Junior has not made it downstairs yet."

"Shall we wait to order our breakfast till Junior shows?" asked the Judge.

"I need something on my stomach," said G.W. "Junior can order when he arrives."

"Very well," said the Judge. He waved his arm in the air to get the attention of the man behind the bar.

The man walked up. "Morning. Name's McSwaim. I'm the proprietor of the tavern. Y'all care for coffee?"

"Yes, and lots of it," said G.W.

McSwaim returned with two tin cups of steaming coffee. "Are you Featherstonhaugh?" he said, looking at G.W.

"I am."

"Not trying to pry into your business, but are you here on a military expedition?" asked McSwaim.

"I am. Why do you ask?"

"I'm telling you this because you're a paying customer. Last night, two men sat near your table and overheard your conversation. They were asking a lot of questions after you, and the other one went to bed. The men are associates of Governor Houston's. They think you're here spying for the Federal authorities back in Washington City. You might want to watch your backside. That's all I'm saying. Now about breakfast, we're serving ham, eggs, and grits. That suit you?"

"We'll both have that. And keep the coffee coming," said the Judge.

McSwaim turned and headed out the side door of the tavern.

"Sounds like you got a little free with your opinion last night," said Cross.

"I've seen all I need to see here," said G.W. "Will you accompany us down to Fulton, then briefly south of the Red River? I've come this far and would like to at least set foot on Texas soil just to see what all the fuss is about."

"I suppose so," said the Judge. "Although the fee for my services just escalated to that of hazardous duty pay."

G.W. did not laugh at the Judge's feeble attempt at humor. McSwaim returned with two plates of food. Then brought the men more coffee. The two made short work of the morning meal. Just as G.W. took the last bite of ham, Junior joined them.

"You need to eat quickly, Junior. We're leaving town right after breakfast. No time for questions. I'll explain after we get on the road," said G.W.

Summer 1835

Chapter 32

"Papa, come home quick! Mama's gonna have the baby," said Billy. "Please, Papa, ya' need to come now. Mama won't get outta bed. She just lies there moanin' and cryin'."

Jimmy Black, who sat at his desk, focused on paperwork, jerked his head upward, peering at his young son. "Okay, Billy. Mama will be okay. Let me tell Dan and Tom to close up shop, and we'll be on our way," he replied.

Black rose from his chair and walked from his office to the forge area where he found Dan and Tom working on some metal hooks. "Dan, I need you to close up shop today. Billy came to get me. It seems Anne's going into labor. I need to get home. I'll see you bright and early in the morning. Tom, can you get word to your mama that Anne's getting ready to deliver another grand-baby?"

"I'll take care of things here. Go tend to Anne," said Dan.

"I'll go tell Mama that Anne's going into labor," said Tom.

Jimmy grabbed his hat and took his son by the hand. "Let's go, Billy." Black opened the door, and he and the boy went outside to where his horse, Socks, was standing in the corral adjoining the shop. He led Socks by the halter underneath the lean-to where he kept the tack, took off the halter, and put on the bridle. Then he threw a saddle blanket over the horse's back, followed by the saddle which he snuggly girded in place. He opened the gate and led Socks outside the corral.

Black lifted Billy up and placed him on the front part of the saddle, and then he climbed on behind him. "Giddy up, Socks. Let's go to the house." Black kicked Socks gently in the side and made a clicking sound with his mouth. Socks cantered down the road towards home.

In no time, the two were riding up to their home. The elder Black swiftly jumped down off Socks, then lifted his son to the ground. Billy ran into the house, yelling, "Papa's here, Mama. Everything 'i'll be alright now!" Black tied Socks to the front porch post, entered the house, and quickly made his way to the bedroom. Two young boys and one young girl were standing by the bedside, tears streaming down their little faces. A boy toddler sat in a nearby crib, sucking on a sugar-teat. Anne was lying on the bed covered with a quilt. She was moaning loudly and mumbling unintelligible words. Her complexion was chalky. She clenched and unclenched her teeth.

"Billy, go fetch Doc Smith. Tell him Anne's having the baby. The rest of you kids, go to the front room. Your mother needs her rest." Jimmy touched Anne's forehead with the back of his hand. Her skin was hot to the touch and clammy. "Anne, I'm here now. Are you thirsty? Can I get you some water to drink?" She moaned and moved her head side-to-side ever so slightly. "I sent Billy after the doctor. He'll be here soon and take care of you. Don't worry." *I hope that's true*, thought Black to himself. *I've never seen her like this during the birth of the other children.*

Jimmy sat down in the cane bottom chair near the bed and nervously waited. While he waited, he prayed out loud. "Lord, I've never been a religious one, but I need your help now more than ever. Please help my precious Anne deliver a healthy baby, and help her get through this. I need her, Lord. This family needs her. Meeting her and making her my wife was the best thing that ever happened to me. I know I'm a sinner and unworthy, but please, Lord, I beg you not to take her from me. I'm begging, Lord." Black sat quietly with tears rolling down his cheeks. *What's taking Doc so long?* Just then, he heard a buggy approaching the house.

Billy came running across the front porch, throwing open the door. "Doc Smith's here, Papa."

Doc Smith came walking into the bedroom, carrying a well-worn leather bag. The silver-haired doctor walked to the bed and grasped Anne's limp wrist, checking her pulse. "How long has Anne been like this?" he asked.

"Well, she was not feeling well last night," Jimmy said. "She only ate a few bites at supper. Said she felt tired and was a bit achy. Said she may have worked a bit too hard doing the wash and cleanin' house. Billy came and got me at the shop about an hour ago telling me she was unable to get out of bed."

Doc Smith looked over the spectacles perched on the end of his nose. "Looks like some sort of fever – not sure. You and the boy to step outside while I examine her. Get word to the Shaw house and have her mother come here. You'll need a woman's help around here for a few days."

"Doc, you know how things are between Shaw and me. I'm not sure he'll let Mrs. Shaw stay here to help us."

"She'll stay. Now send the child."

Jimmy and Billy left the bedroom and pulled the curtain closed that separated it from the main room. "Billy, run to your Grandma's house and tell her that Doc Smith wants her to come over. Tell her your mama is sick, and she needs to come quick. Your Uncle Tom was supposed to tell her Anne's ready to have the baby, but I don't want to take a chance on her coming over."

"Yes, Papa." The boy ran out the front door, the door slamming behind him. The Shaw house was several blocks away. It would take a while before the boy would return.

Jimmy sat by the fire and continued praying for Anne's recovery and that Shaw would not prevent his mother-in-law from coming to help. His nerves were getting the best of him. His mind was turning over all the possibilities of what could happen. *What will I do if Anne dies? How will I raise all these children and run a business without her? How can I live without her? She's my life. I live for her. I need to quit thinking the worst. Doc Smith will bring her through. God surely must answer my prayers.*

He decided to make a pot of coffee and have a smoke to calm his nerves. *I need to focus on something else.* He got up out of the chair, went over to the shelves in the kitchen and retrieved the coffee grinder and the heavy cast-iron kettle. He dumped some roasted coffee beans in the mill and proceeded to grind the beans. He then dumped the grounds into the pot, filled it with water, and placed it on a hook over the fire in the hearth to boil. He reached up to the mantle and grabbed his corncob pipe. He then retrieved a wooden bowl next to his pipe, removed the lid and scooped a bowl full of tobacco. He returned the container to the mantle, tamped down the tobacco with his thumb, and placed the pipe stem in his mouth. He grasped a long twig standing next to the hearth, lit the tip of the twig in the fire, and then lit his pipe, puffing rapidly.

Black returned to his chair by the fire, puffing his pipe and blowing smoke into the air, watching the wisps of smoke vanish into the air. *Life is like a wisp of smoke*, he thought. *We are here for a brief moment on this earth and then like smoke, we're gone without a trace...no...no... that's not really so. If we're lucky, we leave behind our children – our precious angels.* The sound of a horse and buggy approaching the house interrupted his thoughts.

He got up from his seat and went to the front door. Just as he opened the door, in ran Billy yelling, "Grandma's here, Papa. She's here to help Mama!"

Lizzie Shaw walked through the door to her daughter's home. "Hello, Jimmy. I came as quick as I could. Take me to her."

"Doc Smith's still examining her," he replied. "Let me take your coat." Black took his mother-in-law's shawl and hung it on a peg in the wall near the front door. "Doc should be out soon. How about a cup of coffee? I put on the kettle, and it should be boiling by now." He could see steam rising from the spout of the kettle hanging over the fire.

"Coffee will be fine," she replied, wringing her hands nervously. The tension in her voice was noticeable.

Jimmy grabbed a couple of tin cups from the cupboard and set them on the kitchen table. Returning to the cupboard, he retrieved a small crock bowl used to store eggshells. Taking a spoonful of the eggshells, Jimmy walked over to the hearth. Using a metal hook, he grabbed the metal arm holding the kettle and swung it from over the fire. Removing the lid, he dropped the eggshells into the boiling coffee to settle the grounds. Using a towel, he carried the pot to the kitchen table and poured the steaming coffee into the waiting cups. The smell of the fresh brew filled the air. Jimmy set a small container of sugar on the table.

Lizzie Shaw walked over to the table. Jimmy pulled back one of the ladder-back chairs, allowing her to sit, then gently pushed the chair closer to the table. She took a spoon and added some sugar to her cup of coffee, then gently stirred, allowing the coffee to cool. The two adults sat silently for a minute or two, sipping their coffee.

Finally, Jimmy broke the silence. "I'm afraid," he said, his voice quivering slightly. "Anne seems very ill. I've never seen her like this with the delivery of the other young 'uns. I don't know what I'll do if something happens to her."

"We felt the same way when you took her from us a few years back. But I've seen how you've treated her over the years. You're a good husband and father, Jimmy. You've provided a good living for Anne and my precious grandchildren. I only wish that William would admit that. His heart is filled with such hatred for you. I truly thought he would've changed by now. A more prideful, stubborn man I've never known." She bowed her head briefly. When she raised her head, tears were rolling down her cheeks.

"What did her father say when you told him you were coming here?" said Black.

"I could see the concern on his face when he heard Anne was having difficulty. He didn't try to stop me. I think he's relieved I was coming to check on her."

Jimmy stood and fetched the kettle from the fire and refilled his cup. "Would you like some more?" he asked Elizabeth.

"Not now – maybe later," she said.

Jimmy put the kettle back on the hanger and positioned it near the fire, then returned to his chair. "Does he not realize how many women die giving birth? Does he not wish to see her?"

"I know he's very concerned. I'm surprised he didn't come with me. I think he's ashamed of the way he's treated her...and you...and the whole family for all these years. But he cannot admit he made a mistake. He would never admit that."

"So because of his stupid pride, he'll stay away while his daughter lies here...suffering? And he calls himself a God-fearing man? May God forgive him."

Just then, the curtain hung in the bedroom doorway parted, and Doc Smith walked out. He walked up to the table where the husband and mother were sitting. Jimmy rose from his chair.

"Hello, Lizzie," said Doc. "Glad you came to be with the family. Where's William?"

Elizabeth Shaw opened her mouth as if to speak, but no words came out. Doc shook his head side to side as he stared at the floor.

"Have a seat Doc. Care for some coffee?" said Jimmy.

"Suppose so – may have a long night ahead of me." He sat down at the table. Jimmy poured him a cup and placed it in front of him. Jimmy pushed the bowl of sugar in front of him. "No thanks," Doc replied – his face grim.

"How is she, Doc?" Jimmy asked reluctantly.

"She's pretty sick. She has a fever...her pulse weak. Not sure what's wrong." Doc took a sip of his coffee. "All we can do at this stage is to pray. She's having early labor contractions – not close together yet. We need to get this baby delivered. Then let her rest. Maybe later we can get her to eat and drink a little. Lizzie, maybe you can make some chicken soup? Some broth would be good for her. This family will need something to eat in any event." He took another sip from his cup. "Jimmy, get a bucket of cold water from the well, and I'll keep a cold compress on her forehead. Only time will tell now." He took a large gulp of his coffee. "I'll stay with her as long as I can. I know it'll be hard but keep the young 'uns away from her. She needs rest for now." Doc took another long drink from his coffee cup. "I need to get back in there. Have to get this baby delivered. That will help Anne more than anything else I can do at this time." He got up from the table and headed back to the bedroom.

"Jimmy, go out in the yard and ring one of those hens' necks," said Lizzie Shaw. "I'm going to make y'all some of the best chicken soup you've ever put in your mouth. Now go on. You're not doing Anne or your kids any good moping around here. Tom will drop by soon. After we eat, I'll have Tom take the children over to my house. Grandpa and their aunts and uncles can spoil them for a bit. Besides, they don't need to be here while Anne's having the baby."

Before Jimmy went out to kill and pluck a chicken, he showed Lizzie where the cornmeal and other ingredients were stored. Then he went out back to wring the neck of the slowest chicken he could catch. A couple of hours later, Jimmy, Lizzie, and three of the children were all sitting down to a hot bowl of chicken soup with a side of steaming hot cornbread. The toddler was sitting in a high chair, chewing on the stewed chicken meet and mushy carrots. The kids ate heartily, and so did the adults even though they were all concerned about Anne. After they were done eating, the kids somehow talked their grandmother into a game of checkers by the fire. Tom arrived while the checker game was underway. With the kids distracted by the checker game, Jimmy filled Tom in on his sister's condition. Tom's visage clearly reflected his concern. After consuming some soup and cornbread, Tom loaded the children in Jimmy's wagon and headed back to the Shaw home. The sun was setting, and the western sky was a fiery red.

* * *

Loud moans and screams filled the house for several hours. Jimmy sat quietly by the fire, reading Anne's well-worn Bible. Finally, the piercing cries stopped, and the sound of a baby crying came from behind the curtain. Jimmy leaped from the chair as if shot. Lizzie stood at the ready with a clean blanket prepared to receive her newly born grandbaby. Doc Smith walked through the curtain with a tiny baby in his arms. He handed the baby to Lizzie, who quickly bundled it in the blanket.

"Jimmy, you're the proud papa of another beautiful baby girl," said Doc Smith. "The baby's healthy."

Jimmy stood next to Lizzie, ogling his baby girl. "How's Anne?" he pleaded.

Doc Smith stood quietly for a minute before answering. "I'm concerned. She's sleeping now, but she's frail. The delivery was hard on her. There's nothing else I can do but pray. You and Lizzie should make her comfortable and check on her frequently. See if you can get her to drink any water or chicken broth. Keep a cool compress on her head." The kind doctor retrieved his bag from the bedroom.

Jimmy handed him his hat. "Doc, I'll settle my account later."

"No worries, Jimmy, I need some work done on my buggy. I'll be by to see you when we get Anne back on her feet. I'll be back in the morning to check on her." Doc looked over to Lizzie. "You tell William that it's time he woke up and smelled the coffee. He needs to...he ought to...oh, you know what to tell him." Doc walked outside, and Jimmy closed the door behind him.

Lizzie, baby in her arms, and Jimmy walked into the bedroom to check on Anne. She was asleep. Her breathing was shallow, her complexion pale, and her bedcover soaked with sweat. She was mumbling in her sleep as if she was dreaming. Her mother walked to the nearby crib and lay the newborn baby on its back. She pivoted and sat in the chair beside the bed. Lizzie reached over, took hold of Anne's hand and pulled it to her bosom.

"Anne, it's me, your mother. Can you hear me? We love you, Anne. Jimmy and your children love you. They need you. You have a beautiful baby girl that needs you."

There was no response, but Anne seemed to relax some. The mumbling ceased for a minute or two.

Her mother continued, "Anne, your father loves you. He misses you so much. If only you will get well, I know he'll change his ways and be a father to you again. And a grandfather to your children. Please, Anne, please get well." Lizzie began to sob uncontrollably. "My dear, dear child – we love you so much."

Jimmy fell on his knees by the bed, brought his hands together, fingers pointing toward Heaven, and bowed his head. "Lord, I beseech you, please heal my wife. She's a good and faithful servant. Her family here on Earth needs her. I know I'm a sinner and not worthy of your grace, but please, Lord, please hear my prayer. Please allow Anne to walk this Earth for a while longer. Amen."

Jimmy continued to kneel beside Anne's bed. He placed his hand over her heart. Her heart was beating rapidly. He continued to pray silently. A few minutes passed, and he sensed his mother-in-law standing up from her chair. Jimmy stood.

"I have to do something," Lizzie said. "I can't just sit here doing nothing. I'll bring a cup of chicken broth. Maybe you can get her to drink some. Anne needs to eat, and she loves my soup. And we need to change her bed linens. Her quilt is soaked with sweat." Lizzie left the tiny bedroom.

Jimmy grabbed another quilt from a trunk at the foot of the bed and replaced the one covering Anne. Lizzie returned with a cup of hot soup. Anne remained asleep. There was no noticeable change in her appearance. "Anne, your mama made some delicious chicken soup made just for you. Wake up, Anne. You need to eat so you can get well." There was no response.

Lizzie walked in and handed the cup to Jimmy. "Try to get her to drink some broth, Jimmy. I'll take the baby to the kitchen and wash her with a cloth. Need to get this afterbirth off her."

"Call her Sydenham. That's what Anne wanted to name a baby girl," said Jimmy.

"Sydenham – what a beautiful name," said Lizzie. She walked to the crib and picked up the tiny baby. "Come with me, Sydenham. Let's get you cleaned up." The two left the room.

Jimmy sat in the chair beside the bed. He gently placed the rim of the cup next to Anne's lips and tried to get her to drink. The broth dribbled down her chin and onto her gown. He tried again to no avail. Anne seemed to be sleeping peacefully. *Maybe rest is the best thing for you,* he thought. He set the cup on the nightstand, stood, and left the room.

Lizzie was at the kitchen table, drying the baby girl with a soft cloth. Jimmy walked up next to the table and admired the beautiful girl. Lizzie placed a cotton flannel diaper on Sydenham, then wrapped her in a clean quilt. It was getting late.

"Why don't you get some rest?" Jimmy said to Lizzie. "You'll need to be rested tomorrow to help tend to Anne, the baby, and the others. You can sleep in the loft where the kids sleep."

"The baby needs to be fed. Anne's not able to breastfeed right now, so I'll have to make do tonight. Tomorrow, we'll see if Anne improves. I may have to find a wet nurse in town. Tonight, I'll mix some butter and sugar and feed her through a cloth teat. Then call it a night."

Jimmy blew out the bear-oil lamps in the kitchen. Lizzie sat in willow rocking chair in the glow of the fireplace feeding Sydenham, the butter and sugar mixture. He returned to Anne's bedroom, blew out the lamp on the nightstand, then sat in the bedside chair. The distraught husband talked to her quietly for a while. Her breathing seemed a bit more relaxed, but he wasn't sure. He leaned his head over, laid it on the edge of the bed, and soon dozed off weary from the long day.

Chapter 33

Jimmy awoke the next morning from a nightmare to the sound of the cock crowing. It was still dark outside. At first, he was unsure where he was or what day it was. He raised his head off the bed. His back was stiff and aching from slumping over all night. He looked up. The nightmare was real – Anne was lying in front of him. She appeared to be deep asleep, but she did not appear to be breathing. He placed his hand over her mouth and nose. He felt no air movement in or out of her nose. He put his hand on her heart. There was no heartbeat. He touched her face and arm. Her skin was cold to the touch. He shook her and called her name. He shook her harder. She showed no response. His worst fear had come to pass. His darling Anne had gone to sleep forever. Black wept.

* * *

Saturday afternoon, Pioneer Cemetery.

"Friends and family of Anne Shaw Black, we are gathered to pay our respects and to honor the short life of our dearly departed," said Reverend Stevenson. "Anne Shaw Black no longer dwells with us sinners on Earth. She resides with her Heavenly Father for eternity. Praise the Lord." Several "amens" were mumbled by mourners gathered at the gravesite barely audible above the sniffling, weeping, and crying. The somber quiet was interrupted by the loud cawing of some pesky crows perched high in the nearby pine trees.

"What do we know about this good woman? We know that she loved the Lord and loved her family. Anne is survived by her loving husband, James Black, and her children, William, Grandison, Sarah, John, and Sydenham. She was the oldest daughter of William and Elizabeth Shaw. By all accounts, she was a wonderful daughter, sister, wife, and mother."

"I see the heavy-hearted family here today. I see those shedding tears and weeping at the loss of this precious loved one taken from us so prematurely. The Holy Bible tells us it is okay to mourn the loss of this wonderful young woman, but that same Bible tells us it's time for rejoicing and celebration. For we know that the soul of this faithful servant now resides in her heavenly home with her Lord and Savior, Jesus Christ. While we mourn the loss of this loved one today, let us also celebrate her short life and her victory over death."

"What does the Good Book tell about a faithful wife? In Proverbs twelve, verse four, King Solomon tells us that 'A worthy woman is the crown of her husband.' Solomon goes on to say that the price of a virtuous woman is far above that of rubies. Indeed, her husband and all who knew Anne would agree with the wisdom of King Solomon. No doubt, the void created by her untimely death cannot be filled. Many of you are wondering why God would take this wonderful woman and faithful servant from us at such a young age? Friends, we know not the will of the Lord. We know not God's plan for us on earth -- nor should we question the Lord's will."

"Perhaps the Word of God can help us understand his actions. In Isaiah fifty-seven, one, the prophet tells us that God sometimes takes good people away to avoid the evil that is yet to come. In Ecclesiastes chapter seven, verse two, God affirms that death is the destiny of all men. Death is inescapable. However, in that same chapter, the Lord provides believers with a glimmer of hope that the day of death is more precious than the day of one's birth."

"Why does God's Word, make such a claim? The New Testament provides the answer. God's only begotten son, Jesus Christ, shed his blood on the cross to wash away our sins. But Jesus's death at the cross was not the end of the story. On the third day, he arose from the dead. His victory over death provides us all with an opportunity for eternal life -- a gift from God free to all who believe. All who believe in Jesus will never die. Family and friends, take comfort in knowing that your loved one is now in heaven, rejoicing with family and friends that have gone before her. To all present today that are unbelievers, Anne would want me to share the message of salvation with you. Before it's too late, repent of your sins and accept Jesus as your Savior."

"Let us pray. Heavenly Father, please welcome this good and faithful servant into your loving arms. Provide strength and comfort as only you can to all who are deeply pained by her loss. May they mourn her death as they should but provide them the peace and understanding to know she is in her eternal home free of pain, suffering, and sorrow. May her life be an example to all present today that they will honor her memory by forgiving those who have transgressed against them as Jesus forgives our transgressions. In Jesus's name, we pray, Amen."

Chapter 34

It was a brisk, November day. Large flocks of geese were flying high overhead in their characteristic "V" shaped formation heading south to escape the advancing cold front. The brightly colored leaves in the hardwood forests were turning brown and rapidly falling from the trees. The days were growing shorter, and the sun's daily arc was low in the sky. Dark clouds appeared on the distant southwestern horizon – a storm was definitely brewing Texas way.

Four horsemen rode from the northeast into Washington about mid-morning. The lead horseman was dressed in buckskin breeches, a buckskin shirt, and wore a coonskin cap with the black-striped tail dangling from the back of the cap. His long, Kentucky rifle lay cradled in his arms.

"How much farther to Texas, Davy?" said Will Patton.

"This here town is Washington," replied Crockett. "I reckon we're about a day's ride or there 'bouts from the Red River. Texas is t'other side of the Red. We'll spend the night here. I don't know 'bout you fellers, but I could use a hot bath, a hot meal, and a warm bed tonight."

The other three men audibly agreed with their folk-hero leader.

"I hear there's a tavern in town by the name of Black Bear. Sounds like my kind of place," said Colonel Crockett.

The men rode along the dirt road through the small town, catching the eye of the nosy passers-by, eventually arriving at the Black Bear Tavern. Will Patton dismounted and tied his horse to the nearby hitching post. "Let me go in and make sure they have room for us," said Will. He returned a few minutes later. "Davy, owner by the name of McSwaim, says he can accommodate us for the night providing we is willing to double up. I didn't figure that would be a problem – except for the unlucky one who has to bunk with Abner. Smells so even flies won't go near him."

All the group except Abner laughed heartily.

"I think all of us might do with a bath," said Davy. "Not just Abner."

Will plucked some dry straw from a nearby clump of dead grass. He fashioned two long straws and two short ones and placed them in his fist. He gave Davy first pick. Davy drew a long straw. Abner Burgin and Lindsey Tinkle took their turns, each drawing short straws. "Well Davy, looks like you and me lucked out," said Will.

The men carried their limited belongings to their rooms. Then Abner and Lindsey took the horses to the nearby livery stable. Davy and Will went to take turns getting baths and shaves. Abner and Lindsey soon followed Davy and Will's lead. The four men, feeling rejuvenated, then walked down the street to Block's Mercantile to buy a few supplies. The general store was doing a brisk, noonday business. Abraham Block, being the salesman that he was, introduced himself to the four strangers. Upon realizing Colonel Davy Crockett from Tennessee was in his store, Abe Block became even more eager than usual to help his famous customer. They purchased some hoop cheese, crackers out of the barrel, and some venison jerky for the noon meal.

The four men sat on some benches in front of Block's store, eating their noon meal. After the men finished off the noonday morsels, Davy reached into a buckskin pouch slung around his neck and fished out a handful of pecans and passed them around to the men. "Compliments of Mr. Block," said Davy. While the men sat eating, passers-by would stop and stare. Some would point. The more outgoing ones walked up and asked to shake the hand of the famous Davy Crockett. Davy, relishing the attention, eagerly shook hands and seemed keenly interested to learn the names of his local admirers.

Finished with their noon meal, the four men decided to return to the tavern to have some spirits. Tomorrow would begin the long trek to Texas, and they decided to make the most of their short respite. As they approached the tavern, they noticed a large crowd had gathered outside the front entrance. "Davy, looks like word has spread you're in town. I hope they don't want to throw a party like they did back in Little Rock," said Will. "I was looking forward to a good night's sleep in a real bed."

As the four men approached the tavern, a man in the crowd shouted, "Here he comes, here comes Davy Crockett!" The group quickly turned and looked in the direction of the approaching men. One of the men in the group walked towards Crockett and his party. With hand extended, the man said, "How do, Colonel Crockett. Name's Reverend Stevenson. I'm the pastor at the Methodist church here in town." The two shook hands. "Word is your heading to Texas. Thought you might like to know, I'm a close personal friend of Moses and Stephen Austin, the impresarios of the first Anglo colony in Texas. On behalf of the citizens of Washington, Arkansas, I wish to welcome you to our young but growing town."

"Thank you kindly," said Crockett. "I didn't expect such a welcome."

"Colonel Crockett, your reputation is well known here as it is elsewhere in the country. But many of our citizens hail from Tennessee and Kentucky, and you're revered by them as a true pioneer hero."

"We had a warm welcome in Little Rock several days back," said Crockett. The people there insisted on throwing me a party at the Jeffries Hotel. I'm honored and at the same time, humbled."

"Would you mind speaking to the crowd?" said Stevenson. "They're curious about what brings you to our town. By the way, three of our best marksmen are here in the crowd. I believe they are hopeful of enticing you into a shooting contest. I'd not be surprised if some wagering has already taken place on the possible outcome of such a contest."

"Being a man of the cloth, I'm sure the good reverend would have no interest in who the winner of such a contest might be?" asked Crockett.

"Certainly not," said Stevenson. "Well, at least not from a monetary interest. I might prefer to see one of our locals win the contest solely for parochial reasons."

"Hmmm, boys, it seems I'm like that old coon once was that now sits atop my head," said Crockett to his fellow travelers. "Looks like I've been treed."

"Splendid," said Stevenson. "Why don't you stand in the back of that wagon so that everyone can see you?" Stevenson, Crockett, and his three travelers made their way over to a wagon near the tavern. Stevenson helped Crockett climb into the back of the buckboard. The crowd continued to grow as more and more people made their way to the inn.

"Folks, I'm not much on making speeches," said Crockett. "But since y'all came out here on such a cold day to see my Tennessee friends and me, I s'pose it won't hurt me none to say a few words. Let me first say, if'n I could rest anywhere, it would be in Arkansas, where the men are of the real half-horse, half-alligator breed such as grows nowhere else on the face of the universal earth." The crowd let out a cheer. "And only the Good Lord knows, I might yet bring my family here, but right now, I'm on my way to Texas. You see, some folks back home are spreadin' rumors 'bout Ol' Davy. These so-called gentlemen are saying I'm turnin' tail and runnin' off to Texas 'cause I got whipped in my last run for U.S. Congress. Well, that just ain't so, folks."

"While serving the good citizens of Tennessee in Congress, I heard tales about Texas. That Texas is the garden spot of the world. The best land with the best prospects for health, and I do believe it is a fortune to any man to go there. There is a world of country there to settle. So I told my family to stay behind in Tennessee while I go see Texas with my own two eyes. Afterward, if'n I like what I see, I would return for them."

"While I was in Congress, some folks expected that 'cause I'm from Tennessee, I was to bow to the name of Andrew Jackson...even at the expense of my conscience and judgment. Such a thing was new to me, and a total stranger to my principles. I have always supported measures and principles – not men. Even though I fought beside Ol' Hickory in the Creek Indian War down in Alabama and he helped me get elected to my first term in Congress, we didn't always see eye-to-eye on things. I didn't like the way our President was dealin' with the Five Civilized Tribes – forcing them off their legally owned land 'cause other folks wanted it. And forcing them to move west across the Mississippi."

"Folks, I want people to be able to get what they need to live – enough food, a roof over their heads, and an education for their children. That's why y'all are here on the frontier and why we uns are heading to Texas. Jackson's not the only one tough as old hickory wood. I'd rather be beaten and be a man than to be elected and be a little puppy dog. I've acted fearless and independent, and I'll never regret my course. I'm that same David Crockett, fresh from the backwoods, half-horse, half-alligator, a little touched with the snapping turtle; can wade the Mississippi, leap the Ohio, ride a streak of lightning, and slip without a scratch down a honey locust tree! Now, if you good folks only remember one thing about Ol' Davy, remember he was a man of principle and beholden to know man!" Crockett paused.

At first, the crowd stood quietly, not sure if Crockett was finished. Then the gathering let out a loud cheer. Most people clapped loudly. A few looked angry and stood silently with their arms crossed.

"Now, some of you like Ol' Hickory better than me. And that's okay. We can agree to disagree. I understand that some of you local marksmen have challenged me to a shooting contest. Now I did a fair amount of braggin' in that book I wrote about my life. I guess it's time for me to put up or shut up. And for those of you that don't like me, now's your chance to take me down a notch or two. You can place a wager on one of the local shooters. But I warn you folks, when it comes to my shooting, me and Ol' Betsy, my Kentucky rifle are the best in the land." The crowd let out another huge cheer.

Crockett jumped down from the back of the wagon. Will handed Betsy to Davy along with his powder horn and shot pouch. Davy told Will to find anyone taking bets and put down twenty dollars on yours truly. Stevenson directed Davy over towards a large oak tree standing to the side of Black Bear Tavern. Someone had leaned a long plank of yellow pine wood long-ways up against the tree. At the top of the plank, a large V was drawn with a piece of charcoal on the upper end of the plank. A rope was strung along the ground forming a straight line about thirty paces from the target plank. Three men stood along the rope, rifles in hand, staring intently at Davy as he approached them. The four men shook hands. Reverend Stevenson soon joined the shooters.

"Men, I'll be the judge of this contest. You will each get two shots at cutting the "V" on the plank against the tree. After each man shoots, the plank will be replaced with a new one. Each man's shots will be marked and measured on his plank. The man that places two holes inside the "V" and closest to the bottom will be declared the winner. If any ball strikes outside the "V" or off the plank, that shooter will be disqualified. Our guest of honor, Colonel Crockett, will shoot last. Any questions?"

There were none.

The first shooter carefully loaded the muzzle of his rifle. He placed his toe against the rope, took aim, and squeezed the trigger. The flintlock smacked down on the pan, sending sparks into the black powder. *BAAAAANG!* Black smoke and the smell of sulfur filled the air. The smoke obscured his view of the target. He reloaded, waited for the smoke to clear, aimed, and fired again.

Two young boys scrambled and retrieved the plank for scoring. A man with a metal divider compass measured the distance between the bullet holes and the vertex of the V. Reverend Stevenson looked on to make sure the measuring was honest. One round had left a hole through the plank three inches high of the middle of V. Another hole lay two inches below the V. Shooter number one was disqualified.

A new, yellow pine plank was placed against the tree. Shooter number two – a man with a long, black beard – stepped up to the rope. He took aim and fired his first shot. Smoke again filled the air. Someone yelled, "Your beard's afire!" The shooter gently brushed the sparks from his beard, reloaded his rifle, aimed, and fired again. The plank was retrieved, and the results were again measured. Both bullet holes were inside the V. One hole was an inch and a half from the vertex. The other was two and a quarter inches from the mark – a good score – admittedly hard to beat.

Shooter number three took his turn shooting at the target. Like number one, he was disqualified. Finally, it was Davy's turn. He walked over to examine the three planks leaning against a wagon. He looked at the second shooter's target and slowly shook his head from side to side. He then let out a low whistle, doffed his coonskin cap at the second marksman, and scratched his head. "Now folks, that is some mighty fine shootin'. Mighty fine. Yessiree. I just don't see how me and Ol' Betsy here can possibly beat that," said Davy as he looked at his trusty rifle. "Well, old gal, we got our work cut out for us. You've gotten me out of some mighty tight spots before. Let's see if you can do it again."

Crockett stepped up to the rope. Davy pried open a brass-covered chamber embedded in the curly maple stock of his rifle and removed a couple of oil-soaked, buckskin patches. He lightly adhered the sticky patches to the back of his hand, closed the brass lid, and placed the butt of the gun on the ground. He took the powder horn hanging around his neck and poured a deliberate measure of powder down the barrel. Crockett plucked one of the buckskin patches from the back of his hand and placed over the opening in the barrel. He then reached in the leather pouch hanging at his side, pulled out a small lead ball about the size of a marble, and placed the lead ball on top of the cloth patch. From the leather pouch, he retrieved a flat piece of wood, put it over the lead ball, and smacked the board with the butt of his open hand. This forced the patch-covered ball into the end of the barrel. Crockett extracted a lengthy ramrod from just below the barrel of his gun. Holding the barrel near the end with one hand and holding the ram-rod in the other hand, with a series of up-and-down ramming motions, Davy forced the ball and patch down the barrel. When the ball hit bottom, Crockett tamped the ball with three solid tamps. Crockett replaced the ramrod in its holder next to the barrel. He then hoisted the rifle into a horizontal position. Lastly, he poured a small amount of gunpowder into the pan near the trigger of the gun, then he closed the pan. The weapon was ready to fire.

Crockett placed the butt of the gun snugly against his right shoulder. He pulled back the flintlock, aimed down the barrel, carefully sighting in the target. He exhaled, slowly counted to three, and slowly squeezed the trigger, avoiding any jerking movements. *Baaaaaang! Thud.* The sound of the lead ball striking the target was clearly heard by all. After the smoke cleared, Davy eyed the target, confident he had made a good shot. He reloaded and fired again. A faint sound was heard in the distance but not nearly as loudly as after the first shot.

The eager young boys retrieved the plank from the tree and returned it to the wagon for judging. There was only one visible hole on the plank, but it was less than a quarter-inch from the charcoal point of the V. The four shooters had gathered at the back of the wagon. Reverend Stevenson turned to Crockett. "Colonel, one of your shots cut the V dead center and is a mere fraction from the mark. There's only one hole, though. Your second shot appears to have missed the board altogether."

"Reverend, I'm afraid you're mistaken. You see, my second shot hit smack in the middle of my first shot. That's why there's only one hole. Looks like I'm the clear winner of this here contest. My hats off to my fellow shooters. You folks have some fine marksmen here in your midst."

The crowd had pressed in close around the shooters and Stevenson. The good reverend just stood there, mouth agape, unsure how to respond, not wishing to offend the honored guest and legendary figure by calling him a flat out liar. The second shooter, the man with the next best shot, stepped forward. The reverend thought the shooter would start a fracas for sure. Instead, the shooter extended his hand to Crockett and said, "that was some mighty fine shootin' Davy. You bested us for sure." Davy shook the man's hand vigorously.

Reverend Stevenson regained his composure. He grabbed Davy's right hand and raised it in the air. "I declare the champion of this marksman competition is Colonel Davy Crockett of Tennessee," said Stevenson.

The crowd let out a loud cheer. "Hooray for Davy Crockett! Hooray!"

Davy tipped his hat to the crowd. "Folks, we have a long journey tomorrow as we head down to Texas. And it would behoove us to hit the hay early tonight. But seeing how y'all have been so kind to us, we'd be happy to tip a mug or two with any of you in this here tavern."

The crowd slowly dispersed. The other shooters and several of the men made their way inside the tavern. Many stepped forward to shake the hand of the great Davy Crockett. Finally, Davy freed himself from the gawkers, turned to Will, and whispered, "Did you get my bet down?"

"Now, Davy, have I ever let you down?" replied Patton. "I got your bet down and put another twenty down on my account. I didn't get any odds but at least doubled our money."

"Fair enough," Davy said to Will. "Let's have some ale, some supper, and call it a day. Whaddya say? This trip to Texas is paying off so far." Davy slapped Will on the back with his right arm. The two men turned to join the raucous crowd inside Black Bear Tavern.

* * *

The next morning, the four horsemen awoke before dawn. They hurried to get on the trail before another gathering formed. It was a clear night, and the stars shone brightly in the night sky. A heavy frost was on the ground. The men retrieved their horses from the stable.

"Are we riding south to Fulton and Dooley's Ferry?" Will asked Davy.

"I think not," said Davy. "A fellow mason talked with me last evening in the tavern. Said he'd heard through a friend that some bushwhackers might be awaiting us down Trammell's Trace from Fulton. It seems they want to make a name for themselves. A fellow told me we can ride due west towards Fort Towson, then turn south into Texas to a town called Jonesboro. There we can head south on another branch of Trammell's Trace. Besides, I'd like to drop in on Capt'n John Becknell, who lives over near James Clark's place."

"Who's John Becknell?" asked Abner.

"Capt'n Becknell is the man who blazed the Santa Fe Trail that opened up trade with the Spanish way west of here," said Crockett. "I'd like to shake the hand of Becknell. He's my kind of folk."

The four men rode along quietly for a bit down the Fort Towson Road. Lindsey was dozing in the saddle. As they rode along, hardwood and pine trees gave way to a natural prairie. Will broke the silence. "Did you ever in your life see so many stars. A feller can pert-near see forever out here. Hey! Look over yonder direction," as he pointed in a southwesterly direction. "Look at that shootin' star! 'Cept it don't act like any shootin' star I ever saw. It's hardly movin' – and it's got a mighty long tail." The other men looked in the direction Will was pointing.

Davy said, "By gosh, Will, that ain't no shootin' star. I believe that's what they call Halley's Comet. Heard a trapper talkin' about it back at the tavern."

"Comet? What's a comet?" asked Abner.

"All I know is that comets stay visible in the same general part of the sky for weeks at a time," said Davy. The ancients believed that comets were a sign from God that something was about to happen. Sometimes good things but mostly bad."

"Well, let's hope somethin' good will happen for our sake," said Abner. "I done had my share of bad luck."

The other three sat quietly, admiring the unusual sight in the sky.

Davy thought to himself, I hope you're right, Abner. For all our sakes, I hope you're right.

1836

Chapter 35

March 6.

"How's Colonel Bowie?" asked Davy Crockett as he stood in a small room beside the wood and rope bed on which lay Jim Bowie.

"He's running a fever, sir," said the young soldier tending to the ill man. "He's been restless – tossing and turning – sweating – having nightmares. He yells out in his sleep, the name of his deceased wife and children. And sometimes he's cursing someone."

"See if you can wake him," said Colonel Crockett. "I wish to talk to him."

"Colonel Bowie, wake up, please. You're having a nightmare," said the young volunteer as he shook Bowie to wake him.

"Huh...wha...where am I?" said Bowie.

"Sir, you're at the Spanish mission called the Alamo. We're surrounded by General Santa Anna's army. We think they'll attack very soon – maybe at sunrise. How do you feel, sir? Take a drink of water?" The soldier held a dipper of water in front of Bowie's face.

Bowie raised his upper torso and propped himself on his elbows. Sweating profusely, he grasped the dipper and drank slowly. He looked around the room getting his bearings. "Bring me something stronger than water."

"Yes, sir," said the soldier as he quickly left the small room.

"Hello, Jim," said Crockett. "Heard you were in a bad way. Had to see for myself."

"What's our situation Davy?" said Bowie.

"Santa Anna's army is closing in like a noose around our necks. It's bad, I won't lie to you, Jim. You and me have been in some tight places before but none tight as this."

Bowie laid back down in the prone position and stared up at the ceiling as the gravity of the situation settled in. "You think any of Houston's or Fannin's men will get here in time to help us?"

"Afraid we got the last reinforcements we're gonna get," said Crockett. "I snuck out of Santa Anna's noose a few nights ago and met up with about thirty men from Gonzales. Brung them back with me."

"You still got a family back in Tennessee, Davy. You should have kept going. Nobody would have faulted you for that."

"I've never run from a fight, and I ain't starting now," said Crockett.

"Never ran from a fight, but I ran from my family," said Bowie. "My beautiful wife and precious boys all died near here in a cholera outbreak. I should have been there when they were fighting for their lives. I wasn't. I've chased after fortune and treasure all my life, but I had something more valuable than gold and didn't appreciate it till it was gone. You have any regrets, Davy?"

"More than a few, Jim. More than a few. Every man does."

"Damn it, Davy, I wish I'd met you when we was younger. We would have had one helluva time riding gators, wrestling bears, and howlin' at the moon."

"Reckon so, Jim, reckon so." The soldier returned with a jug interrupting the two men's conversation. "It's almost daylight. I best go check on my men. See you after this is over." As Crockett was exiting the tiny room, he turned his head to take one last look at Bowie.

"You know where to find me," said Bowie. "I ain't going anywhere for the time being. Now hand me that jug, son."

Crockett broke a brief smile as he turned and continued outside. Bowie placed his parched lips around the mouth of the jug and tilted the bottom up. BOOM! A cannonball exploded nearby, shaking the room. Dust and debris fell from the ceiling. Bowie spewed grog from his mouth and coughed. "Hand me my saddlebag, son, and that rifle leaning against the wall. Now get your tail outside where you can help the others. I won't be needing you for a while." Bowie placed the long rifle beside him on the left side of the bed. From the bag, he removed a pistol and three of his big knives, placing them on his right side. Colonel Bowie propped himself up against the wall behind the bed, turned up the jug, and chugged down several gulps of the strong drink. He rested the jug on the bed, took a deep breath, and closed his eyes. *Now come on, you devils. I'm ready for you. I've been fighting demons all my life, and I'm finally going to get rid of you for good.*

* * *

Easter Sunday, April 3rd, 1836.

Every pew in the wooden chapel was full. Those arriving late to the Methodist Church had to stand in the back and along the side aisles. Most everyone was dressed in their Sunday best. Many had recently purchased or made their outfits for this holiest of days. The ladies all wore bonnets or bow covered hats of bright spring colors. All of the men had their boots or shoes gleaming with a fresh coat of polish. Even the children in attendance were clad in their best Sunday attire.

Reverend Stevenson stood in the pulpit, ready to deliver the Easter message about the death and resurrection of Jesus Christ. The crowd was ready to hear the old, old story. They were not prepared for the message that the pastor was about to deliver.

Reverend Stevenson stood solemnly behind the rostrum. He stared over the crowd, cleared his throat, then stared at his well-worn Bible as if searching for inspiration. He then looked up and began. "Good people, I stand before you this morning with a heavy heart. On this glorious day, this Easter Sunday, a day for celebrating the death and miraculous resurrection of our Lord and Savior, I must first share some sad news with you. A member of our congregation shared a fresh copy of the *Arkansas Gazette* with me this morning. It seems a terrible tragedy has befallen our brethren in Texas. Between 150 and 200 brave men, women and children were brutally massacred in a Catholic mission in San Antonio by the Mexican Army led by General Santa Anna." A loud gasp went up from the congregation.

"Yes, I said women and children too, were murdered by this army led by its bloodthirsty general," continued the Reverend. "Several of the brave souls lost in the massacre are known by us here in Washington." The Reverend paused for a moment. "Many of you recall back in the fall when Colonel David Crockett from Tennessee passed through our town on his way to Texas. It appears Colonel Crockett was among those killed in this brutal attack. He was there bravely leading a troop of men resisting the Mexican Army, many of which were also from Tennessee." The crowd again let out a gasp of disbelief.

"Colonel Jim Bowie is also among the dead. As some of you know, our local blacksmith, Jimmy Black, who is present here today with his lovely children, is the maker of knives carried into battle by Colonel Bowie. William Travis, the commander of a group of regular soldiers, was killed, as were many more brave souls who refused to surrender to this cowardly general, Santa Anna."

Many of the women were openly weeping. Some of the men sat staring into space as if in disbelief. Some were visibly angry and mumbling about seeking revenge. The young children were distressed by the show of emotion by the adults, unsure what all of this really meant.

"Just like all of you here in this sanctuary today – like my good friends Moses and Stephen Austin – these Texians went southwest seeking a new life for their families. We can only pray that these brave pioneers did not shed their blood in vain. Jesus Christ shed his blood on the cross on a little known hill called Calvary, so that our sins would be forgiven. Just like these brave Texians, Jesus committed no crime. He was sentenced to death for what he represented. A threat. A threat to the way of life of the corrupt Pharisees and Sadducees. Jesus would not renounce his principles. He would not turn against his Father in Heaven. He knew that he was to be the sacrificial lamb whose blood was shed so that we could all have eternal life. Turn with me to the Book of John, chapter twelve, verses twenty-three to twenty-five, 'Jesus answered them, "The time has come for the Son of Man to be glorified. Most certainly I tell you, unless a grain of wheat falls into the earth and dies, it remains by itself alone. But if it dies, it bears much fruit. He who loves his life will lose it. He who hates his life in this world will keep it to eternal life.'""

"Let us pray that something good will come from the bloodshed by these brave men, women, and children at a little known place called the Alamo. Just as Jesus died so that we can have eternal life, perhaps the death of these brave souls in one of God's churches will lead to a better life for others."

* * *

July 1836.

Jimmy was in his shop, working feverishly on a new batch of knives. His business was booming more than ever since the Alamo. Settlers were stampeding to Texas now that it had gained its independence from Mexico. It seems every traveler through town wanted a "Bowie knife" like those found near Jim's body in the old Spanish mission. Jim fought valiantly to the death using his namesake knife to take several of the unlucky Mexicans with him. Jimmy wouldn't have expected anything less from the man.

The events of the last few months in Texas were the talk of the town. Folks talked about what a colossal blunder old Santa Anna made when he massacred those brave folks at the Alamo. "Remember the Alamo" became the battle cry for the small rag-tag army led by Sam Houston that finally defeated Santa Anna's much larger army at the San Jacinto River. Rumors were rampant about what really happened down in Texas. Some wondered why Sam Houston had not come to the rescue of Travis and the others trapped in the makeshift fort. Some said Houston was too far away, and his army was not large enough to fend off the much larger Mexican Army. Another story was that Houston had ordered Travis to leave San Antonio before he became surrounded by the Mexican Army, but Travis ignored Houston because the two men generally disagreed on things. What's done is done, and Texas was now a republic.

Dan was at the forge, getting it warmed up. Tom was putting iron blanks into the crucible – getting ready to pack them with some charcoal dust. Black was overseeing both men. They were preparing to make some blister steel.

"Hello, in there?" It was the familiar voice of Jimmy's old friend and former partner, Dr. Isaac Jones. Black had bought out Dr. Jones's interest in the shop some time ago. Dr. Jones was very pleased having made a nice return on his investment.

"What a pleasant surprise," Jimmy said to Jones. "I haven't seen you in a while. What's been keeping you so busy?"

"I've been dabbling in politics. Maybe more than dabbling, I guess," said Jones.

"Let me guess. You've been a part of the delegation from here working on getting Arkansas admitted into statehood?"

"Someone tell you?" said Jones.

"Now you of all people know you can't keep secrets in this town. Too many busybodies," said Jimmy. "Let's go into my office and have some stale coffee. "Besides, we're slowing progress here."

"Stale coffee? How could I pass up such a tempting offer," said Jones. "I hope it's at least hot."

The two men walked into the office. Black grabbed the pot off the cast iron stove and poured a couple of cups of coffee. He handed one to Jones. "Have a seat."

"So business is good, I hear?" said Jones.

"Knives are selling faster than we can make them. Jim Bowie, may he rest in peace, was a Godsend to me," said Black. "Now what can you tell me about getting Arkansas admitted as the twenty-fifth state of these United States? Last I heard about a couple of months back was that Governor Fulton was trying to block the passage of the Arkansas Constitution."

"You heard right. The stars finally aligned for me. Some of the local planters, lawyers, and merchants went to Little Rock and greased the wheels of the legislature, so to speak. But national politics helped our cause more than anything. The Missouri Compromise worked in our favor, it seems. Michigan was petitioning to enter the Union as a free state. To keep the balance of power in the U.S. Congress, the Democrats needed a southern slave state to come in at the same time. Arkansas was the best candidate. Timing is everything. Rumors were that Florida might be ready to enter the Union as a slave state but likely did not meet the population requirement. Fortuitously, we conducted a special Sheriff's Census about a year ago that demonstrated Arkansas could meet the population threshold. There's a bit more to the tale with Jackson deciding not to run for president again and the Whigs making a serious run at the White House, but you've probably heard more about politics than you wish. How's your young family adjusting to life without Anne?

"Mrs. Shaw found a nurse-maid for me. The woman has a newborn of her own and needed to earn some extra money – so I hired her to stay with the children during the day. She's very kind to the children, and they seem to be gradually getting over the loss of their mother. I wish I could say the same for me. I think of Anne every minute of every day. Thank you for asking. I know I've told you before, but I'll repeat it – thank you for having faith in me and helping me start my own business. I can never repay you for all that you have done for my family and me."

"Nonsense, Jimmy. I made a solid return on my investment. Maybe I should have retained my interest in the business given your current success," said Jones. "Now, I must be on my way. One of the women in town has a baby that's due any minute."

The two men shook hands, and Dr. Jones exited the shop. Jimmy stood quietly for a moment. He was thinking about how Dr. Jones was more like a father to him than his own natural father. He turned and headed back to the forge.

Fall 1837

Chapter 36

The crescent moon was high in the night sky. The sun would not rise for another three hours or so. The man approaching the Black home on foot felt confident he would go unnoticed. He was wearing leather moccasins to make it easier to stalk his unsuspecting prey. A dog a few houses away started barking. *Damn dog. Don't turn back. I've waited a long time for this night – too long.* The man slowly approached the house. He walked down the left side of the dark house towards the rear. A cord of Firewood was stacked neatly against the back of the house near the rear door. The stalker grabbed a sturdy, round stick of wood from the pile. It fit nicely into his hand. He swung the makeshift club and struck the palm of his open hand. *Yep, this should do the job.* He stepped onto the log step and stood quietly at the back door. All the man could hear was his heart pounding in his chest and his rapid breathing.

He gently unlatched the back door and entered the rear of the dark house. The intruder knew the kids would be sound asleep in the loft. He could hear the sound of Black snoring from the ground-floor bedroom. He slowly and quietly approached the bedroom. A heavy cloth curtain hung in the doorway to the bedroom. The intruder lifted the firewood club above his head -- his palms were wet with sweat. He gently pushed aside the curtain and entered the small bedroom. Black lay on side with his back towards the intruder, slowly snoring. Black seemed to be mumbling as if dreaming.

The first blow had to be forceful and on target. The assailant did not want Black to cry out, awakening the sleeping children. The intruder had strong muscular forearms. He brought the club down hard and fast on Jimmy's head, like a hammer striking an anvil. Jimmy let out a low groan. The attacker struck again and again – landing three hard blows to Black's head. Blood flowed freely from a gash in the side of Black's head. Black appeared to have stopped breathing. A look of calm slowly crossed the intruder's face. *You're no longer a thorn in my side. I regret the day I ever met you.* The intruder quickly retraced his steps and exited the rear of the house. He tossed the bloody club on top of the woodpile, then made his way back down the street. The distant dog let out a low, mournful howl.

* * *

The following morning.

Black's oldest boy, Billy, ran the all too familiar route to Doc Smith's house after finding his father lying in bed on a bloody pillow. The young boy was not sure if his father was dead or alive. The doctor quickly arrived and began examining Black. Jimmy was alive but badly wounded. The doctor applied some salve to the open wound and then bandaged Jimmy's head. The head was badly swollen on the left side. The left eye was swollen shut. There was not much the doctor could do but wait and see if Black would pull through on his own.

The doctor went out to the kitchen to talk with the children. The Browns who lived next door sat in the room with the children who were sobbing and crying. They had lost their mother a few years earlier and now faced the prospect they might lose their father. The wise old doctor explained the situation to the children and the neighbors. He said it would be a wait and see matter for several days to see if their father would pull through this. He explained that their father's brain had been damaged in the attack and was lucky to be alive.

"Should we fetch the children's grandmother to come tend to the children?" asked Mrs. Brown.

"Not yet," said the doctor. "I'll notify the sheriff first and let him know the situation." The old doctor, like most in town, knew the history between William Shaw and Black. The doctor had his suspicions about who might be behind the attack. He wanted the sheriff to have a chance to talk to Mrs. Shaw before she was alerted to the attack on Black. "Can you and Mr. Brown help out till I can get someone here to take care of the young ones?"

"Yep, we can help out for a bit," said Mrs. Brown. "We think the world of Jimmy and the children. I was a good friend of Anne's, God rest her soul."

"Very well then," said the doctor. "I'll be back a bit later to check on Jimmy. I'm going to see the sheriff – then to my office for a bit."

* * *

Sheriff Will Sanderson rode his large, dapple-gray horse up to the Shaw home. Arriving, he hitched his horse to the post out front. He walked onto the front porch and knocked loudly on the door.

A minute later, Mrs. Shaw opened the front door and said, "Why, Will, what brings you here? Is something wrong?"

"'Fraid so, Lizzie," replied Sanderson. "Mind if I come in?"

"Course not," said Mrs. Shaw. "Come in, please." She opened the door wide, and the stocky sheriff walked into the front room.

"Is your husband home?" asked Sanderson.

"Will, you know he's been at his shop now since daylight. He's there like clockwork."

"Thought so, Lizzie – just checking," said Sanderson.

"Now what's wrong, Will? What brings you here today?" said Mrs. Shaw.

"Get to that momentarily, Lizzie. Was William here all night? Did he leave the house last night?" asked Sanderson.

"No, Will, he didn't leave the house last night." She paused a minute. "Now he woke up the middle of the night with stomach cramps. Said he had to go out back to the privy but returned to bed shortly after that. Said the cramping was gone."

"'Bout how long was he in the privy?" asked the sheriff.

"I don't rightly know, Will. I dozed off and woke back up when he was crawling into bed. I reckon a half hour or so. Don't rightly know."

"How was he acting this morning?" asked Sanderson.

"Same as usual – in a hurry to get to the shop," said Mrs. Shaw. "Said he still had the trots, though."

"Might as well tell you why I'm here," said the sheriff. "'Fraid I have some bad news. Somebody attacked your son-in-law last night while he was asleep – beat him within an inch of his life. He's lucky to be alive. Longways from being out of the woods, though."

Lizzie Shaw slumped into a nearby chair. She bowed her head and began to weep, using her apron to wipe the tears from her eyes. "My poor grand-babies," she said. "They've had so much heartache." She sat quietly for a moment, continuing to wipe her eyes and nose on her apron. "Surely you don't think William did this awful act?"

"Everyone in town knows about the feud between Shaw and Jimmy," said the Sheriff. "Don't know anyone else with an ax to grind with him."

"Sheriff, I think you best leave now. Besides, I need to get over there and help my son-in-law and my grandchildren. They need me."

"Just doing my job, Lizzie," said the tall sheriff. He walked out to the front porch and put his hat back on his head. "I'll stop by the shop and visit with William. Get his side of the story." Sanderson got on his horse and rode off.

* * *

Shaw happened to be standing in front of his shop, talking with a local planter when he saw Sheriff Sanderson and his dappled gray horse lumbering down the road. Shaw had expected the Sheriff to show sooner or later. "John, I hate to cut our conversation short, but I see our High Sheriff coming up the road," said Shaw to the planter. "I've been repairing a bridle for him, and best fetch it from the shop. The Sheriff's not one to tarry. I'll have the wagon parts ready in about a week." The planter, from the rear seat of a covered carriage, called for his driver to take him to Block's Mercantile. The driver popped his buggy whip and slapped the reins causing the large strawberry roan gelding to start with a lurch. The driver turned the wagon away from the shop and headed down the road towards the mercantile. As they passed the sheriff on the way, the planter tipped his hat to the sheriff.

Shaw stood patiently awaiting the sheriff's arrival. Sanderson reined up his horse a few feet from Shaw. "Good morning to you, Will," said Shaw.

"Nothing good about it," replied Sanderson. "Got any idea why I'm here?"

"Has your horse thrown a shoe?" asked Shaw.

"I'm here on official business," said Sanderson as he stroked his bushy mustache a couple of times with his thumb and forefinger as if assuring it was securely attached to his weathered face. "Were you home all night?"

"I was. Why do you ask?"

"I'm asking the questions," said the sheriff. "Lizzie says you had the back door trots last night. Says you were gone from her sight for quite a while. Any chance you trotted down to Jimmy's house and smacked him over the head with a piece of stove wood?"

"Why would I go and do a fool thing like that?"

"Well, sir, I can think of a few reasons. It ain't exactly a secret about how you feel about Jimmy."

"He's the father of my grandchildren. Besides, if I did such a thing, why would I tell you I did?"

"That's what I thought you'd say," said the sheriff. "I had to ask. Just doing my job."

"Not very well, I'd say," replied Shaw.

"Ain't you going to ask how Jimmy's fairing today, or do you already know?"

"How's that scalawag doing?"

"He's alive at the moment. He's lying in bed with one helluva headache for now. By the way, I think Lizzie may be over there taking care of him and the children."

Shaw made no reply but raised his eyebrows and blinked his eyes rapidly a couple of times.

"You a bit surprised to hear he's still alive after that clubbing you gave him? I guess Jimmy will remain a thorn in your side a bit longer."

"Will, if you have proof I clubbed him, arrest me. Otherwise, I've got work to do." Shaw turned and headed back inside his shop. The sheriff stroked his mustache twice with his thumb and forefinger, tugged the reins of his horse to the left, and rode back toward town.

Chapter 37

Several months later.

Black slowly recovered from his brutal attack. Unfortunately, he lost sight in his left eye and only retained partial sight in his right eye. The blow to the side of his head had severely damaged his vision. Even before the attack, his eyesight had been deteriorating from years spent staring into a hot forge in a dark room. Dan and Tom did their best to keep the shop going, but the mainstay of the shop was knife making – not blacksmithing. Although Dan and Tom had assisted Jimmy with specific tasks in the knife making process, neither had ever performed the more critical steps. Jimmy had always kept the hardening and tempering of the metal to himself. It was his trade secret. Dan and Tom attempted to make a few knives, but the quality was not the same.

Fortunately for Jimmy and his young family, he had a tidy sum of money put away to live on. His eyesight was critical to his work. He had to see the metal change colors to harden and temper the knives. He got word to his old friend and benefactor, Dr. Isaac Jones, that he needed to talk with him.

Dr. Jones arrived at the Black home on a cold, wintry Friday afternoon, anxious to hear from his old friend. Jones knocked on the front door. Billy, the oldest son, let the doctor in and led him to the kitchen at the back of the house. Jimmy was sitting by the hearth. A fire was blazing. Jimmy sat staring into the fire, the light though blurry, was comforting to him -- he hated the dark. Fear overcame him at night – suffocating fear. At such times, he would feel panicky, his breath would quicken, his palms would sweat. It was all he could do to control his emotions.

Dr. Jones walked up to him and placed his hand on his shoulder. "How are you, Jimmy? You look stronger than when I last saw you."

"I'm progressing, but my eyesight is not. That's why I called you. A planter that's a regular customer of mine told me about a doctor in Cincinnati. Says the physician is known far and wide for helping folks with eye problems. I'm desperate to get my sight back and prepared to travel to see this doctor. What do you think?"

"Cincinnati's a long way to travel to see a doctor based on hearsay. I'm well acquainted with a New Orleans physician that has a solid reputation helping people with vision problems. Why don't you at least stop in New Orleans and allow my friend to examine you?"

Jimmy sat quietly, contemplating his friend's advice. "The planter said the Cincinnati doctor is a miracle worker. I'm desperate to get my eyesight back – for my family's sake. I'm prepared to spend the money to make the journey -- by steamboat to Cincinnati."

Jones decided not to belabor the point sensing that Jimmy had his mind made up and was simply looking for confirmation of his risky plan. "What will come of the children?"

"Their grandmother will take good care of the children while I'm gone."

"You're willing to leave the children at Shaw's? Did the blow to the head affect your reasoning too? Everyone around town believes Shaw's the one that attacked you -- everyone except the sheriff and the county prosecutor."

"Shaw won't raise a hand against those grandchildren," said Jimmy. "He's mean as a cottonmouth snake, but he's not that crazy. Those grandchildren are all that he has left of his beloved Anne. And you're wrong about the sheriff. Sanderson knows Shaw did it, but he doesn't have enough proof to convict him in a court of law."

"Maybe you're right. Now how can I help you?" said Jones. "At least allow me to take you to Fulton in my carriage so you can catch the next packet boat."

"That would be gracious of you. I wanted your opinion about my plan. Would you mind checking on the children from time to time? I'm not sure how long I'll be gone. The journey alone will take over a month."

"You should plan on being away for several months," said Jones. "Your convalescence could require considerable time, assuming the doctor can help you."

Jimmy sat silently, staring trance-like into the flames. A tear rolled down his cheek. *Why do bad things keep happening to me? Why? Have I not suffered enough on this earth?* He finally broke the silence. "I must make the journey. This blindness is intolerable. I need to see the undistorted faces of my beautiful children. Allow me a week to make the arrangements. I'll send word when I wish your help getting to Fulton."

"Very well," said Jones. He again placed his hand on his friend's shoulder. I have grave reservations about the merits of this scheme. Jimmy seems to make brash decisions at low points in his life -- always running from a fight. "I'll await your response." Jones turned and left the Black home.

1838

Chapter 38

Months later, Dr. Jones receives a letter.

July 4th, 1838

To My Dear Friend, Dr. Jones,

I hope you are well. I find myself still in Cincinnati on this 62nd birthday of our country. Unfortunately, I am not in a celebratory mood. The doctor here is a fraud. My eyesight is not any better and may be worse than when you last saw me. I will give the doctor credit for one thing – he has successfully fleeced me of most of my money.

I should have heeded your advice and sought out the New Orleans physician you urged me to see. I plan to travel to New Orleans on the next packet boat heading south. I pray for better results in the Crescent City.

Please tell my children I love them and miss them. I hope to see them very soon.

Your friend,

Jimmy

P.S. An acquaintance here kindly aided me with this letter. My penmanship is a bit lacking at the moment, as you might guess.

Months later, in another letter to Dr. Jones.

November 18th, 1838

Dear Dr. Jones,

I will be brief. The doctor in New Orleans has done his best. Perhaps if I had arrived here sooner, things might have turned out differently. He says it's now in God's hands. What has God ever done for me? My eyesight is no better, and I am weary. I will be returning home soon. I expect to arrive before winter, assuming the water level permits. Please tell my children I shall see them soon.

Yours truly,

Jimmy

Dr. Jones sat behind his office desk. After reading the letter, he crumpled the paper into a tight ball, making a fist. Jimmy slammed his fist onto his black walnut desk, then slowly walked over to the fireplace and tossed the ball into the blazing fire. He watched the letter be quickly consumed by the flames, leaving only the smoldering ashes. He placed his left hand on the heavy oak mantlepiece and grimaced. *How much more bad news can this poor man take? How much misery can one man stand?* Even if Jones knew how to get a letter to Jimmy, he did not have the heart to tell him the truth about what awaited him on his return home. The poor man would find out soon enough.

After the riverboat from New Orleans docked at Fulton, Black disembarked and quickly hired a driver and a wagon to carry him home to Washington. He was champing at the bit to see his children. The last leg of his journey from Fulton north to Washington took most of the day, so Jimmy took advantage of the slow ride to catch up on the goings-on around the southern part of the county. Based on his lengthy conversation with the wagon driver, Jimmy was left with the impression that not much had changed in the months that he had been away from the frontier community. He would soon learn that he was sadly mistaken.

Upon arriving in the town of Washington, Jimmy directed the driver to his home. Approaching the house, Jimmy's knees and legs quivered with nervous anticipation of laying eyes on his children. He hoped they were as excited to see him as he was of them. When the wagon lurched to a stop in front of the small frame house, the driver jumped down, grabbed Jimmy's bags from the back, and carried them to the front porch. The driver then helped Black down from the carriage and up to the front porch of his home.

As the driver stepped to the front door to open it, an elderly woman opened the door from the inside. "Who are you?" said the woman. "What are you men doing on my front porch?"

"My name is Jimmy Black, and this is my home. Who are you and what are you doing in my house? The sheriff is a personal friend of mine, and I shall summon him if need be."

"Mr. Black, you are mistaken," said the gray-haired woman. "Me and my husband bought this house fair and square at a public auction on the courthouse steps. I have a quitclaim deed to prove it."

Black stood silently for a moment, unsure what to do next, then turned to his driver. "Please load my bags back onto the wagon."

The driver did as asked and helped Black back onto the seat on the buckboard. The driver then climbed up and sat next to Black. "Where to, Mr. Black?" said the driver. Jimmy directed the driver toward the middle of town.

* * *

The wagon pulled up in front of a white-washed, wooden building. A sign out front read, "Doctor Isaac Newton Jones."

"Help me down," said Black. "Then unload my belongings, and you can return to Fulton. I'll be okay here." The driver helped Black to the front stoop of the office. The driver unloaded the bags and a trunk. Black-tipped, the driver who promptly turned and climbed back into the driver's seat of the wagon.

"You sure you want me to leave, Mr. Black?"

"Yes, yes. Dr. Jones is a good friend of mine. He'll tell me what's going on here."

The driver snapped a buggy whip, and the team of horses leaned into the harness with a start, and the wagon was off.

Black entered the front room of the office, where Dr. Jones soon greeted him. Dr. Jones crossed the room, clasped his old friend's hand with both of his hands, and shook it vigorously. "Welcome home, Jimmy. I was becoming concerned whether I would ever lay eyes on you again. You are a sight for so...er, a sight. You must be exhausted. Please have a seat." Jones helped Jimmy into a nearby oak chair.

"Beyond exhausted," said Jimmy. "My trip was a complete failure. Two doctors were unable to restore my eyesight. One was a phony – the other – legit. I'm afraid my situation appears hopeless. And I have pretty well exhausted all of my money in the process. The only thing keeping me going are my children – I must see them soon. I'm confused, though. I just came back from my house -- there was a strange woman there. Said she bought my house at a public auction. Surely this is some sort of a mistake. What do you know about this?"

Dr. Jones stood quietly. He shifted his weight on his feet. He then pulled a handkerchief from the breast pocket of his long-tailed coat and wiped the sweat from the palm of his hands. Jones pulled up another chair and sat across from Black.

"So how was your trip from New Orleans and Cincinnati?" asked Jones, ignoring his friend's question for the moment.

"Long...and difficult. Of course, I traveled by packet boat from Cincinnati down to New Orleans. I stayed there for a couple of months under the care of your physician friend. When I realized my cause was lost, I caught a boat from New Orleans to Fulton. On the leg up the Red, I recalled the first time we met some fifteen years ago. It seems like yesterday. A lot of water has flowed downriver since. Now, what about my house? What's going on here?"

"I've more bad news for you, I'm afraid. No sense in mincing words. Since you were gone so long with no word as to your whereabouts, Shaw petitioned the court and was named the guardian of your children. A while later, the judge awarded Shaw custody of your estate to provide for the well-being of your children. Shaw sold all of your property – your house and shop – at a public auction held on the steps of the Hempstead County Courthouse."

"So it's true? The woman was telling the truth?" said Black in disbelief.

"Sadly, it's true," said Jones.

Black bowed his head and shook it slowly side to side. "Well, at least my children have been taken care of. Please take me to them. They're all I have left in this world. I thought of them every minute of every day. That was the only thing that kept me from...that kept me alive. I need to see them this instant."

"Shaw has fled to Texas – not sure whereabouts. He's taken his family and your children with him, I'm sad to say."

Black sat quietly, not fully comprehending what he had just heard. His lower jaw quivered as if he was attempting to speak, but no words came from his mouth. "NOOO...this can't be...I don't believe you. Please take me to my children...NOW!"

"I wish I could, Jimmy. I wish I could," mumbled Jones. "No one in town has heard from Shaw since he left."

"What about his blacksmith shop?" said Black. "Why would he just up and leave his business?"

"More bad news, I'm afraid. Tom Shaw up and moved to Texas while you were gone. Shortly after Tom left town, a blacksmith passing through town offered to buy Shaw's shop. Shaw jumped at the opportunity. Seems Shaw was ready for a fresh start in a different place; too many painful memories for him here. His business had been in decline for years. As you know, you siphoned off a considerable amount of his business. Ever since Texas gained its independence from Mexico, the flood of settlers moving to Texas has been relentless. I suppose he felt opportunity was greater south of the Red. Who knows? Maybe he felt a fresh start in a different town would help his family heal some deep wounds. Seems Shaw convinced your children you weren't coming back to Washington – that you had probably been institutionalized or died due to complications from your injuries – not sure which. In any event...they're gone, Jimmy. Texas is a big place. Finding them would be like looking for a needle in a haystack."

Black placed his head in his hands and began to weep. Jones put his hand on Black's shoulder. "I'm truly sorry, Jimmy. I wish I could have prevented this from happening, but Shaw kept his plans quiet. I didn't learn what had happened until he'd left town."

"Why me? Why is this happening to me?" cried Black. "I don't understand. I can't take it anymore." Jones sat quietly. Black continued to sob, head in hands. Eventually, Black ceased his weeping. With his hand, he wiped the tears from his face.

"He won," said Jimmy. "Shaw finally got what he wanted all these years. He beat me."

"You're wrong," said Jones. "There are no winners here. You've both lost. Shaw became consumed with hate. He lost his beloved Anne. And what a steep price he paid for so little gain. All for the sake of Shaw's stubborn pride. No sir...there are no winners here. 'Vanities of vanities, all is vanity.'"

Jimmy looked up at Jones with red, swollen eyes. "Where have I heard that saying?"

"From the Good Book," said Jones. "Ecclesiastes. Some scholars think it was written by King Solomon, the wisest man who ever lived. Solomon reminds us of the folly of man. Solomon built up great riches on earth, but his quest for riches did not bring him happiness. He gained the wisdom to know such a quest only leads to emptiness and vexation of the spirit. Vile sin in the world leads us all to misery at points in our lives. Earthly goods cannot satisfy the soul. Only a life lived for God can lead to true and lasting happiness."

Jimmy seemed to take a small bit of comfort from Dr. Jones's words. He sat quietly in his chair, thinking. "I'm lost. Like a rudderless ship adrift on the ocean."

"Listen, Jimmy. You can wallow in the mud like a pig – growing to love it – or you can crawl out of the mud. It's your choice. You've been knocked down – received some hard blows – but you're alive. God did not guarantee us a number of days on this earth, but we should cherish each day we wake up. Now I'll climb down off my high horse."

Jimmy sat quietly – shoulders slumped. He made no reply.

"Since I received your letter that you were coming home, I've thought about your plight. I spoke with my wife about your situation. We've prayed as a family about this. I...we...want you to come live with us in our home. At least until you get back on your feet. You're welcome to live with us as long as you like. I don't want you to give me an answer now. You have a great deal to absorb. My wife's preparing supper. A good home-cooked meal and a sound night's sleep in a feather bed will do you some good. We can talk again tomorrow or in a few days after you've had time to think. Now let's get your baggage loaded into my buggy."

* * *

Dr. Jones owned two homes – one in town and a much larger home on his plantation south of the Red in Lost Prairie, near Dooley's Ferry. Dr. Jones's plantation home, he had more room to house his new guest. Plus, Jones felt it would aid his friend in his recovery if he were away from the town and his old familiar haunts. Besides, Jimmy was friends with one of the Buzzard boys that lived on a plantation nearby. Dr. Jones reasoned it would help Jimmy's recuperation to have more frequent visits from his old friend, Jacob Buzzard.

After Jimmy was settled in at the Jones plantation, Dr. Jones continued treating Jimmy's eyes. His mood also needed attention. Dr. Jones tried all the therapies he personally had learned or read about with limited results. One day, Jones decided to try some remedies he had heard about through an old Choctaw Indian that lived west of Jones.

Jones found Black sitting in a willow chair on the long porch in front of the plantation home. It was a fall day, and Jimmy sat in the evening sunlight. He was in one of his somber moods.

"Jimmy, we're going to try a new remedy today," said Jones.

"What would that be? A musket ball through the head?"

"Glad to see your sense of humor is returning," said the doctor.

"I wasn't joking," replied Black.

"My Hippocratic Oath requires me to first do no harm. I think that rules out a bullet to the head," said Jones. "I consulted an old Choctaw shaman a few days ago. He told me about some cures used by his ancestors for generations."

"So you're going to scalp me instead?" said Black.

Jones tried to ignore the comment but caught himself smiling. "I've made a tea from the leaves of Saint Andrew's Cross – it grows wild in the woods hereabouts. I'll drop this tea into your eyes a few times each day for a fortnight. I've also made a tea from the roots for you to drink. You'll drink the tea each day while we treat your eyes. The tea may help elevate your spirits. Now tilt your head back."

Jones used a small glass tube to drop the greenish tea into both of Black's eyes. He then handed Black a cup of the root tea. "Now drink it down quickly. It has a rather pungent smell and taste."

Black took the cup and turned it up, swallowing the reddish-brown liquid. Black grimaced. "Tastes like horse piss. So I guess you plan to poison me rather than shoot me?"

"Since you mention it, the thought has occurred to Mrs. Jones on occasion. She told me just the other day that if you maintain this melancholy state, she might just serve you some poison mushrooms or put some witch hazel in your tea. So be warned."

Black jerked his head and stared at Jones with a surprised look on his face. "Was she serious?" he asked.

"You'll have to ask her," said Jones. "But I'd tell her you're not fond of mushrooms, should she serve them anytime soon."

* * *

Jones treated Black's eyes every day for weeks. Black's eyesight did not immediately improve, but his mood did. Everyone in the household noticed that Jimmy seemed much more pleasant and congenial. *I wonder if that old shaman's root tea did this? Or maybe letting him know Mrs. Jones had her fill of him got his attention.*

Whichever, I'm thankful for the change – so is everyone else – especially Mrs. Jones.

* * *

Days turned into weeks and weeks into years. The patient-doctor continued to treat Jimmy's eyesight with little results. Time, however, worked wonders on his spirits. Over time as do most who've had their vision impaired, Jimmy began to accept and adapt to his handicap. Eventually, Mrs. Jones gave birth to three boys -- Junior, Daniel, and Littlejohn. From the birth of the children, Jimmy doted over them. As the babes grew into young boys, they called him "Uncle Jimmy," and he savored their affection. Jimmy saw this as one of those rare second-chances in life, and he treated the boys like his own.

He especially took a liking to young Daniel. Maybe it was because Daniel enjoyed listening to his stories about the early days in Washington, his travels, and his time spent on riverboats. Young Daniel hung on every word out of Uncle Jimmy's mouth and could while away the hours listening to the pioneer's tales. Junior and Littlejohn, on the other hand, got bored sitting for too long and had to be continuously entertained.

Jimmy, being the resourceful old blacksmith, was adept with his hands in spite of his limited eyesight and regularly made things to entertain the young boys. He would send the boys to fetch objects and then work his magic. From a squash vine or a short hickory limb, Jimmy would make whistles. From the limb of a bois d'arc tree, he would make a bow like that used by the Caddos. The arrow shafts were made from light-weight river cane. The arrow points were those found in the many fields surrounding the plantation. He would carve for them, replicas of his Bowie knives out of soft cedarwood. When the boys were not away at the Washington Academy for Boys, they could be found with Uncle Jimmy learning useful frontier skills.

* * *

It was fall. The cotton was in full bloom at the Jones plantation. The slaves in the fields busily stuffed cotton into long, canvas sacks they drug behind them. The fluffy white bolls were being loaded onto wagons with high, wooden sides for the trip to Dr. Jones's cotton gin in town. Uncle Jimmy was sitting beside the main house on a split-log bench near a fire pit. The fire felt comforting to him on the chilly, fall day. Black liked sitting near the fire. It reminded him of better days when he was at his forge, making beautiful, shiny knives from ugly black iron.

Jimmy was startled from his daydream by the distinctive sound of a large horse galloping down the road toward the main house. The rider reined in the horse next to the front porch, quickly dismounted, and walked briskly to the front door. The old, gray-haired house servant let the man enter the Jones home. A few minutes later, Black heard Mrs. Jones scream, followed by deathly quiet. Black grabbed up his walking cane and began making his way up the well-worn trail to the house. He was met halfway by young Daniel. Daniel was sobbing uncontrollably.

"Daniel! What's wrong, Daniel? Tell Uncle Jimmy. What happened?"

Daniel continued sobbing. Black put his hands on the shoulders of the young man. Daniel stared at Black, tears streaming down his cheeks. "He's gone, Uncle Jimmy. "He's gone."

"Who's gone. Daniel?"

"Papa. Papa's dead."

Black stood quietly, not believing his ears. *My dearest friend, Dr. Isaac Newton Jones, dead? Could it be true?* "This can't be. What happened, Daniel?"

"A boiler blew up at the cotton gin and killed him. Billy, the head slave at the gin, told Papa the boiler was cracked. Papa didn't believe him. Papa was stoking the boiler with firewood when it exploded. My Papa's gone to heaven." Daniel began to cry again.

"Let's go sit by the fire," said Black. The two walked back to the fire pit and sat down on the log next to the fire. They sat quietly for a few minutes.

Jimmy broke the silence. "Daniel, your papa was a great man. He'll be sorely missed by many – especially his family and most of all, me. You may not fully understand what makes a man great yet, but one day, you will. I met your father on my first trip, upriver to Fulton. He helped me open my own blacksmith shop when I needed a backer. He picked me up when I was knocked down. He believed in me when my own father-in-law didn't. Isaac Newton Jones didn't have to take me in and treat me like one of his family, but he did. I've often pondered this. Why? Why would a great man like your father befriend someone like me? I never asked him why though I was tempted to several times."

"I'll share a story with you about your papa that few people know. He shared this story with me a few years back. Before you were born, Colonel Davy Crockett passed through these parts on his way to Texas and his untimely death at the Alamo. I know you've heard of Davy Crockett – another great man. Colonel Crockett and his fellow travelers spent the night here on this plantation as honored guests of your papa's. It seems Ol' Davy was low on cash. Colonel Crockett had a gold watch which he traded to your papa for a silver watch and thirty dollars boot. Later, after your papa learned of Crockett's death at the Alamo, he mailed that gold watch along with a note of sympathy to Crockett's grieving widow in Tennessee. He didn't ask for nor expect any compensation in return."

"That is...err, was...the way of Dr. Jones. He lived by the Golden Rule. I know your heart is aching. I'm sad as well. I know the sense of loss is overwhelming, but, as time passes, the ache will lessen. You'll always miss your pa, always, but you can honor him by mirroring his life. If you do, you will find greatness. He's smiling down on you from Heaven, and your memory of him will light your path when days grow dark. And believe me, dark days will come again. I've been knocked down many times in my life -- from the time when I was eight, and my Mama died, leaving me in the hands of a step-mother who wished I was dead. When life knocked me on my butt, I tucked tail and ran. I ran all my life until I met your pa. He saw something in me – not sure what. I've thought long and hard about things over the years. You see, being a man is a lot like one of those knives I used to make. All men start out as a piece of impure iron with no useful purpose. The blows and challenges men face are like the forge, the anvil, and the quench. If a man is up to the challenge, he will be forged into a knife with a purpose. A lesser man will bend or become brittle and will end as a piece of scrap. What makes the difference is the skill of the blacksmith. The good Lord showed me mercy, and your pa, who encouraged me along the way, kept me off the scrap heap. Just you remember that through the rest of your days."

Summer 1870

Chapter 39

Daniel Jones returned home from his law office to find his wife, Margaret, sitting in the parlor, fanning herself, and drinking a glass of lemonade to stay cool. It was a sweltering hot July day. The windows were open wide, but there was little breeze to stir the humid air. Daniel walked into the parlor and threw his suit coat over the back of a winged-backed chair. He held a rolled-up copy of the *Washington Telegraph* in his hand. A pesky horsefly buzzed in front of his face. Jones swatted at the fly with the paper but missed.

"How's your day been, dear?" asked Margaret.

"It was an uneventful day," said Daniel. "No one to prosecute today. No court. Good thing. The jury wouldn't have paid any attention to me today. Too darn hot. It seems I can't even give a fly justice today. Where's Uncle Jimmy?"

"He's in his room. Hasn't been downstairs all day," said Margaret. "Have you noticed he's getting more senile by the day?"

"I've noticed," said Daniel. "I'm going upstairs to check on him. I'll take him a glass of lemonade. It's one of his favorites. Right up there with buttermilk biscuits and sorghum syrup."

"How well I know," replied Margaret. "He asks for his precious biscuits and syrup almost every day. I thank God for Dottie B. She seems to like cooking biscuits as much as Jimmy likes eating them."

Daniel climbed the stairs and walked down the short hallway to the last door on the left. He knocked.

"Who's there?" asked Jimmy.

"It's me, Uncle Jimmy," said Daniel.

"Thank God. Get in here, Daniel. Been waiting all day to talk with you." Daniel opened the door and walked into the room. Black was sitting in a well-worn, oak rocking chair near an open window. The sheer curtains hung unmoving in the still air. "Got something on my mind."

"Brought you some lemonade," said Daniel.

"No time for that now. Got something to tell you."

Jones set the glass on the small table beside the rocking chair. The old blacksmith paid no attention to the lemonade. Jones pulled up a nearby straight-chair and sat down, facing Uncle Jimmy. "What's so important that you'll pass on a glass of lemonade?"

"I should have done this years ago when your papa was alive. What a selfish old fool I've been. Time to right the apple cart. I owe your family much – too much. Only thing of value I can give you is the secret of my knife-making. It's a fourteen step process. Or is it twelve? It'll come to me. Now fetch some paper and something to write with. I'll tell you the process – you can jot it down. Yep, should have done it a long time ago."

"Now Uncle Jimmy, it's okay. You don't owe me anything. You're part of the family. You've been like a father to me since Papa died."

"Shush. I've got to do this, Daniel. Never told a soul 'bout my process. Not sure how long I'll be around. Got to do this 'fore it's too late. What ya waiting on? Get moving. It'll be dark soon."

Daniel turned and left the room to get some writing paper and a pencil from his downstairs study. He quickly returned and sat down at the table next to Black.

The old, gray-haired man, sat quietly, rubbing his brow with both hands. "Gimme a minute – I'm thinking."

"Take your time," said Daniel, who sat patiently waiting.

Uncle Jimmy continued rubbing his brow with both hands. His forehead grew redder and redder with each passing moment. "It'll come to me. Gimme 'bout an hour. Now go downstairs so as I can think."

Daniel got up from his chair and walked to the door. He turned and looked at the frail old man who sat frantically rubbing his forehead. He started to speak but didn't. He left the room.

An hour past. Daniel returned to Black's room. The old man was still rubbing his brow. "Are you ready now, Uncle Jimmy?"

"No. Gimme another hour. It'll come to me. Just need some quiet. I need to think."

Daniel left the room again.

Another hour past. Daniel returned to the room again. He crossed the room and looked at Black.

"Uncle Jimmy! You're bleeding!"

The old man had rubbed so hard and long that his forehead was bleeding. Daniel ran to the washbasin against the far wall and grabbed a towel hanging on the back of the basin. He quickly immersed it in the washbasin and rung out the excess water, then he scurried back to Jimmy. "Move your hands, Jimmy. Need to stop the bleeding." Daniel gingerly dabbed the wet cloth against the old man's brow. The white towel began to turn red. Daniel then pressed the cloth against the old man's wrinkled forehead to stem the bleeding. "What are you doing, Jimmy? You have to stop this. Now."

Tears formed in the old man's eyes. "My God, my God. I've waited too long. It's gone. It's left me. Like smoke up the flue."

"It's okay, Uncle, it's okay. Let it go. Now let's get you to bed. I'll bring up a poultice to put on your wound." Daniel helped the old man up from his rocking chair and into his bed. Daniel pulled the sheet up to Black's chest.

"But...but...I need to give you this. It's all I've got left. I need to repay you for all your family has done for me all these years."

"You owe us nothing, Uncle Jimmy. Your debts are forgiven. You've been a good and faithful friend. Now rest." Daniel walked to the bedroom door. He turned and looked back at the frail old man lying in bed. Daniel could see Uncle Jimmy moving his lips, mumbling to himself. Daniel said a silent prayer for the old man. *Give him peace, Lord. He's fought the good fight.*

Epilogue

The paths of James Bowie and James Black crossed in the small frontier town of Washington, Hempstead County, Arkansas Territory circa 1830. We remember Bowie as the frontier hero who died at the Alamo and for the many colorful exploits throughout his short but adventurous life. James Black, on the other hand, would have been forgotten at his death but for the efforts of one Daniel Webster Jones, the 19th Governor of Arkansas. Black, befriended when but a young man by the governor's father, Dr. Isaac Newton Jones, lived the latter portion of his life in the younger Jones's Washington home. Years after the death of Black, Governor Jones kept the story alive about the frontier blacksmith and the role he played in making the famous Bowie knife.

Black's role in making the Bowie knife is not without controversy. Some say that Bowie's own brother, Rezin, made the famous knife. Others believe an unidentified Louisiana blacksmith made the knife. The timeline and facts underlying my fictional account of the crossing of the two men's paths in the town of Washington support the plausibility of the Governor's story. This is one of my primary motivations in writing this story.

The town of Washington reached its pinnacle during the Civil War when it became the Confederate capital of Arkansas following the Union Army's invasion and occupation of Little Rock. Following the Civil War, the residents of Washington made a disastrous short-sighted decision – choosing not to allow the Cairo and Fulton Railroad to lay its tracks through their community. These myopic leaders felt the railroad would be the ruin of their fair city. Being spurned by the Washington citizens, the railroad chose to locate its station about eight miles to the southeast in the town of Hope, which eventually became the county seat. The settlement founded at the strategic intersection of the Southwest Trail and four lesser-known ancient trails chose not to be a crossing for the most significant road of commerce for the next 75 years – the railroad. Thanks to the efforts of some citizens with foresight during the 1950s, many of the historic structures in the town were preserved where visitors can step back in time at Historic Washington State Park.

-- Kim O. Davis

www.ingramcontent.com/pod-product-compliance
Lightning Source LLC
Chambersburg PA
CBHW031941110726
47902CB00001B/259

* 9 7 8 0 9 9 1 3 9 4 3 3 3 *